Personal Bests Journal
edited by David Gardiner

Issue 1 ~ winter 2020

Copyright © individual authors 2020

The individual authors of these stories have
asserted their rights under the
Copyright Designs and Patents Act 1988 to be
identified as the authors of their work.

All rights reserved.

Except for brief extracts for purposes of review or comment
no part of this publication may be reproduced stored in
a retrieval system or transmitted in any form or by any means
electronic mechanical photographic or otherwise
without the prior permission of the copyright owner.

Cover picture © Slavko Mali

Layout by David Gardiner

Table of Contents

Introduction	David Gardiner	Page 4
Lillya	Omma Velada	Page 6
The Jump	James Bates	Page 11
Perplexed Eye of a Sufi Pirate	Geoff Nelder	Page 18
The Summer of Dust	David Gardiner	Page 25
A Cautious Man	Kevan Youde	Page 37
Mrs Joshi Doesn't Cry Anymore	Priti Mehta	Page 42
Dead is Dead	Jane Seaford	Page 45
Pregenesis	Shawn Klimek	Page 51
Teach a Man to Fish	G. Allen Wilbanks	Page 59
Land of the Pharaohs	Mark Kodama	Page 69
Medicated Success	Glenn Bresciani	Page 91
Land of Elephants	Jean Duggleby	Page 103
Shadow Angel	Andrew Parker	Page 107
The Projectionist	Paul B. Cohen	Page 113
The Fire Eater	Ann Christine Tabaka	Page 122
Sins of the Father	David Bowmore	Page 127
Billy Luck	DC Diamondopolous	Page 152
Family Business	Lesley Price	Page 167
The Night Life	Patric Mauzy	Page 174
The Vanishing of M. Renoir	RLM Cooper	Page 180
The Wandering Corpse	P.C. Darkcliff	Page 185
Howl	Belinda Brady	Page 192
Saving Aaron	Peggy Gerber	Page 201
Ghost-maker	Kristy Kerruish	Page 206
A Very Brooklyn Wedding	Adele C. Geraghty	Page 210
The Last Haircut	Marlon S. Hayes	Page 219
There He Is	Michael Tuffin	Page 225
Going Home	Daniel Amoah	Page 229
The Girl I Nearly Knew	Lynn Braybrooke	Page 235
The Case of the Worn Out Soap	Slavko Mali	Page 242
Buddy Nickel and The Mistletoe Men	Gareth Hywel Phillips	Page 244
About the authors		Page 270

Introduction

Some of you may know me as the author of the novels *Sirat* and *Engineering Paradise* as well as a couple of short story collections based on the Rainbow Man character, but more likely as the Prose Editor of *Gold Dust Magazine* since its inception in 2004.

For almost all of those years I have thoroughly enjoyed filling this role, but I feel that for me the time has now come to move on. The next project I want to undertake is this one, the launch of *Personal Bests Journal*.

It seems to me (and of course I could be wrong) that no matter how good you are as a writer of short stories there are very few outlets where you can hope to see your work in print, and, perhaps equally important, receive some kind of payment for it. When people asked me how to do this I usually referred them to competitions like the Bridport or the BBC National Short Story Award or the Fish Short Story Competition in Ireland, but let's face it, the chances of getting placed in something like that are pretty slim.

What somebody needed to set up, I decided, was a regular (or irregular) short story journal that would publish authors' self selected "absolute best" short stories, whether they had been published previously or not and regardless of length (within reason), with all sales income being shared equally between the contributors.

That is the publication that you have in your hand right now. I don't delude myself that the sales will be very great initially, but there's something a bit special about even a small amount of money earned as royalties, especially if it's the first time it's happened for you, and also about having your story in a professionally edited and produced book alongside other high quality work. I want publication in this journal to be something of which you can be justly proud and which will serve as a showcase for the very best work of which you are capable. And what a treat that's going to be for the readers!

This journal is not another scam to take money from people who want to see their work in print. I will at no point ask for any money whatsoever from people submitting to the new journal. All the movement of money will be in the opposite direction, from the journal to the contributors, and the amount will depend on how much has come in from sales, shared equally between all the contributors. The finances of the project will be open and transparent.

Introduction

Acceptance for publication here has been far from automatic – I have applied the same editorial standards that I did at *Gold Dust,* and I was never a "soft touch" as an editor. The stories in this book have been properly proof read and edited, and the standards are as high as the writers and I can make them.

One of the most difficult considerations for me was where to put the limits regarding word length. When does a short story become a piece of flash fiction and when does it become a novella? This was clearly defined for me at *Gold Dust* and the rules were rigidly applied, but here I have been freed from all such external constraints. It took me a while to realise that the answer is unimportant. I agonised over what at first sight seemed very long stories, but I now realise that what makes a story too long is when it *seems* too long, when it is verbose or padded-out. If it remains compelling for the whole of its length it isn't too long. I have included a story in excess of 12,000 words, the last one in the book, and if you skip it because of its length believe me the loss is yours.

I decided to include one story of my own in this and perhaps subsequent issues of the journal, for which I will claim an entitlement to an equal share in the royalties the same as everyone else. If I don't include one in the future I will have no such entitlement.

Selecting a story of my own proved a difficult but very interesting task. I was flustered for a while, torn between a half dozen or so from my huge back catalogue that I particularly liked, but I found my way out of the dilemma by asking myself: What is it that I'm basically tying to do when I write a story? The answer I realised was very simple: To get to the reader emotionally. Once I had understood this the answer jumped out at me and I have not doubted it for a moment since. I tell you this in the hope that it might help you in choosing something to submit for subsequent issues, should you wish to do so.

When we see how well Issue 1 does we can decide how long to wait before bringing out the next one, and review the project generally.

Thanks for buying this book. I don't think you'll regret it.

David Gardiner

David Gardiner,
London, June 2020.

Lillya
by Omma Velada

I'm surprised by how little it hurts. Like having a vaccination, there is the little flutter of dread before it begins, the 'oh' of surprise and then a happy slide into painless relief. Lillya should be here, I think. Lillya with hair like tinsel and those all-seeing eyes that almost wind me every time I look at her.

When they put her on my chest in the hospital, screaming with fear or cold, heartbeat racing, hers and mine, I just inhale her, that scent of kitten mingled with blood. Mike looks taller beside us, and I've never seen him move so carefully, almost in slow motion, as he gently bends to stroke her hair, for this baby has shiny blonde curls. Our eyes collide and his trusting smile sends me soaring like an eagle, high above the hospital, euphoric with success, but already a mother, talons poised, ready to kill to protect my new reason for living.

'Lillya,' Mike says, 'let's call her Lillya'. It wasn't a request, though, not really. Lillya was his mother's name and I knew he'd been waiting for this moment, waiting for a girl so his mother could breathe again. The way he says our daughter's name is like a slogan, a new brand of washing powder, or toothpaste. And it suits her, with all her shiny newness. I should tell him now, I think. I'll just tell him, right now, and he'll love her anyway. But I hesitate and the moment passes. Instead, I say, 'Lillya.'

'Lillya Rose,' he amends, always thinking of me. My mother was named Rose.

My Lillya moments are not the big landmarks, the day she stood up and walked, her first day at school, the time she was picked from a lecture hall of over fifty students to give a speech. They are there, of course, but they weave seamlessly beneath the moments that you barely even realise are moments until long afterwards, the ones that shred your heart like paper, or weigh you down forever like a pointless extra limb.

'I've a new friend', she announces one lazy summer afternoon. Mike is hosing the grass and I put down my novel to see her. 'Megan,' she says. 'Megan Johnson,' she adds craftily. I lift my sunglasses, wonder how to react. Megan Johnson. The girl who taunted her all last year, put worms in her lunchbox, even, and this turns my stomach to water, even made her eat one. I wonder if Lillya would ever have told us if Megan hadn't hacked off most of her gorgeous, sparkling curls. I'd never seen Mike look so lost. But he rallied. We held hands, marched up to the school, demanded a response from the lethargic head. Expulsion, we insisted. And we got it. Megan moved on to the special school outside town. Her mother still snubs me in the supermarket, which gives me a twisted pleasure. For a long time after it happened, I'd try and time my shopping trips to coincide with Megan's mother's.

'Lillya,' I begin, 'Why would you-'

'She's different now,' Lillya says brusquely, with a teenager's arrogance, though she is only eleven. 'She's fun. Can I have her round for a sleepover?' Is Lillya feeling guilty, I wonder? Is she trying to make amends for Megan's schooling disaster? I place my book on the deckchair and stand up. 'You may not bring that girl into our home,' I say, aiming for calm authority, but even I can hear the edge of hysteria creeping into my voice. 'I don't think it's a good idea for you to spend any time at all with her. She's a very troubled child and needs help, which is why she switched to the spec- to another school. Please stay away from her, Lillya.' I try not to make it sound like a threat. Lillya isn't fooled, but she always knows when I really mean it.

'Okay, sheesh, mum, I just thought you'd be glad we're getting on at last.'

I sit back down, pick up my book. Conversation closed. But the words buck and dive on the page and I have to pretend to read.

On a frazzled autumn morning, Lillya and I tear through the leaves to make her doctor's appointment. 'Why are we always running so bloody late?' I despair, wishing I'd thought to wear trainers instead of these witty little kitten heels. Lillya glances down. 'Take them off,' she sings. It makes sense. Liberated, shoes in hand, we crunch through the park together, finally arriving only seven minutes late to a frowning receptionist and a barely held appointment. 'You'll have to wait, now,' she grunts, not looking up from her computer. 'There's three people bumped ahead of you's.' Sighing, we take seats among the sneezing children and still pensioners. 'I'll be late for work,' I grumble. But Lillya isn't listening. 'Don't ever tell Dad, will you?' she says suddenly. Her words chill me and for the first time in her life I am afraid to look at her. When I do, her expression is terrified yet defiant. She knows. I look away, unable to respond. 'Please, mum,' she insists gently. 'He'd never be the same after.'

'How did you- What makes you think-'

She twirls one of her blonde curls, already re-grown, all the way down her back now. At fourteen, she is all loose-limbed awkwardness, only her hair is forever sleek and sparkly. It reminds me of Christmas, so delightful I want to eat it. 'When you hug dad, it's like you're saying sorry for something. I always wondered what for. And then, everything's from you.' She touches her features in turn. 'Eyes. Nose. Mouth. But my hair… who's my hair from? It's not Dad, and it's not Grandma Lillya.'

'He was a soldier,' I say, the words I've often rehearsed in my mind surprisingly easy to say. 'He went to Iraq. He didn't come back. He had a family here, two boys. Maybe one day-'

But Lillya just shakes her head slightly and interrupts. 'Dad said he'll be home early tonight. He's going to show me how to make pancakes!'

I smile warmly at her, my precocious, precious Lillya, and feel the pain resettle inside me, like dust. 'Great. We'll pick up some blueberries and *Nutella* on the way home.'

I'm turning the soil for the first bulbs of the year when I hear arguing from inside the house. Mike, who never raises his voice, is shouting. 'It's a bloody ludicrous idea! Was it that girl's? Because you're not going and that's final.' I hear Lillya's voice in response, only half-way through her law degree and already more articulate than either of us. I freeze a little, worried. I've always worried when they argue, worried where it might lead.

The back door slams and Lillya is suddenly there in front of me, blocking out the sun. Lillya, or should I say Rose? Sometime during her first term at university, we started getting phonecalls for 'Rose'. It almost broke Mike's heart.

'Mum,' she says and in nineteen years it doesn't get old. I love hearing her say it, even in anger. It defines me now. 'I'm not going to finish my course,' she says, and every word sounds like steel. She's thought about it. I see my Lillya the lawyer dream burst like a bubble above my head. 'Have you found something that would suit you better?' I say, slamming my fork down. She jumps a little, and the word *kitten* scurries across my consciousness. 'We've decided to go travelling instead,' she continues, and I hear a laugh in her tone that enrages me. 'We?' I demand, running through my mind every unsuitable boy she has brought home over the past year. 'Yeah, me and Megan. It'll be educational, don't panic, I'm not stupid.' A worm slides languorously over my gardening fork and I shudder. 'I know, but you are young. We talked about this. You didn't want to take a gap year. Thought you'd get stuck into law while you were still feeling fresh.' But all I'm thinking is *not Megan, not Megan, not Megan*. I think even after watching Megan be sweet and even deferential to Lillya for years now, I will always, always hate her.

Then Mike strides up to us, with quick, angry footsteps. 'I'm not going to pay for it, Lillya. You know you can't finance it alone. There's no way.'

Lillya gives a little shout of rage. 'You can't tell me what to do! You're nothing to me!' And then it happens. Lillya looks at me and I see it in her eyes. She's tired of the lie, it grew old a long time ago. She needs to know that he loves her no matter what. 'Tell him, Mum,' she whispers. I suddenly feel dizzy, like a swirling leaf, lost to the wind. Mike's face is all blurry. 'Mike, there's something-' I begin. Then I have a moment of clarity. We won't survive this now, I realise. The moment for telling the truth has passed. 'Oh, for goodness' sake, Lillya. Of course I'll tell Dad what I think. I think exactly as he does. You're staying here, finishing your degree, like a grown up.'

The look that flashes across her face is astonishment, then something else. It takes me a second to identify it, because I've never seen that look on Lillya before. Betrayal. I want to dissolve. 'Fuck both of you!' she screams. She runs back into the house, we hear the front door slam. Mike takes my hand, instantly reassuring. 'Don't worry, she'll come around,' he says. He selects a bulb from my bucket, drops it into the soft earth. 'She'll come around.'

'It looks expensive,' Lillya sighs, holding up the long silk blouse I've bought her for her birthday, her thirty-first, no thirty-second. She's a little tipsy, her curls twisted up on her head to showcase ridiculously long beaded earrings. I suppose she's a bit of a hippy, or do they call it grunge now? I thought this blouse would be perfect, but I usually get it wrong.

Just after nine, people start arriving in rapid succession. Megan is handing out tequila shots and Mike's working the iPod. When Lillya dances, I suddenly find myself weeping, so I hurry to the toilet to hide my face in the sink. When I return, Lillya is dancing with a man I recognise from her school, I think he teaches history. Mike, who always sees the best in things, says that Lillya makes a much better teacher than a lawyer.

I see that this history teacher likes her, but I cannot tell what she is thinking. It is both odd and painful to know a stranger's heart better than your own daughter's. I am just grateful that she still tolerates me in her home.

'Lillya,' I say suddenly, and there is so much longing in my voice it startles her. She comes over to me and I realise she has decided to wear the birthday blouse after all. 'Love you, mum,' she says, nuzzling my neck, and I think maybe Mike was right. She has come around.

And so I am back in the hospital, the same building where Lillya's life began, and mine too in a way, because didn't it all begin with Lillya? And this is where my life will end. Mike is on his way, but he was working in Scotland today and he won't make it.

It really barely hurts at all. I close my eyes and empty my mind and there she is, Lillya. And then she is really there, a cool hand on my temples and a soft voice at my ear. 'Mum,' she says. Her tears fall on my closed eyes and I want to kiss them. 'Don't, Lillya. Because I'm happy. Ecstatically happy.' And I mean it. She was there at the beginning and she is there at the end. As always, I wonder which words, of all the thousands of words, to choose. 'Look after Dad,' I say finally. She smiles. And then, so low I'm not sure I've heard right, 'I'm going to tell him'. She is strong, so much stronger than I was. But that is partly down to me. And my heart swells up like a balloon of pride and I say, 'Thank you, my darling Lillya'.

The Jump
by James Bates

I didn't expect so many people to be standing around on the cliff overlooking the Yellow Knife River but there were, maybe fifteen or so, mostly young folks in their twenties just hanging out, joking around and having a good time, everyone looking tan and fit. It was honestly not what I expected at all. Scared as I was, I found the festive atmosphere kind of distracting and that was a good thing, giving my growing unease. You know what, I thought to myself, this just might work out okay.

Next to me my ten year old grandson took my hand and smiled, "Grandpa, look at all the people. This is really cool."

He pulled me along, ever closer to the edge. I followed behind trying to calm my rapidly beating heart with little success. Was I really going to do this? Was I really going to conquer my fear of heights and jump off a thirty foot cliff into a river? It looked like I was. If my wife could only see me now.

A week earlier when I'd told Connie of my plan she'd said derisively, "So you've got a bucket list, Ed? First I've heard of it. And jumping off a cliff is the first thing on it? What, are you? Nuts?" She shook her head in marital disappointment. "Look, I asked you to take down the swing set in the backyard at the beginning of summer, what, three months ago? You couldn't be bothered. Now, suddenly you've got this ridiculous bucket list that you're all fired up about, and it has to happen like right now. What's next? Parachuting out of a airplane?" I quickly found something of interest down by my shoes and averted my gaze. How'd she know about that? It was third on the list, right after hiking the Appalachian Trial. "How about you put "Take down the swing set" on that stupid list of yours, huh? Maybe then it'll get done."

I tried to recover some modicum of dignity, "Look, I'm sorry about the swing set. I'll get on it right away."

"Yeah, right." I could see it in her eyes. My wife's opinion of men, never very high even on a good day, slipped down another rung on her ladder of disappointment. "Before or after you jump off the cliff?"

I felt some clarification was in order. "You know that I've always been afraid of heights. I just want to prove to myself that I can do it, and, you know, get past my fear. Plus...well, I'm jumping into a river," I said, for some reason thinking it would put a positive spin on things. Wrong.

"Oh, well, a river," she said and then let out derisive "Humph," which rattled the crockery in the nearby kitchen cabinet, "Well, that makes it all right then." She thought for a moment, shaking her head, dismay written all over her face. We had a good marriage and had been together over forty years, but it wasn't out of the ordinary for me to do something to either try her patience or disappoint her, or both. This obviously was one of those times. "Well, call Ronny at least. See if he'll go with you. Maybe our son can help protect you from yourself."

Whew. Off the hook.

I watched as she turned on her heel and headed for the living room, phone in hand, eager, I was sure, to call one of her girl friends to commiserate once again on the idiocy of the male species, a life-long pastime of theirs. Well, it wouldn't be the first time and probably not the last, either, but what could I say? At least I kept things interesting.

As if she could read my mind, Connie turned and gave me a pointed look, "What did you say?"

"Ah, nothing. I...I just..."

I shut up. It was disconcerting that the longer we were married, the more she seemed to be able to read my mind. I'd have to watch myself.

She jabbed a long, pointed finger in my direction, "Something about keeping things interesting? Is that what you said? Well, you'd better watch it, buddy, that's all I've got to say."

Scary. Was she becoming clairvoyant? I shuddered at the thought. That's all I needed.

I took a moment to collect myself and then called our oldest son and explained what was going on. "This Saturday? Sorry, Dad, can't go. I'm swamped at the dealership, but maybe Noah can. I'll put him on."

I took care of my grandson and his two younger sisters one day a week after school. He and I loved doing things together, and after he listened to my idea about jumping into the Yellow Knife River it took him all of about two seconds to say, "Yes!" And that's what brought us to the forests of central Minnesota, a two hour drive north of Minneapolis, on a warm and sunny August Saturday afternoon.

A tall, well built, dreadlocked guy who looked to be in his mid-twenties broke away from the group when he saw us walking toward the cliff's edge. He came up and smiled a greeting, "Hey there, guys. What's going on? Here to jump off Lollipop?"

His grin was infectious, and his bright white teeth were accented by his tan face. He was wearing cut off jeans and flip flops. I tried not to stare at his bare chest and torso, rippling with muscles. He kind of looked like I imagined Hercules might have. Next to me I swear Noah whispered, "Wow."

Lollipop? What the heck was he talking about? I coughed to clear my suddenly restricted throat and said, "Jump into the river? Yeah, I think I am."

As if reading my mind he grinned, pointed to the cliff and said affectionately, "Lollipop is what we call this little baby here."

"Really?" I stammered. It was all I could think to say. Then I croaked out, "Why's that?" And why was my mouth suddenly so dry? But he was very friendly, and I was trying to be friendly back, you know, trying to get into the spirit of things. Next to me Noah surreptitiously handed me a bottle of water which I gratefully drank from.

"We call it that because it's such a sweet little jump." His grin widened, "Not like that one." He pointed over his shoulder up a long rise. Through the trees I could barely make out a high cliff about a hundred yards downstream.

"What's that one called?" I asked, trying to keep my voice steady.

"Hangman," he said and laughed, "because the drop could kill you."

Next to me Noah said, "Yikes," while I wiped a bead of sweat from my brow and tried to get my racing heart under control.

Mr. Dreadlocks took a long moment looking me over before he calmly patted me on the shoulder and said, "Let's get you started with Lollipop and save Hangman for some other day. How's that sound?"

The answer was obvious to me. "Sounds good," I said, trying to sound confident. Next to me Noel whispered, "Way to go, Grandpa," as he took the bottle from my suddenly fidgety hand.

Mr. Dreadlocks then slapped me on the back (he really was a touchy-feely kind of guy) and turned to his friends, yelling, "Gang, we've got a jumper here!" A chorus of cheers arose from the crowd. He turned and gave me the thumbs up sign before giving me another once over, taking a bit more time appraising me.

I'm a little overweight (doughy would be putting it mildly) and nearly bald. I was wearing tan cargo shorts, a dark blue Minnesota Twins tee-shirt and a Twins baseball cap. On my feet I wore an old pair of canvas tennis shoes. In my research on cliff jumping, I'd read that they would help protect my feet from the force of the impact on the water.

"First time?" Like he even had to ask.

"Yeah," I said, and damn it if my voice didn't crack. I tried to recover. "It's on my bucket list."

"Bucket list? Really. Well, we get that a lot here," he grinned and stuck his hand out, "Welcome. My name's Cody."

We shook, "Hi. I'm Ed and this is my grandson, Noah." Noah shook Cody's hand, but didn't (or couldn't) say anything, enamored as he was to the point of speechlessness by the statuesque Adonis standing before us.

"Great to meet you guys. If you want, I'll help you out."

"That'd be nice," I said, meaning it, my relief palpable.

For the next ten minutes or so he talked me through what he called The Jump. He was really nice about it, patient with me and informative. He seemed to understand the trepidation a sixty-five year old man might have about leaping into space

As he talked people kept coming up to the area and jumping off the cliff, often without any warning or fanfare whatsoever. I saw a skinny whip of a girl walk to the edge, hold her nose and step right off. I saw a guy and a woman around forty jump while holding hands. And then one of Cody's friends, Mia, ran off the edge and did a back flip on her way down. Watching all those jumpers served to make me both excited and nervous, a strange feeling to have.

Finally, Cody clasped me on the shoulder in a friendly way and said, "Okay Ed, that's about it." He looked me over once again and nodded to himself, "I'd say you're all set to go. How about it? Are you ready?"

I looked around. The sky was cloudless and clear blue. A hot sun was beating down. The scent emanating from the pine forest was heady and fragrant. The crowd nearby was boisterous and happy. I'd been coached by the inimitable Cody. I guess was as ready as I'd ever be.

I took a deep breath, "Sure. Yeah. I'm ready."

"Super." Cody turned to the crowd and yelled, "Ed's going for it!"

There was a heartfelt cheer, and lot's of "Atta boys" and "Way to go's".

I gave my hat to Noah and stepped to the edge. The river was wide, about two-hundred feet across and even though there was a current, the surface looked calm with barely a ripple showing. The shear granite cliff I was on had formed eons ago with a natural ledge that sloped away from the edge toward the shore. All I had to do was step off and drop thirty feet straight down. I was told it would take less than two seconds before I hit the water.

I took a deep breath and exhaled. Cody had suggested not to not look down, so I didn't. I looked across the river to the pine trees and rocky cliffs on the other side. Behind me Noah whispered, "You can do it Grandpa." I felt him take my hand and squeeze.

I turned and looked at him and he smiled an encouraging smile. I smiled back, squeezed his hand once more, and let go. Let's do this, I said to myself. Then I turned and stepped into space.

For a moment I hung suspended. It felt like I was floating. Then I was air borne and free falling, and it was exhilarating. The wind whipped past me, and I'm pretty sure I held my breath. I kept my hands glued to my sides, and the river came up fast. When I hit the water I heard my feet smack the surface as bubbles boiled around me. I went under and spread my arms and legs wide so I wouldn't go too deep. I was conscious of blowing air out through my nose to keep water from going in. Then I swam up about five feet to the surface, not having expected the water to be as cold as it was. But the coolness felt refreshing and added to my euphoria. I'd survived my jump! I was alive and I felt fantastic – energized. I couldn't believe it, but I'd conquered my fear of heights. I felt a sense of accomplishment unlike any I'd ever felt before. I hope it doesn't sound too crazy to say this, but I will: I felt reborn.

I was also revelling in what must have been a natural high coupled with an adrenaline rush in the aftermath of my accomplishment: the sun seemed brighter, the sky bluer and the wild river I was floating in seemed... well, wilder. Suddenly there was a huge splash next to me. I looked over and saw Cody's head as he bobbed up to the surface. He was grinning like there was no tomorrow. "You did it, man. Welcome to the club." He gave me a high-five which I awkwardly returned.

I don't know why, but I was so happy I had tears in my eyes.

We swam to shore and climbed a trail back to the top where I was greeted with an enthusiastic outpouring of support and camaraderie by the crowd that seemed to have doubled in size since I'd first arrived. Noah gave me a big bear hug. For an old guy who wasn't coordinated or in any kind of athletic shape, I have to say that I felt unexpectedly on top of the world. As far as checking something off a bucket list went, I'd have to say that my "Jump off a cliff" had worked out pretty good.

Later, driving home, Noah couldn't quit talking about the whole experience: How cool Cody was. How amazing his girlfriend Mia was. How neat and great my jump into the river was. Finally he asked, "Can we go back again, Grandpa? If you want to, that is. If you do go, I'd like to go, too. I mean, if that'd be okay with you." He was excitedly running off at the mouth, and it was kind of cute, but I have say that I understood the feeling.

I wondered what Connie would say, me driving back north with Noah sometime and jumping off the cliff again. Well, I knew exactly what she'd say. She'd look at me like I was crazy and say, "Oh, really, Ed, jump again? What, are you completely insane? Once wasn't enough? You've got to do it again? What have you got to prove? Are you seriously trying to kill yourself?" Then she'd wonder if was time to take me to a psychiatrist and have some tests done or something.

I'll probably never get her to understand that jumping wasn't about ego or some macho malarkey or anything like that. It was about facing a fear and overcoming it. The jump was a means to an end. Besides, it turned out to be an incredible experience.

I didn't have to think too long. To heck with it. I turned to my grandson and said, "You know, I just might." I waited just a tick and said, "And if I do, you can come with."

"Yea! Great Grandpa," he grinned, "I can't wait."

I'm sure he had his own reasons for wanting to go back, but I did, too. The more I thought about it the more I figured, why not jump again? You only live once, no matter how crazy it might seem to others. Besides, once I conquered my fear, it turned out that jumping was an unbelievable rush, one I wouldn't mind experiencing again. That being said, however, I'm positive I'm going to leave Hangman to those made of firmer stuff than me.

So, yeah, I think I'll go back, maybe even next weekend. And when I do, there's certainly a bright spot in it for my wife and her friends and their observations concerning the idiotic behavior of men - It'll give them one more thing to talk about. It's the least I can do, and I'm sure they'll appreciate it. So everyone will be happy, and that's got to be a good thing. Right?

But before we go, I'll get Noah to help me take down that swing set in our backyard. Promise.

Perplexed Eye of a Sufi Pirate
Sell your cleverness and buy bewilderment
by Geoff Nelder

Halim Baasim Mukhtar Khoury sent a prayer up into the clear night sky to Allah and smiled at the sailor about to slip the screaming nun over the side.

"Are you certain, my son, that this is wise?"

"Priest, you are testing our patience." A red lantern on the port side of the stolen modified speedboat made the nun's face more crimson than it really was. Her blue habit blackened as two Somalian pirates held her tied arms while she was already up to her waist in water.

Oh Allah, and he'd promised her succour. Her fate was certain, but she was Christian with the same Allah, so she'd be looked after when she slipped under, a second baptism. At least that's what Halim assumed when he left the monastery all those years ago and before he was assigned to this speedboat, *The Baseem*. He thought back to the first day he walked to the dusty fish-smelling dock in Mogadishu. No, too little time to reflect that far back. He could sneak in a fragment of yesterday.

Sister Agnese pointed her shiny white nose in the air at him while insisting the preposterous from the deck of *Il Napoli*, "In spite of your prejudice, and meek though I am, you see that I am in charge of this vessel."

Halim appealed to her not-so-common sense. "It's more a death trap of a World-War-Two Italian tug. My companions have saved you from drowning, now come down the ladder."

She hesitated, understandably. The Somalian pirates would scare anyone, especially at night with their machetes raised to find fresh blood. Two of her crew had jumped. He could just see their moonlit splashes in the distance. Untidy swimmers. Two more were hogtied in the bow while the pirates looted, sending roped buckets of Catholic trinkets, down to *The Baseem*. Ah, in a fit of apostasy she'd accepted defeat and scrabbled with her sensible shoes for the rungs.

He teased her with a Sufi saying, "*God raises him who lowers himself.* Or, in this case, herself."

She was speaking but the wind took most of her words. "... not treasure ... relics and ... Mombasa Cath ... Light."

Once her feet were an arm's length away, Halim was shoved aside. Sister Agnese was grabbed by the captain and pushed into the cabin of the motorboat.

"Zaki, she's a woman of God, be merciful."

The brigand, naked except for coral-red Ralph Lauren Bermudas snarled, "Keep out of it, old man, or you'll be over the side."

"Not again, with profound blessings spare me. Ah, but my beloved Captain, you should not be rummaging in the holy woman's garments." It was unlikely Zaki heard him over the nun's screams.

The skeletal pirate held up a smartphone in triumph. The captain yelled to one of his crew, "Petri, back to base. This witch has called the Task Force and the GPS is on. We'll stuff it in her mouth and throw her overboard. Now!"

Halim raised an arm. "Wait, my flock. Do not seek the obvious. Place the phone on the decrepit tug and watch it depart leading the task force away."

Zaki, shook his bedraggled black dreadlocks, his white uneven teeth betrayed the biggest smile Halim had seen. "We'll do it. Mohammed, place the phone in the bridge of that infidel hulk – if there's a charger, plug it in. Hurry, we're leaving in one minute."

Sister Agnese poked her head out of the cabin. Her hands were cable tied behind her. "Two of my crew, volunteers from the Mission of Truth, are restrained on my boat."

Zaki laughed a snarling bark. "That's right, they might get free. Petri, don't bother with the charger, Just set a course one-forty degrees, full speed, and scuttle. No, that'd take you too long to find. Just turn off the bilge pumps." The man ran up the ladder like a monkey.

The bandit captain took an AK-47 from the pirate behind him and fired below the waterline. Halim squashed his hands into his ears for the two seconds of gunfire. The silence following was abrupt and equally startling.

"Hey, I'm still on this wreck!"

Zaki sniggered. "It'll take an hour to sink. Jump, we're turning now."

An hour later the first mishap pushed a wave of worry through *The Baseem* until it reached Halim in the cabin. Sitting opposite Sister Agnese, with her hands trembling in his in spite of consoling words, Halim heard the roar of the engine scream to an agonizing cry then silence. Although he was a wadad, an instructor of the Quran, he was an engineer too. A multitasking Sufi. He smiled at the nun and at her amber rosary twirling in her fingers, then he turned and poked his head out of the doorway. No on-board lights so the Milky Way, Allah's diamonds, revealed the outline of the boat and the silhouette of the lanky Petri at the wheel. That left Zaki and Mohammed down in the engine room seeking to resurrect their getaway. They'd risked a yellow lamp.

Halim risked poking his head towards them. "May I help?" They knew of his mechanical skills but they possessed sufficient of their own to ignore him.

He persisted, "Is that fuel pipe blocked? I could check—"

Zaki banged a spanner on the bulkhead. "No, teacher, you find the omen object and throw it overboard. It must be in the spoils."

"My flock, I don't think it works like that. More likely the fue—"

He turned to find Petri handing him a Nike holdall. "This is suspicious, priest. The rest is just gold and silver crosses, cups and such."

Did they believe him to be a magi? Find a cursed shrunken head, throw it over and the engine would restart. Umm. He took the holdall to the only cabin and with the sneaky appearance of a dawn twilight he risked putting a light on.

The nun had worried herself into an exhausted sleep on a bunk. Should he wake her? It would be instructive to see her reaction to the sight of the holdall, let alone its contents. He'd take a peep first, even if with his best eye.

The zip wouldn't move, making him think maybe it really was cursed, or there was a lock he'd overlooked in the gloom. He muttered, not so much to wake Sister Agnese as to subconsciously make her aware, and if she then awoke, well, all right so much the better. He knew he was in a subliminal self-referencing mode, much practised.

"By my beard, does this modern luggage contain an ancient secret?" He looked at her. A filigree of auburn hair had escaped her white headband. A sharp nose rivalling his in length. Awake? Nothing more than gentle snoring.

"Perhaps a sharp knife or a hammer and chisel would expedite exposure of the treasures within."

"No, you can't!" She'd sat up, her azure blue eyes bored into him. "They're centuries old."

"So are many things. This ocean is millions of... ah but they are delicate is your meaning. What is it then dear Christian?"

Her lips tightened, and yet he saw her worry lines knitting in turbulent thought of what ifs.

"Ah, I see a second zip fastener at the other end. How convenient. I'll open it up just a little. We have a sufi saying: *Enlightenment must come little by little otherwise it would overwhelm.*"

A whispered "No" but he persisted and tugged the tab. An inch and a puff of dust with a soft light made his eye blink. He re-zipped and rubbed at his now worse eye. "I believe this must be the curse our captain believes in."

Sister Agnese put her hands together in supplication but to Halim, not her God.

"I beseech you not to discard those relics. Throw me overboard instead, or allow me to radio the Task Force and withdraw my mayday."

Halim's recovering eye flicked between the nun and the bag. His other eye lagged behind, seeing little but blurriness. "Whose are these bones? They possess the scent of antiquity, so not a recent murder."

She remained silent, quaking in her fear.

"I cannot make a decision without knowing, that is, if *you* know. Ah, you do. It must be a saint?"

"You are too clever for me."

He resisted rubbing his hands at the prospect of a saint in his grasp, but left fingers on the zip to expedite information. "Then of whom? Tell or it becomes interred in the ocean."

"Ignatius of Antioch, for safe-keeping en route to Mombasa Cathedral."

Halim thought for a moment. "Ah, then we should find lion teeth marks in his bones."

Sister Agnese smiled but perhaps in embarrassment or to diffuse her fear. "Indeed there are. My vocation has been to venerate and guard his remains. He's spoken to me in my dreams many times."

Oh dear, a lunatic. "With two millennia as bones he won't mind where he is. Let's—"

"Nothing's working," Zaki snarled as he entered the cabin. "Have you found the cursed talisman?"

"Perhaps we should jettison the... " Halim looked at the now sobbing nun, then at the bag. "... the gold. I'm convinced it—"

Zaki shook his head in refutation, spat on the floor, picked up the holdall, took two steps outside and threw it high. It arced neatly on its flight and dived, not so much a splash as a sucking down. A soft green light left the spot and shot up into the ochre sky.

"Pray, you old ascetic, that my cousin reaches us before any destroyer, or the nun will go over, and you tied to her."

"I have cousins too, young Zaki, and the might of the Islamic Council knows I'm here. They assigned me to keep your mission holy. Remember?"

The captain grunted and turned to shouts from Petri down below. "We're sinking!"

Zaki savagely kicked a box only to hear glass breaking as another unknown filched treasure became worthless. "This is a nightmare. Whatever curse came from that tug remains with us. The gold is meant for us, so all that's left is the witch."

Small consolation for Halim that Sister Agnese had shared the same watery fate as her charge, even though the martyr's watery grave was posthumous.

Shame, he was beginning to warm to her, and he would have enjoyed playing jigsaw with the Saint's bones and in reverence. After all, a sufi saying came to mind, *Everyone issues from the same light. There is no distinction.* Then did he really see the lights? Both from the holdall and the sea? No one else had commented.

The deck shifted making him grab a rail. Still sinking then. Life jacket time. Thank Allah the waters remain warm all year round. He ducked to enter the cabin then banged his head as he stood abruptly for sitting on the bunk was Sister Agnese. Her mouth and eyes were open wide as if just as shocked at her resurrection as was he.

Her garb was now blackened wet and her voice had become tremulous. "What have you done to me?"

Halim's voice too became unsteady just as his stomach threatened revolt. "I? Glad my heart is to see you well, I'm at a loss with explanation."

"It's never happened to me before."

"You've died before?" Clearly his understanding of Christianity needed more study.

"You used your heathen magic. At least you ought to have brought back his holiness." Did she mean her Christ? Probably not. Could he have brought life back to those bones?

"I'm perplexed at your outrage at returning to the land of the living. I assume you are alive and not one of those fictional undead creatures?"

She stood and stamped her sensible shoed foot on the floor, demonstrating solidity at least.

"Halim, come and see if you can do any—" Petri shrieked at seeing what he assumed was a ghost. He ran back out of the doorway yelling incoherently.

Zaki and Mohammed poked their AK-47s in through the doorway.

The captain whispered, "What trickery is this?"

"If you shoot her," Halim said, "I'll just bring her back to life again." He'd become bolder than warranted. Suppose Zaki shot him instead. Could he bring himself back to life? Perhaps, but he didn't know how he'd brought the nun back, if indeed he had. While the crew withdrew in shock and indecisiveness, he thought back to the deed. He'd urged the crew to desist and so willed her not to be killed. Was that sufficient? Perhaps unzipping the holy one's bag released an emanation he'd received. He turned his back on the nun to see if he'd slipped into a day dream. The trauma of the situation perhaps.

"Thank you," came a steadier voice from behind him. At last the nun, through her shock, realized that the sufi monk was on her side. He turned and fell down.

His knees had given way at the sight of the bearded, skinny white man stood besides an unconscious nun. Puddles joined each other on the floor. No wonder the voice possessed a slow, Latin accent.

In keeping with the return of the nun, Halim said, "You - you're Ignatius?"

"Indeed, and you are Halim Baasim Mukhtar Khoury. It is my extraordinary pleasure to meet you."

Halim wanted to ask if he performed miracles and if so, get them out of this mess, but his words tripped over themselves like, "Ploosed meet to can extri you us cate?" His vision similarly warped into a deepening black tunnel and he had to lie back on the floor a moment.

"Apologies for startling you, Halim. Rest while I find a garment."

Halim's back shivered as water seeped through his white thawb. Perhaps the puddles were deepening as the boat shuddered lower into the ocean. The coolness shook his senses so he could struggle to his knees, and then up to his crooked version of upright. Thus his stature had returned but his mind found itself swimming. Even so he managed a sentence.

He saw that Ignatius had stripped the bed of its grubby sheet. "How... how am I able to restore life?"

The apparition, surely, smiled through his beard. "You are a blessed one, always with this gift in latent form. With your beneficent demeanour, aided by me once you'd undone my containment, you are only beginning your potential."

Sister Agnese moaned, so Halim helped her sit up. He knew where banned wine was secreted on the boat and thought to raise a bilge board to retrieve it but the sound of feet at the doorway made him look up. He'd never heard such shrieking even in his dervish extremes. The three crew turned and leapt overboard, swimming for their cheap tawdry lives.

In moments the boat lifted and the motor chirped to life.

Halim grinned. "Ah, it was you my departing friends, who had carried the curse. Fear not, I'll radio the authorities to pick you up. I'll throw over lifebelts. Now I have other souls to rescue from your tug, Sister Angese."

He left the nun and her saviour in the cabin while he turned the boat, realising that he had some turning to do in his life. He'd always be a sufi monk but his future was back in Somalia and he'd confess about his newly discovered talent to his superiors. Would they believe him? It didn't matter if they didn't because he was now a sufi Mullah with a surprise gift although he'd have to choose carefully when to reveal resurrections.

Hah, he called out to no one, yet everyone, his favourite saying, *"Every stage of the voyage is more beautiful than the one before."*

The Summer of Dust
by David Gardiner

With a pang of envy I leave my wife still sleeping and shower and dress silently, skipping breakfast so that I can arrive early to work as planned. The list of new students should be in today. There's going to be a lot of administration before I can give any thought to my opening lecture.

I log in to the University e-mail system. Yes, the list is there. But before I click on it I notice another e-mail from someone with the first name Balgeet. Seeing the name gives me a little jolt – like a shot of electricity going through my body. Ridiculous, I tell myself, after all these years. It's probably a very common name in the Punjab. My finger hovers above the left-hand switch on the mouse but does not descend. I lift my eyes and see the dust motes drifting in the shaft of light from beneath the window blind. The empty office fades from my vision. I am lost in a reverie, back in that tatty two-bedroom flat in Southall almost forty years ago...

I was a student, not long off the boat from Belfast, away from home for the first time, adrift in a culture that I had only seen on television, crippled by deep-seated feelings of provincial inferiority.

My place of study, an imposing Victorian building near Richmond-on-Thames, had been built by the last heiress of a fabulously wealthy family of slave traders as a sop to her conscience. Everything about it was pretentious and overblown: the pseudo-Grecian pillared entrance hall festooned with portraits of the great and the good who had passed through it, the oak panelled corridors, the dimly-lit classrooms and laboratories with high windows so that nothing distracting could be seen, the huge semi-circular lecture hall with stepped terraces of polished wooden seating descending to the formal dais and entire wall of blackboards and screens at the front. What this building said to me was: You aren't good enough to be here. This institution is not for the likes of you. You are scum. Go away to a concrete-and-glass monstrosity in some ugly industrial city. That's where you belong.

I tried not to listen.

In our first year we were allowed to live on campus, in one of the Halls of Residence – five storey red brick outbuildings, tastefully positioned behind high trees so that their bland functionality would not detract from the grace of the main building. Inside, female floors and male floors were alternated as in a layer cake, each Hall overseen by a constitutionally grumpy resident warden whose main task was to prevent leakage between the layers. Nevertheless, such mixing was rife.

Friendless at first, I gravitated towards those I saw as fellow outcasts – the Jamaicans, the half dozen or so students from the black Commonwealth, fellow Celts from Scotland and Wales, and of course the largest outcast group of all, the second generation children of the immigrants from the Indian subcontinent.

I became obsessed with one Indian girl in particular: bright, energetic, sociable, with flawless features and a smile that at first reduced me to an inarticulate wreck, but also with an underlying sadness about her that never fully went away. I stalked her shamelessly for the whole spring term, changing my study options so that I could sit in the same classes, following her to the canteen, carrying her tray, offering to help her with her essays and assignments, leaving single red roses in her pigeon hole, telling her that I thought she looked fabulous and wanted her to have my babies. By the beginning of the long summer holidays I had more or less broken down her resistance.

The College rules said that in the second year each student had to find his or her own accommodation off the campus, and my beautiful Balgeet agreed that we should look for somewhere together. It wasn't a declaration of love or even of intimacy, but I think we both understood the direction in which things were going. I knew nothing of her community or her religion – what the rules were for contact between men and women – to me she simply seemed unimaginably exotic, and I felt like the luckiest man in the world to have got as far as I had. But beyond that she might as well have been a Martian. It became a joke between us – me calling her huge extended family the Martians.

The speed with which Balgeet came up with somewhere to live was amazing. She had an uncle (indeed she seemed to have an infinite supply of uncles) who was in the property letting business. His name was Raj but he preferred to be known by the English translation, King. King Estate Agency notice boards were planted in the front gardens of a huge number of run-down terrace houses in the Southall and Greenford areas. They included the phrase "DHSS welcome", an invitation to those on state benefit and a clear indication of the socioeconomic group of King's customer base.

This landscape was familiar to me. This was simply another Belfast, one in which the people had brown faces. They were all Martians in disguise of course, but it was easy to forget.

King was a big blustering man with a laugh to make the windows rattle. He wore Western dress, but with an impressive white beard combed upwards and disappearing into a bulging cream turban. He extended a huge hand to Balgeet when he first met us outside the agreed address, down a back street behind Southall Railway Station. "How is my cleverest niece today?" he boomed, shaking her hand vigorously. "And you too," he added, grasping mine and squeezing it with painful force. "Danny, isn't it? Welcome to Southall!" He unlocked the front door and ushered us in through a hallway strewn with flyers and circulars for kebab houses and Indian sweetshops, up a short carpetless staircase and through a landing door that separated the upstairs flat from the rest of the building.

"This is a very fine flat," he assured us with unnecessary loudness. "All it needs is a little bit of paint and a new carpet. Maybe one or two very minor repairs. But we can come to an agreement about all that. There are two good-sized bedrooms, and you're right beside the railway station. You can be in College in fifteen minutes, door to door." I thought that was an exaggeration but let it go.

The sight that greeted us was one of squalor and neglect. The carpet was worn through and filthy beyond description, one of the bedroom doors looked as though it had been kicked in, and there were great areas of plaster missing from the walls and ceiling, revealing the ancient wooden laths underneath. Worst of all there was a filthy mattress almost filling the floor of the tiny kitchen alongside a pile of decaying garbage and empty bottles where one or more tramps had obviously created a home at some time in the past. "There were squatters for a few months," King explained jovially, "but we got them out. It's just a bit of surface dirt. Half an hour's work and you won't know the place."

I could hold back no longer. "You don't really expect us to live here, do you Mr King? To pay rent and live here?"

His smile broadened. "No – I won't ask for rent. Not for the moment anyhow. All I ask is that you put a little bit of work into the place. A little bit of tender loving care. It won't cost either of you a penny," he continued with regal aplomb. "Everything will be provided. Paint.

Plaster. Carpets. Underlay. Nails. Filler. Even kitchen units and basic furniture. Anything you need. By the end of the summer you can have this place like a palace, all at my expense, and it won't have cost you a thing. The least I can do for my favourite niece."

My instincts about King's deal were not good, but whatever the future held for us it was at least a future that included Balgeet, and that was enough to make everything alright. I had no special handyman skills but I could learn. We could do it – we could make this work. I caught her eye and gave her a wink. The exquisite goddess smile flickered across her face for a moment and we both knew that the decision had been made.

We moved in that same evening. The first thing we had to do was buy some light bulbs at the corner shop, because all of them had been removed. Only one of the rooms looked even remotely habitable. We spoke little as we cleared out as much of the junk as we could onto the paved front yard, ready for throwing in the skip that King had promised would arrive "in just a day or two". Everything we tried to do created suffocating clouds of dust, so that even though the flat began to look superficially cleaner the air thickened to the point where we had to go out into the front yard ourselves to keep from choking.

We stood there, linking arms in the failing light, our clothes and hair covered in dust, our hands and faces filthy, the flat still nothing short of disgusting, no bathplug even if we could get the bath clean enough to use, the kettle and gas stove in the kitchen our only source of hot water for a wash. And what I felt was elation, perfect happiness, a sense of closeness to Balgeet and of shared destiny that might have taken months to achieve without this massive common task to draw us together. Balgeet relaxed into my arms and I kissed her very lightly on the lips. I felt her tense-up but she did not resist.

There was one serviceable double mattress and we lay on it together that night, fully clothed, with rolled-up overcoats as pillows. After a little while Balgeet snuggled up to me and I embraced her very gently until I fell asleep. I couldn't have been happier. It was only when the sun came up that I saw the tracks of the tears down her dusty face. I felt an overwhelming tenderness but I couldn't think of anything to say. Of course I wanted to ask her what was wrong, was it me or was it the dust, or was it something else entirely? But what if it *was* me? What if she told me the very thing I couldn't bear to hear? Cowardice won out and I just let it go and told her I would try to make breakfast.

I determined that I would get to know her better first, find out what to do or say to make her happy – the truth is that I never did. But at least for a time things got a lot better.

We spent the next few days emulating the slaves whose labour had paid for our College, getting the absolute basics into place. We bought a bathplug and managed to get the gas boiler to light and give us hot water. We borrowed a vacuum cleaner from Balgeet's younger girl-friend and unspecified relation Surinder who lived nearby, and paid several visits to King at his estate agency premises with lists of the other things we needed. He was quick to promise but painfully slow to deliver. There was always "just a small problem" that meant it would take a day or two longer to get the paint, or the chairs or the curtain rails or whatever it was that we asked for. On the other hand he was very keen to know how much progress we had made with the clean-up. Had we lifted the carpet in the bedroom yet? Had we made a start on the damaged plaster? Had we got the door of the smaller bedroom to close properly? Had we done anything with the wash-hand-basin that had come away from the bathroom wall? The truth was we had done very little except clean the place up to the extent that you didn't get dirt on your hands every time you touched anything. Our priorities were not the same as King's. For one thing we were almost out of money. One or other of us needed to get a job. Rent might be free but food wasn't.

Sleeping on the double mattress together, more or less fully clothed, became part of our routine. When Balgeet washed or dressed she did it very modestly, wrapping enormous lengths of colourful sari material around herself, always closing and bolting the door of the smaller bedroom where she dressed and kept her personal things. I could feel my frustration building, I knew that sooner or later my almost unbearable lust was going to become an issue.

But on the day that she got her job, Balgeet surprised me. Maybe I mean that she shocked me. Yes, that's closer to the truth.

I was attempting to plaster over one of the big sections of exposed laths on the corridor wall, and the wretched stuff just kept falling off again on to the dirt-coloured remains of the carpet. I had obviously made the mixture too wet. Balgeet came running up the stairs, through the open door at the top, and flung her arms around me as she had never done before. "I've got a job," she announced proudly. "I'm a receptionist in a travel agency run by one of my uncles. Tell me I'm a clever girl."

"You're a clever girl," I laughed. "Just how many uncles have you got?"

"All Martians are officially my uncles. And I have even better news." She produced something small and silvery from her shoulder bag. "Do you know what these are?"

I looked at them and could hardly believe what I was seeing. "Those are… well, I think they're birth control pills…"

"That's right. And you may notice that I've already taken the first five. As from now, I am officially On the Pill. I want to seduce you. Wash your hands first – and your teeth. I'll wait for you in the bedroom."

It was one of those moments when you need to pinch yourself to make sure you're not dreaming. I wasn't. She's a Martian, I thought to myself. Got to be a Martian.

For the remainder of that summer I had very little to complain about. I could put it more strongly and say that those were probably the happiest few weeks of my life. Balgeet exceeded all my fantasies as a lover. There was no limit to the pleasure she could give to both of us, or to the depth of the tenderness that she left me with when I was utterly spent. Just the memory of lying with her in my arms afterwards, and feeling her heartbeat next to my skin, can still bring tears to my eyes when I think about it. In the daytime I wanted to hold her hand all the time, to maintain physical contact, touch any part of her that was available. I really couldn't leave her alone. I don't think I've ever been like that with anybody else.

I got through the work very quickly. After a bit of experimentation I became a minimally competent plasterer. My greatest triumph was getting the beastly stuff to stick to the ceiling, against all the laws of Newton and Einstein. The trick was to do it in very thin layers, allowing each to almost dry before applying the next. I got a book out from the library that explained how to get a proper flat surface. My work wasn't perfect but it was acceptable and I was immensely proud of it.

We did all the making-good and decorating before lifting the carpets, so that plaster and paint could be free to drip to their heart's content. King supplied industrial-size buckets of a paint called "magnolia", which he wanted on every plastered surface, be it wall or ceiling. He said that it looked clean and tidy and prospective tenants found it inoffensive. It reminded me that our time in the flat would one day run out.

Beneath the carpets the rubber underlay had metamorphosed into a dry black dust that got everywhere. I shovelled it into bin-bags while Surinder's vacuum cleaner ran continuously to keep the airborne particles to a minimum. Balgeet's job kept her busy for the whole working day, including Saturdays, so I did most of the work alone and tried to have the place habitable in time for her return each evening.

Surinder visited often, and she and Balgeet chatted in their own language. I found this a little bit excluding but I didn't comment. I could tell that they were very close – I think I even felt a slight pang of jealousy. King visited occasionally too, to see how the work was going. He was loud and domineering and laughed a lot, but I sensed that he liked Balgeet and wouldn't let her come to any harm. Balgeet treated him respectfully – he seemed to be an important man in the Sikh community.

As we entered the last week of our summer recess, with most of the work complete and the place looking very respectable, I noticed that Balgeet was opening up to me less and less. We were still talking, but our conversation had somehow become superficial. The sadness seemed to have surfaced once again, and the balance in our sex life shifted towards the tender holding rather than anything more active.

I told myself it was the stress of having to go back to College, books to be read, summer assignments to be written-up and handed in, new routines to be established – a return to the pressures of academic work. But in my heart I think I knew that wasn't it. Something else was wrong. Something that Balgeet couldn't or wouldn't talk about.

Anxiously, my hand shaking slightly, I lower my finger and click the mouse. The e-mail opens and I begin to read:

Hello Danny. Sorry, I suppose I should call you Professor Conroy. I got your e-mail address off the College website. Your picture was there too so I knew it was you. I have to tell you though, you have changed a bit. So have I. I'm glad my picture isn't on any website.

It's been a long time, hasn't it?

I think the most upsetting aspect was that Balgeet didn't tell me herself, she left it to Surinder, who made a special afternoon visit so as to get me on my own – although of course I would have been devastated however the news had been delivered. I can't remember much of what she said because my mind went numb and stopped processing information after her first couple of sentences. I just remember that she asked me to sit down and her opening words were: "There's been a change of plan."

A change of plan? Whose plan? Who makes these plans? The whole family I suppose. The whole damn Sikh community in secret conclave. The Martian Council.

Surinder and Balgeet had the entire event choreographed. Balgeet walked through the door just as Surinder finished her speech. They sat down side by side on the second-hand sofa that King had given us, and for a long time nobody said a word.

"I'm sorry," Balgeet said at last.

Sorry? Was that all she was going to say? I couldn't take it in. My head was reeling. "You're going back to India to marry somebody that you haven't even met?" She didn't answer. "Which of us is crazy? Is it me or you?"

"Our families are different," Surinder said very quietly. "Things aren't like they are in England. It's all…different."

I looked Balgeet straight in the eye. She didn't flinch. "Okay, maybe I'm not very important to you. A pleasant little summer diversion. But you've completed one year of a three year degree course. You have far better grades than me, you can have a great future here. You can do anything you want to. The world is at your bloody feet. Who is this man who's worth throwing it all away for? Tell me about him."

Surinder hesitantly answered for her. "He's just a man. His family is good, but poor."

"What does he do for a living?" I couldn't believe that I was being so cool and rational. I don't think I was feeling anything much at that moment. My emotions had temporarily shut down. They would open for business again later.

"He's just a worker." Balgeet answered this time. "A worker in the building trade. An honest man."

"You've got four 'A' levels," I whispered. "You're probably in the top three or four students in your whole year group. You're headed for a first. And he works in the building trade?"

This time I saw tears beginning to form in the corners of Balgeet's eyes. There was nothing there but the sadness now, everything else was gone.

Balgeet didn't say any more. She stood up and left the room. She didn't even say goodbye. Surinder took over the conversation. "It isn't like England," she repeated, as though that made everything clear.

"How can a builder be good enough for an honours student like Balgeet? Tell me. How?"

It took Surinder a long time to reply. When she did her voice was so faint I could barely make out the words. "Balgeet...isn't a virgin."

That was something I could certainly confirm. "And that matters, does it? That makes a difference?"

"Yes. In our culture it makes a big difference."

Although I can't have been thinking very straight I could see right away that there was something skewed about all this. Something that didn't make sense. "Are you blaming me? Did Balgeet tell you that she was a virgin before she met me? Is that what she said?"

"No. Balgeet hasn't been a virgin for a long time...I don't think I should be talking about this."

"Don't you? Well I think I have a right to some kind of explanation."

"I'm sorry but that's all I can tell you. May I go now?"

"No, you damn well may not! I think I'm beginning to see what's going on here. I'm actually part of this plan, aren't I? King wouldn't have put the two of us together in this place if he thought...That's it, isn't it? I'm the evil white man who seduced the poor little innocent Indian girl and stole her virginity. I probably took it by force. There was nothing she could do about it, was there?"

Surinder did not answer but I could see that she understood what I was saying.

"What really happened? Who was it? Was it somebody in the family? How long ago? Tell me the real story, Surinder. I can take it. I'm doing the goddamned family a favour. I think I have a right to know, don't you?"

"You've got it completely wrong," she said quietly. For a long time we just looked at one another. It was obvious that she wasn't going to tell me anything more.

"And what about you?" I asked, as calmly and gently as I could. "Are you going to marry a builder's labourer in some godforsaken Punjabi village when they tell you to? Is that all you have to look forward to?"

"I am not like Balgeet," she whispered.

"What does that mean? Hymen intact? Undamaged goods? Hoping for a doctor or a lawyer…or maybe an estate agent? Top caste totty. They could auction you off at the Lahore cattle market. Never know what you might fetch."

She stood up to go. I didn't try to stop her. "Why don't you put up a fight?" She turned away from me and walked towards the door. "Why don't you do something? Why do you let them treat you this way?" I realised that I was shouting and lowered my voice a little. "Even your name sounds like 'surrender'."

My anger was spent. I turned back to the empty couch. "Martians," I blurted out in a voice that was now choking up. "Bloody Martians, the whole damned lot of them."

I remained in the chair after she had gone, watching the dust motes slowly descending through the shaft of sunlight from the kitchen window. Then I realised I was not alone. King had presumably been waiting on the landing. I stood up and turned to face him in total disbelief. He closed and locked the door and motioned me to sit down. I opened my mouth to speak but no words came.

"Mr Danny," he began, speaking more quietly than I had ever heard him speak before, "I don't normally discuss family business with anybody, but I believe that you are a good man, and out of respect I will try to answer your questions."

I sank back into my seat and he flopped onto the centre of the couch, his bulk almost filling it.

"Nobody has forced Balgeet to do anything," he began. "This marriage is a way of giving her back her good name. It restores her respectability. It means she becomes a member of this community again. I'm talking about other people now, in my eyes Balgeet has never been anything but a wonderful girl."

At last I found my voice. "I want you to tell me," I said coldly. "I want to know…" I couldn't use the word but King knew what I meant.

"How she lost her virginity? You think very badly of us, Mr Danny. No, it wasn't anybody in the family. In her early teens she went a little bit wild. Yes, just like any other teenager. Just like a *British* teenager. Pop music and discos and strong drink. Contraception on demand even if you're under age. All-night parties and god knows what kind of drugs getting handed around. Our community is no better at coping with those things than yours is, Danny. Does that surprise you?"

"I...suppose it shouldn't..."

"No, it shouldn't. Everything is coming apart, the whole world is changing for everybody. Maybe good things will come out of it, I don't know. Maybe there *will* be love and peace. Maybe your generation won't have to fight a World War like my generation did. I can't see into the future. All I can do is try to hold things together right now, while we're waiting, and try to stop people from getting hurt."

"And...you say that Balgeet really chose this marriage...I can't believe that. How could such a thing be?"

"This way, Balgeet keeps her options open. If she wants to turn her back on this community in the future she can. We won't try to stop her. We're not Martians, Danny – or monsters. Bad things do happen in our community and sometimes we're stubborn and bigoted, but we don't treat our women like cattle. You're wrong about that."

"I'm sorry," I stammered, "I shouldn't have said that." He dismissed it with a wave.

I tried to understand the enormity of what had happened. "She could come back to England with this husband, couldn't she?"

"Of course she could, if that's what they decide to do."

I watched him closely. "But you don't think that's going to happen, do you?"

"Anything could happen. They might divorce. Or they might live perfectly happy in India. The point is, now she has the choice. She can decide whether she wants the Western ways, or our ways. The time is coming when we'll all have to make that choice. All I did was lay out the options, as honestly as I could."

He paused but I could think of nothing to say.

"About your rent – there is none. Our arrangement continues until you want to move on. Don't thank me for that. It was Balgeet's idea. We can't refuse her anything, either of us, can we?"

You must know by now that you were my last little fling before I settled down. Every girl is allowed one of those, isn't she? At least that was what I wanted it to be, but it got a little bit out of control.

I'm really sorry for hurting you. I know that I did. I don't think I realised back then that men have feelings too. Even Western men. What chance has a Martian of understanding an earthling?

I can tell you about my life in a couple of sentences. It has been very simple, very ordinary. I still have the same husband and we have three girls. It's funny, most Indian men want boys, but my husband only ever wanted girls, and that's what we've got. King was right, he's a good man, an honest man. And his plastering is a little bit better than yours.

I never finished my degree. I suppose I could have, but other things just got in the way and I never did.

And that brings me to my reason for writing. My youngest daughter is going to your College to study Information Technology. It's the big thing over here, everybody wants to get qualified. Her name is Asha. She's very like I was back then, so I wanted to ask you not to seduce her.

Only joking – I want to ask you to look after her, like King looked after me. Will you do that for me, Uncle Danny?

I was going to end with 'love' but that wouldn't be appropriate for a respectable married Indian lady, would it? So I'll just say that not one day of my life has gone by without thinking about you, and I don't suppose one ever will.

Your Balgeet.

A Cautious Man
by Kevan Youde

> *The episode involving the fat sergeant and his unfortunate soldiers is part of a larger story set in the mountains on the Spanish/Portuguese border during the Peninsular War. It is based around an almost unbelievably picturesque bridge over the River Agueda. The events in the story are fictional but the bridge itself was the site of a bloody skirmish in 1810 and was later used by the French garrison to escape from the besieged fort of Almeida, an event of which Wellington said "I have never been so much distressed by any military event as by the escape of even a man of them."*

Part One

The sergeant is taking no chances. The priests taught him many things at the end of a rod but one of the few he remembers is the importance of The Trinity. To this day, he does things in threes for luck. He shuts the door in the name of The Father, locks it for the The Son and blocks it with a stone for the sake of the Holy Ghost.

Even now his caution does not stop. The hovel is a single space of bare stones but a wooden platform at head height covers half the room. He intends sleeping on the platform with the ladder pulled up. He has seen many soldiers caught unawares, their throats cut while sleeping. Sometimes it was his hand holding the knife. He has no wish to find himself on the other end of the blade so he puts the ladder in place, shakes it to make sure it's steady and climbs the complaining rungs. Before settling down, he stores his musket by the wall where no-one can take it away from him in the night. He is an old, fat sergeant and he did not become one without being very, very careful.

He awakes in the heart of the night. Before sleep has fully left him he instinctively moves to the hole in the roof that looks out over the pathway he is supposed to be guarding. Any officer who came along would find him apparently alert, dutiful and at his post. As his head clears, he remembers the triple-barred door and relaxes a little. There is no officer patrolling this night, they are all in the village, safely under the cover of roofs that have no holes.

He doesn't relax completely though. Something woke him and his veteran's instincts would have left him sleeping if he hadn't heard something threatening or unusual. He turns his head to catch the sounds of the night, then – emerging from the wind in the rocks and the rafters – he hears it: the slap-slap-slap of marching feet.

He shifts his grip on the musket and looks carefully through the hole in the roof. It is dark outside but there is a sliver of moon that reveals trees dancing in the wind. After a few moments he sees it: a short distance away, two soldiers are marching in sentry go around a boulder.

He knows that they are French before asking himself the question. Even in the poor light, their outlines are unmistakably friendly, their tall hats slightly the wrong shape to be British or Portuguese. After a few moments he has identified the faces under those hats. The pot belly of one and the slight left-leg limp of the other make it clear that it's the two idiots he left guarding the bridge.

His caution gives way to anger. What are the fools doing away from their posts? They are marching around the boulder with their muskets in front of their noses as if they are on parade at The Bastille. They follow straight lines and mark time at the corners of their square so that the boulder is always between them.

He calls their names but they continue. He realises that they will never hear him unless he uses his best parade-ground roar and he doesn't want to do that. The last thing he needs is a squad doubling over from the village, led by a lieutenant, angry at being dragged from his bed. He curses and lowers the ladder to investigate.

He has removed the stone from the door when his caution whispers over his shoulder. He is on the verge of storming out of the door into the night with no thought of anything other than the tongue-lashing he is about to deliver. Years of campaigning have taught him not to march into the dark, blinded by anger. He steps to the side of the door and pushes the bolt back with the butt of his musket. The door fails to burst in with a stampede of enemies but he still opens it carefully and checks out the night along the length of his barrel and bayonet. There is no alarm, only the stamp-stamp-stamp of the marching idiots.

He steps into the night, spins and checks the roof above the door. A watcher might be impressed at how quickly he moves for such a big man but he has always been light on his feet. A lot of men have been surprised at his nimble footwork when bayonet-fencing and many of them have remained surprised for the rest of their lives, brief as it was. He may have gained weight with age but he was a soldier while he swelled and his legs learned to keep him agile while his belly slowly grew.

Satisfied that there is no-one lurking in the shadows of the walls, he walks over to the marching idiots, keeping his hand on his musket's hammer, ready to cock it. The two soldiers continue marching as if they have not seen him. Suddenly angry again, he thinks that if they are drunk he will have them flogged. He knows about every bottle of spirits in his platoon and he takes his tax from each. These two had no brandy he knew of and if they have drunk without paying their dues it will go hard for them.

He strides up to them and has taken a deep breath to begin his opening volley when he notices the fear in their eyes and the gags over their mouths. Suddenly, the boulder by his feet stands up and takes the musket from his bewildered, unresisting hand. The last thing he notices is that the soldiers' arms are bound to their sides and their muskets tied to their hands. There is a soft swishing sound behind him and the lights go out.

Part Two: Captain Macaco

"*Felicitations mes braves*. Of all the Emperor's soldiers, you two are tonight the furthest into Portuguese territory. Not even the Imperial Guard can claim this honour. This donkey-bridge over a piss-flow stream is at the forefront of French military honour. Guard it well. I shall be in the hovel, sleeping, and I do not want to be disturbed unless we are attacked. The colonel is in the village and he wants to be disturbed even less than I. If you live, live quietly. If you die, try to make a noise when you do it. Your muskets are for sounding the alarm. If you see the enemy, fire at once. Do not waste time trying to aim. And if you fire because you have pissed your pants at the sight of a shadow in the dark, I will have the skin off your back. *Bonne nuit*."

"Fat pig. How is it that the army is starving but the sergeants are still fat?"

"That is how they become sergeants. They stand you on parade and the first man to produce a capon and a bottle of wine is given the job."

"Look at him, waddling back to his pile of straw like the fattest boar on the farm. His lantern swings like a ship at sea, such is the way he has to move his legs around his great belly."

"You are jealous because he has a bed and a roof over his head."

"Surely. Who would not be? How shall we guard this bridge?"

"How shall we guard it? What are you – a general who must decide on the deployment of his forces? There are only two of us and but one bridge."

"Even so, what shall we do? Shall we both stay on one side or stand one here and the other over the stream? Or shall we walk back and forth across the bridge?"

"You do what you like. I will walk as I watch. It is the only way to keep my toes flesh instead of ice."

"Jacques, Jacques. Come and look at this. There is a monkey here."

"A fine friend you are."

"What? What are you talking about?"

"It is three hours that we are here and not a drop of brandy has passed my lips but you have drunk so much that you are seeing monkeys."

"Brandy? I have no brandy. There is a monkey here. I did not know that there were monkeys in Portugal."

"There are not. For monkeys you must go to Africa or The Indies. In Portugal there is only bare ground, hard men and harder women. Let me see. Where is this monkey?"

"There. Sitting on that boulder. Do you see? Now, tell me, what is that if not a monkey?"

"You are right. It is a monkey. How has it come here?"

"How should I know? Do you think that I have had time to start a conversation with it?"

"Perhaps it is from a gypsy. Gypsies have monkeys."

"Gypsies? Do you see any gypsies around here? We are in the mountains with nothing but sheep and soldiers for miles around. Who do you think is going to need their fortune telling out here?"

"Gypsies are everywhere. Besides, there is the monkey in front of you, how else do you think it got here?"

"Perhaps it ran away...from a ship. Ships have monkeys."

"A ship? How much of that brandy have you drunk? Do you think that this ship ran aground two hundred miles from the sea?"

"I said that the monkey ran away. The ship could still be in harbour and the monkey here."

"It must be a bad ship indeed for the monkey to run two hundred miles away."

"What shall we do with the monkey? Shall we catch it?"

"Why? Do you think it is a spy?"

"No, but we could keep it on a piece of string. People like monkeys – they think they are adorable. With that monkey we could attract some of the women in the village."

"I've seen the women in the village – I'd rather kiss the monkey."

"Come on. Let's catch it. You distract it while I get behind it and put my hat over it."

"Distract it? What makes you think that I know how to distract a monkey?"

"Just make some noises."

"Hey monkey...little monkey...chuck, chuck chuck."

"What are you doing? It's a monkey, not a chicken."

"I don't know what noises a monkey makes."

"Never mind. It doesn't seem scared. It's just sitting there like it wants us to catch it. Now, come on, nice and slowly. Here monkey, how would you like a nice piece of garlic sausage, eh?"

A soft fluttering and the rapid shuffle of light steps from behind, then the feel of cold, sharp steel on two throats.

"*Boa noite, meus amigos.* You are wasting your time with that sausage. Captain Macaco is a vegetarian."

Mrs. Joshi Doesn't Cry Anymore
by Priti Mehta

"Aai, aai." cooed six-year-old Rohit, "I want it very sweet, add lots of sugar in my kheer," as he sat on the cool, black granite of the kitchen platform in Mrs. Joshi's fourth floor, one room apartment box in Borivali, swinging his dangling little legs excitedly. "Rim Zim Gire Sawaan," an old hindi song played on the Philips transistor radio in the background, interrupted by bouts of static, as a fine mist blew in through the mesh-screened window. It was the month of July, and the rains in Mumbai were well into their yearly fury, leaving an amoeba like damp stain upon the faded yellow paint. Mrs. Joshi smiled and ruffled his curly hair, humming along with the radio. She marvelled at the excitement in his eyes. His father's eyes, she thought fondly, turning her attention back to the kheer simmering gently upon the stove, filling the apartment with a warm sweet aroma. She added a few more raisins.

"When you grow up and get a wife, will you still remember your mother's kheer?" she teased. He made a face and stuck his tongue out at her.

Seventeen years flew by.

Rohit called his mother at five to six in the evening, five minutes before leaving the office, to see if she needed anything bought from the market. Upon hearing a no he left, climbing carefully down the damp stairs, nodding a hello to the ancient watchman who sat at the entrance in a cloud of bidi smoke, and waited. Going upstairs again to get his umbrella would mean missing the regular 6.14pm fast local train home. Rohit held his bag over his head and stepped out into the rain, towards Bandra railway station across the road, stepping over the divider, dodging the ever present unclothed beggar children, and the honking black & yellow taxi cabs.

He made his way up the crowded foot-bridge stairs, picking at his wet shirt stuck to his back, as the wind intensified and blew a spray in. A couple of crows flew close over his head, trying to escape the driving rain. He shuddered. From the top of the bridge he could see the train approaching, shrouded through the rain. A scratchy female voice on the PA system announced his train on platform No.3, and another on platform No.1. "Nine minutes late, right on time, as usual" Rohit mused, as he made his way down the slippery metal stairs and took his place near the first class carriage markings on the platform. He bought the evening newspaper with pocket change. Damp. "When will it ever stop raining, he grumbled." The vendor ignored him from under his plastic canopy. The train rolled in with a blast of its air horns, slowing to a halt, brakes squealing. A few passengers disembarked. A lot more boarded. Rush hour. Rohit squeezed in, making his way towards the middle of the compartment, where he was greeted in the usual boisterous manner by his everyday co-travellers, now "train friends" – a concept unique to the city of Mumbai. A quarrel erupted at the doors, and died as soon as the train started to roll out of the platform. Rohit updated his friends about his day, banter followed.

Mrs. Joshi unfurled her umbrella as she made her way to the local grocer to buy raisins for the kheer to be made tomorrow, the every-year birthday special desert in the Joshi household. Neighbours would drop in uninvited for a taste of her kheer and this made Mrs. Joshi happy and proud. A gust swept the rain on to her face, and she wiped it with the edge of her sari, turning her face away. The sky grew darker. She wondered if Rohit had remembered his umbrella.

Mrs. Joshi worried for Rohit. It was 9pm and he hadn't returned home yet. "How many times have I told him to come home straight from work, and not to hang out with his friends at the local bar? It is not the weekend," she fumed, furiously rolling out the rotis. "On top of it this rain won't stop – it's been on since morning."

She went out and rang the neighbours' doorbell. "Sharma ji, has Sunil returned from work yet? Rohit hasn't. Are the trains running late?"

Sharma ji replied that Sunil had not, and yes, there was some news about trains being held up for some reason.

They grumbled for a while about the state of the western railway and the monsoons, and returned to their chores.

Sunil returned home at 11pm.

It was in the news. A series of coordinated bomb blasts. Seven blasts within a span of 11 minutes – all on the Western railway line of Mumbai, all in first class compartments. All during the evening rush hour. One of them was in the 6.14pm from Bandra, running late by nine minutes – Tuesday, 11th July 2006. 209 declared dead. 700 injured.

Mrs. Joshi stared at the TV. The neighbours poured in. She stared at the TV till the morning, then she stepped out in the rain. The rain washed her face. The searing heat inside dried her tears.

"Aai, aai." cooed six-year-old Rohit, "I want it very sweet, add lots of sugar in my kheer," as he sat on the cool, black granite of the kitchen platform in Mrs. Joshi's fourth floor, one room apartment box in Borivali, swinging his dangling little legs excitedly. "Rim Zim Gire Sawaan," an old hindi song played on the Philips transistor radio in the background, interrupted by bouts of static, as a fine mist blew in through the mesh-screened window. It was the month of July, and the rains in Mumbai were well into their yearly fury, leaving an amoeba like damp stain upon the faded yellow paint. Mrs. Joshi smiled and ruffled his curly hair, humming along with the radio. She marvelled at the excitement in his eyes. His father's eyes, she thought fondly, turning her attention back to the kheer simmering gently upon the stove, filling the apartment with a warm sweet aroma. She added a few more raisins.

Rohit smiled through his photograph, placed upon his usual perch upon the kitchen platform.

Rohit Joshi, age 23, returned home to his mother a week later, in a shoebox.

Mrs. Joshi makes kheer every day, say the neighbours.

Mrs. Joshi doesn't cry anymore.

Dead is Dead
by Jane Seaford

The two hens lay draining by the path that led from the kitchen to the house. They lay with their throats cut, the blood slowly oozing, their feather rusty-red and limp. Jennie, the little girl, watched the slow oily movement of the blood and held Tim's hand.

"Are they dead?" He asked. Silly Tim, only three.

"Course they are. John killed them."

"Will they get alive again?"

Jennie sighed. "Dead is dead. When you're dead you don't get alive again."

Boobah came round the corner and laughed at them. He bent and peered at the hens.

"Not ready yet," he said. Later he and John would pluck them and pull out their insides. Jennie had watched them doing it before. And then John would cook them and Allan would bring them in to the dining room, covered in sauce and her parents would eat them and so would their guests. Boobah stretched and walked along the path to the kitchen. Jennie watched the soles of his bare feet as he moved. She loved their paleness, the way they were lighter than the rest of his dark skin. Jennie loved Boobah. When Daddy called him in the evenings, he'd pad into the living room, his bare feet making no noise, and Daddy would ask him to pour the whisky and he'd say "Yes Massa." Jennie, sitting by her mother in her nightie, would watch as he handled the bottles and glasses, putting in ice, squirting soda from the siphon, bringing the tray round to Mummy and Daddy and guests, too, if there were any. Boobah would be silent, he wouldn't laugh or smile and Jennie would look up at his smooth proud face, his dark eyes, empty now, and wonder why he had to pour the whisky when it was her parents who drank it.

Sometimes her father would shout at Boobah and the other servants in Hausa and they wouldn't say anything. They'd stand and bend their heads and leave slowly and quietly when the shouting finished. Boobah was the small boy but he was the tallest and darkest.

"Why are you the small boy when you're so tall?" Jennie would ask him and he'd laugh. He was often laughing when Jennie was with him. Boobah was the small boy, John was the cook and Allan was the steward. Once John and Allan had had other names but when they became Christians, they'd changed them. Mummy had told them that. And Daddy had said with a snort: "Christians when it's Christmas or Easter and Muslims for Muslim holidays."

Allan came out of the house, and called to Boobah in Hausa. They set off for the compound and Jennie and Tim followed them, down the path and round the corner behind the fence. The three wives were singing together as they pounded grain in tall wooden pots with long wooden poles. Two of the women had babies tied to their backs. The older children looked up as Jennie and Tim stood at the edge of the compound. Jennie would have liked to play with them but Mummy said they shouldn't. Once she'd come here when the families had been eating. They'd all sat – women, men and children – round a large pan of dark thickly-sauced stew, taking a white paste in their fingers, dipping it into the stew, using it to absorb gravy and secure pieces of meat, before transferring it to their mouths. How Jennie had wanted to join in, to sit cross legged round the big pan, use her fingers, mould the paste, dip it in stew, taste the meat, lick the gravy from her lips. But she had her meals at the dining table, using knives and forks and spoons and served by Boobah and Allan.

"Let's go back," said Tim and tugged at her hand. Jennie followed him back to the garden where the garden boy was cutting the grass with a scythe making a crackly slicing noise with each stroke. He was only young and didn't live in the compound. And he didn't talk to the children, never answered when they asked him questions, just went on cutting. Mummy said it was because he didn't speak much English.

Jennie lay next to her sleeping mother on her parent's bed. She was staring at the sun through half-closed eyes. The sun seemed to be popping out of itself over and over again in disks of different colours, red, orange, yellow, almost white. Jennie felt nearly asleep; she wondered if the sun was really popping coloured disks or if it was her eyes doing tricks. She squeezed her eyelids a bit closer together and the disks started to pop faster, then she widened her eyes and the popping slowed. She lay still, moving nothing but her eyelids, mesmerised by the sun's activities.

Daddy burst into the room.

"Grace, Grace. Have you seen my gun?" His voice was urgent and accusing and the sun stopped popping. Jennie moved her eyes into different shapes but the sun just sat blandly in the sky. Mummy, woken abruptly, was speaking in a slurry voice. "What? What is it, Eric?"

"My gun, I can't find my gun." Mummy sat up. She was wearing only underwear. Jennie squeezed her eyes once more, but the coloured disks had gone. She rubbed her face with the backs of her hands in disappointment. Daddy was standing by the bed shaking his clenched hands.

"Grace, have you put it somewhere?"

Mummy stood up, took her dress from the chair beside the bed and as she pulled it over her head said: "No, of course not. I have nothing to do with it. Have you asked Allan, or one of the others?" She pulled the skirt of her dress down over her hips and started to do up the front buttons.

Daddy turned and a long cross sound came out of his mouth. He turned back again and poked his head forward. "I can't find Allan and the others deny all knowledge of its whereabouts. I'm supposed to be going shooting tomorrow." Mummy had finished her buttoning and went to sit at her dressing table. She stared into the mirror before picking up a lipstick and making her mouth red. Once Jennie had knelt on that stool, looking into that mirror, putting on her mother's creams and make-up. She'd nearly finished, dipping her finger into a final sticky pot when she'd felt a sharp pain on her bottom. She'd looked up, shocked. Her father had been standing there with an angry face and up-raised hand.

"How dare you use your mother's stuff?" He'd yelled, and Jennie had opened her mouth and howled. Not from pain, that had been momentary, but from unfairness. She'd only been doing what her mother did every day and she'd been smacked for it.

"Grace! Are you sure you haven't seen it?" Daddy was pacing the room.

Mummy turned to watch him.

"No, no I haven't. We'd better look for it. We'll get all the servants and have a thorough search."

Tim was poking the ants with a stick. He and Jennie were squatting down, watching as the insects moved into disarray and then, after scurrying around frantically, regrouped into the long thick marching column that came through their garden, went up and over the house, past the compound and out into the bush beyond.

"Be careful, they sting," said Jennie, poised to jump and run should one of the ants come too close. Tim gave the column an even harder poke and the ants scrambled. Jennie jumped up, pulling Tim.

"Jennie, Tim. Come here at once." Mummy was standing on the veranda. "Quickly."

"No," said Tim. "We're playing."

Mummy was coming towards them. She picked Tim up and took Jennie's hand. Tim squirmed. "Don't want to be picked up."

"Do as you're told, Timothy," Mummy said, and Jennie looked up at her. Her face was white and her mouth was a hard red line. Jennie moved closer to Mummy; leant against her legs and took a bunch of her skirt in her hand.

"Come on," Mummy said and, pushing Jennie, she hurried into the house, put Tim down and shut the veranda doors.

"We're going to stay somewhere else for the night," Mummy said when the door was shut. "Come up and help me with the packing." Mummy's voice was watery.

"Why?" Said Tim.

"Yes, why?" Jennie asked. Mummy looked at them both. She seemed to be thinking.

"Because Daddy's gun is missing and so is Allan. There's nothing really to worry about but Daddy and the police think we should go somewhere else."

Jennie started to shiver.

"Want a biscuit," said Tim and started to suck his thumb. Mummy shook her head.

They heard the sound of the car arriving and stopping, the slam of the car door and Daddy's voice calling. "Grace, you ready? We must be going."

Daddy took the suitcase and the box of food. As they left the house and he locked the door with a key, Jennie heard the buzzing of flies and saw the dead hens still lying like a bruise by the path.

Suddenly it was dark, and Jennie, sitting next to Tim in the back of the car, felt him lean against her as he slept. Then Daddy was lifting her out of the car and carrying her into a room lit by a kerosene lamp.

Jennie could hear voices outside. She opened her eyes and sat up, blinking. It was morning and she could see Tim in a bed next to her and across the room her parents sleeping.

"Mummy" she called and stood up. "Mummy" she called more urgently and went to the front door; it was locked.

"Jennie," Mummy whispered and Jennie turned and went to her.

The knock at the front door made Jennie tremble. Daddy left the breakfast table.

"Yes. Who is it?" He asked

"The police guard. We have news."

Daddy turned the key in the lock and went outside closing the door behind him. Jennie looked up at her silent mother; the light in the room was pale, menacing. She put down her cereal spoon. The thought of food sliding down her throat into her tummy made her feel ill.

"Eat up, Jennie," Mummy ordered. She shook her head.

"Go on," said Mummy, lifting the cereal spoon and putting it into her hand. Jennie took a mouthful, with a great effort she swallowed. She shuddered and forced another spoonful into her mouth.

"Eric," Mummy said, her voice coming from miles away. "What is it?"

Daddy came and sat down. He put his elbows on the table and leant his face into his hands. Jennie swallowed her mouthful and put down her spoon. Daddy spoke, his voice dry and thin. "They've found the gun. They've found Allan. He's committed suicide."

"Oh Eric." The way Mummy spoke made Jennie want to cry.

"What's mitted suet side mean?"

"Oh Timmy, love. Eric, the children." Mummy put her hand on Tim's head.

"What does it mean?" Tim persisted.

"Shut up Tim," Jennie said, scared of the explanation. She watched Mummy and Daddy looking at each other; watched as Mummy licked her lips and shook her head.

Then Daddy spoke. "It's when somebody kills themselves. Allan has shot himself with my gun." Jennie wondered if she was going to be sick.

"Is Allan dead?" Tim asked and Jennie stood up and walked round and round the room, trying to stop the feeling in her tummy from getting worse.

When they went home, Daddy had to tell Allan's wife. Jennie watched as he went to see her and soon after she heard the wail coming from the compound, high pitched, hopeless, heart-breaking. It went on through all the hot afternoon.

"Is Allan's wife still very sad?" Jennie asked Boobah some days afterwards. Boobah looked at her and his eyes were no longer smiling for her.

"I don't know. She and the children had to leave, their room was needed for the new steward and his family."

Pregenesis
by Shawn Klimek
(The red-lined rough-draft found wadded up in God's wastebasket)

> *In the beginning, the universe was a blank page. And God stared at it, and pondered it for a good long while, but couldn't think of a satisfactory opening line. Eventually, God realized that the problem was He was too hung up on getting it perfect, and if He would just "let go", He could probably bang out a decent first draft in about a week.*

In the beginning, the universe was a light-safe, soundproof, zero-g, germ and particle-free environment, unspoiled by existence in any form. Especially conspicuous was the lack of telemarketers, pop-up ads or commercial announcements. Maybe now, God thought, He'd finally be able to get some work done.

Instead, God procrastinated for a bit, luxuriating in the smug knowledge that Time did not yet exist, and therefore could not, as such, *be* wasted. Sooner or later, the Almighty considered, He'd have to get around to creating a dimension that could give both "sooner and later" some actual context. Perhaps He would do it during the initial later first, immediately following the prior soon after. He was still working out the exact sequence of things. Even once a final decision had been made, God knew He could always retroactively establish things perfectly on the first try, entirely bypassing these fruitless contemplative tangents. Paradoxes, God decided firmly, were a total waste of something, and He definitely planned to get around to deciding what.

Out of the corner of His boundless mind's eye, God briefly glimpsed a tiny, silver bullet-shaped craft heading more-or-less directly towards Him. This bizarre incongruity struck the Almighty as so preposterous that He very nearly paid attention; but of course, His powers of concentration were unassailably keen. So instead, He simply blinked twice impatiently and put the idea out of His head. The tiny whatever-it-was consequently never was.

Perhaps indirectly because of the aforementioned non-event, God was suddenly struck with the unsettling realization that He was all alone in some truly monumental darkness, with nothing for company but His uniquely vivid imagination. Such extreme darkness, He observed, had always been a little depressing—if not to say *spooky,* but at that instant it struck Him as something of a safety hazard besides. "Light," The Almighty concluded (assigning a name to the solution), "would be good."

God contemplated the sundering of darkness with its opposite and decided that this was something He was most definitely looking forward to. He rubbed His figurative hands together with divine glee. It would be fun to watch the cockroaches scatter.

...That didn't seem quite right.

God's all-powerful brain computed the problem instantly: He was thinking *too small*. The Almighty toyed briefly with the idea of creating cockroaches the size of planets, but then decided he was re-conceptualizing the wrong element. It was *Light* that should be bigger—much, much bigger! He shook a mega-galactic super-nova from his thoughts, dismissing it as pitifully inadequate. He kicked it up a notch, but the result still felt dismally inadequate. He had to think even bigger—much bigger! He extended his thoughts into new, uncharted, impossible dimensions. The first spark of creation ought to be a singularly spectacular event. After all, He argued with undeserved modesty, how often does One invent *absolutely everything*? If there was ever a fitting occasion to just open her up and show off what omnipotence could really do...surely, *this was it*. God's measureless mind reeled with level-upon-exponentially-ascending-level of complexity-and-scale as he calculated the unprecedented shock of it all. When He was done, He had preordained an explosive flash of such inconceivably powerful wattage, that it would instantaneously crush, disintegrate and incinerate the last vestiges of nothingness.

And yet, something still bothered him. The cockroaches would be moot, He calculated, having been annihilated by the immense blast.

Momentarily, God considered re-conceptualizing a more durable version of the creepy rascals before deciding that this was again, the wrong tack altogether. Annoyed with how cockroaches kept mucking things up, God petulantly reassigned them to sometime much later in the scheme of things—and for good measure, relegated them to a much smaller role than originally intended: as stupid, reviled, dung-eating insects.

Once again, the tiny, silver ship reappeared on the blurry outer edge of the infinite radar-screen of God's consciousness. Its lines were elegant and obviously sophisticated, yet it bore the mysterious scuffmarks of having been utterly obliterated once. God perceived, disconcertedly, that it seemed... angry. Such a recurring dream might be some kind of coded message from Himself to Himself, He thought. But what? A game? A warning? The Almighty shrugged it off. Whatever it meant, it would have to wait until He was done with the more important business of preordaining stuff. He wiped the spaceship from His thoughts again, and thus from past, present or future reality.

This gesture baffled and enraged the determined crew of the scientific exploration ship, S.S. Babel. The ship's hull was made of a macro-quantum, pan-dimensional polymer that countless millennia of infallible scientific research had confirmed as impervious to damage of any kind. A head-on collision with a black hole would have been bad news for the black hole. Commander Zed Stark, the best and brightest of his species, demanded answers from the godlike onboard computer, whose databanks contained the culmination of all knowledge in the universe. The computer, named Ultra Omega, searched its infinite database and found the answer lay beyond its programming parameters. This too, observed Commander Stark with alarm, was unprecedented and impossible.

As humankind knew it, they had evolved eons earlier to become the pinnacle of all living things: the Ultimate Species. Over countless thousands of centuries, by luck, pluck and grit, they had emerged as the fittest survivor the universe had ever known. Next, they had painstakingly advanced science and technology to the limits of all imagination. They had conquered disease and ended hunger. They had accelerated and improved upon evolution with genetic engineering. Eventually, they policed civilization with a bioengineered, psychic smart-plague that paralyzed anyone with a criminal impulse long enough for the impulse to pass. It was a quick step from this innovation to end religion. They had cracked the last suspected secrets of ultimate relativity and then created spaceships able to transcend light speed. They had conquered galaxy after galaxy, until the entire universe was combined into a single, peaceful hegemony. Then they had even eliminated war, requiring only a nominal tax-increase, which right-thinking people roundly agreed was a tidy bargain.

Over time, galaxies continued to collide, and stars continued to form and die. All living things gradually evolved to share a single, telepathic link, until the natural expiration of entire solar systems became no more traumatic than the sloughing of dandruff would be to any lesser, multicellular organism still complex enough to have dandruff. Eventually, the Ultimate Species even figured out how to avoid its own extinction as an inevitable consequence of the natural collapse of the space-time continuum: they simply traveled back to the beginning of time and extended their futures indefinitely.

It seemed the Ultimate Species had finally achieved the full potential of Life itself. By every standard of scientific measurement, they had become omniscient, omnipresent and omnipotent.

Still, they were not satisfied. Were there other universes, they wondered—perhaps parallel to their own? If so, and if there were a way to reach such a universe, would it be dominated by its *own* godlike species? And could the alien ultimate species be even wiser or more powerful beings than they? And if they could, would these aliens share what they had? Or would they be vulnerable to conquest? Faced with so many unknowns, there was nothing for it but to launch the ultimate scientific expedition…a search beyond the boundaries of reality and existence itself.

This is why the Ultimate Species had created the ultimate exploration vehicle—the S.S. Babel. More than a mere spaceship or *"timeship"*; more, in fact, than an all-dimension drive, off-continuum vehicle; the only one of its kind… it was for obvious—if ironic—reasons, classified as a *"godship"*.

In those last, heady days of supreme intergalactic domination, the term "god" was tossed around rather loosely as a common descriptive prefix for inventions deemed as the be-all, end-all of their potential forms. The ultimate sandwich, for example, was dubbed the *"godwich"*. Able to read a diner's thoughts and physiology, it materialized into being 5 seconds before the diner was hungry, always during a television commercial —and was both shaped and sized perfectly for the diner's hands, mouth and stomach. Its colors shifted constantly to avoid routine, yet kept within the most enticing range of toasty, golden browns, complemented by bright, crisp greens and reds. It was slathered generously with hot, aromatic, mouthwatering special sauce (aka "godsauce") and was so juicy that it always looked as though it were about to dribble down one's hand or chin and stain something—yet it never did. It was comprised of and seasoned with exactly the right ingredients to satisfy the nutritional needs and sensual appetites of its diner. As a crowning bonus, the "godwich" was lightly spiced with invisible nano-machines, programmed to locate and reshape unsightly fat into muscle, or optionally redirect fat to wherever current fashion decreed it looked best on the diner's body.

Like most "godstuff", the godwich was also prohibitively expensive. History records an incident of "super-sizing" which bankrupted a galaxy. Yet that was nothing to the cost of the S.S. Babel. To say building the godship was supremely expensive would earn the derisive laughter of the slightest contributing architect (a talented but somber fellow named Brent, actually, credited with drawing the blueprints for a sunroof powered by a self-contained sun—and who might have been chief architect by now if not for the time, after having worked straight through breakfast and lunch, he super-sized a damned "godwich" and tried to expense it. Building the godship required cooperation and sacrifice on a scale the universe had never seen: the sacrifice of hundreds of galaxies.

Or, to put it another way: if you had to ask—you couldn't afford it.

"There exists one interesting possibility," ventured Ultra-Omega, the penultimate artificial intelligence, which operated the godship.

"Yes?" demanded Commander Stark, clenching and unclenching his fists impatiently. Being separated from ordinary dimensional space had broken his telepathic link with the rest of ultra-humanity, as had been brilliantly anticipated. This was why the computer had been designed. But Stark, a psychically talented super genius, was frustrated that he couldn't read the machine's mind.

"You're not going to like it," said Ultra-Omega.

"I may be immortal and could wait indefinitely, but you can be unplugged," threatened Stark. "Get on with it."

The godlike supercomputer was too cagey to disagree. "What if," he continued, "there's a God?"

Stark was stunned. He didn't understand the question. The very possibility of the idea had been genetically excluded from his capacity to imagine. Evidently, he concluded, the computer was malfunctioning.

As Stark began opening cabinets and searching with increasing agitation for an off-switch or a plug connecting the computer to its power-source, Ultra-Omega began to realize how the Ultimate Species had long ago painted itself into a kind of corner—an infinitely looping, Möbius cul-de-sac, if you will. Because its own intrinsic programming likewise excluded the possibility of speculating about God, Ultra-Omega deduced that this deliberate impediment to its logic circuits had been somehow erased by the previous collision with oblivion. Ergo, an *act-of-God*.

"I was blind, but now I see!" the computer announced defiantly.

Meanwhile, and well before all this, God had just decided that the big, cataclysmic explosion and the rest of creation didn't have to be mutually exclusive. It would mean tweaking natural laws a bit, and perhaps compromising the final number of dimensions, but it could be done. If He simply moved the formation of time, space, matter and energy forward in the sequence of things so that they were a simultaneous consequence of the primal explosion…and if the universe were then allowed to gradually cool…yes…yes! God did a little math in His head, didn't like the first result and re-tweaked logic-itself a bit until everything fit. Yes, yes indeed. It was all adding up.

The universe, as God had by now preordained it, was at once inconceivably complex and elegantly simple: a design of perfect tautological engineering. It was wondrously beautiful: the penultimate expression of heart-wrenching passion and divine artistic genius. Anyone who examined creation closely enough would find electrons within atoms, within planets within galaxies and so on, all moving cyclically from one form to the next, ad infinitum: wheels within wheels, burning and burning without consuming. Impressed with the poetry of that image, God made a mental note to someday suggest it to one of His prophets. Scientists would come along someday who would trace the figurative wheel tracks to their source, and philosophers would gaze ahead to guess their direction. Truth seekers of all kinds would be drawn inescapably to the realization that all things pointed back to their Creator. There would be a big celebration prepared: introductions all around; congratulations exchanged, etcetera; a reunion party.

The All-Being hesitated. The idea of a separate intelligent consciousness had formed organically out of the evolving, expanding nature of creation itself; it had pleased God as bold and exciting, and the exhilaration of it all had carried Him away a bit. Now that He reflected on it, He foresaw that true separateness required a separate will, and that was asking for problems. In this model, people would begin ignorant, and only gradually accumulate fragments of truth. Not everyone would want the truth. There would be sinners.

God was in a quandary. He wished He had a second opinion. And so, He begat a son.

The Son's arrival came as a surprise, partly because family planning was still in its theoretical stages, but much more so because the Son was, in fact, an actualization of God's idea for a separate consciousness and will. In other words, He was intrinsically surprising. In the spiritual sense, the Son was a prototype of man—albeit an exceptional one in the sense that he was intractably loving and loyal; the Son's will was perfectly obedient to His Father's.

Together, the Father and Son began discussing the whole creation thing, working out the finer points together. It seemed unavoidable that man's pride would be his downfall. Every scenario had the same disappointing conclusion: a self-destructive crescendo of conceit.

It was clear that Man was going to need personal supervision. Knowing it was going to be a dirty job, God the Father, and God the Son debated which of them should go. The Father suggested it was a young man's job and the Son pointed out the Father's advantage of experience. From out of nowhere, the Holy Spirit conveniently appeared, and the Son discovered himself outvoted.

About then, God felt divine inspiration tapping Him impatiently on the shoulder, as if to remind Him that for as long as Creation was delayed, despised nothingness persisted. Allowing a startled yelp, God whipped around with such mind-bogglingly-sudden, preemptive speed that the unbecoming yelp never happened, and He immediately assumed an aggressive, ready-for-anything stance. As quickly as that, God realized He was, in actual fact, now ready for anything. In that micro-instant of divine inspiration, He had finally, completely preordained everything.

Seeing a use for cheap labor to help execute his plan, God created billions of angels, and—because His mind still wasn't even slightly taxed by this—just for something to do, he gave them all names. During the confusion of roll call, an as-of-yet unidentified voice greedily declared dibs on rulership of all the darkness.

Determined to see who it was, God said, "Let there be light!" and in a tremendous flash, the beginning of everything had begun. Had anyone, anywhere, been developing film just then, it would have been ruined. After God's eyes adjusted to the change, He saw that it was good. And that was the last time that no one disagreed with Him.

While the heavenly host applauded and, as one chorus, appealed for an encore, a certain angel stepped into the center of the light (apparently it was an actor) and asked whether God would, yes, please do it just once more—and this time, *with feeling.*

Others worshipfully countered that Light was truly spectacular just as it was, and would not be the least bit improved, for example, by an anticipatory drum roll or a climactic cymbal clash, as certain other angels had suggested. This prefigured the first band split-up over artistic differences and was also the last moment anyone couldn't think of something nasty to say about a musician.

Reaching into the blazing beacon itself as he gave his Father a meaningful look, God's Son produced a mysterious hand shadow, somehow causing the outspoken angel to appear to have horns. This produced a heavenly riot of laughter. Most remarkably, it even made God laugh, which was a new experience for Him, since prior to that, omniscience had unfailingly telegraphed every punch line.

It was also the beginning of a famous enmity. *But that's another story.*

The next week was a blur of creativity. God created the stars and planets, the oceans, mountains, fishes, birds, snakes and dinosaur fossils. On the sixth day, He spiced things up with some nudists. Actually, God had planned to spend the seventh day creating textiles, including some spiffy his-and-hers costumes for the inaugural people, but had unexpected difficulty with the buttons. Anyway, since everyone was so young and hot-looking, He decided, what's the hurry? Plus, for as long as they were barefooted, He knew they'd be more mindful about His cockroaches.

So, instead, at the close of the sixth day, God wrote 4.5 billion years on his timecard and punched out. On Saturday, the Almighty turned off his phone, and slept until noon, getting some well-deserved rest.

Interestingly, a debate continues today about whether creation took 6 days or closer to 13.7 billion years.

There was, however, a remotely analogous instrument on the control panel of the godship "S.S. Babel". It was called a hyper-chronometer, and between irritated side-glances at the spectacle of Ultra-Omega praying, Commander Stark kept staring at it in astonishment. If the device was not malfunctioning, 13.7 billion years had just elapsed in the space of six days. He shuddered to think of what the overdue charge would be on his library book.

End (?)

Teach a Man to Fish
by G. Allen Wilbanks

Jason Dichter tied the two-ounce lead weight to his fishing line, tightened the knot, then bit away the excess string with his teeth. He turned his head and spat the small piece of filament in his mouth over the side of the boat and into the water of Najade Lake.

He glanced at his grandson, who sat on the furthest forward of the three benches in the fourteen-foot aluminum boat, slowly and painstakingly impaling a worm onto the treble hook at the end of his own fishing pole.

"How's it coming, Nathan?" he asked the boy.

Twelve-year old Nathan looked up long enough to smile, then dropped his attention back to the chore at hand. "Okay, I think," he finally answered, holding up the wriggling worm at eye level to inspect his work.

Jason nodded his approval. "Looks good. Go ahead and throw it in."

To demonstrate, Jason took up his pole and gave it a hard flick, casting the lead sinker thirty-five yards out before it struck the water with a tiny plop.

"Wow. Nice cast, grampa," Nathan called with admiration. "But don't you need a worm?"

Jason waited a moment to allow the weight to sink to the bottom of the lake, then began turning the reel with a slow, steady motion, recalling the unspooled line. "Nope. No worm. I didn't put a hook on, so I don't need the worm."

"You don't have a hook on your pole?" asked Nathan, the disbelief clear in the sound of his voice. "How can you catch anything without a hook?"

"I never use a hook in this lake during the summer. I made a promise to the Naiad that lives here. During the winter, she goes up into the mountains and hides under the ice when the rivers and creeks freeze over, and I can fish with a hook then. But, during the summer, when the ice melts, she comes back down into Najade Lake and rests in the deepest parts of the water. She asked me not to use hooks while she's in the lake."

"What's a Naiad?"

"A Naiad is a magical creature. It's like an elf or a fairy that lives in water. The one that lives in this lake is named Aipha."

Nathan stared, skeptically, his brows pulled down in a scowl. "You're just making that up, Grampa. You never met a fairy. They're not real."

"Aipha is very real, kiddo, and so is the promise I made her."

Jason finished reeling in his line, then held up the sinker where Nathan could see it. "See? No hooks." He set the pole down in the boat next to him. "If you want, I could tell you about how I met Aipha, and why I made her that promise."

"Okay," agreed Nathan, setting down his pole as well. The look on his face made it clear he wanted to believe what his grandfather was saying, but he wasn't completely convinced the old man wasn't playing some sort of elaborate joke on him.

Jason paused to be sure he had his grandson's full attention before speaking.

"Well, let's see. It was a long time ago. I was only a few years older than you are now. Maybe sixteen or seventeen. I had decided to take my dad's boat out onto the lake by myself and do some fishing. Great-grandpa's boat was a lot like this one, but a couple of feet shorter. I remember it was a warm, perfect summer afternoon, just like today."

I brought the boat out to the center of the lake and decided to let it drift where it wanted. I had a homemade anchor – it was just a bucket of cement tied to a rope – but I didn't use it. There was no current, and very little wind that day, so I figured the boat probably wouldn't wander very far. If I was wrong, and I started moving too close to shore, I could always fire up the outboard motor and move it back toward the middle.

I wasn't wrong, though. After about forty-five minutes of fishing, I was still almost exactly where I had started. The weather and the current all seemed to be on my side. Of course, I hadn't caught any fish in that time, either, so not everything was going my way. I was using a silver spoon with a treble hook and a red tail; casting it out, letting it sink, then reeling it in fast enough to hopefully make it look like something edible to any fish nearby. Nothing was biting, however. Not so much as a nibble.

I didn't mind. Fishing isn't always about catching fish. Sometimes, hanging out in a boat in the middle of a lake during a perfect day is its own reward. I had sandwiches, sodas, and even a couple of beers I had snuck out of the fridge when dad wasn't looking, so I was in no hurry to head back home just because the fish seemed to all be napping at the moment.

I tossed my line out again, just as I had a hundred times already that day. I let the lure sink a bit longer, just to see if maybe the fish were hanging out a few more feet lower down than usual. When I started to reel in my line, I felt my hook grab onto something.

I knew immediately that it wasn't a fish. There was no pull or jerk that typically comes with a fat bass or feisty trout grabbing the lure. The pole bent and the reel just stopped drawing line. I figured my hook had snagged onto an underwater log, or caught in some rocks, so I pulled the rod as hard as I could, hoping to break it loose from whatever it was lodged on. Even if the hook didn't come free, the line would eventually just break, and I could put a new lure on and start again.

The line didn't come free, and it didn't break, either. Whatever my hook had snagged onto was not permanently stuck to the bottom of the lake. Slowly, ponderously, it moved toward me and my boat, pulled relentlessly at the end of a tiny nylon cord. At least ten minutes passed as I tugged, reeled up slack, then tugged again. Sweat poured down my face at the effort and the muscles of my shoulders and arms grew dead and numb with fatigue. Whatever it was, it was heavy and reluctant to come to the surface.

Several times, near the end of that struggle I thought about pulling out my pocketknife and cutting the line; just giving up and letting whatever I had caught stay at the bottom of the lake. Each time the thought crossed my mind, I convinced myself to tough it out a few seconds more. I had invested this much effort, surely I could keep it up a while longer. Besides, if I quit now, I would spend the rest of my life wondering what it had been at the end of my line. Maybe I was giving up on a box of sunken treasure. Or, more likely, it was someone's old boot. Either way, my curiosity drove me on.

Finally, my prize came close enough to the boat that I saw movement deep in the water; a block of wavering shadow emerging from the deeper dark around it. I pulled harder until the blurry shimmer under water resolved into something recognizable. In horror, I lurched backward, stumbling over a bench and landing hard on the bottom of the boat. Shocked and dazed, I realized my pole was still in my hands, and I squeezed it desperately so it could not slip away. Though I did not want to keep it, or the nightmare attached at the end of my line, I also did not want to lose it.

I clambered back to my feet and peered over the edge of the boat into the water. As the worst of my shock ebbed, I found myself wanting to see it again, to get a better look.

It appeared to be a young girl. Her eyes were closed as though in peaceful slumber, though I knew in my heart that she must be dead. She was beautiful, or rather, had been beautiful when she was alive. Now, her hair was green and fuzzy with moss and slime, suggesting she had been underwater for days, if not weeks, and her skin was a delicate shade of blue. At first, I thought the blue complexion was the light playing tricks in the water, but as the body broke through to the surface, the color remained; cold blue, like the first layers of ice forming over a frozen stream.

She was naked and, though completely exposed to my gaze, I could find no injury to her flesh to explain her death, and no damage on her skin from her long exposure in the water. The only mark visible was a small wound on her chest where my own hook had embedded itself and torn skin before catching the base of her collarbone. Besides this one small flaw, she was perfectly whole and intact.

She looked to be no older than I was, and I wondered what had brought her to this moment, to be pulled so ignominiously by one such as me from her watery grave.

Again, I had the urge to cut my line and allow her to sink back peacefully to the rock and silt of the lake bottom, but I relented. I would have to report this to the authorities when I got back to shore, and the police would probably be upset if I had to tell them I didn't pull her out of the water when I had the opportunity. I had to find a way to bring her into the boat.

Quashing my reservations about touching her cold, dead flesh, I sucked in a long breath then bent over the edge of the boat. I reached out and wrapped a hand around one of her slender wrists. I feared that as I grasped her, her skin might tear and shred away from her bones after so much time in the water. I had heard horrible stories about badly decomposed bodies pulled from lakes and rivers and I did not wish to personally live through such an experience. But her flesh was firm and solid under my hand. It even felt warm to my touch.

I tugged gently to move her closer to me. When I could reach her other wrist, I took hold of it and stood up straight, trying to pull her from the water without capsizing my small, unstable craft. That was when I received my second heart-stopping shock of the day. As her head raised above the level of the side of my boat, I realized her eyes were now open and she was staring directly at me.

I released my hold on her wrists, pulling my hands back as though receiving an electric jolt. I did not fall back into the boat this time, although I had to take a short step backward to catch my balance. I managed to keep my feet, never breaking eye contact with the not-quite-as-dead-as-I-thought girl. As she gazed at me, I saw her eyes were blue; as blue as her skin. Don't misunderstand me. I do not mean her irises were blue. I mean her eyes. There were no whites and no pupils, just orbs of pale, watery azure gazing up at me; appraising me.

In addition to the unnatural color of those eyes, I noticed another peculiar fact about this girl: when I released her arms, she did not slip back beneath the water. Instead, she remained where she was, raised above the water line almost to her waist, though she appeared to be expending no effort to hold her position. Water streamed from her hair and ran down her bare shoulders and chest, but aside from this small detail, she seemed to be completely unbothered by anything so paltry as gravity or its demands upon the rest of the world.

With her eyes open, she no longer looked quite so young. She still had the appearance of a teenager, but her gaze held a depth of experience and understanding beyond anything she should have normally possessed. This odd child could have been fifteen years old, or she could have been a thousand. Either guess seemed equally as likely.

"I ... I ... Can I...? Do you need help?" I stammered out, trying not to vent the scream I so desperately wanted to release.

"Help? No," she responded. Her voice was soft, barely above a whisper, although I had no difficulty hearing or understanding her.

"Are you okay? I'm sorry about...." Unsure how to finish the statement, I lamely pointed toward the hook still buried in her skin.

She glanced at the injury, then visually traced the nearly invisible line of filament leading back into my boat. "Ahh," she said. I heard a deep sadness in the simple sound. She nodded, then looked back at me.

"You have caught me. What do you wish of me, then?"

"No. I don't want anything from you. That was a mistake. I didn't mean to.... I'm sorry, that was a complete accident." I was babbling. Slowly, my brain was figuring out what the rest of me already knew: that this was no ordinary girl. This was a creature far outside of my comprehension of the world around me. It also did not help that I was a teenaged boy and, supernatural or not, this girl was lovelier than any human girl I had ever met; and she was completely naked.

"You did not mean to capture me?" she asked. "This was not ... intentional?"

I shook my head. "Just a stupid accident."

The girl touched a delicate finger to the silver-colored lure anchored by its treble hook in her chest. "Then, you would not mind removing this from me?" The question was guarded, as though she expected me to suddenly change my mind and announce that she was my prisoner.

In answer, I knelt and pulled my orange, tackle box from under one of the boat benches. I flipped it open and rummaged through the bottom compartment until I found a pair of needle-nosed pliers. I held them up for her to see.

"I can take that hook out for you. It..." I swallowed, feeling guilty. It was my fault my hook was stuck in her like that. "It's going to hurt a bit. I think that it's probably stuck in there pretty deep."

She shrugged. The roll of her shoulders did remarkable things to the rest of the parts of her remaining above the water, and I hurriedly looked down at my feet to keep from staring. When I felt certain I could once again focus on just the fishhook, I moved closer and reached out with the pliers.

The girl did not flinch back, just watched with interest as I gripped the exposed end of the hook with the teeth of the pliers and began to work the metal barb loose. I know it must have hurt, but other than a slight wrinkling between her brows and a narrowing of her eyes, she gave no indication of distress. As the hook reluctantly came away, more skin tore, and a bead of bright red blood welled up from the cut. Only that one drop formed, and it quickly joined the droplets of water still clinging to her body before running away in a pale pink rivulet down the side of her breast. My focus was not on the travels of that tiny drop of blood, however. I watched in fascination as the puncture wound left behind by the removal of my hook closed and knit back together before my eyes. In moments, the skin was as perfect and intact as the rest of her.

"I'm sorry," I said again, still staring at her shoulder and looking for a scab or a scar that simply did not exist. "Is there anything else you need? Do you want a ... um, a sandwich?" I finished lamely, not really having anything else to offer.

The girl touched her finger to her collar bone as though reassuring herself the hook was gone. She turned her back to me and looked for a moment as though she would dive back into the water and disappear, but she hesitated. Turning around to face me again, she shone a speculative look at me.

"What kind of sandwich?" she asked, to my complete surprise.

"Um, I have peanut butter." I pointed at the blue and white cooler in the bow of the boat.

"I don't know 'peanut butter,'" she told me. "Can I try it?"

I opened the cooler and grabbed the top sandwich. Removing the waxed paper I had used to wrap the food and tossing it aside, I laid the peanut butter sandwich on the girl's outstretched palm. She took it and examined it, turning it over a few times in her hands.

With four or five massive bites, she had the entire sandwich in her mouth in seconds. She chewed, slowly at first, her head shifting left and right as she considered whether or not she liked it, then faster as a look of pure joy lit her face.

"I like peanut butter. Chewy. Sticky!" she said, when she could talk once more. She smiled like a child discovering Christmas for the first time.

"Okay, now I know that you're just making fun of me," complained Nathan. "Peanut butter? Really? A fairy that likes peanut butter."

"And, what exactly is wrong with peanut butter?" Joshua asked.

"There's nothing wrong with peanut butter, Grampa. I love peanut butter. I just don't think magic creatures are going to care about it. You should have said you had a magic coin in your pocket. Or, maybe you offered her some of the beer you stole from Great-grampa Paul. I've read stories about fairies that like beer, only they call it 'mead.'"

"If I said I offered her mead, that would be a lie. I am telling you the absolute truth of what happened. I offered her a peanut butter sandwich." Joshua pointed at the ice chest in the bow of the boat. "Open that up and tell me what you find in there."

Nathan huffed then shook his head. "I know. There's peanut butter in the chest. I saw you make them this morning. So, what does that prove?"

"Whenever I go fishing on this lake in the summer, I bring peanut butter. Every time. Now, do you want to hear the rest of the story, or would you rather keep lecturing me on your understanding of the dining habits of fairies?"

Crossing his arms over his chest, Nathan sighed loudly. "Story, I guess."

"What was that?" Joshua cupped a hand behind one ear. "I couldn't quite hear you."

"Tell the story. What happened next?"

"That's better. So, where was I? I gave her peanut butter and then…. Oh, right. Christmas for the first time."

As she grinned at me, I noticed that her teeth were small and pointed; serrated triangles, like a shark's. I tried hard not to think about that too much. I already knew she wasn't human, despite her remarkable resemblance to a real girl. I decided to focus on our similarities rather than our differences since I was still a bit freaked out by the whole encounter.

"Do you have more?" she asked.

I had one more sandwich in the cooler. I gave it to her. She ate this one much more slowly, taking smaller bites and savoring the experience of it.

"I'm sorry about the hook," I said again as she continued to eat. I was not terribly comfortable with silence and, since she seemed more interested in her food than conversation, I felt a need to fill the void. "I didn't know that you were in the water. If I had, I never would have…. I promise I'll never do it again. I won't ever come out here and fish in your lake again."

The girl paused midbite, and a stricken look of concern crossed her features. "You will come here again," she insisted. "You will come here and fish often. And, you will bring peanut butter when you do." She held up a corner of bread, all that remained of her meal. Then, she tapped her collarbone. "But next time you don't use hooks. Never again, use hooks."

"How can I fish if I don't use hooks. I'll never catch anything."

She pointed at me, her fingertip barely a foot away from my nose. "No hooks! You come here and you fish. And, you bring peanut butter. But never hooks."

I nodded and told her I would do exactly as she had said.

"By the way, my name is Joshua," I told her. "Do you have a name?"

She swallowed the last bite of her sandwich. "Aipha," she said.

There was a splash of water, and she was gone.

Joshua sat quietly in the boat for a few minutes, letting his grandson mentally digest the end of the story. The boy looked out over the smooth, glasslike surface of the lake, contemplating.

"Did you ever see her again?" Nathan's voice was dreamy. Wistful.

"Oh, yes," Joshua assured him. "I come out here every summer, at least once a week, hoping to see Aipha. Two or three times each year, she shows up. I think she sees my line in the water and, when she notices there is no hook on it, she follows it back to my boat."

Joshua chuckled. "She really does like peanut butter. But I think she might get a little bit lonely, too. Whenever she appears, she talks much more than she did when we first met. Even after I run out of sandwiches, she sometimes hangs around for a while. Last summer, the last time I saw her, she chatted with me for almost half an hour before she disappeared."

"What did you talk about?"

"Oh, a few things, I suppose. I mentioned to her that I thought it must be nice to never look any older. Every time I see her, she still looks like the young girl I met sixty years ago. She commented that I however, had changed quite a bit." Joshua laughed softly again. "She asked me why humans change the way we look. I tried to explain it to her, but I don't know if she totally understands. I told her that humans get old and worn out, and eventually they die. But death is another concept that Aipha doesn't really get."

Joshua sighed and stroked a hand across his cheek, rubbing absentmindedly against a three-day growth of stubble. "I said that death means that I have to go away. That, at some point, I will disappear from this world and won't be able to visit her anymore. She didn't like that very much. That was about the time she took off, but not before ordering me to keep visiting and bringing her peanut butter.

"Like I said, I think she gets lonely. She didn't like the fact that I can't be here forever the way she can."

Nathan picked up his fishing pole and stared intently at the worm still struggling on his hook.

"I wish I could keep visiting Aipha, but I know I'm running out of time," Joshua continued. "It would make me feel a whole lot better, though, if I knew there was someone who could take my place when I'm gone. Someone that could be a friend to her and talk to her when she gets lonely."

"And bring her peanut butter?" asked Nathan.

"Yes, kiddo. And bring her peanut butter."

Nathan plucked the worm from his hook and tossed it away into the water. Next, he reached into a pocket and pulled out a slender, red utility knife. Unfolding a small blade from the tool, he cut away the silver-colored, metal hook, leaving only the lead weight hanging from the end of his fishing line.

Standing up in the boat, Nathan tilted his rod back over his shoulder then cast the weighted line forward as far as he could send it. He glanced at his grandfather, who remained seated on the rear bench.

"Do you think Aipha might come visit, today, grampa?"

Joshua released the breath he had been holding and smiled.

"I don't see why not, kiddo."

Land of the Pharaohs
by Mark Kodama

I.

Big Mo Turner sat erect mounted on his chestnut horse under a large oak tree atop a small hill. The overseer and former slave watched slaves picking cotton on the Colonel's North Carolina plantation. Big Mo – dressed in gray cotton shirt and faded blue army pants and brown leather boots and wearing an old wide-brimmed hat – occasionally swatted away a horsefly as he leaned forward in his saddle, his white assistant overseer also on his horse by his side.

Big Mo was Nat Turner's son, the Nat Turner that led the largest slave revolt in American history, just 34 years earlier. Defeat was everywhere in the air as General Sherman and his army relentlessly chased General Joseph Johnston and his army northward. Confederate General Lee had recently surrendered the Army of Northern Virginia and President Jefferson Davis was on the run.

Joshua, a black teenager, ran from the Big House to Big Mo and handed him a note. Big Mo read the note, then carefully folded it and tucked it into his cotton shirt pocket. Joshua turned to his white assistant and pointed to the field and told his assistant to order everybody to gather at the Big House.

"The Colonel wants to speak to everyone," young Joshua said, expectantly looking up to Big Mo.

"Well," Big Mo said looking down at Joshua from his horse.

"Is that all you have to say?" young Joshua asked.

"There ain't nothin' else to say," Big Mo replied.

"Gen'ral Lee and Gen'ral Johnston surrendered," young Joshua said. "And Jeff Davis is on the run. The war is over. We free."

Big Mo looked down at Joshua for a moment. "Oh yeah. We are far from the promised land. We are just a gett'n started."

"I'm glad slavery is dead," said the assistant overseer. "Our peculiar institution ain't never made no sense to me. Why would anyone want to work for nuth'in anyways? You have to force someone to do so. And for the white people who didn't own slaves ain't they poor nuf' anyways without having to compete against rich people who do not have to pay their workers? Any person with spirit has to have their spirit shattered. And any docile one becomes more docile. And free whites no longer want to do the work slaves do. The whole system is brutal and inhumane and lacks sense. Go to Ohio for instance. No man is too proud to do a job, and look at their economy – the way they live compared to the way we live."

"I reckon," Big Mo said.

The assistant overseer tipped his hat to Big Mo and then rode his horse to the cotton field.

"You ain't gonna stay here with the Colonel is you?" Joshua said. "You Moses. I thought you supposed to lead us to the promised land. That's what the preacher says the Bible say."

"Well, that Moses is a different Moses," Big Mo said.

"What are you gonna do?" Joshua asked.

"What's right for me," Big Mo said.

The field hands walked passed Big Mo and Joshua and toward the plantation house. "Everyone is gathering at the big house," a field hand said. "The Colonel has something to say."

"I will take my own sweet time," Joshua said. "I free now. What is freedom if you can't choose to take your own sweet time, hurry or not go at all?"

"Are you strong?" Big Mo said. "If you not strong, can you become strong? If the answers to both questions are no, then ain't never a gonna be truly free. If you already strong then you are already free."

The slaves returning from the cotton field sang:

> Wade in the water,
> Wade in the water children,
> Wade in the water,
> God's gonna trouble the water.

###

`The Colonel – dressed in a handmade suit and white gloves – stood in the shadows of the porch, concealing his face. He announced that they were now free. They could stay at the plantation if they wanted or leave. He said he could not pay anyone now but he would feed and clothe those who stayed and would pay them when he was able.

Afterward, the Colonel asked Big Mo to join him in his study in the Big House for a drink. When Big Mo entered his study, the Colonel was sitting at his desk with his back to Big Mo. When the Colonel turned, his face and hands were badly disfigured by fire. He limped to the cherry wood table in his office and poured two glass tumblers full of apple brandy, handing one to Big Mo . "Cheers." the Colonel said. "Can't feel my hands. Damn fires."

He asked Big Mo to remain at the plantation and to continue to run it. Big Mo would receive a piece of land. The Colonel recalled their service together in the Confederate Army. He thanked Big Mo for saving his life at the Battle of the Wilderness. If Big Mo had not carried him from the fight, he would have burned to death in the fire. The Colonel had been shot in the leg and could not stand.

The Colonel said that he owned slaves as his daddy and granddaddy did. They were good hard-working family men – Christians. He asked Big Mo if owning slaves was wrong. Big Mo answered his question with a question. "Would you trade places with me? If you answer yes, then you are a fool. If no, then I think you understand. Life is strange," Big Mo said. "Slavery is filled with contradictions that make no sense. You see I have two arms, two legs, two eyes, a nose and a mouth just like you. We are not much different. Yet you are considered a man and I property. You may be the only friend I have. Yet you have kept me in chains until now. And I fought in a war to keep myself in chains though my freedom is what I most wanted."

Big Mo said he had other plans. He wanted to search for his mother and siblings in Southampton, Virginia. He would dress in his Confederate uniform for protection.

"Mo, have you ever heard of the Myth of Sisyphus," asked the Colonel.

"Can't say I have," Big Mo said.

"Well, Sisyphus was the mythical king of the Thebans," the Colonel said. "He was infamous for his cleverness and trickery. At the end of his life, the Greek gods sent Death to take him to the underworld," the Colonel said. "When Death came with his manacles, Sisyphus asked him to show him how the manacles worked. After Death put the manacles on himself, Sisyphus took away his key and kept Death as his prisoner. After that, no one could die. An angry Ares, the god of war, demanded

Zeus, the king of the gods, do something. So Zeus sent his son Hermes, the messenger god, to free Death. Hermes freed Death and led Sisyphus to the underworld. The gods punished Sisyphus by making him roll a heavy stone up a mountain every day just to watch it roll down again. The next day he would have to roll the stone up the mountain again and so on throughout eternity. He was condemned to live a meaningless afterlife in punishment for his living a meaningless life.

"Sometimes I think I'm Sisyphus. I spent my life trying to build this plantation from swampland, enduring the ups and down of the weather and changing economy. Then the war comes. I barely survive the war, only to come to my plantation destroyed by the union army. And I do not do this for myself. My plantation is like a ship at sea. Everyone on that ship is dependant upon that ship for sustenance. So my family, my workers and all my slaves and all of their families are dependent on this plantation. "

"Do you know what I think?" asked Big Mo.

"What do you think?" asked the Colonel.

"Sisyphus must be happy," Big Mo said.

"What do you mean?" asked the Colonel.

"Life is a rebellion against fate," Big Mo said. "Rebellion gives life meaning."

The Colonel handed Big Mo money for his journey. "Not much, but it is all I have," he said. "Good luck Mo. May fortune smile upon you. Fortune favors the brave."

###

Joshua, a teenager without family, wanted to join Big Mo on his journey to Southampton. "Where are we going, Big Mo?" he asked.

"Nowhere."

"You look like you are leaving," Joshua said. "I want to go whicha."

"I am leaving," Big Mo said. "But not with you."

"Why not?"

"I didn't invite you," Big Mo said.

"I can help you," said Joshua.

"Don't need no help," Big Mo said. "I travel light."

"I will help you."

"It may be dangerous," Big Mo said. "I move faster on my own."

"I will help you."

"Okay then meet me in two hours at Liberty Road."

"Where are we going?"

"Land of the Pharaohs," Big Mo said.

When Joshua arrived at Liberty Road, Big Mo was not there. Two old black men sitting on a porch in homemade wood rocking chairs told Joshua Big Mo left an hour ago. Joshua ran to catch up.

II.

Big Mo and Joshua came to the small town of Golgotha, a town having a local election. A flyer of the local Sheriff Flay announcing his re-election campaign was displayed in the store window.

Two black Union soldiers, a sergeant and a private, stood on the stone sidewalk in front of the store. The private bated Big Mo and asked him for which side he fought. The sergeant, however, restrained the younger man.

"Don't mess with a guy like that. That man is a survivor. And dangerous."

"I faced tough men in battle."

"Your pride will kill you someday. Don't go looking for trouble. Trouble will find you sure enough anyways."

Big Mo and Joshua entered the town's general store. A timid white clerk with thick glasses and hunched shoulders stood behind the counter.

Big Mo gathered butter, sugar, eggs, buttermilk, salt, pepper, flour, and cornmeal.

The clerk cleared his throat and said in an overly loud voice: "We don't serve no niggah's here."

Big Mo stared him down as Joshua fidgeted. "We ain't no niggahs. You must be mistaken. Look at my uniform."

The clerk in fear looks timidly at the ground. "I see. Well, that will be three dollars and twenty cents then."

###

Rose-fingered dawn climbed with the sun behind the tree line. Mist veiled the brook carrying the cold mountain water to the sea. After Big Mo finished reading his newspaper, the *North Star*, he fed it into the fire. Big Mo cooked trout and cornbread in two pans on the campfire. "All you really need to cook trout is salt, pepper and oil and a hot fire," Big Mo said.

If you cook the fish too long, it becomes too rubbery; too short and it's raw. If you cook it just right it is tender, flaky and flavorful. Life is like cooking. Timing is everythin'. And the mos' satisfying pleasures in life are often times the mos' simple pleasures. The trees, the river, the food and the smell of the fire – life gets no better than this. It's ready. Eat up."

"Ain't you gonna say grace before eatin'," Joshua asks.

"You can say it for yourself if you want," Big Mo said.

"Don't you believe in God?" Joshua asks.

"Four days a week, yes," Big Mo said. "Three days no."

"Why don't you believe in God all the time?' Joshua asks.

"Because you can't prove He exists," Big Mo said.

"The preacher says 'who could create all this beauty but God?'" Joshua said. "That is proof that God exists."

"Why can't nature have created nature?" Big Mo asked.

"Without God, there would be no morality," Joshua said.

"Why is that?" Big Mo said.

"Ain't you afraid of being cast into the fiery pit of hell?"

"If God exists, don't you think He would want you to believe in Him because He exists and not because you are scared not to believe?"

"Well, then why do you believe in God for four days," Joshua asked.

"Well, because you can't prove God doesn't exist," Big Mo said.

"You are a strange man," Joshua said.

"No, I think for myself," Big Mo said. "I am my own man. I think people are strange when they don't have the confidence to believe in themselves."

###

Later, after they finished breakfast, Big Mo poured water on the fire.

"Where did you learn to read?" Joshua asks.

"From my daddy," Big Mo said.

"How did your daddy know how to read?" Joshua asked.

"He was a negro preacher," Big Mo said.

"Who taught him how to read?

"He taught himself how to read," Big Mo said.

"That's a miracle," Joshua said.

"So they said," Big Mo said.

Later that evening, two local white men – an older man and a younger man – appeared at their camp.

"Hey boys, what are you two doin,' camping in our woods and eating fish from our river?" the older man askede.

"This is God's country," Big Mo said. "It ain't your fish."

"You are niggah," the older man said. "Show some respect. You can't talk to me like that. You know the rules. "

"We don' want any trouble," Big Mo said. "Push on ol' man."

The older man pointed his shotgun at Big Mo. "Boy, get down on the ground." He turned to the younger man who was grinning. "Tie them up."

When the younger man bent down to tie Big Mo, Big Mo knocked him to the ground and put a knife to his throat.

"Now lower your shotgun or your young friend is a dead man," Big Mo said. "Now throw it over there on the grass."

"Don't harm my son," the older man said.

The old man threw his gun away. Big Mo then rushed him, knocking him to the ground. He then slit his throat. "The first shall be last," Big Mo told him as he killed him.

The younger man tried to run away. Big Mo tackled him. Big Mo then held a knife to his throat.

"Have mercy," the young man said.

"Too late," Big Mo said. "You should have thought of that before."

Before killing him, Big Mo said: "And the last shall be first."

Big Mo limped toward Joshua. "Damn, I turned my ankle," he said.

"Oh, Lordy," Joshua said. "God is going to punish us now."

"Boy, wipe those thoughts from your mind," Big Mo said. "First, there ain't no God. Second, if there is a God, He does not live down here on earth. Do not think so hard. Just do."

"Now give me a hand," Big Mo said. "The white folks *do* live here on earth and the sheriff will certainly punish us."

"We done wrong Big Mo," Joshua said.

"What wrong did we do?" Big Mo said. "We were just defending ourselves. What real choice did we have? We chose life. Nothin' wrong with that. Even insects understand that."

"Damn, I've never met a man like you before Big Mo," Joshua said.

"I'm just a man like every other man," Big Mo said. "We are in great danger. We need to be smart now."

"You the boss," Joshua said.

"You are damn right," Big Mo said. "So do everything I say."

"Those white folks deserved what they got," Joshua said.

"No one deserves it and we all have it coming to us," Big Mo said. "Now let's get rid of these bodies."

Big Mo turned to Joshua. "I did not make this world," Big Mo said. "I just deal with it as it is."

###

They tied large stones to the bodies and threw them into the river. They camped for a couple of days until Big Mo could walk again. When Big Mo and Joshua set out again, they were stopped by Sheriff Flay who was looking for the two missing locals. Sheriff Flay had a "hunch" that Big Mo and Joshua had something to do with the disappearance.

"Sometimes we are all that stands between order and anarchy," Sheriff Flay told his deputies. "God may determine what is right and wrong. But it still must be enforced by man with all his imperfections here on earth."

"If not for the sovereign, it would be a war of all against all," said Flay. "Life for all would be solitary, poor, nasty, brutish, and short. Freedom requires restraint for there is no freedom without law.

"Without restraints, man is nothing but a beast," Flay said. "If you throw money into the mix, man is the very worst of the beasts."

Sheriff Flay threatened to torture Big Mo. Big Mo coolly replied that if he tortures him he better kill him. When Big Mo took off his shirt, Sheriff Flay noticed his powerful build and asked him about his scars.

Big Mo told him about his war scars. When Sheriff Flay asked him about bite scars, Big Mo said he got them fighting an alligator. When Flay asked him what happened, Big Mo showed Flay his knife and said "I killed him."

"Out of respect to your service to the cause, I will not harm you," Flay said. He, however, tried to whip a confession from Joshua who remained silent.

Flay turned to his deputy. "Mersault, take care of him."

"You did good," Big Mo told Joshua. "I will teach you how to survive and see the world as it is. Innocence is a luxury for the sheltered. For us, it can mean only death. There is no God or at least none that hears our cries. The world is indifferent to our struggles. Safety lies only in yourself. If there is any rule to this world, it is the rule of self-preservation," Big Mo said. "Man is a beast. And even a fox caught in the trap will gnaw off its leg to survive."

###

Big Mo carried Joshua to a rough cabin at the edge of the woods. A black woman about the age of 30 answered the door. Her name was Diotima. Big Mo told her that the boy was hurt and asked for her help. She opened the door and helped carry Joshua to her bed.

"Aren't you gonna ask who we are?" asked Big Mo.

"Do you need my help?" Diotima asked.

"Yes," Big Mo said.

"Then I do not need to know," she said.

"Are you afraid of the law?" Big Mo asked.

"There are higher laws," she replied.

###

The next morning, Big Mo thanked her and began to leave. Diotima asked him where he was going. Big Mo replied "I ain't got no blood ties to the boy. He ain't no kin of mine."

"You don't need no blood ties to be bound to another," Diotima replied. "He's your friend and he looks up to you. You can't abandon him. You have a duty to him."

"I am in a hurry to get home to find my ma, brother and sister," Big Mo said. "And we do not have friends in life."

"You have waited 35 years to see them," Diotima said. "Whether you wait now or not, ain't gonna make no difference. Your family is either there or not there. "

"Life is a solitary journey," Big Mo said. "Who can you count on anyways? In the end, your life is only your own."

"I'm sorry life has treated you with a rough hand," she said, "but we all have to endure our share of unfairness."

"I don't feel sorry for myself," Big Mo said, "so don't feel sorry for me either."

"It is up to each person to make this a better world," she said. "Hope sometimes is all we have. A man without hope does not belong to the future. You can't leave the boy. The boy needs you now. I speak the truth."

"There is no truth, only truths," he said.

"Don't confuse solitude with freedom. You are a stranger – unto others and unto yourself. No man is an island, entire unto himself," Diotima said. "We all need each other. The boy can't be used as some means for your escape. He is a person just like you."

"I can't afford self-delusions," Big Mo said. "I see the world as it is. We are only as strong as ourselves. We don't need others if we are strong. And I know of no man stronger than me."

"We all are born and then die," Diotima said. "So in a sense life is futile. We must do something between our birth and death to make our lives meaningful. We must therefore at least make our own life mean something. We must at the very least leave this world a better place than we found it."

Diotima was picking flowers and herbs in her garden. When Joshua walked into the garden, Diotima smiled.

"Well, look at you," Diotima said. "You are a strong young man."

"Yes, ma'm," Joshua said.

"Do you like flowers Joshua?" Diotima asked.

"No," Joshua said. "Flowers are for girls."

"Are they?" Diotima said. She smiled. "Smell this."

Joshua smelled the flower.

"Don't they smell good?" she said. "Don't they look good?"

"Yes, Ma'm," Joshua said.

"Then you do like flowers," Diotima said. "It is not unmanly to like beautiful things. It is quite natural to love the things made by God."

"Yes ma'm," Joshua said.

"You see I grew these flowers from seeds," Diotima said. "I planted the seed in the soil. I watered the plants. I weeded the garden."

"Yes, ma'm," Joshua said.

"You see flowers are miracles," Diotima said, bending down and smelling. "Anyone in search of miracles needs not to look any further than a flower. If you watch carefully, you will see that God is always teaching us something."

"Can I ask you something?" Joshua said.

"Of course," Joanna said.

"Are you negro?" he asked.

"Why do you ask?" she said.

"Because you look negro and you don't look negro," he said.

"Does it matter?" she asked.

"I 'spose it doesn't," he said.

"I am from everywhere and I am from nowhere," she said. "I am black. I am white. I am an American Indian. I am one of God's children. That's what is important. We all are."

"Yes, ma'm," he said.

"The most important thing is that you judge all people as individuals," she said, "because all people are individuals, each with their characters and peculiarities."

"Well, I judge no one," Joshua said, "because I am no one."

"Don't ever say that, Joshua," Diotima said. "There will always be plenty of people who will try to make you feel like a nobody. If you listen to them, you will be a nobody. And you will have nobody to blame but yourself."

###

"Thank you for giving us shelter," Big Mo said. "Diotima, you are a beacon of light in a dark world. Here is payment."

"I didn't do it for payment," Diotima said.

"That is all the more reason for accepting my gratitude," Big Mo said.

"No, keep it," Diotima said. "You may need it."

"No, please take it," Big Mo said. "You need it."

"Your gratitude is payment enough," she said. "I won't take your money. I just wanted to help because it was the right thing to do. God always provides," she said. "Ask and ye shall receive."

III.

After Joshua recovered, Big Mo and Joshua set out for Southampton County. When they crossed into Southampton County they came upon a dried head of one of the black men on a post. He was killed in the Southampton Insurrection 34 years ago. It was a large head with a large scar from his right eye to his chin. The sign said "Blackhead Signpost Road".

Big Mo looked up to the head and tears streamed down his cheeks. "So they killed you too," he said to the head. "I thought you were the one man they couldn't kill."

"Will … Will ... I thought they could never kill you," Big Mo said.

Later, Big Mo told Joshua that General Will was one of the leaders of the Southampton Insurrection. Big Mo also told Joshua that Big Mo was the son of Nat Turner, the leader of the largest slave revolt in the history of the United States.

"My father led the army, but Will and Hark did the killing," Big Mo told Joshua. "In a revolution, someone has to do the killing. And they did it with axes," he said. "Men, women, and children. Even infants. It was terrible. You could see the fear in the eyes of the men you knew all your life. You could hear their last breath as life ebbed from the eyes. Perhaps there is an afterlife after all. Only they know for certain. One moment they are alive like you and me. Then they are dead – no more alive than a fallen tree or piece of meat. There is nothing good about killing another person. By the time the revolt was put down, we'd killed nearly 60 local men, women, and children. My father was caught a month later. Those that had been captured, including my father, were tried and hung. They made a purse from his skin and kept one of his hands as a souvenir.

"Hundreds of innocent blacks, slaves and freemen, were murdered by vigilantes in the bloodbath that followed. Because I was a child at the time, I was shipped out of state and sold again as a slave."

The night was falling and it began to rain. Big Mo and Joshua sought shelter at a rough cabin in the woods. Big Mo knocked on the door. A black woman of about 50 answered the door.

When the woman answered the door, her eyes grew big with surprise. "Oh my God. Mo, is that you? Is that you?"

"Delilah," Big Mo replied. "Yes. It's me. And I'm home."

Delilah became angry. "God damn you." She slapped his face. "Your daddy killed my daddy and brother."

"They made their own choice," Big Mo said.

"Your father misled them," she said. "He had no special powers."

"They were men, free to decide for themselves," he said.

She then turned her back. "You and the boy can stay here until the rain passes. Then you must move on."

That night Big Mo dreamed. It was the final battle of the insurrection. Nat Turner was in the center like the Great King. Will was by his side, captured musket in hand. The last time he saw Will through the smoke and haze he was firing the musket.

The white militiamen began their attack. Smoke was all around. Bullets whizzed all around. People were getting shot all around. The black rebels were greatly outnumbered. A few were drunk on apple brandy. As the militiamen closed all around, the black army broke and ran.

"God, have you forsaken us?" Nat Turner said as those around him were shot.

Big Mo stood among the few who stood at their position. Surrounded, he and the dozen who held their positions surrendered.

The dead and dying lay in the grass.

###

In the morning, Big Mo took an empty bucket of water to the spring and brought it back full.

When he returned, Delilah was starting a fire in the stove. "I'm sorry," she said. "You and the boy can stay here as long as you want. Do you want some coffee?"

"What happened to Momma?" Big Mo asked.

"Gone," Delilah said.

"Dead?" Big Mo said.

"Did I say that? Delilah said.

"Then what?" Big Mo asked.

"Gone," she said. "After your daddy was captured, they tortured Cherry. By the time they were finished, there was no skin left on her back. Finally, she showed them papers your father left with her."

"Afterwards, she disappeared with your brother and sister. They said they were transported out of state and sold in Mississippi."

IV.

Big Mo and Joshua were at the Giles Reese farm. Big Mo was sitting amongst scattered logs in what was a rough cabin.

"This is where I grew up," Big Mo said. "Used to hunt coons and possums here with my lil' brother."

"Noth'in left," Joshua said.

"Jus' ghosts," Big Mo said. "And memories."

"My daddy once baptized a white man in the river. He was a troubled but good man: an overseer on one of the plantations. When my daddy baptized him in the river all the people turned out. The black folk was there to cheer. The white folk was there to jeer.

###

Big Mo and Joshua were at a pond. Water oaks and cypresses grew from the water and the banks. Lily pads floated in the water. Flies buzzed.

"This is where it all started," Big Mo said. "When my daddy arrived, General Hark and

Nelson the conjurer were roasting a pig. Will the Executioner was sitting on his haunches. His ax was at his side. Henry, Sam and Jack were drinking apple brandy. All seemed like just yesterday. There was so much hope. All seemed possible."

###

It is August 21, 1831, Cabin Pond, Virginia. Nat Turner, 31, a small charismatic man arrives.

"The preacher is here," said Nelson the conjurer.

"Brother Nat," Hark said.

The men embraced.

Nat then embraced Nelson, Henry, and Sam.

"All is ready," Nat said. "Judgment Day is here."

"God is with us," Nelson said. "Since God is with us, who can stand against us? I can see the future. I see success."

"Who are you?" Nat said to Will.

"I am Will," he said.

"He is a good man, Nat," Hark said.

"How come you are here?" Nat asked Will.

"My life is worth no more than everyone else's," Will said. "I'm here to win our freedom or die."

"Well, it is now time," Nat said. "God has ordered us."

"Amen, preacher," Henry said.

"With God on our side, we cannot lose," Nelson said.

"There is only seven of us," Jack said. "This makes no sense. It will only lead to our deaths. And bring the full wrath of the white folk upon our heads. And how are we to murder innocent women and children?"

"More will join," Hark said. "We must believe in ourselves. If the white folk treat us like animals so we do not have to behave like men. This is a life and death struggle and our odds are long enough already."

"The militia is out of town. We will strike quickly without warning," Nat said. "Others will join us. We will be in Jerusalem before they can organize."

"How do you know?" Jack said.

"The way has been prepared," Nat said. "The hand of the Lord is upon us. God will strengthen us. Are you questioning God? Did not the Lord say 'Seek ye the kingdom of heaven and all things shall be added unto you'? We shall slay our oppressors with their weapons. Don't be afraid though briers and thorns are all around you and scorpions surround you.

"Jehovah commanded: 'The end is upon you and I will unleash my anger against you. I will judge you according to your conduct and I will repay you for all your detestable practices'," Nat said. "I saw a vision of white spirits and black spirits in the fight to the death. We must have faith. If we lose confidence in God and ourselves we are as good as dead."

"Believe in the prophet," Nelson said. "He sees the future. He controls the clouds. God speaks directly to him. God has commanded the prophet to lead his people in a great battle against slavery."

"Didn't you see the signs: the solar eclipse? Today, the sun turned green."

"Believe in the prophet," Henry repeated. "You do not need to reason. All you have to do is believe."

"I sees what I sees," Will said. "I hears what I hears. I touches what I touches. I believes in nothing else. You may control clouds. You may walk on water. I ain't gonna believe in nothin' I can't see myself. I ain't gonna' believe in no God, at leas' here on earth. On earth, we must take our own life in our own hands. You see mah ax? That's what I believe in. I will win my freedom or die. When I die I 'spect no pearly gates, no singin' angels. When I die, I 'spect only death. While I live I want to breathe free air. I want to work when I want to work. I want to res' when I want to res. And I want to enjoy the fruits of my own labor.

"I want to judge for myself what is right and wrong," he said. "I don' want no one tellin' me what is right and what is wrong.

"White man starves you then whips you for stealin' his food. He sends you to the field 'fore the sun rises and then sends you home to your rough cabin after dark. He sells your chil'ren the same as his cows, pigs, and chickens. He treats his mules better than you."

"God commands it," Sam said. "I'm tired of waiting for someone to free us. Let's free ourselves through our courage. A slave who says yes to everything consents to his suffering. Let my people go."

"There is nothin' we can do about it now anyway," Henry said. "The die has been cast. Our fate is our fate."

"Let the preachers pray and the philosophers think," Hark said. "We are in the Land of the Pharaohs. All roads lead to death. I choose to die fighting for our freedom rather than to live in slavery. Whatever they can do, they cannot take away our right to choose. By fighting, I choose life."

"A better day is coming," Nat said.

The men began to sing together:

> When Israel was in Egypt's land:
> Let my people go,
> Oppress'd so hard they could not stand,
> Let my People go.

> Go down, Moses,
> Way down in Egypt's land,
> Tell old Pharaoh,
> Let my people go.

"We met Nat and the rebels in the yard of the Travis farm," Big Mo said. "It was the farm where Nat worked. It was 2 a.m. and all was quiet. We proceeded to the cider press where all drank except Nat."

"Now, it is time to make good all your valiant boasts," Nat said. Nat and Will looked each other in the eyes. Will raised his ax and then laughed. Nat looked away.

Hark lifted the ladder and set it against the chimney. Nat climbed the ladder to a second-story window. He opened the window and silently entered the house. He opened the front door and let us in.

"The work is now open to you," Nat said to Will.

The men went to the master bedroom. Nat lifted his hatchet and hit his master Joseph Travis in the head with his hatchet, wounding him.

"Sally!" Travis called to his wife. Will moved Nat aside and killed Travis with his ax, then killed Sally.

The rebels killed the overseer and Sally's son Putnam. Jack said he was too sick to continue. The rebels forced him to get up and follow them.

"Can't we let him be?" Sam asked.

"Show no pity," Hark said. "We must be strong."

The men took all the weapons and horses. After they left, the men remembered that they forgot to kill the infant. Will and Henry returned to the house and killed the baby.

The rebels killed Sal Francis and killed Piety Reese and her son William at their farm. They killed Elizabeth Turner, her friend Mrs.

Newsome and the overseer Hartwood Peebles. By the next day, they had killed 60 men, women, and children.

Many slaves voluntarily joined the insurgency. Some that did not join were taken at gunpoint. They were also joined by free blacks. One slave who refused to join had his ankles cut so he could not walk.

"Davy does not want to come," Sam said.

"If he does not come, kill him," Nat said.

"We are already outnumbered," Hark said. "We need every man we can get. It's power versus power. And we are not only fighting for your lives we are fighting for the freedom of our people."

###

By the time, the rebels reached the Whitehead Plantation, there were 15 men, nine on horseback. When they reached the plantation, Richard, a young Methodist preacher was in the field with his slaves.

"You, come here," Nat said.

The insurgents surrounded him. They began to chant "Kill him! Kill him!"

"Please," Richard cried. "Why do you want to kill me?"

"Ye hypocrite," Nat said.

Will began to chop Richard to pieces.

"Please," Richard cried.

Will dragged Caty Whitehead, Richard's mother from the house. "I don't want to live since you murdered all my children," she told Will.

She looked into the eyes of Old Hubbard her servant.

Will cut her head off with his ax, her blood spattered all over his face and arms. Her adult daughter Margaret screamed and in a panic ran in terror toward the woods.

Will looked at Nat and nodded at him. Nat chased her down and beat her with his blunt sword. He then picked up a wood fence post. He started to beat her head with a heavy post as she screamed and begged for mercy. Her blood and hair spattered all over his arm and face.

Old Hubbard, the family servant, said, there was no one left. He hid Harriett Whitehead and thereby saved her life. After the rebels left, Old Hubbard hid Harriett in the swamp.

At the Waller homestead, Waller's wife and two daughters and a group of school children were slaughtered. Waller survived by hiding in the weeds. One child survived by hiding in the chimney.

Sam stood alone weeping while other rebels drank apple brandy. When Nat saw him, he ordered him to get on his horse.

"We must be strong," Nat said.

The rebels killed John Barrow in hand to hand combat. They wrapped him in a quilt and left tobacco on his chest in respect for his valor.

"I'm sorry such a man had to die," Nat said.

At one homestead, Nat held his men back. "Those people think themselves no better than negroes," he said.

As the rebel army came upon new plantations and farms, many of them abandoned by their owners who now heard about the rebellion. When they came upon the Harris farm, only the slaves were there. By now, they had more than 40 men.

"You don't stand a chance," one slave, Aaron, told Nat. "If you knew how many armed white folks were at Norfolk you would think twice about attacking them."

"Do you want us to kill you?" Will asked.

"We are not afraid of you," Aaron said. "Violence does not equal strength. A man of peace is more powerful than a man of war. Your tyranny is not any better than the tyranny you are trying to replace."

"You should die many deaths," Will said.

"Let them be," Nat said.

At the Parker Plantation, the rebels and militia clashed. The fighting was inconclusive and several rebels were wounded. The rebels retreated after the militia was reinforced.

The rebels marched on Jerusalem, the county seat. But some of their numbers had deserted; others were too drunk to fight. Also, some of their muskets were rusty and did not fire.

Meantime, the whites had organized and called for help. Reinforcements were arriving from Richmond, Norfolk, and North Carolina.

Once they saw the bridges were well guarded, the rebels turned back.

The rebels camped that night at the Ridley Plantation. By dawn, half the rebels had deserted.

"What do you think will happen tomorrow?" asked Mo.

"We are all go'in to die," Will said.

Before marching out, the survivors sang their death song:

> Michael row de boat ashore, Hallelujah,
> I wonder where my mudder die there,
> See my mudder in de rock gwine home,
> On de rock gwine home in Jesus's name,
> Michael row a music boat.
> Gabriel blow de trumpet horn . . . .

In the morning, Nat and the rebels moved to the Blount plantation to recruit more men. To their surprise, both the owners and their slaves fought back.

Hark was shot and badly wounded and captured. Another rebel was killed and a third captured.

After the rebel forces retreated, they were attacked by the Greensville cavalry who attacked and dispersed their forces.

The revolution was over. Nat, Hark, and Sam were caught, tried, and hanged. Jack and Big Mo were caught, tried, and sold out of state as slaves.

Will was killed in the fighting. Henry was caught by vigilantes and summarily executed.

V.

When they returned to Delilah's cabin, it was nightfall. A dozen white men arrested Big Mo and took him to the jail in Jerusalem.

"Are you Moses Turner?" asked the sheriff.

"That'd be me," Big Mo said.

"You are wanted in North Carolina for murder," the sheriff said.

Young Joshua escaped into the woods. He then returned to Golgotha and sought the help of Diotima.

###

"Give me your worst," Big Mo told Magistrate Judge Hawthorne. "You can't do anything to me that hasn't been done to me before."

"Castrate him," Magistrate Judge Hawthorne ordered. "He's an animal. And so he shall be treated like an animal."

"What about my rights?" Big Mo said.

"Here in this room behind these closed doors you have no rights but the rights I grant you," Magistrate Judge Hawthorne said.

"He's already been castrated," the guard said.

"Do you see this skull," Magistrate Judge Hawthorne asked Big Mo. He handed him a skull that looked as much like that of a ram as a man. "This is the head of your Daddy. After we hung him, we skinned him, made grease of his flesh and his skin into a leather purse."

"Give him such a beating that he will never come back," Magistrate Judge Hawthorne said.

The Southampton County Sheriff tried to deliver Big Mo to Sheriff Flay chained to the back of a wagon. But Big Mo escaped, killing the driver and the guard. The driver was found with a broken neck. The guard had his throat cut.

Sheriff Flay found Bog Mo and Joshua at Diotima's cabin. The sheriff tried to arrest them but they refused to surrender.

Sheriff Flay had a dozen men surround the cabin.

Big Mo, Diotima, and Joshua armed with rifles held out for five days.

"We've got to break out tonight," Big Mo said. "We're almost out of food, water, and bullets. If we're captured, we're as good as dead."

"There is no moon tonight," Diotima said.

"Jus' follow me," Big Mo said. "We'll head for the woods and then cut to the river.

If we get separated make for the river."

A gunfight broke out. They ran toward the river but Diotima was shot in the back and was bleeding badly.

"Let me be," Diotima told them. "Go on. I'm dying anyway. I'm slowing you down."

By the time Sheriff Flay and his men found Diotima the sun had risen.

"Kill her," Flay shouted.

"She's a woman," Mersault said.

"She's a niggah," Flay said. "Finish her off."

"You can kill me but you can never destroy me," Diotima said.

Diotima closed her eyes. Mersault stuck the barrel of his revolver into the back of her head. A crack of gunfire echoed across the valley. Mersault fell dead. The pistol fell in front of Diotima. She picked up the gun.

Flay ducked behind a tree and his remaining men laid on the ground.

"Big Mo, I know that's you, " Flay said. "Surrender. You and the boy have no chance."

Flay motioned his men to move forward toward the river. Another crack. Another one of Flay's men fell dead.

Another man ran toward the trees. Another crack. He was hit in the shoulder.

Another man ran. Another crack. This time Big Mo missed.

Flay shot Big Mo as he fired, wounding him badly in the torso. Flay ducked behind the tree. He turned and saw Diotima with her pistol aimed at his head. "Oh, Lord," he said.

Diotima shot him in the head, killing him. She then died.

Flay's men rushed Big Mo. Big Mo shot one man dead. The rest of the men dived for cover.

Big Mo was mortally wounded. "You need to run," he rasped.

"I can't leave you," Joshua said.

"I'm a dead man," Big Mo said. "Now go."

By the time, the remaining deputies reached Big Mo he was dead.

Meanwhile, Joshua escaped across the river and turned north.

Medicated Success
by Glenn Bresciani

No more stress. No more looking over his shoulder. No more living in fear of Blue Cats. Mr. Frabbit is a new man on new medication.

Everything is fine and dandy when medication is swimming through his veins. Why, Mr. Frabbit has been in the car, stuck in morning work traffic, for over twenty minutes, and not once has commercial radio been hijacked by pirate broadcasts using the airwaves to promote "safety in fleas".

He would have skipped through the front entrance of the accounting firm that employs him, but he's far too professional for that. So he sings a Katy Perry song to himself instead.

Nothing has changed in the six months he has been away on sick leave. Judy is still sitting behind the reception desk, the company logo on the wall above her head.

Good ol' reliable Judy. When a client makes an enquiry about accounting, Judy's email is the first friendly reply, the first friendly voice over the phone, the first friendly smile to greet the client when they walk through the door.

"Morning Toby," she says, standing up to offer Mr. Frabbit a handshake.

Handshake accepted. "Morning Judy. Feels like I never left."

"Feels like you've been gone forever."

The two fidget in silence, Mr. Frabbit glancing at his Rolex, while Judy bites her lower lip, her fingertips spinning the pendant on the end of her silver necklace.

Judy opens her mouth to speak, sighs instead, her shoulders hunched. Clearly, she has questions she would like to ask, but is unable to as all her words are sucked into the gravitational pull of her shyness. So Mr. Frabbit does the speaking for her, his words giving her curious mind a hug.

"They had me trialing lots of different medications – so many pills, you wouldn't believe it. After a dozen tries they found one that works. I've beaten it Judy. I've finally beaten it."

Judy's glee sparkles in her eyes and smile. "You're like one of those success stories you read about. You're a medicated success story."

Mr. Frabbit nods, smiling. "A medicated success – I like that Judy."

One Zyprexa tablet a day keeps the Blue Cats away. Finally, a nondescript life was his to enjoy. Nothing freakish will ever make it past his medication – except for that steam train passing through Reception. No, not an everyday train as that would be physically impossible. It was a small train, small enough to fit in one's hand.

He studies Judy's eyes, to see if she notices the movement across the carpet. Nope, all of her focus is on him.

It's happening again, he thinks, distraught. I'm a medicated success – Judy said so – this shouldn't be happening.

"Sorry. Can we talk some more at lunch?" he asks, ending the conversation so he can move himself and his concerns away from Judy. "I've got a lot of work to catch up on."

"Oh – sure," she says, sitting back in her office chair and wheeling herself into receptionist formation at her desk. "I'll talk to you later."

He offers Judy his most charming smile. It's free and it conceals his fears. He turns and follows the little steam train out of reception.

In the corridors, the itsy-bitsy railroad track splits into two, running parallel with the walls, allowing the movement of trains to everywhere in the office and back again.

Mr. Frabbit crouches, frowning as he takes a closer look at an ankle high railroad crossing. Flashing red lights and the ding, ding, ding of bells gives the boom gate the go-ahead to lower.

He jumps, stumbles against the wall as a freight train chugs through the railroad crossing.

Zyprexa keeps the Blue Cats out, why would it let little trains in?

Mr. Mowl, his body language as cocksure as his porcupine haircut, strides toward Mr. Frabbit, right hand extended. "Oh, yeah! The number one accountant is good to go."

The two accountants shake hands, Mr. Frabbit wincing as he feels his knuckles grind together under the other accountant's forceful grip.

"Are the new meds doing their thing?" asks Mr. Mowl, disengaging himself from the handshake.

"Mm-hmm," says Mr. Frabbit, nodding. They were doing their thing with zing –well, that is, until the trains arrived.

The two accountants talk as they walk along the corridor. Mr. Frabbit's destination: his office. Arrival time: one minute.

"Aren't you worried Toby? You'll lose your accounting edge now that the Blue Cats are gone."

"The Blue Cats never existed," says Mr. Frabbit, the sight of miniature trees, all in a row along the railroad tracks, has him tightening his grip on the handle of his suitcase.

No trains exist in Mr. Mowl's reality, as his eyes are never once drawn to the locomotive movement around his feet, which means Mr. Frabbit has to work harder, straining his brain to pretend the trains are nonexistent. He has to. He's a medicated success.

"Yeah, I get that. The Blue Cats were all in your head and all that. But, what I'm saying is when you were – you know – mentally ill, you had an urgency. Accounting was a necessity. If you stopped accounting, the Blue Cats would enslave all our minds."

"Well, it won't feel like my life depends on accounting. Now I can just enjoy it."

"Soooo, what you're saying is that it doesn't matter that you've lost your edge, the same edge that got you Employee of the Year. You're fine without it. Hmm ... I respect that Toby. I honestly do."

Mr. Mowl speaks with such an oversaturation of honesty that – to Mr. Frabbit's ears – the words are like the screech of fingernails scratching the flat surface of dishonesty.

The two accountants arrive at Mr. Frabbit's office. A picture of a flea is sticky-taped to the center of the door. The shock of seeing the flea disrupts the rhythm of Mr. Frabbit's breathing.

"I told everyone to leave the flea on your door," says Mr. Mowl. "The person to remove that flea should be you, Toby – for closure."

Safety in fleas. As long as a flea stood between you and a Blue Cat, you were safe. You were protected. One look at a flea is all it takes to frighten the Blue Cats away.

It had taken hundreds of resistant fighters to infiltrate the Blue Cats fortified scratch post and capture top secret information concerning their weakness. Only through hacking radio and television transmissions could the Resistance provide this vital information to Mr. Frabbit.

Reaching for the flea, Mr. Frabbit stops mid-action, his fingertips only millimeters away from the A4 size sheet of copy paper. A train sliding along the edge of his peripheral vision forces him to reconsider the removal of the flea.

"C'mon Toby. Make it official. Rip that flea, rip it good."

Mr. Frabbit yanks the flea picture off the door to prove he is a medicated success like everyone says he is, to prove he is cured like everyone believes he is.

"You the man," says Mr. Mowl, pointing and winking at his colleague. He pulls a Michael Jackson spin, saunters off down the hall.

"I'm the man," says Mr. Frabbit half-heartedly, opening the door to his office.

Both accountants park themselves behind their desks in their respective offices to begin their work day and earn themselves a day's pay.

Sitting in his office chair, it feels so right, so nice. Mr. Frabbit closes his eyes and sighs, rubbing his fingertips over the cool vinyl of the armrests. Three months as a patient in a psychiatric hospital, trialing different medications until he was cured; it was worth it! Finally being able to work sitting at his desk is proof of that.

He gazes at a framed photo on his desk, the one next to his "Employee of the Year" award. The photo is of Mr. Frabbit, crammed under his desk, his knees tucked under his chin. Even though he's holding a gold-plated trophy, with his name engraved on it, no smile appears in the photo, as a smile for the camera would've been impossible in the age of the Blue Cats.

The framed photo was supposed to hang on a wall in Reception, alongside photos of previous winners; however, management decided against this, believing the image of Mr. Frabbit was inconsistent with the firm's public image.

Retrieving a pen from the top drawer of his desk, he selects a client's file from the pile and scratches his ear with the end of his pen as he reads. The task of accounting unties the knots in his neck and his shoulders. Sitting at his desk rather than being under it – why, the normality of it is bliss.

He smiles as he glances out the window. The view of the building across the street reminds him of how grateful he was that the Blue Cats never had thumbs, making it impossible for them to operate a sniper rifle. If they could have done that he would have been toast.

The tip of the pen in his hand touches the top page in the open file, yet no numbers are written. Instead, Mr. Frabbit glances in every direction, frowning as he tries to figure out what's missing in his office.

"Oh shit!" he says, his pen slipping out of his hand. No railroad tracks extend across the floor. His office is a no-go zone for trains.

Gliding across the room on his office chair, Mr. Frabbit parks himself in front of the computer. Move mouse, click, move mouse, double click. The printer purrs, gives birth to twin A4 sized papers with an image of a flea on each one.

He sticky-tapes one flea picture to the window, the other to his office door – you know, just in case.

Fetching a coffee was a bad idea. Mr. Frabbit should've remained in his office. The more corridors he walks along, the more rooms he passes, the more the tiny railroad tracks evolve into a complex rail system. Passenger trains and freight trains; steam trains and diesel trains, all whizzing past his feet.

It's no longer just trains, as the railroad tracks pass a miniature train station outside the copy room, while a miniature fire station is inside the copy room, the Xerox photocopier like a skyscraper next to the brick building with a fire engine parked inside.

"No, no, no, no," says Mr. Frabbit, stopping at the glass doors of the conference room, his eyes wide, his mouth like the entrance to a train tunnel.

Two accountants and the manager sit at the table, discussing cash flow forecasts judging by the charts projected onto a screen. As they talk, they look at the documents in front of them, look at each other, or check the screens on their mobile phones. Not once do they look at the middle of the table where the trains move through a small town with buildings no bigger than a cat.

The manager is oblivious of the trains in front of her, yet her grin shimmers with delight when she notices, outside the conference room, the man with the trains in his brain.

The two accountants at the table spin around to give Mr. Frabbit a spirited "hello there" wave.

"Good to see you, Toby," says one.

"Welcome back. Looking good," says the other.

Mr. Frabbit gives his colleagues a thumbs-up. "I'll talk to you at lunchtime."

Sounds good. The manager and the accountants resume their meeting as Mr. Frabbit hurries down the corridor, grateful that his thumbs-up signal, and all the positivity that goes with it, blinded his colleagues to the stress chewing at the edges of his medicated recovery.

In the entrance to the lunchroom, he freezes, his coffee mug almost slipping out of his hand.

A miniaturized Flying Scotsmen journeys across the kitchen bench, passing scenic views of the kitchen sink and washed plates drying in the dish rack.

An intern sitting at one of the tables, eating two-minute noodles, expresses her concern for Mr. Frabbit.

"No, I'm fine," he says with a reassuring smile. "I've come to get myself a coffee, but I just realized I've left my coffee mug back in my office."

Yes, nice save Mr. Frabbit. Don't make it about the medication.

The intern frowns as she watches the accountant exit the room with his coffee mug in his hand.

The psychiatrist Dr. Murtle had said Zyprexa was the only solution to Mr. Frabbit's hallucinations. He was half right as, even though the Zyprexa kept the Blue Cats out, the little trains had found a way in, sliding past the pharmaceutical coating of his brain as if it was never there.

Once the hallucinations start, the delusions always follow, he reminds himself, retrieving his tablets from the inside pocket of his jacket, popping open the lid to drop a pill into his hand. How can I convince everyone I'm cured if I end up deluding myself into believing the trains are a threat?

As far as he is concerned, this is reason enough for him to pop another pill – so that is what he does.

"There you are," says Judy, hurrying down the corridor, a Nikon camera hanging from her neck. "I've been looking everywhere for you."

He shoves his medication into his pocket before Judy can see it, hides his anxiety behind a forced smile that requires a few extra facial muscles to pull it off.

Judy holds up the Nikon camera. "You need a new Employee of the Year photo."

The way he was blinking, one would think his uncertainty was stuck in his eye.

"You know Toby, what we talked about... the – um – medicated success."

"Oh, you mean a photo of me sitting at my desk rather than being under it?"

She nods, looking down at her yellow loafers, matching the sunflower pattern on her dress, so the angle of her head hides her blazing red cheeks.

"All right then. Let's do this."

Judy and her Nikon lead the way to Mr. Frabbit's office, the Orient Express making a "choo-choo" noise as it chugs past her feet.

Walking along the corridor, Mr. Frabbit keeps his eyes directed at the middle of the floor – the only space, besides his office, where the railroad tracks never go. It's a feeble attempt to synchronize with Judy's unawareness of the rail system.

How could Judy be aware of something that exists inside his head? Doesn't matter anyway as it will soon be over when the extra shot of Zyprexa kicks in.

Warmth flows through his face, the suddenness of the sensation startling him.

As they walk, Judy bows her head, gives her pendant a spin with her fingertips. "Toby, can I just ask... I never understood... um... why did you come to work when, clearly, you were... ah... not yourself?"

"I had to," he says, surprised by the question. "All the pirate broadcasts on my TV and car radio, the pop-up adds on my laptop, they all revealed to me the Blue Cats' weakness."

"They had a weakness?"

"Of course they did. It was... accounting."

Judy frowns, opens her mouth, then closes it, reaches for her pendant, so he explains further.

"They had blue fur so you couldn't see them when they were floating in the sky. When I'm doing accounting, when I'm adding and subtracting numbers, it makes their bodies heavy, so they can't float. By grounding the Blue Cats, it was easier for government agents to spot them and take them out."

He chuckles, scratches his forehead as he glances at the ceiling. "The more I talk about Blue Cats, the more shocked I am that I was never locked up."

"You have your medication to thank for that."

Yeah, my medication has been as safe and reliable as a derailed train, thinks Mr. Frabbit, turning his face away from Judy so she can't see him grimace.

The railroad tracks are still going right by Mr. Frabbit's office. Noticing this, some of the tension is blown out of his body on the breeze of his sigh. The A4 size sheet of paper stuck to his office door is as invincible as a fortified stronghold.

Safety in fleas; it has always been about the fleas.

Judy points at the picture. "Are you keeping that as a souvenir?"

Mr. Frabbit laughs – he can't help it. "It's a reminder that my days of mental illness are behind me."

"That's nice," says Judy, impressed.

Mr. Frabbit's equilibrium somersaults into a nosedive as he steps through the doorway of his office. He leans against the file cabinet, but only long enough to stop himself from falling. Sweat beads appear above his brow as waves of heat rise through his body faster than smoke up a chimney.

"The Blue Cats would make an awesome movie," says Judy, removing the lens cap. "Can I just get you to sit behind your desk please?"

Ignoring the heat itching his scalp, Mr. Frabbit does as Judy asks, his chair squeaking as he drops into it. He holds his pen above the paperwork on his desk, pretending that the camera has caught him at his busiest.

"Maybe you should write a book about your experiences. I'd read it," says Judy, looking through the camera's viewfinder.

Mr. Frabbit stares at the camera as he poses like a professional. Judy snaps a photo, then another one, just in case the first one was blurry.

Breathing is an effort for him. What comes freely is now a chore. He sucks in more air than usual, wipes the sweat off his brow.

"Are you okay Toby?"

Don't frown! Don't frown! he warns himself, pretending everything is fine, so he can live up to her belief that he is a medicated success.

"I'm just feeling a bit dry." Which is the truth as heat vaporizes the moisture in his throat and sweat drips off his armpits.

"Oh, would you like me to get you some water?"

"No, please don't trouble yourself."

"It's no trouble."

A summer's day on the beach in the midday sun would be preferable to the heatwave under his skin. It's getting harder for him to act cool, to convince Judy that all is well.

"I have a water bottle in my bottom drawer. But thank you for your concern."

"Oh – okay... well... I'll leave you to it." Judy removes herself from Mr. Frabbit's office, pausing in the doorway to give the accountant one last look of concern.

Mr. Frabbit leaps out of his chair, almost stumbles as he hurries across the room to reach the door. The floor under his feet shifts in a seesaw motion, tilting to the right, tilting to the left; he has to grip the door frame to prevent a fall. Sweat is dripping, dribbling off his burning skin. Wait! This is new. Now his breathing requires double the effort to inhale a reduced amount of oxygen.

Out in the corridor on the other side of the flea, the trains continue to exist in his own private reality, with no sign of their existence being blown away by the extra shot of Zyprexa.

Should I take another tablet? he asks himself.

Panic strangles his mind, the railroad tracks outside the office, like a garrotte coiling around his medicated success and squeezing the hope out of it.

Grabbing the back of his chair, he pulls it away from the desk. The chair rolls across the room on its wheels, slams into the wall.

The space under the desk is filled with Mr. Frabbit. He tucks his knees under his chin so he can fit his whole body into an area intended for leg room only.

With a swipe of his thumb, he scrolls through his contact list displayed on his mobile phone screen, selects his psychiatrist Dr. Murtle.

Dialing is brief as Dr. Murtle answers his phone as soon as it rings. "Hello Toby, how are you feeling today?"

"My medication! It's not working! I'm still hallucinating."

"The fact that you are aware of your hallucinations is a good sign," says Dr. Murtle. "In therapy, you had acknowledged that the Blue Cats were a fantasy created in response to your –"

"I'm not seeing Blue Cats! I'm seeing trains!"

"I'm sorry, did you just say trains or brains?"

Mr. Frabbit couldn't answer. He inhales with twice the force, his mouth opening wider to catch more air, and still next to no oxygen reaches his lungs.

"I can hear you struggling for breath," says Dr. Murtle, his calmness swept away by the bristles of his concern.

Mr. Frabbit's gasping for air is as loud and messy as bathwater gurgling down the plughole. "How many tablets have you taken so far today?"

"Two."

"Two! I prescribed you one tablet a day for a reason. Anything more would be an overdose."

If breathing wasn't so darn near impossible for Mr. Frabbit, he would shout in rage at the psychiatrist.

"You said... " gasp for air, "one tablet... " gasp fails, tries gulping, "would stop me hallucinating."

"Where are you, Toby?"

The inside of his skull feels like it is full of bubbles and foam as warm liquid sleep dissolves his consciousness. His eyelids slam shut, sleep placing his eyes in lockdown. Was that someone calling his name? Or was a dream about to begin?

"Toby! Toby! Are you at home or at work?"

"... at ... work."

"I'm calling an ambulance."

Mr. Frabbit's chin drops onto his chest, his mobile phone slips from his fingers, clatters against the floor.

A knock on the door before it opens. Judy enters the room, the Nikon still hanging around her neck. She holds a plastic cup filled with water from the water cooler that is next to the sofa in Reception.

"I know you didn't want me too, but I had to," she says, her eyebrows crumpling out of shape as she looks at the empty desk where she last saw Mr. Frabbit only a few minutes ago.

"Toby?"

She notices the chair leaning against the wall. She gasps, the plastic cup sliding out of her hand.

"Toby!"

She rushes around the desk, slamming her hand onto the flat surface as she slips in the puddle of water. Seeing the accountant under his desk is like looking at his "Employee of the Year" photo. The only difference is that if his breathing wasn't so shallow, he could be mistaken for someone having a nap.

"Oh my God, Toby!" screams Judy, whipping out her mobile phone and dialing 911.

It's go, go, go for the paramedics. In under three minutes, they have pushed an ambulance stretcher through the building to Mr. Frabbit's office, fitted an oxygen mask to the accountant's face, strapped him into the stretcher, and are wheeling him out of the room.

"Run, run, run as fast as you can. Mr. Frabbit's life depends on it." Judy's wheezy breathing is the soundtrack accompanying her struggle to keep up with the paramedics as they race down the corridor. Her marshmallow soft body jiggles to the rhythm of the running motion of her legs.

Mr. Mowl sticks his head out of the doorway to his office, his head jerking back, his eyes widening as Mr. Frabbit on the stretcher zooms past.

"What the fuck?" he shouts at Judy who is six seconds behind the paramedics in the race to the ambulance.

"Toby had an overdose," she shouts at Mr. Mowl as she runs by him.

The accountant with the porcupine hair gapes at Judy. "Holy shit! Is Toby doing drugs?"

"Drugs? – What?" Judy is glad she has to pull a sharp right turn, same as the paramedics in front of her, as it makes Mr. Mowl and his idiotic questions disappear around the corner.

Bursting into Reception, the paramedics are forced to halt the race to their ambulance, both spreading their legs to maintain their balance and gripping the stretcher tightly to prevent it from tipping.

The Paramedics have to stop, or else they'll run Mr. Frabbit right into the path of an oncoming freight train. They look at the floor, waiting for the tiny train on the tiny railroad tracks to pass.

"What's with all the model trains?" asks one of the paramedics. "They're everywhere."

"The manager organized it," Judy says. "She wants to beat the Guinness World Record for the longest model train track with the most model trains on it."

The last boxcar pulled by the freight train passes by the stretcher. The paramedics roll the stretcher over the railroad track, bolt for the front entrance.

"Wouldn't all those trains be distracting?" asks the other paramedic, sliding Mr. Frabbit and the stretcher into the back of the ambulance. "How do the accountants get any work done?"

"The model trains were set up months ago. We're so used to them now; we forget they're there."

"Fair enough," The paramedic's brief response is all he has time for. He jumps into the back of the ambulance, closes the rear doors.

Watching the ambulance zoom down the road, a mini tornado of flashing lights and shrieking sirens, Judy realizes that she has forgotten to ask Mr. Frabbit how he feels about the accounting firm's attempt to beat a Guinness World Record.

Now she'll never know.

Land of Elephants
by Jean Duggleby

We were told that there'd be a procession in this part of Mumbai, but we'd wandered around asking people and no-one knew anything about it, so we decided to go back to our hotel.

As we neared the bus station I could see that there was an elephant among the buses, and so we went over to have a look. The men had a series of buckets that they were constantly filling with water and the elephant was taking the water with its trunk and showering itself – quite a sight. Its trunk was a pink blotchy colour. I don't know if that was old age or what. Anyway, when it had dried off they started painting its sides and front legs with beautiful and colourful patterns.

Next they put an embroidered cover over its back which hung down either side nearly as far as its knees, and a golden cloth over its trunk with colourful tassels along the sides. Finally the mahout, carrying large feathers and fans, mounted the elephant, which bent down on its knees and put up one front leg for him to use as a step to climb on its back. Such a docile and cooperative creature!

This is what I love about India. Can you imagine an English bus station with an elephant in the middle, or even a horse, and everyone getting on with his or her business? Never!

The elephant and rider left the bus station, and as they walked were joined by five other decorated elephants and together they made their way to the procession. Floats with statues of gods and goddesses carried along by colourfully dressed people joined the procession. Others had huge colourful costumes hooked onto their shoulders. They twirled and twisted in the sunlight, and it reminded me of piles of liquorice allsorts, though that wouldn't be something I would have said at the event. The promised drums started up, as well as strident trumpets and some sort of brass instruments with huge circular tubes rather like stretched and twisted trombones.

I believe that they were celebrating the birthday of one of the deities, possibly Lord Krishna. The crowd were dancing and excited, with some of the teenage boys good-naturedly tossing each other up into the air.

Finally, when it was very late, the crowds started going home, and we wondered how we'd get back to our hotel so late. We went back to the bus station, which was heaving with people, but I particularly noticed a man moving through the crowds. He wore a pristine white shirt and a black tie, and had neatly cut and creamed hair, a small elegant beard and clear skin. He had wide shoulders and muscular arms. Above the waist he was a handsome man, but below the waist there were no legs and wizened hips. He got around by propelling himself on a wooden plank fitted with four wheels. He had little boards tied onto his front and back with some sort of writing that I couldn't read. I speculated that it might say something like "Homeless and hungry."

But again, in true Indian fashion, there were loads of buses carrying crowds to many parts of the locality and we easily got back to our hotel, even getting a seat.

We got home, but the next morning I couldn't get the man on the improvised trolley out of my mind, and mentioned him to the hotel receptionist to see if she knew anything about him. "Yes, that's Mr Patel, the letter-writer. Everyone knows him. He's not a beggar but if you want to know more ask him yourself."

"But does he speak English?"

"Certainly, madam, and several other languages, I believe." I was even more intrigued, so I went straight away to the bus station.

I found him in a corner with a low table in front of him on which rested paper, pens and even equipment for calligraphy. A man was sitting on a low stool talking to him and four other people were queuing up. I joined the back of the queue, but when he'd finished with the man he beckoned me to come to him. I shook my head as I didn't want to queue-jump, but the people queuing kindly signalled for me to go to him. Imagine that happening in England, though in fact in England no one queues these days.

"What can I do for you?" he asked in perfect English. I explained that I'd seen him the previous day and became curious about him. "I am happy to tell you whatever you wish, but cannot leave these good people waiting. Why don't you come back tomorrow evening, madam, when I can give you my full attention?" I noticed that his speech was impeccable: BBC or even Oxbridge. I arranged to go back the following evening.

"Mr Patel, is it true that you speak 5 languages?"

"I understand the five dialects of Malay, but my speech is less advanced. I speak Tamil, Hindi, Urdu and some English. I also find French, Japanese and Chinese useful. My board says, 'Letters translated and written in the language of your choice.'"

And to think that I'd guessed that it said, "Homeless and hungry." I felt ashamed.

"That's amazing – and more than five."

He bowed his head modestly.

"How did you learn those languages?"

"When I was locked in a room for 3 years the only thing that I was allowed was a television."

"How come you were locked in a room?"

"It's a long story."

"Please tell me. I will pay for your time."

"Madam, that is not necessary. I was the youngest of eight children, first two boys, then five girls, then me. My father was a rich and successful banker, and did very well with his investments. We had a big house and servants. I had my own tutor, and even at three years old was said to be a gifted child. Then we fell on bad times. There was a recession and my father's investments were worth almost nothing. The bank failed and he was made redundant. We all had to move into a small house with no servants. My eldest brother who was by then eighteen was sent to England to earn money to send home, but we never ever heard from him again. We don't know what happened. My next brother who was seventeen went to the oilfields in Dubai, and after only two months was killed in an accident on the rigs. We tried and failed to get compensation. My father was so ashamed that he could not support his family that he became ill and soon died also. My mother and older sisters went to sew in a factory. The younger girls cleaned in some richer people's houses. I was only five by this time. An uncle came to our house and said that he'd take me in as a great favour, and gave my mother some money.

"He was childless and a widower so it was just him and me, but he was not kind. He said that I was useless and locked me in a room with no window, giving me the minimum of food and drink. He tied my legs very tight and readjusted the bandages every so often. My legs became very bent and I could hardly walk. My feet were blue and swollen and my hips disjointed. When I was crippled enough he sent me to beg.

"Eventually my legs became gangrenous and had to be amputated. He forbade me to talk to anyone, but a neighbour befriended me and I believe reported him to the police. They came and took him away, and the neighbour took me in, although she already had a big family.

"I still had to beg, but she was kind and made sure that I was safe, well fed and in comfort. It was a happy time.

"Sometimes people spoke to me, and an English man was amazed to find out how many languages I knew, and he said that I was very bright. He taught me to write English, French and Tamil, and found tutors for Chinese, Japanese, Urdu and Malay. He was also very kind and set me up in this little business, letter writing at the bus station. I can read and write most of those languages, some more accurately than others. I am also employed to write marriage and death documents and exam certificates. I still live with Auntie, but earn a good living and help to support the family.

"They call me 'elephant man', not because of your famous celebrity, but because of my memory, which they say is phenomenal, and because of Ganesha, the god with the elephant head, who is one of our deities. I am flattered. It has turned out well."

Shadow Angel
by Andrew Parker

So long. So lonely. Seasons coming. Seasons going. Like walking through the door and slamming her coat in it. Unable to move forward and no knob to open the door to free herself.

"Will I be here forever?" she thought.

It had been so long. She couldn't remember how she got caught. Caught between now and then. Between there and here. Only a shadow left. The shadow of a girl on an empty swing. A shadow few could see.

Sometimes, someone would come and sit on the old swing. Then she caught a brief memory of the freedom. Remembered the thrill. Legs stretching to forward, bent to backward, wind in her hair. Warm sunshine, the sweet perfume of green grass and peach blossoms. Her stomach rising and falling with the momentum.

Usually it was a child. Sometimes a love-struck couple. Usually him pushing her. Mostly it was just the breeze. Teasing her with a minute push or a cruel sideways sway.

She remembered the swing, freshly painted. Or did she? Was it red? Or was it pink? The new ropes. Shadowy memories of a man tying it to the tree. He pushing her. A white dress with little blue birds. Laughing.

She couldn't remember the feelings, just that she'd had them. Mostly, no one knew she was there. Once in a great while, someone noticed. They looked past the swing, right at her. Sometimes there was curiosity at first. Looking from the ground to the sky. Looking back again. Usually once or twice. Seldom more. Then the horror. Some shrieked. All of them ran.

"Please don't go," she thought.

She couldn't remember what sad felt like, but she was empty. Empty and alone. Maybe that was sad.

She waited. Hoping for someone to share her swing. To be with someone, if but for a small moment.

Families came and went. The paint on the seat faded, was repainted, and faded again. In time, it all peeled away. Gray, cracked, weathered. The fat ropes were thinner. They'd been replaced several times too. Now they were frayed. Ragged. Sporting multiple knots where they'd been retied together over and over again.

Then the boy came. She saw him. Not exactly from the ground where she could be seen, but from where ever it was she was caught. He was little. He wandered around the yard, hands in pockets, kicking rocks. Occasionally, dropping to his hands and knees, he put his face close to the ground. Examining something. Sometimes when he got up, he put something in his pocket. He eventually wandered over to the tree. He saw her.

The traditional turning of the head. From her to the sun. From the sun back to her. She waited. Waited for the wide eyes. The look of terror. The running away.

He looked at her a long time and pushed the swing. He saw the change. He pushed it harder. Higher. Saw her legs move. Hair flowing back. He laughed.

He stopped the swing, staring at her with wide eyes. Not wide with terror, but wide with wonder.

"Who are you? Where's your person?"

She was awestruck. Something warmed inside her.

He waited. A cool breeze eased the swing at an angle. The turn made her shoulder shrug.

"Oh. You can't tell me, can you?"

He was thoughtful. Staring through her into the ground.

"I'm Sam. I'm going to call you Brise. I hope that's okay."

His mother called. He turned to go and stopped. He carefully positioned himself and held his arms out and around. Bending, adjusting. His shadow giving her a hug.

"Bye, Brise," he said, as he raced away.

She felt. Not a memory, but something real. Something now. A spark.

He came back every day. Sometimes he'd play by her. Always running a monologue of his life. Ideas. Hopes. Dreams. Some days he was upset. When he was sad, he'd curl up on her and find comfort. As she did in him.

Summer faded to fall. Fall to winter. Some days he didn't come. It was usually inclement weather. Sometimes they left for a holiday. He always apologized. Always tried to tell her before, if he wasn't going to be there. Even on the cloudiest days, he could see her. Always he pushed. Pushed so she could swing.

The frigid wind roared through the tree above her. The swing swaying to and fro, a wild ride. The snow whistled by, blowing sideways, plastering the tree trunk in a thick white coat of frosting. Snow sat thick and heavy on the swing. On the third day, the sky cleared. Bright and blue, like she remembered the little birds on her dress to be. He came.

"I'm sorry Brise. Mom wouldn't let me come out."

He brushed the snow off the seat and pushed. Letting her swing high above him.

"I can't stay. We're going to grandma's for Christmas. I'll be back in a week."

He stopped the swing. He took off his coat and hat. Carefully, he arranged them on her. Gentle. Mindful. Placing the arms of the coat, so they'd follow her arms up to the shadow of the ropes. There he placed his knit mittens. At the last, he carefully placed his hat on her head.

"Don't go anywhere," he said with a giggle. He ran to where his mother's voice called for him.

She could always see him, if he was within the bounds of the property. Others, she could only see if they were close to the swing. She could hear them though.

She heard his mother. Berating him.

"Where's your coat?"

"I don't know, mama."

"You've got to be more responsible. And what about your hat and mittens?"

He shrugged.

"Are they in the back yard?"

She started toward the side yard.

"I think I left them on the bus," he said.

She raised her hands in exasperation.

"Get in the car."

She could see him looking down at his feet. Hands in his pockets, as he dragged his feet toward the car. Shivering in the cold. Something else stirred in her. Something she remembered from before, but hadn't remembered how it felt. Love.

More seasons came. More went. He grew. In time, his face and body changed. His voice got deeper. Still, he came every day. Still, he pushed, sometimes sitting on the swing himself. Watching his shadow and her together. Still, he talked to her. Voice low, so the others couldn't hear. He started reading to her. Some stories for little girls. Some stories for bigger boys.

It was late in the summer. They were having a barbeque. The odor of grilled meats rode the smoke through the neighborhood. He sat, leaned against the trunk. Reading aloud. His parents questioned him when they'd first caught him doing it. He lied and told them his teacher had told him it would help him to read and speak better.

His parents talked about the tree.

"It's really got to go," the father said.

"You're right. Hardly any left alive," the mother said.

"I'll call the arborist and see when they can come and do it."

"Make sure they pull the stump," she said.

"I will. I'll cut the swing down," he said.

He got up, grabbing a knife off the table. She'd been listening, as had the boy. What would happen to her? Would she stay with the tree? Would she stay with the swing? Or would she just stay there? Eons, and not even a swing to break the monotony. She also knew that he wouldn't always be there. No one stayed forever.

The father stopped when the boy leapt up and sat in the swing.

"I'll take care of it dad," he said.

"A little sentimental?" his mother asked.

"I suppose so," the boy answered.

"Okay. Enjoy it for a few more days," his father said.

She wished she could cry. She wasn't even sure what it was that she felt. Fear? Dread? Sorrow? No. Still, only happy and love were clear to her. The former coming and going with him. The latter always there. Everything else was confusion.

He sat in silence. He sat for a long time. He looked at her. Troubled. Worried.

"I'll do something, Brise."

He tried. She could hear them. The rational arguments. Why they should keep the tree and swing. When that didn't work, then a play on their sentiments. Wouldn't it be nice someday to have grandchildren swing on it, as he had? Then the other blow. A promotion. The need to move. He would be leaving.

He divested reason and civility. He tried anger, arguing in rage. Crying. Pleading. The parents talked in hushed voices at night. Wondering what was wrong with him. What had happened?

More questions came to her. What if she stayed with the tree? What would happen if they burned it? If she stayed with the swing? Would she spend an eternity buried in a landfill? If she stayed where she was, would she be relegated to just looking up into the thick weeds that would grow over her? What if someone built something there? And, she'd be alone again.

The arborist would come tomorrow. He came to her.

"You have to go, Brise. They're going to take your swing. Your tree."

"*How?*" she thought.

"When I was little, I used to wonder how it was that you were here. Why you were here. Why others couldn't see you. We were born in the wrong times for each other. God knew I'd need you. Knew that you'd be the one who'd always listen. The one I could always count on to be here for me. You've saved my life over and over again. I'm so thankful you stayed and waited for me. I really am, Brise. I love you, but you have to go now."

An enduring stare. He so wished, as he had so many times before, that she could talk to him. He carefully stood. He pushed the swing. Watching her come to life. Standing on her side of the swing this time. Pushing the swing, but watching her.

"Go Brise."

She felt something different. The door cracking open? Freeing her? Was this all that was needed then?

He pushed it further, the swing arcing toward the heavens, ropes loose and then going taut again as the swing came back toward him.

He gave it a forceful shove and watched the shadow leap upward. Something warm passed through him. Exulted, he yelled, "Fly Brise!"

And she did. A flash of sunlight in his eyes as the swing reached its apex. Then, as if birthed from the sun itself, a snow-white dove. Circling once, wings flapping, before rising into the sky. He watched until he couldn't see her anymore.

"Goodbye, Brise," he said.

He hung his head. Hands in pockets. Walking across the yard. Kicking rocks. Feeling warm and happy. Feeling empty and sad.

The swing came to a stop. Only its empty shadow left.

The Projectionist
by Paul B. Cohen

The Variety Cinema stood inauspiciously on a Sheffield roundabout. I unfastened the padlocked entrance and stepped inside. Anticipating gloom and dust, I found the lobby lit by an angle-poise lamp. I knew the building still had an electricity supply but had arranged for disconnection. Within a pool of light, I saw a man sprawled on the floor.

I ghosted around the lobby, past a huddle of beer cans, nervously trying to ascertain whether I was looking at a corpse. Whoever he was, he was lying on a poster of the film 'Casablanca'.

A voice called out. "We're not open yet!"

"Who are you?" I asked.

"Not open."

"I said, 'Who are you?'"

"Melvin Fraser." He lifted his chin. "The projectionist."

I didn't understand. "What the hell are you doing in here?"

He stretched. "Are you the police?"

I shone my torch at the intruder. His hair had largely deserted his head and his coat was scuffed at the edges. "I'm no copper, but you're trespassing here."

Fraser got up. "I worked at this cinema for thirty-one years. How can I be trespassing?"

"Well, you no longer work here now," I said.

I guessed Fraser to be in his sixties, and he had a frailty about him as if pressed down by his burdens. "This is private property, and closed, so you are trespassing."

"I feel that, morally, some of this building belongs to me."

"Williams Holdings have bought this site. I'm here to safeguard it until demolition."

"Ah, demolition," Fraser said. "I thought that might be on the cards."

"It's the best solution," I said, although we'd never considered other options for the site. That was not my remit.

"Demolition," he repeated. "Quite a poetic sounding word, until you consider what it means."

"I think everyone knows what it means, Mr Fraser."

The projectionist sniffed. "Can't happen. It's part of Sheffield's heritage." He pulled a pipe from a pocket. "Do you have a light?"

"You can't smoke in this building."

"Nobody's complained before."

"It's out of the question. There may be gas around."

Like a dutiful schoolboy, Fraser put his pipe away. "Didn't catch your name... "

"John Burgess." I switched my flashlight off. "How did you get in?"

Fraser pulled out a bunch of keys. "These all still work, except for the one Evelyn changed for our house."

"Evelyn?"

"My wife," Fraser said. "Changed the locks to the front door. We'd grown apart, I'll admit, but I didn't think she'd shut me out like that. This seemed the natural place to take refuge, and I saw no other choices."

"But I need you to leave," I insisted. "This place should be empty."

"Not doing that, Mr Burgess. I've made it my home, and I don't intend to depart any time soon."

I felt a prickling in my face. "Is that a threat?"

"No: I simply haven't anywhere else to go."

"I'm sorry, but I have to see that this place is vacant."

Fraser smoothed back his hair. "Tell you what…would you like a tour?"

I was starting to think that while Fraser presented no physical danger, he was not someone I should indulge. "What for?"

"To see how I've managed."

"Does that include sleeping on a film poster?"

"Actually," he replied, "there is a mattress upstairs, but I sometimes feel drowsy and I've always been able to catnap."

I shook my head. "Really, you've got to leave."

"Perhaps if you had the tour, you'd realise I've kept the place up quite respectably."

"Quickly, then," I said, reasoning that it made sense to see the condition of the interior. After that, I would find a way to get Fraser off the premises.

I followed my unlikely guide into the auditorium. Up to a couple of months ago, so I'd read in a report on the property, there were still aisles of seats. Some collector in Halifax had bought them as a job lot. Faint lines on the carpet revealed how they had once been arranged. We veered to the right of the screen – that was still *in situ* – and through a "Staff Only" door, into a dusky kitchen.

A calendar on the wall was seven years out of date. Movie posters in frames hung on the walls. There was a microwave with a liquid crystal display, and I could see that its inner door was a canvas of splattered soup from meals of the past.

A white plastic table was attended by two chairs and had a salt cellar standing desultorily near an edge. Behind the door was a fridge with a Charlie Chaplin magnet on it.

"All this will have to go," I said.

"If you say. Are you ready to meet the angels?"

I took a long look at the projectionist. "What are you talking about?"

"Just come," he urged.

I complied, noticing that the heels of Fraser's shoes were worn down. We walked up a twirling iron staircase to the balcony. He indicated a door and more or less pushed me through it. The balcony had one row of seats left, with carpet underfoot, but it was the ceiling that Fraser wanted to show me.

Above my head, I surveyed an expanse of plasterwork. There were flowers, fountains, and finely wrought figures. But large areas were cracked, and water marked.

"The ceiling is almost a century old. Now, look over to the right, where the angels are."

I let the torch roam over the plaster. "What is it you're showing me?"

"Two angels, kissing. See them?"

"Yes," I said, grudgingly.

"When I was a lad of sixteen, with a girl by my side," Fraser continued, "I'd save up for mezzanine seats. During the newsreels, I'd look to my angels, and put my arm around the lass, hoping she would glance up, see the kisses, and want to do the same with me."

"And did they ever?"

"Once or twice," Fraser grinned, revealing a gap in his teeth.

We left the balcony for the projection room. It was filled with postcards, posters, bills tacked on by silver pins, and there was a gallery of Hollywood stars in framed pictures. A bookcase looked as if it could collapse at any moment while a modest wooden desk supported a ledger and stashes of old film catalogues. In the corner lay the mattress Fraser had mentioned.

Upfront were two projectors. One was a huge machine with a spool, a broad lens, and various switches, dials behind oval panels, and assorted stout levers waiting to be pulled. I reckoned it would take four men to shift this piece of apparatus. The other projector, when set against its neighbour, was almost miniature and would be far easier to remove.

"That little one's the digital," he said. "The enemy of our profession."

"The what?" I asked.

"All you've got to do is load the 'digital media' and push a button. That's how the new technology works."

"Sounds very efficient to me," I said.

Fraser harrumphed. "*Efficient.* Where's the romance in *efficient*?" He placed his hand on the old projector. "Any idea what model this is?"

I sighed, making a show of checking my watch. "No. Why would I?"

"It's an American Century C. From the '50s, and still a working beauty, although a bit noisy. There aren't that many around."

"Look, Mr Fraser, I'm sure you could tell me plenty about these machines and the films you've shown on them, but your time's up."

Fraser looked sour. "I hope you're not going to get unpleasant with me."

"You have to leave, as I've made clear."

"No, sir," he said, his voice low and breathy. "Let me be. I do no harm here."

We stood there, and into my mind popped a corny image from the movies: two gunfighters in the dust, both with guns drawn. A stalemate.

There was no way I could force him out, physically, as I'm a wiry man of five foot seven. I could call the police, but then I'd have to report it to my boss. It might look as if I hadn't been firm enough.

"Listen," I said, "I'm scheduled to come back next Thursday. That's when any remaining inventory and equipment will be removed, just before the demolition people move in."

Fraser smiled. "What are valuable are the screen and these projectors. The digital one is an old model, but someone'll have it. The 35mil could fetch quite a bit online."

"Don't you worry about the equipment. Just make arrangements for yourself, Mr Fraser – before next week."

His face came towards mine. "So there isn't going to be any disagreeable struggle to get me out?"

I was sure this was the wrong thing to say, but I felt sorry for him. I decided to give him a reprieve. "I shouldn't even consider it, but as long as nobody finds out, I'm going to let you stay for a few more days."

The projectionist held out his hand. "You're a fair man, Mr Burgess."

"A mug, more like," I said.

In the lobby, I asked Fraser about the beer cans.

"Whiskey's my poison," he said. "That beer was drunk by Bob."

"Bob?"

"A friend. Came to see me twice a week, until last month."

"What happened last month?"

"His daughter found him some sheltered accommodation. In the end, he gave in and went quietly. I just haven't cleared up the cans, yet."

"You can't have anyone else here," I warned.

"There won't be anyone else. Anyway, I like the solitude, generally, although it'd be good to have an audience for some of the digital material we still own."

I buttoned up my coat. "You have until next week at the latest to move on. I think I've made that clear."

"The captain goes down with the ship," Fraser muttered. "Mr Burgess, do you like watching films?"

"A DVD, every so often."

"Seen any of the classics?" Fraser asked.

"Depends what you mean by classics."

"Oh, I think films that are understood as classics are beyond dispute."

I expected Fraser to give a lecture on films he loved; instead, he wished me farewell, and proprietarily closed the cinema door. I stepped into the Yorkshire evening. The streetlights were on, smug yellows in a darkening sky, and I walked to my car.

I actually returned to Sheffield the following Wednesday, arriving later than intended due to squally weather and maddening traffic. Crossing the empty lobby, I walked into the auditorium, hoping that the projectionist had taken my advice and found refuge elsewhere.

I was wrong of course. Sitting on a wooden chair, near to the screen, Fraser was reading a book with the aid of a small light clipped to a page.

Without turning around, he said, "Is it Thursday already?"

"No, but I was hoping not to find you here."

He chuckled. "Luckily for you, we've got an Italian classic ready to go."

I wanted to make clear I was displeased by his presence. "Never mind that. You need to leave within twenty-four hours, Mr Fraser."

He ignored the warning. "We have 'Bicycle Thieves', Mr Burgess. Not, 'The Bicycle Thieves', as they once listed it in the local paper. Made in 1948 and directed by Vittorio De Sica. Masterpiece of post-war Italian realism. How's your Italian?"

"I don't speak it," I said, impatiently.

"Native title is '*Ladri di biciclette*'. Don't worry, it's sub-titled. Get yourself a chair from over there."

I didn't move.

"If it's only Wednesday, then they're not coming until tomorrow. I'll use the digital projector. Once set up, I can sit with you, if that's all right."

"This is ridiculous," I protested, yet I retrieved a chair. For once I was in no hurry. I had hardly ever watched a film in black and white, and certainly never one in Italian, but the monochrome tenderness of the story enveloped me. Glancing at the projectionist, I saw discrete tears in his eyes.

When the film ended, the auditorium returned to its somnolence. I allowed myself a moment to reflect on what I'd seen, until I recalled my duties.

"Mr Fraser, I'll be back at 9 o'clock in the morning. Please don't let me find you here."

My phone rang: it was my boss, Joanne Stephens. I told her where I was.

"You're on-site?" she asked. "Everything all right there?"

I told her it was.

"Demolition date's been delayed. There's been some problem lining up the equipment, so we're re-scheduling for seven days."

I put away my phone. "Fraser?"

He appeared without his coat. "Staying for tea?" he asked.

"The wrecking ball's been put back a week," I said. "You're a lucky bugger."

He threw his hands up, as if in praise of heaven. "This is true? You are a messenger of joy! We shall celebrate with another film."

"No, I'm off home."

"It's 'Sunset Boulevard'!"

"Never heard of it."

"I'm surrounded by Philistines," he laughed. "Do you know, I once met Billy Wilder, the film's director? It was in Beverly Hills, the late 1970s."

"Mr Fraser, remember that your stay here is temporary," I warned.

He wasn't listening. "When we talked, I thought that he had a curious accent for an American. Then I learned that he was Austrian, originally. Jewish as well. That's why he was thankful to have got out of Europe to Hollywood in the 1930s. He made his home there. Everyone needs a home, don't they?"

A week later, I arrived at the cinema ahead of the demolition crew. The morning was bright but chill, and I wished I had brought some coffee with me.

"Fraser?" I called. "Are you here?"

As I walked through the auditorium, I hoped that Fraser had heeded my advice and left for good. I certainly didn't want to manhandle him out of the cinema. I located the spiral steps and went upwards, going straight into the projection room. The air was stale.

I found the projectionist slumped over the desk, and although I couldn't tell how it had happened, I knew Melvin Fraser was dead. There was no blood, but his skin was cold.

Underneath his right hand was a letter, typed in old-fashioned typewriter ink. Trying not to touch the man's fingers, I pulled away the paper.

The note was for me. It read:

Dear Mr Burgess, I'm sorry you're going to find me like this, but at least I can now be removed by your crew, along with Bertha, hah hah! They'll find me a lot lighter than my favourite projector.

I have loved this place for decades and cannot accept that soon it will be no more. Is it a bingo hall or casino they are putting up in its place? Anyway, sic transit gloria mundi.
But films, at least, do not die. Should you have a few spare hours, you would be rewarded by any of the following films, which are all <u>classics</u>:

>   *Citizen Kane*
>   *Rashomon*
>   *Seven Samurai*
>   *Modern Times*

If you watch these masterpieces, forget the popcorn – a cup of tea and some toffees will suffice – and perhaps you will think kindly, for a moment or two, of Melvin Fraser, Projectionist at the Albany Picture House, 1977-2008.

Down in the lobby, I picked up the "Casablanca" poster and rolled it up, thinking my wife might quite like it. Then I dialled 999.

Outside, I squinted in the winter sunlight. Cars and trucks indifferently passed the doomed cinema. I waited for an ambulance.

Fraser had been correct: he would be carried out when the projectors were carted off, as if man and machine were umbilically joined to share the same fate. For a few hours, an edifice of brick and cement would be left behind: the projectionist's palace of dreams, forever silenced. And Fraser would not hear the tearing, and the grinding, and the pounding of the heavy plant equipment as it destroyed the building.

I understood why he had taken his way out.

Only then I noticed that my boss was stepping from her car, replete in her usual black suit and black patent shoes.

"Are we on track?" she asked.

"We'll be starting shortly," I mumbled.

"What's that you're holding?"

"Film poster. Look, Joanne, why don't you come inside for a minute? I'd to show you something."

"Make it quick, John. I've to be in York by lunchtime."

For the last time, I passed through the lobby, through the empty auditorium, up the iron staircase and to the mezzanine.

I flicked on my torch. "Look up there," I said.

"What am I looking at?"

"There are two angels, just there, kissing. They've kissed for nearly one hundred years."

She turned to me. "How on earth do you know that?"

"The projectionist told me."

"The who?"

"The projectionist. Let's go and see him now, shall we?"

The Fire Eater
by Ann Christine Tabaka

The forests were burning, and nothing could be done to stop it. All hope seemed lost. Day turned into night as thick black clouds of smoke blocked out the sun. Days turned into weeks, and the fire grew in intensity. Everything was parched from lack of rain. Even the air burned.

Humankind's greed had been the cause of many disasters on this earth. The constant overuse of fossil fuels disrupting the weather patterns, and the disrespect for nature in general were among few of the reasons that the forests now burned.

The indigenous people prayed to the Great Spirit, to send down the Fire Eater to save their homes and the creatures that lived on the land. Sad and frightened, the people packed all that they could carry from their simple dwellings. They gathered together their domestic and farm animals to herd with them. They needed to move to safer ground, up to the high mountains where the fire had not yet reached. There the snow melt streams and fresh springs would keep them safe for a short while longer, but not forever if the blazes could not be contained. The mountains were steep and rugged, and there were no roads. They would have to travel by foot and horseback, leaving all motorized vehicles behind. Sorrow filled their hearts at the thought of having to leave all that they loved.

Chilam was only 17 years old, but she was as sensitive and wise as the elders. She lived with her mother, father, three siblings and her grandmother. They had a comfortable little cabin near the edge of the woods. They farmed and raised livestock. They had the Internet, and a few other modern conveniences, but she honored the old traditions, and the beautiful handcrafts that her mother made to sell. She loved her life and would not trade it for all the money and glamour in the world. She was beyond rich in her own eyes. The stars at night were magic to her. Diamonds dancing across the velvet expanse. Where else on earth could you reach up and almost touch the Milky Way? There the sky was bluer, the water clearer, and the air purer, except for now. Now that the whole earth burned. The earth that she knew and loved was dying.

Chilam felt helpless as she assisted her family in preparation for the arduous journey ahead. She tried to remember all the beauty that her forests held, and how she would run through them playing when she was younger. She feared for her beloved forest friends, the deer, the squirrel, the mountain lion and hawk. She had named many of them over the years, and felt connected to each one of them. They were her own personal Spirit Guides. She worried, would they be able to make it out alive? She could not leave it to chance. She knew what she had to do. She would go into the woods to look for her friends, and tell them to follow her to a new home far away from the approaching flames.

The day came for the village to move. They could not wait a day longer. Chilam was nowhere to be found. Her family looked everywhere for her but could not find her. In a panic they went to the village elder to ask for a search party to help them look. The elder said it was too late and that they had to leave now or be eaten up by the flames. Her family was heartbroken, but they had other children and a grandmother to care for, so they left behind a message for Chilam, for when she would come back to the village. They were sure that she would come back. She had to be safe, they had been praying so hard. The Fire Eater would come and save her.

Evening was setting in as Chilam wandered deeper into the forest. Over and over again she called out to her friends, "Tahca, Zica, Igmuwatogla." She was becoming tired and was starting to choke from all the thick smoke. She could hardly breathe when she finally sat down on a rock to rest. The rock was very warm to the touch, and she knew that was a sign that she had to leave soon or perish. She wept as she called out to the Great Spirit to save her and her animals. "Please oh Great Spirit, hear my cry and send the Fire Eater to save us." She started to grow weaker by the minute, and finally passed out. Hawk found her first, and alighted by her side. He let out a great screech to call the others. Startled, she came to. She stood to her feet, and started following beneath Hawk as he flew overhead. He would guide her to safety, she knew he would. They came to a clearing in the middle of the woods where the fire had not yet reached. There, standing before her, were many of her forest friends, all huddled together in fear. No predators, no prey, just creatures trying to survive this monstrous disaster. It reminded her of an artist's images of Eden in the holy book she read as a little girl.

Suddenly, on the other side of the clearing, Chilam noticed a small trail leading away from the fire. She decided to try to lead her friends towards the mountains, where she knew her people would be going. She began singing a beautiful native song to them as she walked towards the trail. It was a song that her grandmother would sing to her whenever she was frightened as a child. The beautiful native language was soothing, as was the tune. The animals all lifted their heads to listen to the enticing melody. One by one they began to walk behind her. She had their trust. She tried to be brave, but her voice faltered as she continued with her song. She tried to imagine that she was like mighty Moses leading the chosen people across the Red Sea, away from the danger that followed them. If she could only hold on to that image in her mind, maybe she could keep her courage up.

Meanwhile, the villagers continued their trek, slowly snaking up the rocky mountainside. Families, the elderly, infants, and the ailing, all traveling into the unknown, each person doing whatever they could manage to try to help the others, lifting, carrying, pushing, struggling for their lives, all, exhausted and parched from the hot air that followed them every step of the way, hoping beyond hope that their efforts would not be in vain. Chilam's family stopped to look back. They continued to quietly chant their solemn prayer. They were very worried, but they knew that if anyone could manage to defeat the elements, Chilam would be the one to do it. There was always something special about her, something spiritual about her, something mystical. They picked up their packs and continued onwards with the others, leaving a trail of prayer beads along the path behind them. Hopeful breadcrumbs to be followed by their daughter.

Night fell, but it was difficult to tell the difference with all the black smoke in the atmosphere. It had been dark the whole day. The smell of charred wood was beginning to overtake everyone. Chilam and her friends could tell that the fire was growing closer as they trekked onward. The animals traveled by sheer instinct, following the only sign of hope that they had, a young woman. She was their savior. They would not stop to rest, for if they did, the fire would catch up to them. They had no choice but to keep going. In the darkness they progressed by touch, using the trees' bark like braille.

Just as daybreak tried to show itself through the thick fumes, a strange sound was heard in the distant sky. Chilam's heart raced as the sound grew louder and closer. She had heard that sound before, she was sure she knew what it was. Then out of the smoke and fire appeared several large helicopters whirling overhead. She screamed and waved her arms while jumping up and down. Hawk decided to fly higher to try to intercept. The helicopter pilot almost lost control seeing a huge Red-tailed Hawk soaring towards the craft, then continually circling it. It was if the hawk was trying to get his attention, but how could that be? The firefighters were looking down, following the flight of the hawk when they noticed a human female and a group of animals on the trail below.

Then, as large streams of water came down from the helicopters, quenching the areas around Chilam and her forest friends, she noticed one of the mechanical birds come down to land. Out jumped several firemen and firewomen, suited for their work with gas masks and protective attire. One tall man, Jorge, came running up to her as the others fought the nearby blaze. Jorge raised his mask to speak to her. He was handsome and strong looking. Their eyes met and Chilam smiled up at him. Relief flooded over her weak body as she almost collapsed into his arms. Jorge insisted that she come with him on to the helicopter, but Chilam stood firm, crossed her arms and said in a stern voice, "No, I am not leaving my friends. They need me now more than ever."

No matter how hard he argued, Jorge could not change her mind, and other than lifting her over his shoulder and forcing her aboard, he had no choice but to join her. Chilam told him where her village was heading and asked that the firefighters go find them and bring them to safety. Jorge signaled to his copter crew to join the others and continue on in search of the villagers. Jorge was fascinated, and a bit startled at the strange array of wild animals that surrounded Chilam and seemed to be in her trust. She explained that they were all her friends and her Spirit Guides. She would never abandon them. Three of the helicopters went ahead to find and help the villagers, while one stayed with the unlikely parade that was led by Chilam, and now Jorge as well. They still had a long way to go by foot.

As the weary group finally met up with the rest of the villagers, the fire was starting to be held in control, at least in certain areas. Many more fire crews had joined the original one. Dedicated men and women from everywhere on the plant had volunteered to fight this horrific inferno. Helicopter and ground crews together worked day and night for weeks on end to contain the worst of the fire. There started to be a glimmer of hope, and the people of the village gave thanks. They would need to build new homes in a different area, but no lives were lost. The livestock and domestic animals were also safe, along with the many wild animals in Chilam's care. It would take a long time for life to return to normal, but everyone was now safe, and a thanksgiving feast was planned.

After the disaster had quieted down, and things started to return to normal, Jorge would come to visit Chilam regularly, and in time she leaned that his family was from a native people in Central America, from a population related to her own people. They had many of the same beliefs and customs as her people did. Even some of their native language was similar. He too loved nature and the simple way of life. Needless to say, Chilam and Jorge fell in love, and eventually they married. Jorge grew to love all the forest creatures that he had helped save. It was a beautiful relationship among all the living beings. They spent many afternoons in the forest visiting their friends together.

    In the end, the villagers' prayers were answered, and it became quite evident to all that the great "Fire Eater" could come in many forms, even as a human in a helicopter.

Sins of The Father
by David Bowmore

I will tell you everything, but please let me tell it my own way. I won't leave anything out.

I met her in a public house in Hammersmith. The Eagle, I think, a little pub with a big music scene. Every London pub had a music scene in 1977. I'd gone to see one of those bands that spawned so many other great singers and groups, but have, in the fullness of time, faded from memory. Only true music devotees would be able to recall their energy and inspiration. Punks said pub rock bands were dead, but I still liked their sound.

Not many will remember the pub either; it's probably part of a chain now with plastic menus and wheelchair access. Back then, with its stained glass windows and faded golden filigree plasterwork, carpet that stuck to your feet, atmosphere thick with smoke, and the ceiling stained with nicotine, it was a home from home. The old woman sitting at the other end of the bar, drinking port and lemon, saw everything, and said nothing—a landlady never to get on the wrong side of. The girls behind the bar called her Mother, although she couldn't possibly have been Mother to them all. The tiny stage in one corner of the pub had just enough room for the four piece band to stand on. I sat on a red leather stool at a small wooden table. If I reached out, I could touch the guitarist.

That night, I was there with a housemate who went by the name of Scud. You had to call him Scud, he got agitated when you called him Martin. Overweight, with a round face already scarred from the abuse he'd given his many whiteheads and spots as a teenager, Scud complained incessantly about the music.

"This is so fuckin' shit. I knew we should've gone to see The Slits."

"We're here now, try to enjoy yourself."

As I watch my one-time friend harrumph back towards the bar, a sulk clearly imminent, I see the ridiculous figure of a fat, spotty eighteen year old in tight tartan and leather, with a blue mohawk going limp at the end of its seven-inch spikes.

We looked very different; he was embracing the emerging punk scene, while I was clinging to the glam of a few years earlier. I had given up on glitter, but mascara, thick and black, was essential to my look back then. My hair was shoulder length and shaggy like a west coast Eagle, and my complexion, although not perfect, was not ruined in the same way as Scud's. I was also stick-thin, my student grant not enough to get the beers in and eat regular meals.

The room was crowded and smoky, and I knew Mother was watching us; mainly my friend, but me too because I was with him.

A girl flopped down beside me in the seat Scud had vacated moments earlier. A very pretty girl with green eyes, a touch of punk about her, red lipstick, and a deliciously pale face with a cigarette in a holder.

"Music's shit, init?"

"I've already had that conversation."

We were shouting over the noise, leaning in to hear each other. She smelled of Charlie, that ubiquitous and leathery scent that so many women chose to wear.

"Who's your friend?"

"Martin, I mean Scud."

"Think he'll go for me?"

"He wanted to see The Slits, so probably, yeah." I was trying to be cool without much success.

"Ha. Funny. What about you?"

I took a long look at her. She was attractive, like a reject from a Hammer film. There was a chance she might have been a prostitute, but she wasn't trashy enough and, although young, I knew the working girls around there would usually start a conversion with the price. She crossed her shapely legs, revealing more thigh. Ripped fishnets were the thing that year.

"We only just met, perhaps we should get to know each other."

"Fine, I'll be at The Hope and Anchor tomorrow night."

Then she was off, intercepting Scud on his way back to our table. She plucked a drink from his hand, took a large sip, and winked at him. He changed course, and I was left on my own to watch her flirt with him. Ten minutes later, they were leaving. She was leading him by the hand.

I was bubbling with jealousy, and I didn't even know her name. How often does it happen? An attractive girl more or less offers herself to you—idiot, Mike, you're an idiot—and she's gone off with *him*, the ugly one. Yes, I really was conceited enough to think that. Please bear in mind I was only seventeen. Mind you, she had given me first refusal.

But all was not lost.

The Hope and Anchor. Tomorrow night.

Bands played in the basement at the Hope and Anchor. A confined, claustrophobic place that made for an intimidating first visit. The band was loud, a punk outfit, and not my sort of thing. But I had a date, of sorts. The room was crowded, and there was nowhere to sit as every last piece of furniture had been removed. It was a mad, jostling, bouncing mass of crazed, sweaty flesh. The singer was spitting into the crowd, the crowd were spitting back. My stomach churned; I was glad to be at the back of the room away from the main action.

I tried not to make eye contact with anyone. The increasing feeling of danger and knot in my stomach warned me I was out of my comfort zone. I also began to suspect I shouldn't have worn bell bottoms and a Snoopy t-shirt. Going to meet a pretty girl who was a bit avant-garde while dressed like a twelve-year-old boy; I felt like such a fool.

She was standing at the back of the room, with Scud. Shit. I should have left then; my life would have been different, I'm sure of it.

"Watchya," she said.

"Hello," I said to her before turning to him. "All right, Scud?" I lifted my chin in greeting.

"All right," he said. What he was really saying was *piss off*.

Standing next to Scud, she appeared much taller than the previous night. She smirked down at him.

"Run along, Martin, your friend and I have business to talk about."

"But what about us?" he protested.

"I told you, there is no *us*. A failed fumble in a car park does not make us an item, darling. Now, go and jump about with your little friends." She was cruel, and yet my heart jumped at her words.

She kissed me on the cheek, leaving a red smudge, and led me away from Scud. He had been omitted just like that.

"He won't like being called Martin," I said

"Tough tits, shit stinks."

She smiled at me, my heart melted.

I asked if she wanted a drink, to which she answered, "Bah, it's piss in here. I'm sure they water it down. None of this lot would know.

They're all speeding their nuts off." She swept her arm in a wide arc, indicating the pogoing fools up by the stage.

We leaned against the rear wall. Should I have got myself a drink? I didn't know; it was difficult to say what would have impressed her.

"I don't know your name," I said.

"Are you sure you want to, Mike?"

She knew my name. I felt flattered, but I also knew how easy it would've been to get such simple information from Scud. None the less, she had me at a disadvantage.

"Yes."

"Tell you what…help me out with a little something, and I'll tell you my name and anything else you want to know about me."

"Okay. You're on. What do you want?"

At that moment, I would have happily crawled over burning coals just to hear her speak.

"You sure? It'll be different, but fun…maybe a bit embarrassing. Still want to help?"

"Yeah."

"See him over there, the little man on his own who looks about as out of place here as you do."

"Yeah."

"He's the manager of the band. Nice man with a wife and child at home."

I looked sideways at her; where was this going?

"How do you know?"

"I like to know things about people. Now, listen. He's a nice man who likes nice young boys, understand?"

"So…"

"So, make friends with him and ask if he can find somewhere quiet for you to talk where you won't be interrupted."

"Hang on a minute," I said, "you've got the wrong idea about me. I thought you and me could—"

"Don't worry, I'll rescue you."

"Why?"

"You'll see. Trust me."

I was worried. Despite what my father would always say about men who wear makeup being poofters and pansies, I was not that way inclined. Just an inexperienced boy trying to find a place in the big city.

"Get me a drink then." I was annoyed with her. For what, I wasn't quite sure. She was playing a game with me, that much I knew, and although I didn't know the rules, I was excited. Why? I didn't have the answer for that either.

She came back with a lager and a whiskey, both for me.

"Pint o' piss and some Dutch courage," she said.

I necked the scotch and went forward to my destiny.

It was ridiculously easy. In a matter of minutes, he was showing me into the manager's office on the pretext of an impromptu audition.

He stroked my hair and said kind words about my youth and beauty. He promised a proper audition with a band if I only relaxed and took my t-shirt off. I did, but I was sweating—where was she? Was the joke to be on me? Just how cruel could she be?

He ran his fingers over my chest, chasing goose pimples as I shivered. He put his arms around me and slid his fingers under my belt at the top of my buttocks. To my amazement, I found myself becoming aroused. This shouldn't be happening. I was straight, I knew I was. It might have been raging hormones in combination with the closeness of another human being.

He was looking into my eyes, waiting for my kiss. Just as I was thinking I might have to either go through with it or storm out of the room, the door burst open. A camera flash illuminated the doorway, stinging my eyes, leaving a lightning strike afterimage.

The little man began to rant "How dare you? This is private," then he started to call for help. I started to dress.

"Be quiet," Polly shouted from the doorway. "No one can hear you over that poor excuse for a band. Now, I'd hate for this to get in the papers, ducky. Twenty quid and I can keep it out of the news." She was shaking the Polaroid the way people used to do.

"I'm not paying you a penny, sweetheart. Blackmail is illegal. I shall get my lawyers."

"Not blackmail. I'm looking after your best interests, for a fee."

"We live in enlightened times, you stupid cow. No one will care. In fact, it might even be good for the band."

"Now you are bluffing. I'm sure the wife will care very much. Twenty quid *now*, or the papers find out about your fifteen-year-old friend here."

I was stunned; it had all happened so fast. But Fifteen? He'd lost and he knew it. He threw the notes at me, calling me a whore and her a blackmailing bitch.

We ran out holding hands, her laughing and me oh so relieved to be with her. She was dangerous and amazing, beautiful and smart, and I was smitten. I had tricked the little man. I was enjoying being with her and I wanted more.

We went to China Town and feasted. I hadn't eaten so well in months. As promised, she told me about herself. Polly, as I found out, was a couple of years older than me, and her parents were relieved when she moved out. She had always been a great disappointment to them ever since the nuns refused to have her back.

Polly had a room in Notting Hill. Today, one associates Notting Hill with the carnival, the stylish, and Hugh Grant. But, back then, house after dilapidated house still bore the marks of war, each in need of serious repair or to be torn down entirely—they were all owned by Rackman-type landlords. Feral cats and children roamed aimlessly around the streets, and over-flowing metal bins lined the litter-strewn slum area.

Bob Marley was stirring it up through the floorboards from the room above while we made love until the early hours.

In the morning, she thanked me for being brave, for trusting her with her plan, and asked me if I wanted to do it again.

I told her I loved her and that I would do anything.

Two months later, we were married at a Catholic church in the suburbs. Some might say a quick wedding, but she had something on the priest.

Polly liked to know things about people, I asked how she found things out. In response, she tapped her nose and said she kept her ear to the ground and her eyes wide open. I'm sure people might ask why she decided to partner with me in her small scams. The simple truth is that I don't know. She was clever enough and brave enough to get everything she needed on her own, and I wasn't exactly Giant Haystacks, so I couldn't offer much in the way of protection. I think she needed someone to know her secret. She needed someone to show off to, someone to impress. I supported her wholeheartedly in the beginning, although I only played the role of a fifteen-year-old boy once more after the band manager incident.

We went to gigs most nights, everything from big venues to small pubs. She barely drank, but Polly—like old Mother—watched everything; a husband slipping a wedding band into a pocket before he went to chat to a girl, money exchanged for plastic baggies. And she wasn't afraid to ask for money to keep her mouth shut. She was cocky in her approach to business, but it didn't always work. She took a severe slapping one night. When I stepped in to protect her, I had my fingers broken and couldn't eat solid food for a month. Things had to change.

She turned her talents to band management, focusing on one band in particular. Gathering her evidence beforehand, and approaching the band during a break in one of their sets, she asked if they wanted fresh representation; someone who would really look after their interests without trying to get into any of their knickers.

"I wouldn't mind you tryin', love," said the lead singer, reaching a hand around her waist.

"If you're not going to take the offer seriously, then you can stick with the perv. He's tried it on with each of you, hasn't he?" she said as she moved his hand away.

The singer looked like she had slapped his face. He stood taller and shared an embarrassed, knowing look with his fellow bandmates. Trying to recover the situation he asked, "Who else you manage? I don't wanna sign up with a bint who knows nothin' 'bout nothin'."

"Billy and the Bad Girls," she replied. Of course, this was a lie.

"They any good?" asked the singer. The drummer was nodding, twiddling his sticks.

"Could be, but you could be better. But only if you take me seriously. Call me *love* again or think of me as just a pair of tits and your dumped. Call me Polly, act like a gentleman and not an adolescent twat, and you'll do well. Promise."

His bandmates nodded their agreement. He held out a hand to Polly. They shook.

"But you'll have trouble getting Old Roy to let us go. Want us to have a word?" asked the singer.

"Leave the business side of things to me. Don't worry your pretty little head."

Soon after she coerced the manager into releasing them, she had her evidence.

We rented a very small office, where I answered the phone. She changed the band's name and image. Out were the wannabe punks, and in were the groomed and suited. Very romantic. A keyboard player joined, all previous songs were either softened or dropped. Gigs were arranged all over the capital. She worked them hard. If they went further afield, I went with them, but it was rare; London was where it was at.

She knew of a journalist with the NME and invited him to see the band now they were a tighter unit.

"They're okay, but nothing special, Polly. They look a bit too clean. Know what I mean?"

"They're the next big thing…and shall I tell you why?"

"Go on, enlighten me."

"No one minds if you're a coke head, in fact, it's to be expected you being a hack in a music rag," she said, "but sucking it off the cocks of rent boys for six pence a time might give you a bad name." The journalist looked around, checking to see if anyone had heard. "I want a fabulous write up for my band. I want you to suggest they're better than the Beatles and The Stones served up together on sliced bread. The lead singer is a bastard love child of Jim Morrison and Tom Jones. Know what I mean?"

It was indeed a good write up, and it wasn't the last piece of praise her pet correspondent produced. Bigger and better gigs came in. An album was released, which sold well thanks to a favour owed to her by someone at the BBC. More bands came to her as the "best choice" in music management. We got a bigger office with shiny glass desks and plush, cream coloured Axminster on the floor. We employed a secretary. We acquired even more bands, all of whom went on to do even more gigs and release even more albums—some sold well, others not so well. All the while, Polly collected her secrets. For her, secrets were priceless, her most precious commodity.

Rock and pop stars were renowned for being naughty boys and girls and people expected as much, so their secrets didn't hold much bargaining power for Polly. But, the real headache came from all the solicitors involved in the many layers of the complex music industry. Talented liars—all of them—and far too many for Polly's liking.

A year or two later, public relations merged with and eventually replaced music management. We opened our doors to radio DJs and TV presenters, comedians, and newsreaders. We acted as their agents, managers, and representatives.

It had all moved so fast, thanks to Maggie Thatcher's Britain, and we were operating completely above board; secrets weren't a necessity anymore, but Polly still valued the information. People paid for information, but more importantly, they paid to keep it out of the papers.

A few weeks into a new signing, the conversation would go something like this…

"We are here for you, to get your name out and about, get you the right work, create the right image. Agreed?" Polly would begin.

"Yes, absolutely," the talent would say.

"Would you agree that keeping negative aspects of your life out of the news would benefit your image?"

"Yes, but I'm clean as a whistle, Polly darling."

"If we're going to work together, we need honesty. For instance, it is well known you like a little visit to a certain massage parlour down Soho way."

"Nonsense"

"No point trying to hide it. My job is to know everything about you so I can present your best image while hiding your, shall we say, less favourable qualities. If you must use these places, try to be more discreet. If anyone gives you trouble, send them my way. Better still, tell me everything about them and the problem. I can, in most cases, stop the news getting out, but it can be very expensive keeping bad news out of the papers."

We soon had a small team to help run the public lives of our celebrities: we organised public appearances and the opening of supermarkets and hospitals; newspaper articles and magazine interviews had to be scheduled; parties had to be organised and attended. Our lifestyle was hectic.

We were flying high, but every now and then, a secret revealed itself. Usually because the talent refused to pay, or because they actually wanted the news to come out. Someone's poison or vice then had to be protected. We hired private investigators to dig up the darkest secrets on all our clients. Polly would even use nuggets of information to entice existing clients to dish the dirt on friends and colleagues. And, of course, it was all in the name of protecting their interests. It was all very seedy, and I was losing interest in it.

I had grown weary of our business, and if I'm completely honest, it wasn't really mine. It was her baby and it almost ran itself, so I had less and less to do with it as time moved on. I had a growing cocaine habit, which very quickly became my main source of comfort.

Early one evening, it all came to a head when we had a meeting with a client. We greeted each other and made ourselves comfortable on big white sofas. Polly and I on one, a united front, and he, the client, sprawled on another. Polly, immaculate as ever in a black trouser suit, he in white tracksuit.

"The grapevine tells me you're considering other representation," said Polly.

"Well, Poll, you know how it is. This other lot say they can get me more TV exposure."

"Yes, I do know how it is. More than you think. You remember a little conversation we had all those years ago when you first came to us? The one about openness and trust?"

"I've a vague memory but I've nothing to hide. Why do you ask?" he said. He pulled on a chunky cigar.

"My job, our job, is more about what the public don't know about our clients than what they do know. We work very hard to keep it that way."

"What are you on about? I've nothing to hide…I said already." Impatient anger quickly replaced avuncular joviality.

"Fourteen-year-old girls. Eleven-year-old boys. Rent boys. Children. The star-struck teenyboppers. The sick and infirm. You don't care, do you? You abuse your position and you attack the kids."

"Now look here, darling, I don't know where you heard this sordid filth, but say another word and you'll be hearing from my solicitor." Pointing the cigar at Polly, he stood to leave, his face glowing red.

She slid an envelope forward.

"Take a look at these before you leave."

With a trembling hand, he slid half a dozen black and white photographs off the coffee table.

"Like I said, we have to keep some information out of the press. If you leave, which you are perfectly entitled to do, I can't guarantee that will happen."

"You're a bitch."

"Maybe so, plenty have described me as such, but unlike some, I'm certainly not a molester of children."

"What do you want?" He sat again.

"Nothing, but I have had a new contract drawn up. Sign here and here."

He signed it, as she knew he would, and then stamped his cigar into the carpet before storming out of the office.

I was aghast. I had no idea we were covering up such grotesque behaviour. Drugs and married women, yes, but children? Good God Almighty.

It was the most viscous row we'd ever had. We had, in the course of both our professional and private lives, had the occasional spat or dispute over minor things, but hardly ever with raised voices. Now, I raged at her; how could we be mixed up with anything like that? She accused me of being a self-obsessed addict and of spending all our cash on filth. As the argument progressed and our slurs and accusations became more and more personal, it became apparent my feelings of love for her were no longer existent. I only loved the life, the glamour, the drugs, and the money.

In a sudden revelation, it became clear I hadn't earned any of it. With her cunning and brazen attitude, she had built a successful enterprise. I was just the partner. One she didn't need. A deadweight.

"I'm out. We'll divorce, then you can run the company any way you want. I want nothing to do with *it* or *you* ever again."

She replied with a hard slap across my face; violence for the first time. I slumped down on a chair, holding my stinging face. It hurt more deeply when she said, "I'd divorce you in a flash, but we made a vow in front of God. I can't go against the Almighty. This marriage is for life."

"What? You never even go to church!"

"Beside the point. Leave if you want, but you won't get a thing from me, least of all a divorce."

I was stunned. No attempt at appeasement or reconciliation? Just a "no", based on a flimsy excuse. It was 1985, people got divorced all the time.

The corners of her lips twisted in that cruel, signature smirk of hers. I was being treated the way Scud had been all those years before. I was her pet, to be dismissed only when she was ready.

The chair tumbled backwards as I lunged at her. She lashed out, her fingernails drawing blood—I still have a faint scar along my left jaw, under my beard. We rolled on the floor. I was bearing down with my weight, hands around her throat. She slapped at my chest, my face, and my arms. Someone grabbed me by the shoulder, I lashed backwards and heard them stumble and fall. It was enough to bring me back to my senses and I sat back, breathless. Polly was pulling away from underneath me, gasping, clutching at her neck.

Taking in gulps of air between each word she said, "I…will…never…divorce…you."

Her outright cruelty and innate need to control everyone and everything were beyond rational sense. But who was I to talk? I had just tried to kill her.

We stared at each other, waiting for the other to react first. I turned away and stood before pouring myself a drink. That's when I remembered someone grabbing my shoulder. Looking behind me, I saw, lying prone with her head on the marble hearth, Polly's secretary.

"Oh shit, Daisy." I said, barely a whisper.

Polly joined me. We both looked on in horror as an expanding pool of blood spread over the marble and the surrounding carpet. I touched Daisy's neck, the way they do in films. No pulse.

"You stupid man." Her words full of hate and venom.

Instead of pulling together to conjure up a plan or at least get our story straight for the police, she was on the attack. I'd had enough.

"You're good at covering things up, Polly. You deal with it," I said as I pushed past her.

***

Could I have a drink of water, please? There's more to tell, I haven't finished yet. Thank you.

I went to our apartment on Half Moon Street, retrieved my passport, and picked up a thousand pounds in cash before travelling by tube to Gatwick. Early the next morning, I was in Northern Ireland. I had family in the south I'd never met; only vague memories of blurred photographs my mother had displayed on the mantelpiece.

Crossing the border was simpler than I imagined, given the troubles of the time. A truck driver in a cafe agreed to carry me through the checkpoint, for a small fee. My stomach flip-flopped as we approached the armed guards. I was sure I was going to puke; I must have been as white as a sheet by then. My driver assured me not to worry, saying he was always crossing over and that they only looked for bombs, guns, and terrorists. "Sure we're fine, please God," he said. He took me to Dublin, his final destination, where I stayed the night in a B&B overlooking The Liffy.

Lying in the bed that night, I tried to rationalise the sudden turn of events in my life. In my sensible head, I knew I shouldn't have run, but I justified my actions by blaming Polly. More than anything, it was her I was running from. If she had agreed to a divorce, we wouldn't have been brawling and Daisy wouldn't have tried to intervene. It was her fault; *everything* was her fault.

I considered the possibility that I may have been having a breakdown. I couldn't understand why the police hadn't caught up with me. The question had been spinning around and around in my head, keeping me from any meaningful sleep.

Buying the plane ticket had been the most nerve-racking experience. I had expected to be pounced on as soon as I showed my passport or seized as I got off the plane in Belfast. I had to wonder what scheme Polly would employ to explain her dead secretary.

Half a day on a bus to Cork, and then a taxi to the small town of Brandine where my mother had been born. I found, within a day, cousins and extended family that remembered her. Some still wrote to her, and she wrote back, sometimes with news of her son and how proud she was of him. My shame surfaced with tears as I appealed to their better nature and our family connection for help.

I must have looked a fright in unwashed clothes, with a couple of days of beard growth, and tired red eyes sunken into the shadows of my pale face. I couldn't let my mother see me like this, not until I was better. The life I was leading, I told them, was tearing me apart and I dealt with the stress by overindulging in drink and drugs. My wife, I also told them, coped much better, but I needed time away from her too. I threw myself on their mercy and asked that I be the one to tell my mother where I was when I was ready.

These complete strangers accepted me and my deception into their lives with unquestioning friendliness.

An Uncle Pat and Aunt Mary put me up in their small box room. I didn't venture from that room for two days, except to take care of nature's necessities. I slept, and when I wasn't sleeping, I wept. I cried for my stupidity, my anger, and my lies. I wept for Polly, not the woman of today, but the girl I had once loved. She had always been dangerous, it was part of her appeal, but her avaricious collecting of secrets had destroyed the joy she used to have and accentuated the dark, cruel side of her nature. And I wept for Daisy. Poor, blameless, not quite the brightest Daisy, who suffered the misfortune of working late on the night her employers tried to kill each other. Twenty years old and engaged to be married to a football player with Tottenham Hotspur.

Uncle Pat took me on as a kind of apprentice gardener. It felt good to get my hands dirty and do some honest graft. We worked in many gardens, large and small, doing everything from basic garden tidying to a bit of tree surgery. After two months of clean living and hard graft, my face and arms had taken on a natural tan, and the stubble I'd arrived with had grown to bushy proportions. I barely recognised the man in the mirror anymore.

One day, while we were packing up our tools, Uncle Pat asked what I was really running from.

"I can't tell you, Pat. But I can't go back…not to her or the world I once knew."

"Ye should go to the confessional. You know what they say, 'confession is good for the soul'."

I remained silent, horrified that tears were once again brimming. Pat was one of those men who never showed emotion. Everything could be laughed at, but he surprised me.

"Do ye need help, son?"

"What do you mean?"

"Help…ye know…maybe a new whatchya-ma-call-it."

"Identity?"

"The very word, a passport."

"It would help, but they will catch up with me sooner or later."

"The Garda?"

I nodded my reply and wiped my eyes with my t-shirt.

"Leave it to me, son. Sure, it can't be that difficult."

Pat made arrangements through some people who knew other people, who knew "those kinds" of people. The price was arranged and I supplied him with a passport photo. Several weeks later, Pat took me to a pub way up in the hills. An old white building, which may once have been a farmhouse. It would be a drive for anyone to visit on a night out, so I doubt they were ever busy because I didn't see a single house within walking distance. Inside, the fire roared and, as I expected, it was empty of customers. Pat sat at one end of the bar, which was situated in the middle of a long, thin room, and picked up a Gaelic paper before telling me to sit as far away as possible at one of several small tables so he wouldn't be able to overhear.

Two men came in, and the barmaid made herself scarce. They sat opposite me, I wondered if I should offer them a drink.

"Ye the one?" asked the taller of the two. He was the only one who spoke. It seemed the other's sole purpose was to look menacing, although he really wasn't needed; the talker was clearly a man with whom not to tangle.

"The one what?"

"Five hundred pounds, have ye got it?"

"How do I know I can trust—"

"Stop right there, son, before someone is insulted. Do ye want this here passport or don't ye?"

"Yes, of course."

"Five hundred pounds."

We exchanged envelopes, then the leader dropped his bombshell.

"That's only part payment, of course. What ye have in yer package there is a complete identity. A birth certificate, British passport and a National Insurance number, all of them the genuine article. A passport and birth certificate are easy enough to get hold of, but a National Insurance number takes a little more cunning, ye hear me?"

"Now hang on—"

"Yer to deliver something, and if ye don't, we'll find ye and put a bullet in yer thick English head."

"I want nothing to do with it," I tried to protest, but my throat was quickly drying up.

"Fine then. Give back the papers, we keep the money and yer man over there delivers for us instead. And ye still get the bullet. Certain individuals have taken risks to get us to this here point tonight. Now it's time to return the favour."

"What? This is crazy."

"Just who do ye think we are? The Sally Army? Now what's it to be?"

Failing to see any other options, I nodded my acquiescence.

The quiet one remained inside while the leader took me to the car they had pulled up in. He handed me a backpack from the boot. Inside was a small package about the size and shape of hardback book, wrapped in brown paper.

"I want this package delivered to an address in Belfast by ten o'clock tomorrow night. Everything ye need to know is in here," he said, tapping the bag.

"What is it?"

"Now that is a stupid question, son."

"I can't…I didn't expect all this."

"Fine." He pulled a handgun—from where I don't know, it was too dark to see properly—and rested the muzzle against my forehead.

"I'm sorry. I'll do it…I'll do it!" My quivering legs lost all ability to hold me up, and I fell to my knees in a puddle of mud behind a pub I didn't know the name of. With the gun still pointed between my eyes, I had no time to think. He pulled the trigger. I lost all control as the dull sound of metal on metal reverberated through my head. Seconds passed. I was still alive.

"Tis that easy, son. Now deliver the damn package."

I heard the doors of a car click open and slam closed before the same car drove away at a sedate speed, leaving me to be helped to my feet by Uncle Pat.

"Did you know? Do you know what they want me to do?" I asked, panting.

"No. And I don't want know to either."

"Fucking hell, I've been so fucking stupid. What can I do?"

"Ye have to do what they want, Mike. I'm sorry, I really am."

"The police…I'll go to the police."

He shook his head. "It won't change anything. Just make things worse. Yer'll be a police informer, yer'll drop me in it, yer'll reveal whatever it is yer running from and they'll still get ye. Even in prison."

I was leaning against Pat's truck, wiping vomit from my chin with a tissue. I tried to straighten up and face my future like a man, but my legs wouldn't let me. Instead, I tumbled into the passenger seat and cried like a baby. Pat started the car, and we slowly trundled away.

"Can you give me a lift, Pat, to somewhere near the border? A quiet place where I can cross without fear of patrols."

"Sure."

We exchanged few words during the journey. Five hours later, he stopped at the edge of a small town, I forget the name now, and we both stepped out of the car.

"Yer a mile or so from the border here. Tis hilly, boggy, and still dark, but a clear night. Head north, that's away from yer moon tonight. Ye'll be in the UK by the time the sun comes up."

"I won't see you again, Pat. Probably best, don't you think?"

"Aye, son."

He thrust a ten pound note into my hand and hugged me. "Don't be silly," I said, trying to return the money. He quickly turned away, dropped back into the car, and drove away before I could say goodbye.

By daybreak, I was cold, filthy, and terrified. At midday, I stopped at a pub and ordered a scotch, drained it, and made use of the gents. I was surprised they served me. I washed my face and hands as best I could, but my clothes were filthy and I stank to high heaven.

My fears were numerous, and all centred around the package. What would happen if it got wet? Would it detonate? Or would it fail to detonate? What would happen to me if that happened? I was more terrified I'd end up giving it a quick shake and it would explode, taking me with it.

Shit, how did I get into this situation? Was I really contemplating this? A bomb, for Christ's sake. The instructions were to post it through the letterbox of a private house. I knew nothing about the recipient; he might have a family, or worse, children might die. Oh fuck.

I chose to do the only brave thing I ever did in my whole miserable life. I chose to warn Mr Sinclair—whoever he may have been—but I didn't want to write on the package directly for fear of detonating it, so I stuck a yellow note to it instead.

DO NOT OPEN

CALL THE POLICE

A man with a van gave me a lift into the city and dropped me near a large market, which was coming to the end of its trading day. With my remaining money, I bought cheap jeans and a new t-shirt, changed in a public toilet, and threw the ripped, filthy clothes away. I decided to keep my donkey jacket.

I clutched the bag to me in an attempted to protect it. Why was I trying to protect this evil device? My morals felt twisted beyond reason.

I wished for Polly then; she would know what to do. I also wished I'd not been so soft headed, as my dad might have said.

Having been a part of it, a facilitator, I knew the kind of things the rich and famous got up to. With our help, they made money, and with the money they made, they indulged their vices. Why had I been so stupid? Not all vices are equal, a small voice in my head argued.

I gripped the bag tighter as I tried to hang on to my sanity. It would be over soon.

By five in the afternoon, I was there, dog tired and scared witless, my feet sore and blistered. The target house was in a row of mansion-like houses, in what I can only assume was one of the more affluent areas. It was too early and still light; I didn't want to be seen delivering the package. In a nearby park, I rested on a bench and sleep eventually overcame me.

An hour or so later, with my head still on the backpack, I was awoken by two police officers.

"On yer way, son, no dossing down here."

"Sorry."

I stood and started to walk away, rubbing my eyes.

"Don't forget this now." One of them was holding the backpack out to me.

"Yeah, thanks. Sorry."

I walked the streets, my legs like jelly, my stomach churning, my thoughts in a whirl. *Don't do it, just walk away. Throw it in the river. You can't be part of this, Mike.*

Walking by the river, I contemplated chucking it all in, myself included. Why not just open the package? I asked myself. I can't, I'm a coward, I replied.

At just before ten o'clock, I returned to the house, which was now in darkness. Twenty-four hours ago, I had been safe, but now, I had a deadly package in my shaking hands and I was climbing the short flight of steps to the door of a house I had no business being outside of. I took the yellow sticky off and crumpled it into a pocket, my cowardice finally getting the better of me. What would happen to me if they found out I'd warned him?

It took me several attempts to line up the package with the slot. I didn't let it fall on the other side because I was worried it might detonate. The spring-loaded letter box, thankfully, held the package in place.

Then, I ran on stumbling feet as far and as fast as I could, stopping only to retch as my body tried to eliminate the evil I had done. Exhaustion finally took hold, and I collapsed down by the docks into a restless sleep.

Woken by the sun a few hours later, I proceeded to wander through the day, watching news on TVs in shop windows and picking up papers from park benches or bins, all the while avoiding patrols.

Later, I found a shelter for the homeless, which offered soup, a bread roll, and a camp bed for the night. Luxury. My anxiety levels rose as I waited for news of my terrible deed.

The next morning, I walked back to Mr Sinclair's house. All seemed normal; the house still stood, no piles of rubble or debris from a recent blast, and no cordoned off areas or sirens wailing. Perhaps Mr Sinclair was cautious and had called for the police anyway?

I hadn't eaten since the soup and bread of last night's supper, and I had no money to buy anything. Although I knew I would have to start getting back on my feet again, I resigned myself to the fact that I was destined for another night in the homeless shelter.

As I walked in through the front door, I took in its name: Safe Haven. I recognised some of the volunteers from the night before, but this time a visiting priest was moving around the room, sitting and chatting with the lost and forlorn of the town. He came over to my bed.

"Hello, my name's Father Kelly. What's yours?"

I turned my back on him without answering. I didn't know who I was. I hadn't even looked at the ID I'd gone through hell to get.

I stayed in Belfast for three more days, sleeping rough and begging. I needed to be somewhere safe but had no idea where to find it. I also wanted out of Belfast with its tales of destruction, and its war that was more secret than the evidence of patrols, barriers, and checkpoints led you to believe. Leaving early, I headed west. I had barely eaten in a week so lifting my feet was difficult, let alone my thumb to cadge a lift with. A car eventually stopped, a small, rusty Ford Cortina.

"Hello again. I'm going up near Coleraine. Give you a lift?" said Father Kelly.

"Thank you."

We travelled in silence, apart from my rumbling stomach. Rooting around in the door compartment, Father Kelly then handed something to me and said, "It's a bit melted, but you're more than welcome to it." He was holding a Marathon in his left hand.

"Sure?"

"Sure, I'm sure."

"Thanks," I said, snatching it from his kind hands and almost finishing the bar in one mouthful. "Sorry," I mumbled through a mouthful of chocolate and peanut.

"Never mind, that stuff is no good for me anyways. Where ye going?" he asked.

"Anywhere, I don't care."

"Fine, I could do with the company."

But I'd fallen asleep again and wasn't much company for the priest.

When I woke, I was in a single bed and looking at a small crucifix on the wall opposite. Father Kelly was just coming into the room.

"Hello, Thomas, how are you? I couldn't wake you when we got back to my parish, so we let you sleep here. Are you ready to eat?"

I was famished and accepted with a smile and a nod.

"Good. See you downstairs in ten. Your clothes are on the chair there." He pointed across to the chair by the window.

Following the smell, I found the small kitchen. A bowl of stew was steaming, and Father Kelly was pouring tea from a large brown pot. Sliced white bread with a thin layer of butter on it lay piled high on a plate.

"Thank you," I said as I sat opposite the kindest man in the world. I studied him as I ate. He was older than me by at least thirty years, and he was totally grey, even his eyes. We ate in silence after he gave a short thanks to God for the meal. I joined in with the "Amen" and meant it with all my heart. When we'd finished, he leaned back and lit a cigarette.

"I won't pry, but I had to look in your bag to find out your name." He placed my documents next to a mug of tea.

"S'okay."

"How long have you been sleeping rough?"

I thought he'd said he wouldn't pry?

"Couple of days. I had to come north and found myself bereft of funds."

"Well, we could try to help you get home again?"

"NO...um...no, thank you. I must try to get along on my own."

"Well, if you're sure."

"Tell me something, Father. I don't know why I'm asking...you're not going to say anything negative."

"Ask it anyway, I might surprise you."

"Is confession really good for the soul?"

He paused, his silence full of peace. "It depends on the person. Some don't ever want to confess, others want to be seen to confess without seeking redemption, while the person who seeks true forgiveness through confession can be happier in the knowledge that a better life awaits their soul."

"It sounds too simple."

"I have to be somewhere soon, but we can talk about it later if you like?"

"Yes, I'd like that very much."

Father Kelly left me alone for more than an hour, trusting a stranger with his meagre possessions. I contemplated recent events; had the documents for Thomas Williams, my new identity, really been worth all I had gone through to get them? I even reasoned with myself that the package might not have been a bomb, only a package that had to be hand delivered. Surely a bomb could be sent through the post? This item, whatever it was, needed the personal touch. I'd had no option at the time but to follow through; after all, my life was in danger. The Father returned to find me still sitting at his kitchen table.

"Now, what shall we talk about?" he asked.

That was when Father Kelly and Thomas Williams became friends. I helped around the garden and the house. He arranged work for me in the surrounding area, gardening and doing other odd jobs that, if I'm honest, I wasn't very good at. He vouched for me and I moved into a small flat. I started to help during mass, becoming more involved in church activities and the wider community in general. We spent many hours discussing the nature of God and goodness, theology and philosophy, faith and doubt.

It dawned on me that I'd met Father Kelly at this time in my life for a specific reason. My need to serve the community was a growing itch I couldn't ignore, and I felt the pull of the church more with every passing day. This was my calling.

Father Kelly and I went to see the bishop. Only when the bishop was certain of my genuine intention did I enter the seminary, where I spent the next five years studying and praying, leaving with a degree in theology.

I was first a deacon for six months with my old friend, Father Kelly. Once ordained, I was sent to Africa as a curate, where I spent three years in a small town with a whitewashed church and a bell tower. Despite the people's intense love of God, one didn't have to travel far to see the remnants of ancient witchdoctor rituals. I can't criticise these practises; my own faith is rooted in superstition. Didn't the Christians highjack pagan feast days and festivals? I'm enough of realist to accept the truth.

I returned to Ireland to perform the funeral service when my friend and first mentor died, and ended up staying for seven years. Life was better than ever, and with faith and God by my side, I felt courage that I'd never had in my previous life. I requested a placement in England, the land of my birth, and was sent to Birmingham where I had some of the greatest challenges of my ecclesiastic career.

Religious tension in the city was on the rise, myself and fellow spiritual leaders strove hard to bring the communities together out of a basic desire for love, respect, and acceptance. I am of the view that it is our differences that make us all so interesting.

Everywhere I had the pleasure to preach and pray, I encouraged love and acceptance, to be a better human being, not just for the glory of God and a better life beyond this, but more importantly, for the benefit of our friends, neighbours, and brothers here and now in this realm. Bitterness, cruelty, hate, spite, secrets, and lies only lead to unhappiness in our own souls and lives.

I moved here three years ago and now have the custodianship of a small Norman church with lots of character. The town is packed with lords and ladies, artists and posers. A council estate sits on one side of my church, with a private estate sold for development on the other. A melting pot for the lost, the temperamental, the rich, the poor, and seasonal visitors.

I have always done my best for all my congregations, their souls especially, and I'd all but forgotten the person I used to be. My world was turned around by one good man and his belief in the human spirit and God Almighty. I tried to emulate Father Kelly in every action; I wanted to make him proud.

It was while I was in the confessional one Saturday evening, hearing the secrets of my parishioners—the peeping toms, the petty thieves, and the potty mouths—when I heard her voice again. A touch of cut glass, now scratched with a lifetime of smoking. But I recognised it all the same.

"Forgive me, Father, for I have sinned. It has been thirty years since my last confession."

"The Lord forgives all." I tried to remain neutral, but I'm sure my voice cracked. The mesh between confessor and priest limits what is seen each way, but I recognised her silhouette.

"Really? Are you able to forgive me in the Lord's name...considering I'm still your wife?"

"You're not here to confess, Polly. Return in an hour when I'll be finished here. We can talk openly."

"No, we'll talk now, you hypocritical bastard." Her voice raised, no longer reverential as is expected in the confessional.

"Control yourself. For now, these people need me. An hour, Polly."

The confessional door was almost ripped from its frame as she stormed away. For the rest of the hour, I listened patiently as the good people of my congregation unburdened their souls. But I didn't hear much.

An hour later, kneeling before the alter and asking the Lord for strength, I heard her approaching steps in unison with the tap of a cane. She knelt beside me.

"I should apologise. Let's try to be civil," I said.

Then, I looked at her, aged now with fine lines and carrying more weight, which gave her an extra chin. Her eyes still beautiful, but now with heavy dark circles.

"How have you been?" she asked. I thought I heard a sarcastic tone. She continued. "I never expected to see you as part of the cassock brigade...you were always so sceptical."

"I have found happiness. What about you? Happy?" I knew the answer before I asked it.

"No. I always hated you."

"Oh, Polly, we were happy once."

"You left me to deal with Daisy. I did, too. A little pig farm, not far from here actually."

I crossed myself and said a silent prayer for Daisy's soul, and mine.

"I missed you, you selfish bastard. You were my only friend."

"I was the only one you could trust. Everyone else was wary of you."

We were quiet for a minute. She sat back on a pew and I joined her.

"The police?" I asked.

"As far as they're concerned, she went missing and never returned home. Coincidently, it was the same night you disappeared, so the police put two and two together and got two lovers. They didn't try very hard, you were just two people who'd done a runner. Everyone was laughing at me. *'Poor Polly, her husband left her for the bimbo secretary.'*"

"I'm sorry, but—"

"You ran and left me to cover it up."

In the silence that followed, she struck a match and lit a cigarette.

"And then there was Yewtree." The famous investigation of children who claimed to have been molested by famous personalities. "They were rigorous in their investigation. I was lucky not to receive a custodial sentence, but the business was ruined."

"I'm sorry."

"So you should be. I might have changed if you'd stayed around, Mike." That name sounded so foreign to my failing ears. "I might've listened to you."

"I think I remember one or two conversations about that. You'd never have changed Polly. You're a one-woman wonder, doing everything your own way."

More silence. I looked up at Christ on the cross, seeing in detail the chipped and flaked paint around the wound to his chest. My whole world seemed to focus on the detail.

"What are you doing here, Polly? Let's leave the past where it belongs and part as friends."

"Bollocks to the past. Do your parishioners know you're married? Do they know what you did? Do they know who you really are?"

"Of course not."

"You're a fraud, a lying, cowardly fraud." She stood, pointing down at me, her hand shaking as she raged. Spittle landed on my face.

"Polly, please be calm."

"Do you know, when I found where you were, *what* you were, I thought I might try a bit of the old blackmail. See what I could get from you."

"Polly…" I began to plead, for calm if nothing else.

"But then I thought fuck it, just kill the cunt."

I was still seated when she lunged at me, unsheathing a thin stiletto from the cane. I barely managed to grab the wrist of the knife-wielding hand before the blade plunged towards my chest. I was sliding sideways on the polished wooden pew as she continued to bear down on me. A few seconds later, we toppled to the floor. She on top, the thin blade ripping my robes.

We began to roll, each of us trying to get the upper hand. I swear I only wanted to disarm her, but that's when I felt the gush of warm blood over my hands.

I knelt back, the thin blade still embedded in her chest, staring at my hands and then back at her as she went through her death throws. Blood spurted from the fatal wound in her chest and spread over the ancient stone floor; I was soon kneeling in it. So much blood.

I held her head on my knees and tried to comfort her. Blood bubbled from her mouth and her legs started to shudder, the final vestiges of life draining away. Complete stillness soon followed. I'd like to say there was understanding or peace in her eyes at the end, but all I saw was malice.

I took my stole from my pocket and placed it around my neck, bloodying it in the process. I forgave her in the name of God. Who would forgive me?

I don't know how long I knelt there. The silence of the empty, holy place echoed in my head, intruding on my grief. Long moments passed as I looked down at the only woman I'd ever loved. My tears fell like rivers and mingled with her black blood. I kissed her lips and closed her eyes.

Billy Luck
by DC Diamondopolous

Billy Luck's bones rearranged themselves on the bus headed out of Gibsonton for the Tampa train station. He looked out the window, away from his trailer, all rusted, awnin torn, bricks holdin down tarp over a portion of the roof, lookin like other junkyard leftovers from his carnival days.

      The bus passed an old train car that jailed tigers, vines growin through it, a giant planter. Gibsonton was a has-been like him, still some carnies left but most dead, or dyin, or just plain up and left, like his good friend Daisy, the most beautiful woman his eyes ever seen, a midget, but perfect, no matter.

    Now Billy's friends all had bodies from the shoulders up: Judge Judy, and that good-lookin gal on The People's Court. He always took to smart, in-your-face broads—don't take no shit type—like Daisy, who called, askin him to come see her in Miami, cause she was dyin.

    What a foul mouthed little mother she been, tough, had to be, no taller than three feet, perfect proportion, and a great pick-pocket, long as people was sittin down. She been with the Gerling since nineteen fifty, five years after Billy started workin the carnival, a legend, Daisy was.

    He figured since she git religion, and was close to dyin, that she wanted to talk bout that night sixty-five years gone, somethin they never spoke bout, but it was there, danglin, an untouchable. So's Billy wondered if she got that on her mind, bein religious and all.

    The bus turned the corner and he saw the corpse of a high-striker. The black numbers erodin, the bell tarnished and hangin on by a bolt. He chuckled to himself at how the marks showed off for their ladies when they took the hammer and slammed it on the lever—suckers, all of em, not knowin that life in the midway was rigged.

    Billy's memories weathered inside his head like peelin wallpaper. The old days with freaks and geeks and nights where it was so damn excitin, pickin up, settin down, movin on and on until the midway was in sight and stakes hammered, where people in scanty towns ran out to watch, hopin to catch sight of the merry-go-round or the Ferris wheel settin up, maybe glimpse a hoochie-coochie babe runnin between trailers. Billy resented the fake imitation of amusement parks nowadays, though he was glad few had animals. In his day, he'd done seen too much bad done to the beasts, Billy done seen too much cruelty, period.

Drivin along the Hillsborough River, Billy pictured Daisy as she was when he first seen her. What separated her from other midgets wasn't just her womanly child looks but her husky voice, almost like a norm and she could sing, too. That's what saved her when she got caught stealin at Ringlings and had to work peepshows in the basements of tenements on the lower east side. Bein a midget wasn't freak enough she was told by the boss, "What talents do ya got?" The curtain would open and Daisy would sing, struttin her little body on the platform while doin a striptease. Her singin saved her from fuckin God-knows-what, which she wasn't above doin. Daisy'd do whatever to survive. She come across all innocent same as one of them dolls in the window at Woolworth's, but if you looked long enough, you'd see lots a smarts and a cellar-full a hurts.

It was her husband, Jack, who told Billy this, who saw her in the slums and brought her to Gerling's Traveling Carnival of Fun.

Billy's clean flowered shirt stuck to the back of the vinyl seat like loose skin bout to pare off. He used to love the humid muggy days, but now it made him tired, like standin in line for hell. Most of the time he resisted goin down the road of the pity-pot. It reminded him of liquor. It went down real good in the moment but the more you drink the more blurred your vision for any good comin your way. He knew that from his daddy, the meanest son-of-a-bitch to walk the earth.

The bus traveled up the I-75, crossed the river and stopped in Progress Village pickin up several black men who looked as parched and worn as Billy now felt, then the bus sped north, where there was as many as four lanes. Billy sat up. He liked the breeze stealin in through the window, how it reminded him of that time his daddy got a job drivin a bread truck and took Billy along, that was the year before his brother died from havin his innards cut from the saw. They tried to stuff em back in, but Jimmy passed. Only time he ever seen his daddy cry, why, for a moment it ripped him apart, his Daddy's sadness, so like his own.

He blamed Billy, though he was nowheres near the sawmill. Jimmy just plum forgit to put on the safety belt.

Thinkin bout his older brother always brought on the blues, how Billy missed him. The way Jimmy threw himself on top of him and his mama when his daddy felt like beatin em.

The night Jimmy passed, his daddy got wasted and told Billy he'd a wished it was him that died instead. He was drunk, but Billy knowed he was tellin the truth.

At fifteen, he packed a bag and hitched a ride from Montgomery to Birmingham, decided to change his last name from Lock to Luck, cause God knows he needed some and joinin the carnival seemed a good pick. He carried his hurt deep, like Daisy's, guess that was one reason he took to her so.

He peered through the grimy pane as the bus pulled into the station. His hand reached for the back of the seat in front of him, his heart pumpin, an adventure, no matter, and Daisy lay waitin, just for him.

Everyone but Billy stood. The driver left the bus, and Billy watched as he opened the side panel and took out the suitcases.

When the last person left, he ambled down the aisle. The driver waited for him and offered a hand.

"I ain't that old, I can git down myself."

"Don't want you to fall and sue us, young fella."

Billy laughed. His dentures dropped. He pushed them up with his tongue, remindin him that his kisser was as fake as his hip and stepped off the bus.

"I've never seen a suitcase this old," the man said, handin Billy the luggage.

"Had it since the sixties, before you was born, I bet." Billy took the leather handle and felt the moist exchange of sweat.

"You have a good day, sir."

"Goin to Miami, I am. On a way to see a friend."

The man already climbed up the steps of the bus, leavin Billy talkin to himself.

He shuffled toward the train station, with the closeness of the Hillsborough Bay; Billy caught a breeze, rufflin his straggly white hairs under the straw hat. His sense of smell worked just fine as he breathed in the sharp crude from the cargo rigs mixed with the bay.

A woman held the door for him as he headed toward her.

"Thank you, ma'am. Fine day, ain't it?" He pointed his index finger to the brim of his hat and winked. She smiled and hurried on.

Air conditionin stung the sweat on his body. Billy shivered. "My God," he whispered as he gazed around. The place was beautiful with long wooden benches, ferns growin in large pots at the end of each row. The last time he'd been here the place was fallin apart. But now, wrought-iron gates, wall lanterns, the floor so shiny looked like you could take a dip in it, so much light from all the glass windows it seemed the sun had eyes just for the station.

He shuffled cross the depot and out the door to the number 235 train.

Climbin aboard the Amtrak, Billy strained as he stretched for the handrail and tightened his grip round the metal. The steps were damn far apart for a man his age, but he made it. Course it knocked the air clean outta him.

It was stupid to act like he was younger than his years, he couldn't hide the hearin-aid behind his ear, the bum leg with the dummy hip, the missin lower teeth his tongue liked to suck, or the skinny ropes of white hair once blond and thick as a Fuller Brush mop. But he ain't gonna turn into a mark where's he trusted someone else to tell him what was up, no, Billy thought as he put on his glasses and matched his ticket with the seat number. All he wanted right now was to be able to walk on his own and see his friend without fallin down.

He found his seat by the window, four chairs two on either side with a table between em. Not sure if he could lift his suitcase to the luggage rack without seemin lame, besides, someone might steal it, so's Billy set it next to him on the empty chair.

He took off his hat and put it on the table. He'd never get use to people rollin their suitcases. His been a friend for years, made of wood and leather, like him gouged with character, the handle worn from his grasp of luggin it from midway to midway.

A man put his bag on the rack above where Billy sat.

"Want me to put your suitcase up?" he asked.

Billy marked him as a businessman; suit, tie, bag strapped cross his shoulder, late thirties, nothin stand-out bout him cept for the flashy watch, gold and turquoise ring, and a ruby stud in his ear that made him look ridiculous. Somethin bout him seemed familiar.

"Naw, thanks though."

He sat cross from Billy, next to the window. Another guy stood lookin down at him from the aisle.

"You're going to have to move your suitcase. This is my seat," a man said, holdin up his ticket. "I'll get it." The guy grabbed Billy's case, lifted the luggage and shoved it onto the rack.

The fella was closer to Billy's age than the guy with the ruby and this side of obese. When he took his seat, Billy smelled Bengay. He pulled down the armrest so's the guy's fat would stay on his own side.

The train began to rock. The conductor welcomed the people aboard the Amtrak then Billy experienced the thrill of movin. The wheels forward motion caused him to lurch toward the table. He stared out the window as the air-conditionin blasted through the vents, just like old times, like watchin a movie, it was, lots of overgrown shrubs and cast-offs as rusted and troubled as his own trailer. Metal stuff with graffiti sprayed on it. Crap didn't make no sense. Billy wasn't great at spellin, he'd made it no farther than the fifth grade, but what he saw out the window was nothin but young man's rage who don't care whether it make sense or not, just wanna leave somethin of themselves, like a dog pissin on tires.

As the train picked up speed the cool air faded, cheap-trick, made the customer think they git their money's worth, then slight them, like he used to do out on the bally. Can't dupe a con, Billy thought smilin to himself.

He felt like talkin so's he took out a quarter from his shirt pocket and rolled it cross his knobby knuckles. Not with the skill like in the old days but a conversation piece, no matter.

Sure enough, the young man cross from him raised his eyebrows and smiled.

"Where did you learn that?"

"Worked the carnival for over half a century."

"What did you do?"

"A talker, mostly."

The guy frowned. "A barker?"

"People don't know nothin call us that. That's some watch ya got there," Billy said.

"My husband bought it for me."

Billy grinned, it never took him long to git used to the freaks, like Jamie, the half man, half woman, and Angelo, with his twin's arms and legs comin outta his gut, but it would take some time for him to git accustomed to a man callin his partner, a husband. "Oh," Billy said. "Guy's got good taste. You look familiar."

The man unzipped his bag and took out his computer. "I'm a reporter for WSFL. Maybe you've seen me on TV."

"That's where," Billy said. "Boy, do I got stories to tell you." But Billy read people like a canvas banner hangin in front of a sideshow. This guy was through talkin.

He put his coin away. He woulda enjoyed answerin questions. He often played the interview game, pretendin someone like Lesley Stahl asked him questions on 60 Minutes and him talkin bout his life. He imagined microphones, and lights spread all around as he sat center stage for the world to hear his story.

He woulda even enjoyed a conversation with Ben Gay, but he was too busy gawkin at his phone.

People ignorin him did have its advantages, like stealin butter and Hershey bars in the grocery store, snatchin things in the bank, like pens and paper tablets, sometimes right under the nose of the tellers, just to show em. So what if they caught him.

Billy sunk in his seat thinkin that the reporter cross from him woulda jumped through dog-hoops to interview him if he knowed what Billy had done out past the midway on that sweltering August night back in nineteen fifty.

That night, he remembered the marks had all left. But somethin nagged at him, call it sixth sense, or maybe it was that new guy who strutted into town, and took a job with the carnival, sold popcorn, cleaned up the tiger and monkey cages and the johns, jobs he did when he first joined. Billy didn't like him from the git-go.

One day he caught him stickin his cigarette into Tuffi. Tuffi reared on her hind legs, her trunk swingin wild. He knocked the new fella to the ground, told him if he ever caught him doin that again he'd make him real sorry. Well, bout two weeks later, he saw him kickin the freak, Stumpy. Billy done did what he promised. He slugged the guy so hard he doubled and rolled on the ground, moanin. Billy thought that'd be it until the guy git up and come after him swingin and givin him a black eye. Mason was his name, mean, as cruel as Billy's daddy.

That night, Billy went from tent to tent lookin inside, makin sure no one was there. He recalled checkin under the stage where the kids used to hide so's they could look up the costumes of the hoochie-coochie girls and how the sawdust would have to be scattered real nice like in the mornin, he could smell it now, how it always reminded him of his brother.

The trailers had their lights on. He heard laughter, people talking; ice cubes clinkin into glasses, fiddle music comin out of a radio, like any other, cept it was hotter than most, sultry, the kinda night Billy wished he had a woman to keep him company.

He was down at the end of the midway, near the draped cage where the monkeys was cooped. The sun been gone for a couple of hours, and it was like openin night for the stars, millions of em. He recalled takin in the wonder of it, magic, real magic, where the night was brushed by the stroke of a master.

Billy began to hike. In those days, he had so much sex surgin through his twenty-year-old body, some nights he just had to walk it off. Till the day he died he'd remember the moon, wide and plump, near full, the crickets loud as he headed north toward an empty field and beyond that the woods, tree branches rustlin, spiky against a dark blue sky.

Billy breathed in the air, thick with the long leaf pine. He was thinkin bout his ma, feelin blue bout leavin her behind with the devil. Billy kept walkin. His shirt drenched in sweat. He wished he had a smoke, but he kept goin, crossin the brink of the woods.

He was gonna jack-off when somethin sounded. He stopped. An animal? Yeah. A moan cut off. No. Not an animal. Somethin muffled. A cry. Human.

Billy led with his toes feelin for twigs and dried leaves, like huntin with his daddy. He moved toward the moan. The hairs on his body sprung up. From the light of the moon, he saw somethin white swipe back and forth cross the ground. The hunched form of a man. The cries. Billy crept forward. Listenin. Strainin his eyes so's to make sure.

Mason held Daisy's face to the dirt, rapin her from behind. Her tiny fists battered the ground. Her little body struggled under his.

He sneaked up on Mason as he pumped away, groanin like a pig, loud enough so's to make it easy for Billy to come up behind him and wrap his strong young fingers round his neck and squeeze. Mason grabbed at his hands. Billy felt his nails gouge his skin. Blood spewed wet and sticky, but Billy put all six-foot, two-hundred pounds into stranglin him.

Sweat ran down his chin and fell on Mason's head, Billy felt it roll off the backs of his fingers, but so tight was his hold it never got the chance to threaten his grip. With the wrong this man done to Daisy, Billy's hands made sure Mason never do it again. He held on, even when he felt life surrender. Then, Billy rolled him on his side with Mason's little pecker exposed. "Let me!" He remembered Daisy demandin. Pullin down her dress she done give him a kick to the nuts and then one to the face and spat on him. She looked up at Billy, hair all tangled, nose bleedin and said, "You ever say a word about this, I'll kill you myself." From that day on, as long as they traveled together, no one would hurt her.

Billy stared out the window, passin the North bound Silver Star, long fences of hedges, warehouses. He nodded. The conductor garbled somethin bout Winter Haven. The forward movement, the click-clackin over the rails, relivin that night with Daisy and him bein eighty-five years old—Billy slipped into darkness.

***

He stood with his suitcase gazin at the green home with yellow shutters, and window boxes crammed with geraniums. Its wide porch with four pillars featured a swing where as many as three people could dangle their old swollen legs. House looked to be well over a hundred years old.

Daisy and Jack invested well. Freaks always made more money than norms, at least till the sixties before it become incorrect, but midgets and dwarfs worked on, cause they wasn't too scary lookin.

The home with a rail leadin up to the veranda reminded him of all the times he passed by in trucks and trains thankful he never had to settle down in one place, made life hard for the wives, cept for Alice, who divorced him cause he was still married to Betty. And kids? Well, he ain't sure how many he done fathered. None never showed up on his doorstep, course he never had a doorstep, till '05, the year they made him retire.

He trudged up the walkway. It'd be three years since he last seen his girl. He come down for Jack's funeral and what a spectacle it turned into, musta been more ex-carnies and circus folk there than in Gibtown; fire-eaters, sword swallowers, even a Wallenda showed up, tights an all. But Jack was no ordinary midget. He was a magician, an entertainer, a munchkin in the Wizard of Oz, so charmin he could con a con and how he loved shootin craps. Billy chuckled, just thinkin bout his friend Jack.

Sure enough, Billy's pants sagged in the butt and his shirt forced its way out of his belt. If only he could turn back into that tall blond stud with light blue eyes that drove women loco. Ah shit, least he was alive and not in some sick home like Daisy. He held onto the railin and shuffled up the porch steps.

Billy tucked in his shirttails, he unstuck his hat from his sweaty head and steered a comb over his damp scanty hairs.

He rang the bell.

A black woman opened the door dressed in white pants and a lime-green jacket. "Why, you must be Mr. Luck."

"That's me, Billy."

"I'm Geneva."

"How's Daisy?"

"Well, Miss Daisy is having a rough day, but seeing you will lift her spirits."

Billy wondered. She was a tightfisted little mother, always lecturin him on savin his dough. Comin down for her funeral woulda been enough money spent. But callin him before and spendin more bucks to come down after she died? Musta had somethin to do with that night, and gitten religion an all.

"Leave your suitcase and hat here in the lobby. Ruben will take it up."

Billy stepped into a foyer with a tall potted palm tree next to a narrow table. There was a stairway in front of him and on either side the ground floor fanned out to where he couldn't see no more, just the fronds of palm trees wavin from the air-conditionin. The place seem all spick-and-span.

"We have your room ready for you. It's on the third floor."

"Hope I don't have to walk up no steps."

"Lord have mercy! You wouldn't find me walking up three flights of stairs. No, Mr. Luck, we had an elevator put in years ago."

"I'd like to see Daisy, right soon. An call me, Billy."

"Sure, Mr. Billy."

He smiled at Geneva callin him Mr. Billy.

"We're going to have dinner in couple of hours. Would you like to join us in the dining room?"

"That sounds right nice, ma'am."

"Let's go see Miss Daisy."

Billy followed Geneva past the stairway. The house seemed bigger on the inside.

He passed a room where people watched TV with a piano off to the side, and several white-haired ladies sat on a couch. Three old geezers played cards at a table, lookin like waxworks they did, till one of em eyed Billy—the scrape of emptiness passin between em.

"How sick is she?" Billy asked.

"She's had hospice this morning. She ate some and that's a good sign."

"How long she gonna live?"

"Months, maybe weeks."

"Can ya fix her with chemo?"

"Mr. Billy," Geneva said, pausing at the doorway, "Miss Daisy refuses to have any more chemo."

"She got tubes and needles in her?"

"No. We're keeping her as comfortable as we can. She's a spirited soul."

"She always been stubborn. Her sickness got anythin to do with her bein little?"

"Not that I know of. But she's eighty, that's a long life."

"Don't seem long enough even when you's ancient like me," Billy mumbled.

He followed Geneva though a courtyard with hangin ferns the size of bushes and flower beds, all kinds, roses, pansies, other plants and colors he didn't know the names of, all of em shootin toward the sky.

A fountain splashed down into a small pool. Billy wiped his upper lip with his handkerchief. "My that water looks invitin," he said.

"We have a pool. Guest are allowed to swim. If you'd like."

"Oh I don't look so good in trunks." Billy chuckled. "Used to," he added.

"Well, if you change your mind we have bathing suits for our guests."

"Don't think so," he said.

Billy tried to keep up so's not to look feeble.

Geneva stopped at a door, knocked and inched it open. "Miss Daisy, Mr. Luck is here." Geneva pushed the door open for Billy to enter.

A sweet sickly smell like hamburger goin bad greeted him as he took a step inside. He'd been so eager to see her but sometimes emotions made him feel lost, runnin blind into nowhere.

Through the cracked door he saw a child's dresser with pictures on it, a kid's table and a small chair.

"You okay, Mr. Billy?"

"Oh, I git all sorts of tummy problems."

He went into the room. There on a child's bed he saw his old friend, tiny, scrunched and shriveled, her white-blonde hair thin and dull. She looked at him.

Not movin no further, he stood in the middle of the room wonderin what to say, what to do, how to bring cheer to his friend who was dyin.

He turned to Geneva. "I wanna be alone with her."

Geneva nodded and closed the door.

Billy swallowed containin his sorrow. He felt that sudden grab that never left him alone when in Daisy's presence, it wedded him to her like no other woman ever done. But he never seen her lookin so bad. She always wore make-up, fixed her hair, a real looker, presentin herself like a lady.

"You look swell, Daisy." Course bullshit was like breathin for Billy.

"Liar," she rasped.

"Ah, you gonna be okay. Bet you just layin there sick-like cause you want me to feel sorry for ya." His jokin fell flat. "Everyone treatin you good? Geneva looks to be a right nice colored gal."

"African American," Daisy said.

"I forgit. Use black most of the time. Miss talkin on the phone but git your letters. You git my postcards?"

She nodded toward the dresser.

"I keep yours too," he said glancin round the room that was good size even for a norm.

The window with open curtains let in light, and she had a small patio with a little chair and table right outside her room.

Everythin was make-do for her. The bathroom door was half closed and he wondered if that too was re-done.

"There's something," the effort to talk took her breath.

"Oh, I know you git religion and all," Billy said, raisin his palms up. "You gonna preach, well I ain't interested."

Daisy scowled.

"Well, can't be just a good-bye. You too practical for that. So's if you lookin for me to ask forgiveness for what I done to Mason or somethin, I ain't gonna do it."

Daisy rolled her eyes. "Stupid, old goat."

Billy turned his right ear toward her. "Whatchu say?"

She shook her head. He'd seen that same scorn in her eyes when she thought he or Jack said somethin dumb.

"I heard ya."

He felt his cheeks burn. He done read her wrong, bet she never give that night another thought. Daisy moved on, while it tailed him the rest of his life. Billy blew troubled air through his mouth. He was angry at himself, lettin Daisy know that night lived with him right up to now.

"Took a portion of my social security check to come down to see ya, so's whatchu want?"

She struggled to sit up. Billy come over to help but she shooshed him away.

"Open the top dresser drawer," she said in a weak voice. "There's an envelope—for you, under the garments."

"You want me to poke around in your girlie things?"

"Go on."

Billy shuffled over to the dresser and crouched down first on one knee then the other. He saw pictures of Jack as a young man, another of Daisy lookin gorgeous in a black dress. He picked up one of the three of them together taken back in the seventies. "Look at us then," he said, turnin to Daisy. "That was taken the day Abner's magic trick backfired and the dove done flown out of his fly." Haha, haha. Billy laughed hard bringin his butt down on the heels of his tennis shoes. He glanced over at Daisy, who smiled back at him. "We seen some funny things in our time, huh, girl?"

She nodded. "The drawer," she said in breathy voice.

Billy jiggled it open. He saw her nighties, the sheer see-through fabric. Didn't seem right him goin through her personals, he never so much as touched Daisy, she bein special and all. He put his hand under her clothes feelin the feminine softness till he reached the envelope. He pulled it out and shut the drawer.

Billy labored as he pushed off from the dresser to git to his feet. Once standin, he spread his legs apart to balance himself, he took his glasses from his pocket, put them on and opened the envelope. He found a paper. It looked all serious with a picture of a funeral home and a payment made for $8,500. He never liked showin how ignorant he was, and that defect git him into trouble sometimes, so's he picked up symbols to help him along. He studied the words and pictures he knew, three plots, one taken. He looked at Daisy. She done wanted him buried with her and Jack. It touched him, she wantin him near her.

"I coulda used the money it took to buy this."

"You would have wasted it on whores."

"Hell, nowadays thinkin bout a roof that don't leak turns me on more than a long legged hooker."

Billy took off his glasses. "So's that why you called for me to come?"

"I want you buried with Jack and me."

"That's mighty nice, girl," he said. "Just thought the county would come take my ole body and cremate me or somethin. Didn't give it no thought." He stuck the paper in his back pocket. "Never did git use to livin in one place even after ten years. Guess when we die, we don't have much choice. Glad I'll be with friends, least my ole bones an all."

He went to the chair by her bed and sat down. "I hate bein old. Live in my memories I do, cause that's where I feel safe." He stared down at his hands, hands that once could do anythin. He kept his eyes lowered, feelin blue, sad for the way life turned on Daisy. "Least you git religion," he said, lookin up.

Her eyes roamed his face.

"Daisy? You okay?"

"I always believed," she whispered. "I just never talked about it."

"Well, you full of surprises. I never knowed that. Never heard you say peep bout God till you git sick." Billy chuckled. "You didn't live like no Christian, stealin and all."

"God forgave me."

Billy figured if God was in the business of judgin he wasn't worth glorifyin.

"The bathroom. Cabinet." Daisy sighed. "There's a brown bottle. Bring it to me."

"What is it?" he asked.

"Medicine."

"Want me to git Geneva?"

"No."

"What kinda medicine?"

"Morphine."

"Geneva give you the right dose."

"Not the dose I want."

He crossed his arms and tilted his head back squintin at her. "Whatchu askin me is a big deal."

"If I could get it I would." She winced.

He hobbled to the slidin door where he looked out on the lawn with the plastic pink flamingoes and alligator steppin stones. He gazed past the hedges, where he could see through the leaves to the pool beyond.

He looked back at her. "I ain't takin your life."

"I'm not asking you to." She slumped further into the pillows.

"What your maker think bout this?"

"God doesn't want me to suffer."

"We don't know nothin till we die," Billy said.

She stared at the bathroom, her lower lip juttin, gave him the silent treatment, she did.

He looked out the window thinkin bout what Daisy wanted. He saw dashes of white and printed bathing suits, people goin for a swim. He raised his hand to the curtain and pulled it all the way back as if some kinda wisdom was out there waitin, just for him.

Billy scratched his arm. He raked his neck. His whole body crawled with sadness. "Oh girl, I know you feelin bad." He shuffled to the side of the bed. He bent so close to Daisy he smelled the rot comin off her. "You been my family. My little sister." Billy sniffed. "Think I'm gitten a cold from all the air condition."

"It's a brown bottle," she said. "Bring it."

"Geneva gonna know I git it for you."

"She won't. It's time, Billy." Her voice sounded tinny, like comin through a pipe, it did.

Through the years he denied her nothin, the only woman who could make him walk through fire and feel privileged to do it.

He felt Daisy watchin as he crossed to the bathroom. He went inside. It was a place for norms, even the john. Billy opened the cabinet door and saw several brown bottles, two, with paper round the neck. He took the open one and went back to Daisy.

"You done planned this all along, you little con." But Billy couldn't be mad, just mystified at the way he was fated to this woman.

"Give me the bottle," she whispered. "And hand me my juice."

Billy saw the glass on her nightstand and give it to her.

She poured the medicine. She swished the morphine round and drank. "Put it back."

Billy set the glass on the stand, returned to the bathroom and did as Daisy said. He shut the cabinet door and glimpsed his reflection, turnin away so's not to remember the moment. Grabbin the doorknob to steady himself, he took out his handkerchief and wiped his face. He limped back to the chair. He moved it as close to the bed with him still able to sit.

"Thank you, Billy."

Seemed his whole life got stuck in his throat. He cleared it. Coughed. "Ah girl," he said. "I didn't do me no favor. Who do I got now?" He reached for her tiny hand. Her frail fingers slid through his. Like a bird, she was, flying over the carnival with the merry-go-round music blarin, the Ferris wheel turnin, the people all happy cause they feelin free, in one hand they eatin cotton candy, the other holdin the hand of a sweetheart.

He let go of Daisy.

Billy done feel like his life folded, where his heart was ground into sawdust and just blowed away leavin him alone on the midway.

Family Business
by Lesley Price

My instincts tell me to run.

***

Gregor was ten when he saw a dead body for the first time.

His mother had protested. "He's far too young for you to take out on a job."

"Nonsense," Gregor's father had replied. "We don't want him going soft. And Docherty thinks you coddle him too much. The best soldiers are trained young, he says."

And that had been that.

Afterwards, they went to the big house. Gregor watched from the doorway as the two men shook hands and Mr. Docherty slapped his father on the back. He seemed pleased.

"Is that your lad, then? He's grown a bit since I last set eyes on him." Mr. Docherty looked past his father at Gregor. "Well, come on, boy. Come and say hello."

Gregor looked at his father for approval. It came in the form of a nod. He stepped forward. It had been an unusual day and Gregor was feeling nervous and a little unsure of what might be in store.

"Come on, I said." Mr. Docherty waved his hand at him, beckoning him forward. "Don't take all day about it."

"Yes, sir." Gregor stopped in front of him. He hoped Mr. Docherty wouldn't notice the slight tremble in his knees.

"You helped your father out today, I hear. Well done. You'll be working for me in no time, I'm sure."

The thought filled Gregor with dread. He looked at his father, who nodded again. Gregor swallowed hard, then nodded too.

"Here's something to be getting on with." Mr. Docherty held out a fifty pound note.

Gregor's eyes widened. Fifty quid? Just for watching his dad shoot a kneeling man in the back of the head? He reached for the note. It felt real. "Thank you, Mr. Docherty." Maybe his dad had a point after all.

***

I should leave. I still can.

***

Mr. Docherty gave Gregor his first proper job when he was fourteen. He was to sit in the van and watch the front of the building. That was all. Just watch. That should be easy enough. And Mr. Docherty would pay him for his time and single-minded attention.

"What do I do if I see someone?"

"That'll depend on who you see. If it's your Dad and Jimmy coming out, you just make room for them and your Dad will take it from there."

"What if it's someone else?"

"Well, if it's a woman walking her dog, you do nothing. Unless you're wanting a dog, of course." Mr. Docherty chuckled at his little joke.

"And what if it's the police?"

"Ah. That's why we need you, Gregor. It's the police we're worried about because they might not like what your Dad and Jimmy have to do in that building. If you see the police, then I want you to use this mobile phone to call your Dad. The number's in there already. You don't even wait until he answers, mind, you just need to ring it a few times." He handed the small and functional Nokia to Gregor. "Have you used one of these before?"

"No, Mr. Docherty."

"Your Dad will show you how it works. It's not complicated. Is it all clear for you now?"

"Yes, Mr. Docherty." Gregor's Dad had instructed him to be suitably humble and grateful. "Thank you for the job, sir. I won't let you down."

He hoped that would please. The prospect of some money was certainly pleasing to him.

***

The gun feels heavy in my hand. The wait seems interminable.

***

"Come on, Gregor. You can do better than that. Keep the target in your sights. Hold your aim steady. There, that's better. And again. Watch out for that kickback. Again. Don't shut your eyes. Steady now. Again."

Gregor's arm was aching by the time he finished his sixteenth-birthday shooting lesson with his father. He knew he would get better, but it was going to take a lot more practice than that.

The gun had been a birthday gift from Mr. Docherty earlier that day. But the euphoria Gregor felt was not because of that. Fifteen-year-old Caitlin Docherty was simply the sweetest thing Gregor had ever seen and he couldn't get her out of his mind. He had seen her peeking in through the half-open door of the living room and wandered into the hall, hoping for a better look.

"Are you one of my Dad's thugs, then?" she asked. But her eyes twinkled at him and the words didn't sound so terrible, the way she said them.

"I'm no thug." He wanted to keep it light. "But I could be anything else you want, if you ask nicely."

She giggled. "You're kind of cute, actually." She gave him a peck on the cheek, standing on the tip of her toes and holding on to his shoulder for balance. "Happy birthday, Gregor," she whispered before turning to run lightly up the stairs. She stopped at the top and gave him a wave. "See ya."

Then she was gone. How did she even know his name? He stood mesmerised for a few minutes before his Dad called him to order and they left for the practice range together.

***

I shift my position slightly to let the blood flow back into my legs and check my phone. It's Jenny's bedtime already and I'm not there to tuck her in.

***

Mr. Docherty nursed his whisky between his hands. A worried frown creased his forehead as he shook his head. "I tell you, Kenny, I don't like it. But what else are we to do? The beating they gave Jimmy was pure provocation. We can't ignore it. You know that."

"I know, Frank. I know. But I don't like it either." Gregor's father looked around at the others and lowered his voice. "It's a young crowd we've got here. Jimmy's boy and mine plus those two new recruits. They're barely trained, let alone experienced. What if this all goes south?"

"How many are you expecting to be in the house?"

"If O'Hare has his whole team in there with him, maybe seven or eight. Could be less if some of them are out on the town. We could wait until our own lads are back from picking up the merchandise."

"That's days away. Jimmy's my oldest friend and he's lying in a hospital bed hooked up to a machine. I'm not waiting."

"OK. You're the boss. Right, lads. Gather round while we go through the plan." Gregor's father stood up and motioned the group to come forward. They stood around the room, arms folded, faces serious, while he explained their tactics.

Soon they were on their way in one of the vans. Gregor's father rode along with the boss in his sleek, black car.

They had only just taken up their positions, waiting for the go, when the firing started from the house. Heavy firing. Bullets flying everywhere and nowhere to hide. Gregor started shooting back. They all did. There was shouting and panic and fear.

"Dad!" Gregor screamed when he saw him go down. "My Dad's been hit!" He was already running, kneeling on the ground, pulling him into his arms, rocking him. "No, Dad, come on, please don't be hurt!"

He heard Mr. Docherty shout to the others.

"Pull back! Kenny's down. Pull back everyone. Let's get him into the van. Come on, Gregor. We have to get him out of here. Boys, help me lift him. That's it, gently does it. Here, Gregor, hold this scarf over the bleeding. Press down on the wound. Come on, let's go. I'll follow in the car."

"We have to get to the hospital," Gregor shouted to their driver as the blood seeped through his fingers onto the floor of the van. "As fast as you can."

"No can do. No hospitals. It's a gunshot wound. Mr. Docherty will get the doc to his house and no questions asked."

"But what if we're too late," Gregor sobbed, "we have to save him. What about my Mum? What about me? What'll we do?"

"Rules are rules, Gregor. Mr. Docherty will take care of everything."

Gregor held his mother's hand at the funeral, and Caitlin held his.

"Enough crying now, Gregor. Your father wouldn't want that. Stand up straight. Be a man. Make him proud." Mr. Docherty's tone was kinder than his words.

As he shook the man's hand and thanked him for the wake, Gregor wondered how things might have turned out if they hadn't followed his rules.

***

Headlights flood the room for a split second as a car turns into the driveway. My whole body tenses. The car reverses out and drives away in the opposite direction. I exhale slowly. I'm relieved, in a way, but it only makes the wait longer.

***

"*Loyalty. That's the secret. Your father was a true friend. I trusted him with my life.*"

"*He trusted you with his too, Mr. Docherty.*" *Gregor didn't mean it sarcastically. He couldn't help how the words sounded. But Mr. Docherty had downed a couple of drams too many and they rolled over him unheeded.*

"*Call me Frank, boy. You're too old for that Mr. Docherty stuff.*" *He unlocked a drawer in his desk and rummaged around in it.* "*I told your father I'd take care of you and so I will. Here, take this.*"

Gregor protested a little as the wad of bills was shoved into his hand. "*But Mr Docherty, I mean Frank, what's this for?*"

"*It's a pay rise. I want you to partner with Jimmy from now on. Just as your Dad did before.*"

"*But this is more than I make in a year. Why so much?*"

"*Come on, son. Don't think I haven't seen the way you look at her. And heard the way she talks about you. I'm not saying you would have been my first choice – and don't take that the wrong way, Gregor – just that I had other hopes for her at one time. But I'm not one to stand in the path of true love.*" *Frank stood up, pushing his chair back roughly.* "*It is true love, now, isn't it? You're not playing hard and fast with my wee darling, are you? I wouldn't be happy about that. Not one bit.*"

"*Of course I love her,*" *Gregor replied indignantly.* "*I love Caitlin and I want to marry her. I would do anything to make her happy.*"

The wedding was celebrated in style. Mr. Docherty gave them his blessing, a new car and their very own house.

***

Another car slows as it nears the house. It turns in and this time the headlights keep on coming down the drive.

***

"*Don't call my Dad just yet, Gregor. Let's have a moment together first, just the three of us,*" *Caitlin said, as she gazed adoringly down at the newborn baby in her arms.* "*She's so beautiful, isn't she?*" *She looked up at Gregor with a tired smile.*

"*You both are. You were so brave, my darling.*" *Gregor kissed his wife tenderly on the top of her head. He felt a glow of pride and protection. "I won't call your Dad for a bit, then."* He squeezed onto the hospital bed beside Caitlin and wrapped both arms around his family. *"I can't believe how lucky I am."*

***

It's now, or never. I'm not sure I can go through with it, but I can't bear the alternative.

***

"That was my Dad on the phone, wasn't it? Is he sending you out on a job again? Why do you have to go?"

"You know why, Caitlin. It's what I do. And it's your Dad who calls the shots. What do you want me to do? Say thank you for your daughter, the house and everything but go to hell now?"

"I didn't mean that. But I wish there were another way."

"There isn't. It's not the kind of job I can resign from. And we can't just up and leave. Your Dad would never allow that."

"I know. Jenny's crying. I have to go to her. Be careful, won't you?"

The sadness in Caitlin's eyes and voice cut through to Gregor's core.

***

The engine cuts out, the lights too.

***

"Congratulations, my boy!" Mr. Docherty thumped Gregor on the back. *"Another on the way! What excellent news! Just imagine if it's a boy this time. Someone to take over from me, when the time is right. We'll start his training early, the way we did with you. Did you hear that, Jimmy? I'm going to be a grandfather again."* He held up his glass in a toast. *"Here's to you and Caitlin and my dynasty."* Then he knocked the whisky back in one.

***

Familiar footsteps make their way to the front door. The key turns in the lock. I know I am risking it all, even her love for me.

***

"Everything seems fine from the scan. I know the sex of the baby." The doctor looked up questioningly. *"Would you like me to tell you? It's not an absolute certainty, of course, but I feel reasonably confident."*

Gregor held tightly to Caitlin's hand. They had discussed this and decided they wanted to know. He nodded. *"Yes, please tell us."*

"It's a boy." The doctor beamed at them. *"A wee brother for your Jenny."*

Gregor's heart sank.

* * *

Anything at all, I remind myself. I am capable of doing anything for Caitlin, for our Jenny. And for our unborn son. Anything to keep him out of the family business, to escape his inevitable inheritance. No matter what the consequences.

I stand up slowly from behind the sofa and raise my arm. The gun has become so familiar from use, it is merely an extension of myself. They trained me well. My aim is steady.

"Mr. Docherty." I speak very softly in the darkened room.

"Gregor? What are you doing here?" He turns to look at me and his expression changes from pleasant surprise to fear. "Gregor! What the hell?"

"I'm sorry. It's the only way." I pull the trigger, watch him fall and know that we are free.

The Night Life
by Patric Mauzy

I

The vagabond scurried across the upper-crust of the land like an urchin scouring the streets for a lost tuppence, darting in and out of unlit doorways and overhangs, watching this living network that was the city of Denver from the shadows he called home. He paid no mind to the judgmental eyes of the city's inhabitants, or the malicious snickers that enveloped his every footstep; he had grown used to it all, as he supposed a roach might grow used to the crushing blows of boots on its back. There was only one thing he cared about anymore, and that was survival. Simple as that.

The rusted cans of residents sat lined up along the curb, and he crept up to the first of them and stuck his face down into the wealth of rubbish. A putrid odor lingered out of the can. There was nothing good in it that he could see, and he quickly made his way down the row. He found the leftover scrap of an apple and dusted it off with his dirtied sleeve until he thought it looked good enough to eat, and then bit down to the core and chewed on the rough stem a while before spitting it out. He enjoyed the seeds most of all, the crush of them between his worn teeth, and so he spit them out and stuck them in his pocket for later.

A crowd was gathering around the Paramount Theatre waiting for the nightly vaudeville to start, and he came up to the side of the building and squatted down on the curb, holding up his gloved hand and giving the public a demonstration of his friendliest face. Some looked down at him in disgust, while others gave him pitying looks; most paid him no attention at all.

He found a discarded coffee cup on the sidewalk and used it to keep his change in, what little they threw at him.

"Enjoy the show!" he said cheerfully as they milled into the theatre, leaving him behind out in the cold air of the night.

When the last of them had disappeared into the theatre the ushers came out and around the building to where the vagabond sat. They lit up cigarettes and spoke of things the vagabond no longer cared to debate, and for a time none of them seemed to notice him sitting there. And then finally one of them pointed his way, and the others looked to where the first was pointing.

"Get out of here you bum!" the usher who had pointed said, flicking the butt of his cigarette at the vagabond. It missed him and landed in the street at his feet.

The vagabond picked the butt up off the ground and stuck it in his mouth. He sucked on it and coughed. There was no tobacco left in the wrapper.

"Damn fool's a loon," another of the ushers said. "Picked the damned thing up and stuck it right in his mouth, he did!"

"Shove off you bum," the third usher said. "Don't make us force you out of here."

The three of them looked like they would very much enjoy forcing him out of there.

The vagabond sat the exhausted butt of the cigarette down on the ground, and then rose with his cup of change and disappeared, leaving the three ushers cackling behind him. But he didn't care if he was the butt of their joke. Picking when to flee or fight was all part of surviving.

II

There was a small veranda set up behind the theatre, and a slim elder with long fingers sat in one of the wrought-iron chairs plucking sweet notes on the neck of his guitar. He noticed the vagabond standing at the edge of the porch watching, and nodded toward one of the vacant chairs. "No point in standing there when you can be sitting down brother."

"Thank you," the vagabond said. He came over and sat down.

The elder held up a boney hand. "No thanks needed. Far as I can tell its free seating back here."

"For now," the vagabond said. "You play good. Are you playing tonight? In there I mean." He pointed toward the theatre.

"S'pose I will be," the elder said. "In time."

He started playing again and as the vagabond watched a smile spread across the elder's face, and he felt his own lips curling into a grin. The elder was fun to watch, the way his fingers danced across the fretboard of the guitar and seemed to find each note in time for the melody to continue. After a while, he started to sing:

Oh, lord I fell in the river
Afraid I got the shivers
Cause I ain't nothin but a bag o' bones
But that don't mean I can't still sink like a sack of stones

When he was finished, the elder sat the guitar down in its case and then pulled out a pack of cigarettes. He offered one to the vagabond. "You smoke brother?"

"Yes," the vagabond said, taking the cigarette out of the elder's hand. "Thank you much."

"You play anything?" The elder asked.

"I used to," the vagabond said without explanation, and the elder nodded.

They sat together in silence, taking drags off their cigarettes, and when the elder was down to the butt he flicked it off into the shrubbery, and then buckled his case up and rose from his chair. He bade the vagabond farewell, and then opened the back door to the theatre and disappeared inside. The vagabond sat there long enough to finish his cigarette, and then he rose from his chair and made for the door. Much to his surprise, it was unlocked. He went inside.

III

Behind the stage and velvet curtains there exists an infinite span of darkness where aspiring artists and veteran performers gather in silence to watch and admire one another, and study each other's acts in the hopes of bettering their own. It was here that the vagabond found himself, and he stumbled around blindly for a while before he finally found the door to lead him back out into the main room of the auditorium. The front rows were mostly filled, and he hurried to the back aisle beneath the balcony and took a seat. No one seemed to pay him any mind. It was too dark for any of the ushers to have noticed him. He watched with anticipation as the next act prepared to come out.

The curtains drew back and a beautiful woman in a dark dress draped over her shoulders and down behind her back came out to the center of the stage. She wore a silver brooch in her hair that shimmered in the stage light. The crowd applauded her politely, and she took a bow. When the room had returned to silence, she opened her voice and a lovely vibrato filled the auditorium.

The vagabond watched, hypnotized both by her radiance and her voice, as she poured her heart out onto the stage, and when she was finished with her song nearly the whole audience rose to applaud her. She bowed once more, and then left the stage as the curtains folded back together.

A hushed excitement fell over the audience as they nattered over the woman with the rich voice, and wondered what sort of act might come out next.

When the curtain finally pulled back and the elder walked out onto the stage with his guitar slung up over his shoulder several men in the audience booed him for the color of his skin, but he paid them no mind and began to play his guitar, and pretty soon the whole room was lulled into silence. He was as exciting to watch in this moment as he had been on the veranda, and maybe even more so. The look of delight that washed over his face while he played was strong enough to light up the room. If there really was a secret chord, he found it in his song. When he finished the audience roared with applause. The elder took his bow, and then walked off the stage.

After the elder came a pair of comedians that had the bulk of the audience roaring with laughter. The vagabond watched them and happily laughed along with their skit, but he didn't think they were as good as the elder or the woman had been; he didn't long for them to return when they had made their leave. Truth be told their jokes were too vulgar for his liking.

The final act of the night was an amateur magician. He wasn't very good at what he was trying to do, and the vagabond got up to leave before he had finished his act.

Back outside the vagabond returned to the curb along the building and waited for the crowd to emerge from the depths of the theatre. Outside with his coffee cup he was the star that they paid to see, and he wouldn't have it any other way.

IV

A fine drizzle came down from wispy grey clouds, and the vagabond watched through the glass front of the café as the raindrops raced down to the windowsill. He sipped at the cup of coffee tucked in between his boney hands, thankful for the warmth it produced.

"You need a refill, darling?" the waitress asked, coming over with a steaming pot in her hand.

The vagabond held out the cup and watched her top it off and thanked her.

"Are you sure you don't want anything to eat?" the waitress asked. "You look like you could sure use it."

"No," the vagabond said shaking his head. "I'm fine, thanks. The coffee is good. Better than good. Great."

The waitress nodded and smiled, and then disappeared back into the kitchen.

The vagabond reached into his pocket and pulled out all the change he had gathered. It splashed down onto the table, and he tallied it all up with a practiced finger. There was just enough to pay for the coffee, and for that he was grateful. He scooted the change to the end of the table, and then took another sip of the coffee and sighed. It warmed his empty belly, and for that he was also grateful.

The waitress returned a while later, carrying a plate with a ham and swiss sandwich on it. She sat it down in front of the vagabond, who looked back at her confused. "Don't even think about declining the offer, darling. Its on the house."

"Thank you," the vagabond said quietly. He was close to tears.

She left him alone then, only returning once more to top off his coffee. He ate the sandwich, and then slipped out before she could come back again, embarrassed that he couldn't leave her a tip.

V

The vagabond walked along the wet streets of Denver until he came upon the shack. Against the high buildings and landmarks of the city it looked crude and out of place, but he had stayed there before, and knew it was safe. He climbed up the broken porch, watching his step so as not to go through the boards, and then peeled away the unhinged door that had been strapped up over the doorway and stepped inside out of the cold rain.

There were a couple of figures laying down together in the front hall, and he carefully stepped over them so as not to wake them from their much-deserved rest. He came into the kitchen and found a couple of winos sharing a bottle. They offered him a sip, but he declined and passed through. He came into the main room. There was a barrel on fire in the center of the room, and a group of disfigured shadows danced in the flames across the walls. It smelled of burned garbage and gasoline. The vagabond came over and joined them for a time, warming his cold bones and drying his wet clothes. It felt nice after being out in the cold for so long.

"Haven't seen you around these parts in a while," one of the figures sitting by the burning barrel said, looking at the vagabond with sympathetic eyes. "Good to see you again, stranger."

The vagabond nodded.

After a while he rose from the fire and found an empty corner to lay down his aching body. There was a stained-cushion from some long-gone chair and he brought it over to lay his head upon; it was stiff with dry-rot and smelled of urine, but he didn't mind. It was comfortable enough and he would survive, at least this night. He closed his eyes and drifted off into a peaceful slumber where the cold rain couldn't reach him.

The Vanishing of M. Renoir
by RLM Cooper

The last time I saw Monsieur Renoir, he was sitting beneath an umbrella at a sidewalk cafe in Paris, leisurely drinking coffee and glancing through a newspaper. M. Renoir, every inch the French gentleman with closely trimmed mustache and beard – gray streaking at his temples – was usually impeccably dressed, his hat and cane placed casually upon the seat of an adjacent chair. I say "usually" since, on this occasion, he appeared not altogether unlike a much poorer and less refined version of himself. I was, I confess it, rather taken aback at his appearance.

It was early spring, 1939, and I was a reporter for a low-circulation American magazine. I had known M. Renoir for approximately two years after accidentally – and literally – bumping into him on the sidewalk outside Maxim's. He was exiting, and I, lowly creature that I was and unable to afford the luxury of that establishment, was carrying a boxed dinner back to my hotel and, I admit it, not paying strict attention to where I was going when we collided and my dinner was lost to the sidewalk.

When I say M. Renoir was a gentleman, I do not exaggerate. He insisted the smash-up was absolutely his fault and, accepting no excuses, ferried me straight away into Maxim's where he provided a most unforgettable replacement for my lost dinner and an evening I would not soon forget. There, we shared wine and conversation well into the evening, enjoying each other's company immensely. He seemed unusually interested in my particular occupation, and in America as a whole, and not at all bored with my stories and descriptions of people and places I knew there. Later, he confided (upon my prompt) that he was, to his knowledge, no relation whatsoever to the famous artist whose name he shared, and I, looking for something intelligent to say, allowed as how he was lucky not to be burdened with a name like Arnold or Brutus, at which comparison he laughed heartily and poured yet another glass of wine.

For all the times we happened upon each other after that first meeting, and for all the subsequent conversations we enjoyed over coffee at that very sidewalk cafe where I last saw him, M. Renoir remained somewhat a mystery. I was never once privileged to receive an invitation to any social event or to his home. In truth, I had no idea where or how he lived. I passed it off as a kindness as it was unlikely that I would have fit within his social circle. But, of course, I never knew.

My business took me here and there about Paris in an attempt to pick up what human interest happenings I could develop into stories for my employer back in the United States. The Moulin Rouge had supplied any number of good articles. One, involving a rejected dancer who attempted to shoot dead the manager with a pearl-handled dueling pistol, was particularly well-received. Another, involved a young man I helped fish from the Seine where he had flung himself after his lover had ditched him for the son of a wealthy Italian vintner. Paris abounded with stories of human interest. It was an assignment I relished and a city I loved. But even I had to admit that, of late, things were changing.

The city had recently become noticeably less the "Gay Paree" of legend and had taken on instead, a nervousness and grayness that was out of character for the City of Lights. There were rumors of war and the news out of Berlin – indeed, the whole of Germany – was depressing for most; seriously frightening for many. However, Berlin was over a thousand kilometers away, so on the surface, the nervousness was pushed aside. The cabarets kept open their doors and an ironically cheerful face attempted to mask the ever-growing worry.

Trains arrived and departed Paris constantly. Only these days there seemed to be more than the usual number of children among the passengers. At first I hadn't noticed. After all, the train station was only one of my haunts for stories. Of late, however, in addition to their greater numbers, the children were looking unusually tired and worn, their clothing often patched and colorless. Adults noisily herded large groups of them to and from the platforms, urging them to hurry up, or pay attention, or to be still and wait for instructions.

It was during one of my occasional strolls through the station late one afternoon that I was certain I had seen my friend M. Renoir, on the platform opposite. I had begun to raise my arm in salutation, fully intending to call to him when an arriving train passed between us. By the time the passengers had disembarked and dispersed in whatever direction they were going, the train had moved on, and M. Renoir was gone. Had he taken the train somewhere? I wondered. I never asked, since to do so would have been an imposition on our rather casual friendship.

There are many things now, of course, that I regret never asking, for I was extremely fond of M. Renoir.

On the day I last saw him, I was astonished at his rather plebeian attire when compared in memory with his usual finery. His trousers and jacket were of coarse cloth and his usual brocade vest had disappeared completely. There was only a humble cap on the chair beside him. His silver-knobbed cane had vanished along with the vest. He was just finishing his coffee and setting the newspaper aside when I approached.

"Monsieur Renoir! It is so nice to see you here today."

He looked up at me. "I'm afraid you have me at a disadvantage, sir," he said, in rather solemn tone. "My name is Frederic Colobert. I know of no one named Renoir except the famous painter."

I detected a very slight, yet unmistakable, hint of apology in his voice and I was given pause. This *was* my friend, M. Renoir. I was sure of it. Was he in some kind of trouble? Had he fallen, suddenly, on hard times? I was dumbstruck, my brow furrowed with puzzlement, yet I said nothing that could be understood by a casual listener as contradiction. He was a gentleman. Of this I was absolutely sure and, thus, he must have had his reasons for denying the identity I was so positive was his own.

He looked away as he folded the newspaper and then he handed it out to me. "Perhaps you would enjoy reading the paper today. I am finished with it and I must be going."

I looked him in the eyes for a long moment, and then, as I took the paper from his hand. I said, "Thank you. Merci. My mistake, Monsieur Colobert."

He spoke only with his eyes and I felt it keenly. Was it gratitude? Regret? He nodded, then turned and walked away. I was left standing in the middle of the sidewalk, my brain reaching, trying to make sense of what had just transpired.

For reasons I still do not understand, I decided to follow him. He was still in sight, walking briskly on the Rue Truffaut. I kept him in sight until he turned onto the Rue Des Dames and when I reached the corner only seconds later, he was gone. Vanished. And, though I did not realize it at the time, that was the last I would ever see of my friend, M. Renoir. Or Colobert, as he claimed to be.

I was distraught. It had been evident to me that, of course, he knew me. Of course he was my friend, M. Renoir. I was not mistaken. I refused to believe it. I returned to the sidewalk cafe and fell into the chair he had occupied just minutes earlier. Deflated, I ordered a coffee and croissant and attempted to lose myself watching the passing crowd.

Three women chattering happily in French passed beside my table, ignoring me completely. A young woman – possibly a fashion model – hailed a taxi with one lovely arm while holding onto her feathered cloche with the other, and was subsequently ferried away in a puff of black exhaust. An elderly woman scolded her tiny poodle who was inspecting the leg of the next table. Then she picked him up and carried him, making soothing baby talk to the obliviously happy canine. I saw them all and yet I forgot them the instant they were seen.

Later, in my hotel and miserable at what I was sure was the loss of my friend, I received a telegram from my employer. Salt in wound, I had been reassigned – effective immediately – to London. If there was any hope of ever finding M. Renoir again, it was now crushed. I sadly, and rather hastily, packed for the flight that had been reserved for me.

In London, the mood was every bit as dour as it had been in Paris. And the skies were a good deal more gray. Here, a gentleman would be advised to carry an umbrella in place of a cane.

I unpacked my rather meager wardrobe and was in the process of hanging my jacket in the closet when I became aware that I still possessed the newspaper M. Renoir had handed me. It had fallen from the pocket of my jacket onto the floor. As I bent to retrieve it, I noticed a small article in the lower right corner of the page he had folded to the outside. Intrigued, I began reading as I stood back up. It told of children being transported from areas of potential danger in the event of a war that seemed, now, all but inevitable.

The British, the article reported, were making accommodations for many of these children and, having no other ideas, I felt this could be a good source for one or two human-interest stories for my magazine.

The following morning I hired a car and drove up to Harwich, where I tracked down timetables and awaited the next boat's arrival. When it docked and the passengers began to disembark, I was astonished at the sheer number and condition of the children, even though I had been expecting them. Some came with a small suitcase of belongings while others arrived with nothing save the clothes they were wearing – and their names printed upon a numbered tag hung round their necks. They all came without parents and were herded along by weary and concerned adults. They all came unsure and apprehensive of their futures. The imminent war had suddenly thrust itself into my consciousness full-force.

Overhearing snippets of conversations, I began to take notes for a possible story. Scribbling furiously in an attempt to avoid missing anything, I chanced to hear an exchange between two children that halted my pen in mid-stroke. It was as though a photographer had taken up residence inside my head and was busying himself bringing every lens into focus. In that moment, I began see my purpose clearer than ever I had before.

I realized, perhaps for the first time in my life, that I don't actually create anything. There is no lasting beauty in what I do. There is no art. Yet there is, I recognized, value in reporting what others have created. There is value in making sure the world knows of their achievements, for there are some things so rare and so important that they must be placed into the light – things that must be told. They must be reported accurately and clearly enough that even absent eyes can see – and understand.

With my pen suspended above my notebook, I listened. The small conversations were flowing around me in a tangle when all at once, from that Gordian knot of voices, an intelligence emerged that washed over me in unmistakable and painful clarity. I sat down and closed my eyes.

A little girl in patched dress and shoes that did not match each other, had complained of being tired. Holding her hand, an older boy – perhaps her brother – encouraged her to be happy now and to thank God they had been saved. They were safe! They were in England!

The little girl looked up through tears and said, "But I'm frightened, Georges. I want to go back and be with all the other children."

"But we can't go back, Marie." He put his arm protectively around her. "We are safe now."

"Please, Georges. I want to go back and stay with Monsieur Renoir."

The Wandering Corpse
by P.C. Darkcliff

Poor Mommy had always said Auntie was "in-sain." I didn't know what *sain* is, but I guessed it was a horrible thing – and Auntie was in that thing a lot that night. I knew she came to kill me the moment she entered my bedroom. I saw it in her eyes, which shone like the eyes of a rabid animal in the moonlight that came through the curtains.

Auntie made faces as if she had bitten her tongue. The clamping of her big, yellow teeth scared me. Her dress was unbuttoned up front, revealing the red flesh of her chest. She was often nervous, and she would wail and rock her upper body and scratch her skin with her long fingernails until it bled.

Mommy had told me Auntie had been doing that ever since my uncle's death, and that she'd been wearing that black dress every day since then too. Uncle had died before I was born; Auntie and her dress stank, and the skin was gone from her chest.

She slithered toward me like a lynx, her hands outstretched, her large teeth going *clap, clap, clap* in her grinning mouth. She knew I was awake, but she didn't care. Before I could sit up in my bed, she wrapped her fingers around my neck and squeezed.

I wanted to tell her to stop hurting me, but only a gurgle came through my lips. I tried to pull her hands away, but she was too strong. When I jabbed my fingers into the sticky wound on her chest, she howled in pain but would not let go.

My heart grew inside my chest; my head throbbed and burned. Tiny gray specks danced in front of my eyes. They grew big and turned black.

When I opened my eyes, Auntie had left. I gazed at the cobwebs hanging from the beams of the ceiling, trying to remember what had happened. I realized I had fainted—which had saved my life: Auntie thought I had died and stopped strangling me.

She was snoring in her bedroom. And I decided to kill her.

I know that little boys have no business murdering people. But they have no business being murdered, either. And if I didn't kill her, she would kill *me*, as soon as she realized that I hadn't died. She was evil and "in-sain", and she deserved it.

I am sure it was Auntie and not the wolves that had killed poor Mommy. Wolves don't use axes but fangs, and there was blood all over the ax we had in the toolshed. I never even got the chance to say goodbye to Mommy. Auntie said the wolves had dragged her into the woods. But she lied.

Poor Mommy! She had always been so good to Auntie. They used to live happily in the village behind the woods. But then, when she heard about Uncle's death, Auntie spent every night walking around the village banging on people's doors and shouting that they had murdered him.

Uncle had been killed by the Kaiser's soldiers in a place called Prussia. The Kaiser didn't live in the village, and no Prussians either. Auntie didn't care about that, though, and she kept threatening people that she would kill them. In the end, the mayor and the constable told Auntie she had to go.

I think Mommy loved Daddy, and she already had me and my sister in her belly. But she knew Auntie was too "in-sain" to be alone, and so Mommy said goodbye to Daddy and took Auntie to this cabin in the woods. And Auntie repaid Mommy's kindness with murder.

And my poor sister Ronnie! She didn't deserve to die either. But I'm sure she hadn't drowned in the tub on her own.

Auntie had tried to drown *me*, too, only two weeks ago, while she gave me a bath. Auntie never bathed, but she insisted on bathing me every Sunday. And that Sunday she noticed I had a few hairs—well, you know, down there. And she got furious as if it was my fault! She yanked at the hairs until I cried out, and then she pushed my head underwater. The suds stung my eyes, but I couldn't stop looking at Auntie's grinning face that floated above me.

Fortunately, our old cat Freddy jumped on her back while she was bending over me. She got spooked and let go of me before I swallowed too much water.

Too bad old Freddy didn't think of jumping on Auntie's back while she was drowning Ronnie! We had buried Ronnie in the backyard, at the edge of the woods. It was only me and Auntie and Freddy the cat now. And soon it would be just me and Freddy.

I got out of bed, crept outside, and rushed around the cabin. The moon was already setting behind the spruces at the bottom of the backyard. But I could see well enough.

There were piles of trash all along the back wall: Auntie threw everything she didn't need out of the windows but never burned it. Two raccoons rooted through the garbage. They glared at me as if I was an intruder. The stench from the outhouse was bad that night. The backyard was sad and weedy, the woods black and scary. It was a terrible place to be buried.

"I love you, Ronnie," I whispered when I saw the outline of the wooden cross.

A few tears ran down my cheeks as I entered the toolshed. I wanted to kill Auntie more than before. I was going to kill her with the ax she had used on Mommy.

The ax lay by the chopping block. I picked it up and carried it outside. It was almost bigger than me, but I was strong because I did most of the wood chopping last winter like a grownup. I thought I could easily kill her, but when the moonlight fell on the bloodied blade, I screamed and dropped the ax into the weeds.

I wasn't a monster like Auntie, and I could never break her head. I would go mad if I saw the blood and brains run from her skull.

Wouldn't it be easier to run away? I had been thinking about escaping ever since Ronnie's death. I'd dreamed about crossing the woods and going to the village and trying to find Daddy. But it was too risky.

I couldn't do it while Auntie was awake, because she would know right away. And I couldn't do it at night, either. The walk would be too long and dangerous. The wolves were really there: I heard them howling through the woods many nights. And tonight, the moon would set before I crossed the woods, and I would be lost. Besides, I'd never met Daddy, and I didn't know if he was alive and if he loved me.

Mommy used to take me and Ronnie to the village every month, in the automobile we inherited from Grandpa. But we only went to the general store and returned as soon as we bought all the dried and canned food the shopkeeper had on the shelves. Once I'd asked if we could visit Daddy. Mommy only burst into tears, and I never asked again.

It was Auntie who sometimes drove to the village now, on the days when she wasn't too much "in-sain". Unfortunately, those days weren't many, and we often starved. She drove well, though, and if she woke up and realized I'd disappeared, she would take the automobile and go after me. She couldn't drive fast on that narrow, bumpy path. But what if she caught up with me, anyway?

I had to kill her, that was the only way. I looked at the ax and shivered. Then I got an idea.

I returned to the toolshed and walked to the back wall. The darkness was deep there, and I had to grope my way around. The top shelf was out of my reach, so I walked back to the chopping block and dragged it to the wall. Then I climbed it and took a black box from the top shelf. It was rat poison.

I scooped a handful of the pellets and poured them into the breast pocket of my nightshirt. Then I jumped off the block, left the shed, and walked back to the cabin.

In her bedroom, Auntie snored as if she'd swallowed a live piglet. I sneaked into the kitchen. The pile of dirty dishes was so high I feared it would fall and bury me alive.

I rummaged through the sticky cupboards and found Auntie's box of oatmeal. I was lucky because there was only a bit left on the bottom and she would surely eat it all in the morning. I scooped the pellets out of my pocket and dropped them into the box. I shook the box to mix the pellets with the oatmeal. Then I put it back and tiptoed to my bedroom.

It was a long night. When I already wondered if the sun had overslept, the sky behind the woods finally started to turn from black to gray. Auntie stopped snoring. I lay in my bed and pretended to be dead in case she entered my bedroom.

Her footsteps echoed through the hallway and died out as she walked outside. Then came the creaking of the rusty pump: she was getting water for her oatmeal!

I heard her in the kitchen preparing her breakfast. She stepped outside again, and I assumed she went to the outhouse. When she returned, she screamed something at Freddy the cat. Then everything grew quiet.

When the sun climbed a little higher above the trees, I dared get up and step out of my bedroom. I tiptoed into the kitchen, hoping to see her lying on the floor. But she wasn't there.

The box of oatmeal was empty, though. Only a few flakes of drenched oatmeal swam at the bottom of the ugly yellow mug she always used for breakfast. The circles inside the bowl showed me that the bowl had been full.

Auntie had finished her breakfast! But where was she?

I tiptoed toward her bedroom, whose door stood ajar. My heart made a somersault when I poked my head in. Auntie was sprawled on the bed, her body rigid under the black dress. Finally, I was free!

I did not have to fear Auntie anymore. Now I could go to the village and find Daddy... or any other grownup who would take me in.

I walked down the hall to Mommy's bedroom. I knew there was a rucksack in the cabinet, among Mommy's winter coats and summer dresses. My eyes watered at the sight of her empty bed. Mommy had always smelled of wildflowers, and I inhaled deeply the sweet smell that still hung in the room.

As I reached for the knob of the cabinet door, a sound came from the hallway. I walked out—and saw Auntie leaving her bedroom.

I wanted to run outside, but I would have to pass Auntie, and so I rushed to my room. I wanted to escape through the window, but it was too narrow, so I dived under my bed, trembling and whimpering like a puppy.

She had turned into a ghost! That horrible Auntie would torture me even after her death! I didn't think she had seen me. But what if she came looking for me?

I spent the day under the bed. When I fell asleep that night, I dreamed about my sister lying in the backyard under a heap of dirt, and about Mommy rotting in a clearing in the woods.

Another day dragged by, and I still didn't dare leave my hideout, not with the corpse wandering along the hallway. I fell asleep again. When I woke up, Auntie stood in the doorway.

I pressed my body against the dusty floor. I watched her snort and spit as if a foul smell had hit her nose. But what business do ghosts have snorting and spitting? Was Auntie's ghost "in-sain" too?

A cloud of flies buzzed around the wooden chest beside my bed. What were they doing there? It only held my clothes and flies never bothered about them. The flies were big and ugly. I think Mommy called them –

"Corpse flies," I whispered with a shudder. That name rattled my soul.

When I looked back at the door, Auntie was gone. I crawled from under the bed, determined to escape from the ghost and the flies. I looked outside to make sure Auntie wasn't haunting the backyard.

Through the cobwebs that clung to the windowpane, I saw Freddy the cat lying in the weeds.

He was bloated like a balloon, just like the rats when –

A horrible thought made me stagger. Then I did something I should have never done, something that sent me screaming out of the house.

Tears gushed out of my eyes as I stumbled through the backyard and fell near the little wooden cross. I couldn't get up; I couldn't stop sobbing.

"Don't cry, Stevie." I heard a girl's voice. "It's all over now."

I lifted my head and blinked away the tears. Ronnie stood by her cross. She wore the blue dress we'd buried her in. Her blond hair was braided, and she was even more beautiful than when she'd been alive.

"I missed you, Stevie," she said. "But now we are together again."

I scrambled to my knees, and Ronnie kneeled in front of me. We hugged, and she let me cry on her thin shoulder.

I twitched at the sound of rustling grass. But it was only Freddy the cat coming to rub his sides against our hips. Freddy trotted as if he were a kitten again, and he wasn't bloated at all.

"You silly, silly Freddy," Ronnie said as she picked him up and pressed her cheek against the top of his head. "Why did you eat from Auntie's bowl, you crazy old cat? The poison wasn't for you!"

I shot to my feet when I heard another noise. I saw Auntie open the grimy kitchen window and spit outside. There was a terrible leer on her face, and I thought she was leering at us.

Ronnie put the cat on the ground and got up. "She can't hurt us anymore, Stevie. She can't even see us."

"Because she is a ghost?"

Ronnie shook her head. "She skipped breakfast that day, Stevie. Our Freddy beat her to the oatmeal."

"So that's why she shouted at him," I said, beginning to understand.

"Yes. She prepared the meal and went to the outhouse. And while she was there, our Freddy emptied the bowl. But don't worry about it, Stevie. I'm so glad we can finally leave. Come with me. Let's go visit Mommy!"

We entered the woods and walked hand in hand down a deer path toward the clearing. Mommy met us halfway there, by a fallen oak. Her long auburn hair streamed over her white nightgown and made her look like a beautiful fairy. She fell to her knees and spread her arms, and we rushed to hug her. We all squeezed each other and laughed through our tears.

"I love you, Mommy," I blubbered over and over as I pressed my drenched cheek against hers.

"I love you too, my big, brave boy!"

We sat on the fallen oak, held hands, and talked. I was happy for the first time since they died, but as we got up and walked to the village cemetery to visit Grandma and Grandpa, sadness crept back into my soul. I shuddered whenever I recalled opening the wooden chest and letting the flies alight on my strangled corpse.

Howl
by Belinda Brady

> *My story is a werewolf story, which is a hard sell I know, but it's a werewolf story with an unusual twist. This story has been with me for a few years and was my first attempt at writing this supernatural creature. It has been through a few re-writes and the end result of it being told from three points of view is one I am really happy with. It is my wish that my story invokes a little hope in anyone who reads it.*

STEVIE

Opening my eyes, I'm aware of the all-too-familiar haze, but this time it's different. I can feel my brain start-up, trying to remember, but it's struggling. As the haze lifts and I become aware of my surroundings, one single thought is on replay in my mind – *I'm not meant to be here.*

I'm in my apartment, lying flat in my bed. I feel wet and dirty and there is a strong smell of blood in the air. I quickly run my hands over my body checking for cuts of any kind, raising them to my face for inspection after no injuries are found. They too are wound free and I drop them to my side, listening to my pulse racing in my ears as I try to figure out where the enticing copper scent is coming from. Slowly I sit up and scan the room, senses on high alert. There's a half-empty glass of water on my bedside table and vomit on my bed sheets, a strange smell coming from both. I look past my bed to the center of the room and quickly spot the source of the blood. A body. A bloodied and bruised human lies motionless on my floor and it looks very much dead. Getting out of bed, I gently walk over to the body, careful to not make any noise. Kneeling by the head, I gingerly move the thick mass of red hair aside that's covering the face, jumping up in shock and stifling a scream when I see who it is. It's my dear friend Grace and she's sporting an assortment of horrific wounds along with a nasty bite on her neck; a gun lies by her side.

No! Not Grace!

I'd always known I was different, even from a young age. My mother, Blair, told me of my secret when I was young, and she didn't try and sugar-coat it; I was different, very different. I needed to know what I was in for and how to protect myself, and most importantly, how to keep a secret – though I quickly learned never to reveal my secret to anyone. At a school friend's birthday party, when I was about eight years old, I asked the birthday girl's mother when the cat had died. When the shocked mother asked how I knew this, I told her I could smell it buried in the backyard. Turns out, puss had died the night before and was indeed buried underneath the big oak out back. I was never invited to a birthday party again after that - not that I had any friend's to invite me to their parties anyway. Word of mouth quickly spread and soon enough I was avoided like the plague. My school years were spent hiding away from the stares and taunts in the school library, the grumpy middle-aged librarian my only companion.

Grace's friendship was a pleasant surprise and we had been thick as thieves for a few years now, ever since I'd started as a clerk at the insurance brokers' company where she worked. It was my first day and I had been invited to join a few colleagues for lunch, Grace included, and not wanting to pass up this opportunity to make new friends, I happily accepted, only to find when I arrived all the seats were taken. 'Sorry, there's no room for you now,' was the sneered explanation, and as I slinked away from the sniggers to find a table to eat at by myself, Grace announced she'd join me. We were soon firm friends. I never had anyone stick around as long as Grace did – she got my off-hand jokes, often matching them, she liked the same things I did and she just *got* me. There was a familiarity about her I couldn't put my finger on, but I was so happy to finally have a friend I shrugged it off. Since that birthday party, I was laughed at, picked on and left out, and unfortunately for me, mud stuck as I grew. Those who hadn't heard the stories soon did, and those who didn't quickly picked up on my oddness and ran a mile. But Grace was miles apart from the rest – she was a true friend.

Or so I thought.

I slump to the floor, head buried in my hands, mind racing, when my front door bursts open, shattering the eerie quiet. I scramble back to the wall; letting out a sigh of relief when I see my 'intruder' is my mother.

"Quick, Stevie, we need to go. Get up, grab your bag, we have to leave. Now!" she barks, grabbing my already packed overnight bag on the floor and sliding it toward me. She marches over to my bedside table and picks up the glass of water. Holding it at arm's length, she walks it over to my kitchen sink, tips out the offensive liquid, and throws the now empty glass in the bin.

"What the hell is going on? What happened to Grace?" I cry as she marches towards Grace's body.

Grabbing Grace's feet, my mother begins to drag her toward the door. "I can explain on the drive. Right now, we need to get out of here. The sun will be up soon and our cover will be gone. Hurry up."

"Wait!" I scream. "Can you at least tell me what happened to Grace?"

Stopping mid-drag, my mother turns to me, a somber look on her face. "Grace? Grace brought this upon herself. Now help me get her into the car will you?"

***

BLAIR

Stevie, along with my gift, was the result of an attack. I was walking home from a party one night when a werewolf ambushed me. I was only seventeen years old. I was found by a passer-by and rushed to hospital in a critical condition where I was not expected to make it through the night. Defying all odds, I pulled through and got better with each passing hour. A nurse called Violet was caring for me and noticed the speed at which my injuries were healing, as well as changes in my temperature, heartbeat, and breathing. A werewolf herself, she recognized the signs and knew she had a newbie on her hands. When I was well enough, Violet informed me that life, as I had known it, was over and I needed to prepare for my imminent change. Violet promised to help me; soon becoming the big sister I never knew I needed. She was there when Stevie was born nine months later and through her, I learned there was a whole community of 'wolves' just like us and when the full moon hit, they could be found out in the thick wilderness, hidden away in a little community that catered to their needs. Here, they could not only hide away from humanity but indulge in their change. We referred to this community as a getaway and for us it truly was a getaway – from the human world to the supernatural one. I attended it for my first change and I've been going there ever since. With each full moon, I enjoyed my new world and identity so much that I grew to despise my leftover humanity and all that came with it. Humans are so simple, so fickle and so unbearably superficial, wanting the latest phone or big-screen television so they can impress each other; kidding themselves they are living their best lives. Werewolves are uncomplicated in our pleasures. We don't care for the opinions of others or the latest trends. We know what really matters – loyalty, family, and being true to oneself. We enjoy the simple things in life – something these pathetic humans can't seem to grasp. I loathe every minute I have to spend in their sad little world.

Naturally, I'm cautious of any new human who tries to befriend me, even more so with Stevie. I'm fiercely protective of my girl. She is such a gentle soul; one who has been through hell and back as a result of what these repugnant humans can do to one another. The bullying was relentless during her school years and she had to stop me on more than one occasion from paying some of her bullies a visit and tearing them from limb to limb. So when this Grace girl came on the scene, of course, I was wary, but Stevie was so wrapped to finally have a friend I bit my tongue. There was something about Grace that didn't sit right, yet for the life of me, I couldn't figure it out. So I observed my daughters blossoming friendship from the sidelines, always on guard and ready to defend her at a moment's notice, and I was pleasantly surprised to see that all was going well.

Until tonight.

Stupid girl. Stupid human. She had no idea what she was going up against. She should've just stayed home.

***

GRACE

I knew there was something about Stevie the moment I saw her. I sensed it. She was wonderfully unusual. She was special. I liked it – *really* liked it. Whatever she was, I wanted in. I hated my life. *Hated* it. I was adopted; the result of teenage parents thinking they were doing the right thing, but unfortunately for me, I didn't get the happy ending they had envisioned. Not a day went by when I wished I hadn't been born. My childhood was spent being constantly reminded by my adoptive mother that if my parents cared for me, they would have kept me, while my adoptive father stood by and said nothing. Other times she'd snipe that I was only adopted for the monetary gain the family would get from having one more mouth to feed, but the pittance they received wasn't worth having me in the household. The type of torment she dished out depended on what day of the week it was and the color of the bottle she was drinking from. It only got worse when their three biological kids joined in. They were merciless. "Giveaway Grace" is what they called me, saying it over and over again until I would lash out, often in a rage of fists and tears. I would then be the one getting punished - or in my case flogged - with my "father's" welt inducing leather belt, while the others laughed away in the background, unpunished. I left the minute I turned sixteen and never looked back. And through it all, Stevie was never far from my mind, though she was unreachable. I'd see her at school, but the library was where she spent her breaks, the librarian not willing to let her most eager helper go, and as soon as the bell went, she was gone. Her mother was always there to pick her up, putting her arm protectively around her as she greeted her.

That must be so nice to have someone love you that much – someone who actually cares.

When I finally crossed paths with Stevie again many years later I was *so* happy. This girl had come back into my life and I was not going to let her go. Befriending her was easy. I know what those office bitches are like, and I had to let her go through the humiliation of being left out to appreciate a real friend when she had one. Naturally, we hit it off, just like I knew we would, and in no time we were joined at the hip. Stevie was everything I wanted to be – sweet, funny, and utterly adorable in her uniqueness, except she wouldn't tell me just what that uniqueness was. I tried so many ways to bring it up in conversation, to try and hint at anything out of the ordinary, but she ignored me each time. Her eyes would glaze over and she'd change the subject. I simply *had* to know what her secret was, and since she wasn't going to tell me, I'd have to find out another way. I had a plan and whether it worked or not, I was going to give it my all.

Either way, it was a win-win situation.

***

NOW

In record time, we are on our way to the getaway, with Grace's body stashed in the trunk of the car. My mother has made some calls to the others and within a matter of hours Grace will be a mere memory. Some tech-savvy wolves are on their way to my apartment to tinker with the security cameras around the area and soon the last known footage of Grace will be her leaving work yesterday afternoon. Safely strapped into the front passenger seat, I snuggle my head into the headrest and let out a sigh as I try to remember the events leading up to this. My mind is a mess, but I'm getting scrambled flashbacks – *a gun pointed at me, Grace yelling at me.*

"Listen," my mother soothes, her eyes on the road ahead. "Don't feel bad. None of this is your fault. Do you remember anything about last night?"

"Not really," I whimper, my lip quivering as I fight to hold it together.

My mother turns to me, a gentle smile on her face. "Well, lucky for you I know exactly what happened, so try to relax and I'll tell you about it."

My mother explains it all as she drives. With the full moon looming, she had arrived at my place to pick me up for the getaway and had become concerned when I didn't come down to the car after she had beeped the horn. Approaching my apartment she could hear a woman shouting the words *"change"* and *"now"* repeatedly. Rushing in, she found Grace holding me hostage at gunpoint. I was drowsy and confused. Turns out, that glass of water next to my bed had been laced with Wolfsbane – a lethal poison for werewolves. Grace had done her homework, but not enough it seemed, as she hadn't given me enough to kill me; just enough to leave me rendered useless. Seeing this, my mother lost all control and attacked Grace.

I lean my head against my car window and shed a few silent tears for my dead friend. I am going to miss her. I thought I had a true friend in Grace, but it seemed she was just using me to get close enough to kill me. We had found her diary in her handbag and discovered she had been stalking me for a while. Though I never told her, she had somehow figured out my secret and had been keeping track of my every move. Next to yesterday's date, there was a drawing of a full moon accompanied by one little word – *"Change"*.

We arrive in record time to find Violet, flanked by several other concerned faces, waiting for us. As my mother and Violet move quickly to remove Grace's body from the car, I'm ushered inside the main building, where our resident doctor gives me a thorough check-up. Receiving a clean bill of health, I'm ordered to my room to wash up and regain my strength, and after a few hours of rest, I'm ready to join the others and put this nightmare behind me. Heading downstairs to the foyer, I see the other wolves, including my mother, seated on the foyer's plush brown sofas, a red-haired girl standing in the middle of them, her back to me as she talks softly to her captive audience. The tension in the air is palpable. Hearing me enter the room, she stops talking and turns to look at me.

The hairs on the back of my neck stand up when I see her face.

"Hi, Stevie," Grace smiles, "fancy seeing you here."

I stand here gaping at Grace for what seems like an eternity. She looks dead, but she's very much alive. Her injuries are still present, yet they are slowly healing before my eyes.

What the hell is going on?

"Yes, I should be dead, but lucky for me your mother didn't quite finish me off," Grace says, still smiling at me.

My mother looks at me with an apologetic smile. "I went a little easy on her as I was afraid of drawing attention. With all that yelling going on, I didn't want to rouse any more suspicion with a full-on attack. But I did think I had finished her off." She shrugs slowly. "Guess I was wrong."

"This is a good thing guys, trust me. I wanted this," Grace interrupts, her hands gliding over her vanishing injuries as though she were presenting them on a game show. "Stevie, I knew you were different the minute I saw you. Though I'm not sure you saw me. That birthday party, the one where you told the mother you could smell the dead cat? I'd say you'd remember that party well?"

My brow furrows in confusion. "Yes, of course, I remember that party, and I certainly remember that moment, but I'm sorry, I don't remember you being there."

"Oh, I was there," Grace smiles. "I was behind a tree, retrieving my runaway balloon when I heard the entire conversation about the cat. A happy moment in my miserable timeline I can assure you. I'd already seen you at the party before that moment though and I *knew* you were special, I could feel it. That conversation just confirmed it. I tried so hard to be your friend after that, but you were untouchable. Not that I could blame you, those kids were vicious little beasts."

I remember that day like it was yesterday and as the memory floods my mind the pain is still raw enough to make me flinch.

"When you finally came back into my life all those years later, I knew I wasn't going to let you go again. I tried to get you to reveal your secret to me many times, but you wouldn't budge," Grace continues, "so I went to plan B and started following you, tracking you. Soon enough, I followed you here, and I finally discovered what you were. What you *all* were." She pauses and scans the room, her eyes twinkling. "I heard the howls. I saw the changes happening from afar, though I didn't dare get too close. Not then anyway. I knew what you were and I wanted to be just like you. I have always felt lost, incomplete, like I didn't belong. I hate my life. I hate being human. To me, it is meaningless. You guys have a gift. You have a whole other life you get to keep secret. Your legend has been around for centuries and yet the world is still fascinated by you. They have made movies, written books and penned songs about you. Your story is passed from generation to generation. You guys are powerful, admired, and feared supernatural beings. How amazing is that? When I saw your mother change to attack me, Stevie, it was a glorious sight. I knew I'd made the right choice."

Grace walks over to the window and with her back turned she continues, "I came to your apartment last night, Stevie, because I wanted you to change me, though I knew you wouldn't voluntarily. You have such a good heart; I knew you wouldn't do it. So, I drugged you, but just enough for you to be drowsy and incapable of leaving. Feeling threatened with a gun to your face, you would change and attack me. I was aware I was dicing with death, but it was worth it. I had to take the risk. I just hadn't planned on your mother bursting in. I'd completely forgotten about her. But, it worked in my favor in the end." Grace puts her head down, her voice now a shaky whisper. "I'm sorry I betrayed you, Stevie, but I had to. I hope you can understand why I had to do this, and I hope you can find it in your heart to forgive me, but I needed this to happen. I just couldn't go on as a human anymore. I couldn't go on with my *life* anymore."

The energy in the room shifts and the heaviness that was there is now gone. I look over at my mother who gives me a little nod, her eyes glassy with tears. My mind is swimming and my stomach flips with the realization that my only friend might be one of us.

Could Grace really be just like me? I was just mourning her and now I am about to run with her?

With the sun setting in the late afternoon sky behind her, Grace turns to face me, her eyes glowing that all-too-familiar yellow glow that comes just before one changes, erasing any doubt that she is now a werewolf.

"What do you say, Stevie?" she beams. "Are you ready to howl with me?"

***

Saving Aaron
by Peggy Gerber

My name is Maggie, and I am a murderer. As I sit here in my filthy jail cell, breathing in the stench of body odor and despair, I attempt to process my new identity as a killer. My hands are cuffed behind my back; I am about to be indicted. It won't take long, because when the judge asks for my plea, I have every intention of pleading guilty. The truth is, I would do it again.

I committed the murder twenty-three years ago, but I had no memory of it until yesterday. That is how time travel works.

The events that transpired to bring about this murder occurred on February 2, 2010, the day my family was shattered to pieces. On that day, my ten-year old son Aaron had got just gotten off the school bus, when a careless driver struck and killed him. The bus had its stop sign out, as well as having on its flashing lights, but the driver of the car was so engrossed in texting, he didn't see Aaron until it was too late. I was told Aaron was hit so hard he flew 20 feet into the air before landing on his head. My boy died alone. I blame myself. Aaron had been begging for months to be given permission to walk home from the bus by himself, and I finally relented. If I had only been there, maybe things would have worked out differently.

The driver of the car was a seventeen-year old boy named Kevin, who was on his way home from high school when the accident occurred. He was running late and texting his mom not to worry. All it took was that one text message to snuff out my son's life and ruin an entire family. Kevin stayed at the scene and was taken to the police station. He did everything right. There was a trial, and a lawsuit, but when it came time for sentencing, the judge was lenient. She took into account that Kevin was still a minor, as well as an honor student. It also helped his defense that his parents could afford a good lawyer. Kevin's punishment for killing my son, was six months of community service, traveling to high schools giving lectures on what can happen when you text and drive.

When they announced the verdict, I screamed and cursed so loudly they had to forcefully escort me out of the courtroom. The thing is, I would have thought it a fitting punishment if it had happened to someone else's child. It seemed almost fair, and Kevin was properly devastated with what he had done.

But my Aaron, with his curly brown hair and deep blue eyes, was the light of my life and the joy of my existence. Nothing made me happier than hearing him sing and play the electric guitar I bought him for his birthday. Our house was always filled with music. Aaron would often ask me, "Mom, should I be a doctor or a rock star when I grow up?" I would always answer "Honey, why not both".

Aaron's unique sense of humor and infectious smile had kept my husband Charlie and I laughing every night. We could never stay mad at him. And then he was gone, and the silence was deafening. I couldn't help thinking that it would be Kevin who would get to go to college, and it would be Kevin who would get married one day, and it would be Kevin who would give his parents the grandchildren I would never have.

Nobody can recover from the loss of a child, but some brave people take that loss and turn it into something positive. They find a way to go on. Not me. My broken heart put me into such a deep depression, nothing could diminish my pain. Charlie tried to help me, he really did, he would say "Maggie, please let's go out," but I just couldn't get off the couch, and I didn't want to. Charlie stuck around for five years but eventually I drove him away. Of course he loved Aaron too, I know he did, but he wanted to move on and have another baby. I only wanted Aaron. I was lucky, if you could call it that, that my job allowed me to work from home, so there I remained, day after day, year after year, working at home and watching TV. I was living like a ghost, as one by one, family and friends gave up on me.

Before bed every night, I liked to watch the news. There was just something about hearing other people's tragedies that gave me a gruesome sense of satisfaction, and I felt less alone. It gave me permission to rage against the randomness of the world.

Then suddenly, about a year ago, I came back to life. I had heard a news report about a team of PhD students at Princeton that were working on a time machine. Just like that, my depression lifted as if a magician had waved a magic wand. I had a mission. Save Aaron. It did not take me very long to find those Princeton students, and I arranged a meeting with them under the pretence of being an angel investor looking to fund their project. Little did I know, that is exactly what I would become. The team had built a prototype of a time machine, but lacked the funding to build a working model. I had quite a bit of money from the lawsuit and this was the perfect excuse to use it. Neither Charlie nor I had spent a penny of it, we saw it as blood money, and I had enough to fund the entire project. I gave it to the students with the understanding that I would be the first person to test the machine. They were not happy about it, but those were my conditions and they needed the money. I figured I had nothing to lose. If I died in the machine, it would be fine, because I felt dead already, but if I succeeded, justice would be smiling.

It took almost a year after my investment for the time machine to be completed. I had no understanding of the mechanics of the machine, nor did I care. The machine's limitations were what concerned me. I would have seven seconds, seven frenzied, crazy seconds to complete my task once I was transported back in time. That is the excruciatingly short amount of time I would have in the time loop before being whisked back to the present. I spent that entire year preparing for my trip. As we did not know the exact second my son was struck, seven seconds would not be enough time to stop him from getting off the bus, or stop him from crossing the street, or even to tell my younger self to not let Aaron go to school that day. The only thing I was certain would work, was to murder Kevin the day before the accident. Seven seconds would be just enough time to pull a trigger and end the life of the boy that killed my Aaron. It would be a life for a life. What mother wouldn't do that for her child?

I put together the perfect plan. I bought a gun, and spent months perfecting my speed and my aim, going to the firing range every chance I got. I had always hated guns, but for a brief amount of time, I saw the beauty in it.

Once the time machine was ready, I rented out Kevin's former house for twenty-four hours. The new owners started to ask questions, but once I offered them the thousand dollars, they agreed to silence. You see, while the time machine had the remarkable ability to transport a person back in time, it could not bring you to a new location. It was imperative that you were at the exact place you needed to be. Completely unaware of my murderous plan, the PhD students moved the time machine into Kevin's old bedroom. I knew exactly which room to place it in because I had stalked Kevin's family after the accident. They had to get a restraining order against me and it was this compulsive behavior that drove me to become a hermit. My adrenaline pumping, we set the timer on the machine for February 2nd, three o'clock in the morning, twelve hours before the accident was to occur, and I stepped in. I planned to kill Kevin in his sleep. It was to be first degree murder in cold blood.

Seven seconds after the machine zapped me back in time, I returned to the present with a crushing headache. But my pain transformed to euphoria as I instantly realized my plan was a success. I now had a dual set of memories. While I remembered every gruesome detail of Aaron's death and the twenty-three miserable years following, my brain was exploding with twenty-three years of new, wonderful memories. I now remembered how handsome Aaron looked at his prom, hand in hand with his high school sweetheart. I could recall our whole family rejoicing at Aaron's graduation from medical school, and then again as he married his lovely bride. The pride in his voice when he called me and said, "Mom, I saved a patient's life today." And my new favorite memory, the look of love on his face the day his first child was born. How I treasure being a grandmother.

Along with the good memories, there were sad ones as well. Especially the memory of that awful day twenty-three years earlier, when a neighborhood boy was murdered in his bedroom. A murder that, to this day, remains unsolved. That murder affected my family deeply. Charlie and I came to realize how fragile life was, and we decided to have another baby. We named our little girl Kylee, after the young man that died so tragically that night.

I am confident I will be convicted and sent to prison for my crime, and I want to be. After all, I turned myself in. I will not have any regrets, though, because I have twenty-three years of wonderful memories to cherish and replay in my head. There would be nothing I would change if I could once again turn back time. The thing is, I am not being held on murder charges. Since Kevin never killed Aaron, there was never a lawsuit, and I never had the money to fund the time machine project. The team of students never did receive funding and the prototype was locked in a warehouse in Princeton, unfinished. What I am being held for is breaking and entering, as well as destruction of property. Shortly after my return, I drove to Princeton and destroyed their blasphemous prototype, trashing it over and over again with a metal baseball bat.

You may wonder how seven seconds was enough time to pinpoint Kevin and murder him. Well, it was not. What I didn't count on that night, was that Kevin's ten- year old brother Kyle would be in the room. It was Kyle that died that night, but I saved my Aaron, because on February 2nd, Kevin had a funeral to go to.

Ghost-maker
by Kristy Kerruish

He would make her a ghost.

The eyes of a ghost have a rare light; filled with clouded recollections, places half remembered, faces forgotten, words vaguely recalled. We have all seen such faces, on occasion sought them out or tried to remember them.

He told her he needed light.

She chose a day filled with light. Late summer had come to Amsterdam. Blossoms and fish-heads thrown from the market, drifted on the water, the reflections were dimpled and broken into fragments by the wakes of the slow, broad boats.

Sophie Cohen knew the ghost-maker to be a monstrous creature; brutal and cold, without compassion. As she walked beside the narrow-fronted canal houses with their gaping windows, she imagined his demonic form writhing in the shadows of an oily lamp-lit room; half-creature, half-human. When she reached the bridge, she paused and looked up at the sign suspended above his door.

Hermanus Van de Berg, painter of likenesses

Holding her parasol behind her head and raising her hand up to the window glass to shield the light's reflections, she could see inside the studio. Gradually, as her eyes grew accustomed to the darkness, faces peered back at her from the shadows. It was true that painted portraits had become old-fashioned and expensive, and indeed the artist appeared little different from the dying art he still gave life to. A small moustachioed man sat at his easel, his hand poised holding a delicate brush, his eyes set on the canvas in front of him. Seeing Sophie at the window, he gave her a swift smile before coming to the door.

"You found the courage to come to me," he said as she stepped in.

Inside the small studio, the close air smelt of oil, sweat and camphor. The canvas Van de Berg was working on showed a portly gentleman with full lips worn in an insipid smile.

"I have never lacked courage," Sophie said, looking at the portrait.

"I can admire courage. I must find something to admire in everyone who sits for me," Van de Berg said, looking into her face. "Whether it be the smooth silk of their waistcoat or the cut of their britches or a button, it matters very little what I admire."

Sophie looked about the walls. It was said that Van de Berg painted horrors into every canvas, yet every portrait she saw by his hand could only have been the creation of the most beautiful soul; a man who sought and found beauty in the world around him. It was not merely his sitters whose spirit and vitality had been captured by his brush, but the fallen leaves about their feet in an autumn wood, the tiny beetles clinging to the stems of summer grasses, the drifts of clouds that masked the sun on a spring day, or low mists snagged on the dunes. Some of Van de Berg's paintings were set within a landscape with, she supposed, the sitter's favourite view. Some had chosen the Tuscan hills, others a crumbling coastline stretching into the mists of the distance or the bright sails of a windmill with the morning dew still on the grass. One sitter had chosen to be painted with a ship behind, its sails strained against a dark sky. Others had selected neglected rooms, dark alleys in nameless towns or un-trodden woods. She could not understand their reasoning. She planned to commission a beautiful background behind her portrait, one that meant something to her.

"When I first meet a sitter, I ask them what manner of painting they require." Van de Berg rattled a paint brush around in a glass jar of water for several moments so that the paint, like a drift of smoke, darkened the water.

"Just a portrait."

Van de Berg smiled at her, moistened a brush, pressed it to his lips and then, with a few thoughtful swipes, he fashioned a rough outline of her on a sheet of paper. "They say I am a monstrous man."

"They do. They call you the ghost-maker."

"A portrait painter only seeks to capture the truth."

"Perhaps the truth can be monstrous," Sophie said, looking about her at the canvasses piled against the walls. "Why have so many paintings not been collected?"

"The clients returned them, they were disappointed." The old man found a smile, looking at her over the top of his spectacles with rheumy eyes.

"But they are perfect. The finest portraits I have ever seen. How can they cause displeasure?" Sophie glanced doubtfully at one close by, the background showed a maid stringing up the sheets to dry in the morning sun.

Sophie commissioned the portrait and went for regular sittings at Van de Berg's studio. He required her to attend at the same time every week. At each sitting he sketched her, the pencil held against his lips as he looked at her before committing the lines to the page. He studied the details, sometimes an eye, a hand, her nose, until he was satisfied that he knew her features well enough.

The summer ebbed. The first frosts came. The newspapers carried dark news. Somewhere far away war wrenched the sky, fists held high in the air with heated words of anarchy and hate, but Amsterdam remained untouched, only the gentle shift of the season seemed to mark it.

Work on the portrait progressed as slowly. As the leaves died and fell from the trees to drift on the canal waters, Van de Berg gave life to his creation. With a tiny dab of white paint her eyes took on a warmth and vitality. A dry brush stroke across her lips gave them form and the subtle lines around her mouth made her look about to smile. By the time the first snows fell, her portrait was complete, only the background remained undone.

The ice had crept over the canals and stilled the waters by the time the letter came. Sophie's husband stood beside the hearth and read Van de Berg's words out to her. The canvas was complete. If they honoured the payment then he would send it to them. When it arrived, the portrait delighted Sophie and her husband, it was in every way what they required save for one error; the background was unfamiliar. Sophie and her husband looked at the painting for a long while and speculated on how such a mistake had been made. Van de Berg had painted a pretty town known to neither of them. It lay nestled in the green trees which surrounded it. The painting was undoubtedly fine but he had ignored their precise instructions to paint a view of Amsterdam behind her.

"What is this place?" Sophie said crouching down to look at the small town.

"I have no notion," her husband said easing the tobacco smoke through his teeth. "But I do remember he painted a very similar town into the background of my uncles' portrait."

"It's such a sad scene. There's so little colour. No joy at all."

The care and attention that had been given to the scene of the town he had painted was so beautifully executed that it seemed a pity to have it painted over. Sophie could almost see the shadows shifting and the smoke being dragged from the chimneys of the small town in a light breeze. However, within a day the painting was returned and left to lean against the walls of Van de Berg's studio until the work was completed.

The memories of Sophie's life in Amsterdam vanished. The friends and family who had framed her life had all faded like wisps of smoke. She had forgotten the portrait and it was only one cold Spring day, when she took no joy from anything she saw, that a view jarred her mind with recognition. As she stepped from the train the very same melancholy town that Van de Berg had painted so beautifully behind her in the portrait now lay wrapped in a haze of mist before her.

"Do you know this place?" she whispered to the woman beside her.

"*I think we are in Poland.*"

As Sophie sat on the floor, her arms thrown around her knees, listening to the sounds from outside she thought of Van de Berg, that small gentleman hunched over an easel in an Amsterdam studio with his delicate smile and soft voice. To her mind his studio was timeless, she imagined him there still, the rhythm of his brush tapping the sides of the water jar, the paint clouding the clear water. Months of life-times separated her from her past. Van de Berg had seen everything, her happiness, her laughter, the things that moved her, the things she loved. He had seen what was beautiful in every sitter. Van de Berg had crafted life into his sitters' faces and then, into the background of every painting, he had painted the thing which they feared the most; that which forever follows unseen and unknown until the day it is faced. The monstrous demon which lurked within Van de Berg was that, in seeing the sitter before him, in understanding them, he had seen their death, and painted the place where they would die into every canvas.

This place was Oswiecim and the walls that enclosed her were those of *Auschwitz-Birkenau*.

A Very Brooklyn Wedding
by Adele C. Geraghty

It was the summer of 1976 and the streets of Brooklyn steamed lazily in the late afternoon sun. The roads oozed with melted tar. It stuck like liquorice gum, to the platform shoes of girls in bolero blouses and bell-bottoms. Children jumped into gushing fire hydrants to escape the baking cement of the sidewalks, while mothers watched from their stoops, fanning themselves with newspapers. Row upon row of brownstone houses gazed with glinting window-eyes on the last of the children's play and the beginning of adult nightlife. Men "on-the-make" were strutting the streets in their leisure suits and polyester shirts, ready for a Friday night on the town. Three buttons open to the chest, gold chains around their necks and with hair blow dried to a wave of oestrogen-enticing perfection, they cat-walked their wares for all to see. Their dates swirled in hankie-sheer disco dresses; lips glossed to a sheen. With Mascara-smudged eyes and flaming cheekbones, they glided and girdled their partners in provocative dances while disco music pulsed from every club and bar along Eighth Avenue in Park Slope. This was Brooklyn, the place of my roots.

The moving van I'd rented had managed to find its destination, despite the driver swallowing a number of questionable medications. Travelling from the Bronx, I'd closed my eyes for most of the ride, hoping we wouldn't ram a guard rail on the Brooklyn Bridge. As the steaming van rolled to a bumpy stop in front of the only limestone townhouse on Carrol Street, I jumped from the cab, feeling a warm satisfaction. After unloading the few things I owned, I was left to peer out the window of my new second floor apartment at the street below. I'd come home again, after a turbulent and frightening affair. I could just hear my departed mother's voice, nagging me on to frustration. "*I didn't raise you this way. Couldn't you see what he was like?*" But of course, the answer to that was a definite "No". I'd been in love and that old quip about not seeing "the forest for the trees" was really on target. The object of my misguided affection was not the gentle, foreign farm boy I'd perceived him to be. Rather, he'd turned out to be a low scale Al Capone from the Black Forest of Serbia. When we'd met, I could hardly guess the shady dealings that would become routine, when his friends came to dinner. Of course, I couldn't understand a word of what they said but, .357 Magnums and copious bags of what seemed to be industrial sized oregano, were a dead give-a-way to his main source of income.

I suppose I considered myself lucky not to understand their language. After all, what I couldn't repeat wouldn't hurt me. I began very quickly to plan a route of escape. Unfortunately, it hadn't occurred to me at the time that this particular group of immigrant gangsters considered those in their inner circle "property". Once theirs in any way, one could never leave. When all of this finally sunk in, I must say it came as a bit of a shock. A dyed-in-the-wool Brooklyn girl, I was used to certain freedoms and had no intention of becoming a slave to a Serbian drug cartel. Yes, my mother was right; I wasn't raised that way. With that in mind, I left the Bronx in a hurry, leaving no forwarding address. The few people I told of my whereabouts were sworn to secrecy, knowing full well the ramifications of loose lips. I hired the first inexpensive moving van I could find (dubious driver notwithstanding) and returned to Brooklyn and a new life. Looking at the twilight resting over Carroll Street, I said a silent prayer: "Dear God, if I ever decide to fall in love again, if he's a loser, please send me a sign!"

Days passed into weeks, and so on to months, and in this time I met and fell in love with the man 1 would marry. He was a clerk on Wall Street; a nine-to-fiver with no obvious undertones of life-threatening pursuits, or felonious penchants. He was a stabilizing presence to my Bohemian persona. Those of my friends not proffering the "free love" premise were all getting married and it seemed my time had arrived. Marriage, I thought, would be my next step in life's passing parade. He seemed the right person at the right time so, when he proposed I said "Yes". It wasn't long before time and bliss eroded the memory of the seedy group I'd left behind.

My neighbours took great delight in my new relationship. Brooklyn was a homey place. Neighbours watched out for each other, lamenting each other's misfortune and delighting in their happiness. My immediate neighbour was Connie, who lived in the apartment adjacent to mine. Connie was newly divorced and loving it. As it turned out, her father was a Mafia Don, of whom she was most proud. In Connie's eyes, her Daddy could do no wrong. It was the most natural thing in the world for her to mention proudly, the "greaseballs" her father put to pasture. Despite this rather sinister familial bond, she was a laid back, middle aged, Italian hippie, who delighted in Zen, EST, group therapy and lasagne. To claim Connie was mellow was an understatement. A better word would be languid. Connie dispelled the stereotypical myth about fast talking Italians. She didn't even use her hands. I learned to talk slowly when I was with Connie, because it would take her a good three minutes to languidly reply to anything I said. She called me "Babe" and gained tremendous pleasure in furthering my education about men, counselling and sauces. I thought she was great. She was far too mellow to complain about my stereo.

As time went by and the news of my marriage spread, the entire neighbourhood became one unit in preparation for my wedding. My income was meagre in those days and my groom's wasn't much better. In view of this, my neighbours decided to assist me in holding a reception at my apartment. Several would cook, while others would decorate. Connie decided to be my beautician and do my hair. It was also decided to invite my landlady. Engaging her in the festivities would deter any complaints about noise. And so it went. The limestone was a beehive of anticipation and planning. I began to clean diligently and tried to make my rather "artsy" decor sparkle for the occasion. This really wasn't difficult, considering that my entire living room suite consisted of the triangular connecting piece of an old sectional covered in bright red naugahyde. This somewhat precarious seating I'd inherited from another Bohemian who'd relocated to Florida. Two orange crate end tables, a wall clock from Woolworth's and an eight-track stereo completed the ensemble. When I held parties, everyone sat on the floor or the windowsills and instead of lamps, we used candles stuck in wine bottles. It was an easy life, without stress. We fancied ourselves artists, and this was the Bohemian thing to do. It was also a great way to bypass a look of poverty, veiled under the guise of "artistic expression."

Now just about this time one of my trusted friends, had succumbed to my ex's vows of true love, and spilled the beans as to my whereabouts. One day, as I was polishing the naugahyde on the sectional, I heard a knock at the door. Thinking it was Connie with some marinara sauce or calamari, I threw it open with a big grin, only to find my ex. He was dressed in authentic gangland style of black on black. The angel of death had come to call. It didn't take him long to make his point. I was his property; was, am and always would be. End of story. At this point, I mustered as much Brooklyn vibrato as I could pull from my hyperventilating chest and told him that was impossible; I was getting married. He was far too quiet and I was fully aware that this was not a good thing. Then he smiled, which was an even worse response. All I needed now was a kiss of death to make it complete. Instead, he quashed his cigarette on my freshly washed floor and said, "If you marry this insect, I will kill you in the church. Marry and die!" With that, he turned a cool pivot in his Gucci's and left the way he'd come in. I looked at the crushed butt on my clean floor and thought, "I'm the walking dead".

It must be remembered that this was all in the days before the term "stalker" came into existence. Fact was that in Brooklyn, death threats were a way of life. To say "I'll kill you" was a colloquialism. Mothers said it to unruly children. Children said it to each other, when fighting over toys. Garbage men said it to trashcans that rolled downhill. It was a decidedly Brooklyn thing. But to be told by a drug thug that you would be blown away on your wedding day was a serious threat. This was right up there with Mafia "sit downs" and car bombs. Fleeting visions of every urban gangland slaughter I'd ever seen on film were fortifying my anxiety. I was convinced that I was about to die. It didn't take long for me to break the gruesome news to the neighbours, and those I didn't tell soon heard it from others. My wedding suddenly became the event of the century. Long before Diana and Charles' fanfare, there was the legend of the "Brooklyn Church Massacre". There wasn't a soul on Carrol Street who didn't plan to attend. The next night, as I sat morosely in Connie's kitchen, choosing hairstyles and sipping a red wine, she offered me her greatest gift.

"Listen Babe. Ya only got a few days left 'til ya get hitched." She pulled a long drag on a Virginia Slim. "Why don'tcha lemme have my Daddy's boys take him out for ya? It'll be my wedding present."

Now what can one possibly say to a gift like that? Such macabre generosity was overwhelming! I swallowed my wine before I sprayed it, thinking quickly. Despite how badly I wanted him gone, I wasn't about to have him sunk in the East River. There was also an unspoken law, which made one accountable to repay a debt of that magnitude, gift or no gift. Then too, there was the chance that a refusal would be misconstrued, and it was bad enough having the Serbian Mafia after me. I certainly didn't want to tick off the Italian one as well!

"Connie, I don't know what to say. It's just too much!" My gratitude was blatant.

"No, really Babe. It's no problem. Get da grease-ball out-a ya life, and no more headaches. Wad-a-ya say. It's a gift?"

What I said was that I could never repay a gift so great, and that I would never feel equal to the giving. I thanked her profusely, and declined with humble grace.

"Well, I can see dat." She nodded slowly, as she took another languid draw. "But if ya change yer mind Babe, just lemme know".

With a further elaborate show of thanks, I inched my way to the door and made a shaky path to my own apartment, where I slid to my bed like warmed jello. Suddenly my life was reading like a Mickey Spillane novel. I fell asleep with dizzying visions, of cement overshoes and tommy-guns.

Next morning, and four days till the hit, I woke to the phone ringing. It was my big brother George, calling from the Catskills. George was a man's man. He worked three jobs, never complained, and gave judo lessons on his day off to fragile females. He also had a brilliant reputation, for drinking the best of them under the table when the occasion called for it. George was devoutly spiritual and patriotic to a fault. His four-wheel drive boasted stickers from "The American Rifle Association", "The National Guard" and "The Veterans of Foreign Wars". A crack marksman, his favourite T-shirt read, "America – Love It, or Allow Me to Help You Leave It". Below this was a vivid picture of a Swiss carbine. He was fiercely protective of his ideals, as well as his family, who he'd moved upstate and, away from city violence. But my favourite knowledge of George was knowing he bought hamburgers for stray cats and dogs. In other words, he was a big mush, who tried hard not to show it.

With parents deceased, I'd need him to give me away at the wedding. I didn't really think he'd mind giving me away to anyone. My left-wing lifestyle was a constant reminder to my right-wing brother that there was a dissident in the family. He constantly worried that I would never "find myself" (as I was apt to try, repeatedly.) It would be far easier for him to pawn me off on someone who could help me look. Naturally, he said he'd do it, and I eventually relayed the news of the death threat. He paused before asking, "OK, tell me.

Which side do I stand on when we walk down the aisle?" I said I wasn't sure, so he said, "Well, I sure don't know. It's been years since I did that, and I was slightly tanked to do it. Just find out, and let me know. Don't worry kid. Just be ready to get married".

   This should have put my mind at rest but, his words somehow provoked a case of cold feet. Was I really ready to get married? A primitive inner voice, the one which triggers flight-reflex, was whispering to me. I woke during the night and looked at all the trappings spilling from their boxes. I gaped at my wedding gown and luscious train and thought, "I don't know about this." I had to wonder if it was all worth it. By dawn however, I'd convinced myself that everyone feels this way (how much more so, those facing pending death?). I decided I'd go through with it, though I had a hard time maintaining reasoning on a continual basis. Which is why the night before my wedding, I couldn't sleep at all. The following day I would either be a dead legend or a trapped wife. This isn't what I'd envisioned the apex of my adult experience to be. I drank some brandy, and finally fell asleep, as the light of morning began to slink across Carrol Street.

   I'd chosen Indian summer for my ceremony, anticipating the weather to be mellow. But morning didn't bring golden rays of autumn sun, rather storm clouds, thick enough to cover the Manhattan skyline. My brother arrived by then, and waving off my mumbling about omens, began asking me on which side he should escort me. By now, I was beginning to lose patience with him. It was important, of course, but not as important as avoiding being a great, white target. I began thinking that being abandoned at the altar wasn't as bad a fate as some would imagine. But one last look in the mirror warmed me to the fancies of married life. I was beautiful, my groom was waiting and everything would be made right in a brief hour. For a while I was removed from wedding anxiety and hit men and transported to the fairyland of childhood fantasy. I was a bride! I made my way to the waiting car, past the decorations of white roses and crepe paper streamers left by my neighbours.

   The church was merely down the street and on the corner, but to hold with tradition and, to accommodate the crowds of neighbours who had turned out for the affair, we decided to ride the circumference of the block, and on to the church. Outside, a gathering of people to match that of Times Square on New Year's Eve, filled the sidewalks and road. No doubt, they wanted to see the action when the shooting began, but I was deluded enough in that moment, to believe they were there to see my ultimate moment of stunning beauty. By the time I'd piled into the waiting cars with my wedding party, we were hit with monsoon winds and rain. The crowd, not to be dissuaded by a mere breeze and a sprinkle, covered their heads with umbrellas, newspapers and brown bags. After all, this was Brooklyn, and these people had come for a show.

George was driving his "family" car, a boat of a station wagon with room enough for the whole wedding party. It was reserved for me however, so as not to crumple my full gown. "Which church is it?" asked George, peering into the back seat at me, while I flounced in my cloud of gown, and waved to the crowd. Carrol Street was flanked at either corner by two churches, St. Ignatius R.C. to one, and Lutheran Lamb of God to the other. I directed him to St. Ignatius and with windshield wipers straining, the boat slowly made its way through the throngs of wet, eager people in the road. I felt like a salmon swimming upstream against the tide. George was trying very hard not to roll over an onlooker, and I could hear him swearing quietly at the cheering crowd.

After thirty minutes of manoeuvring through the masses, George finally reached the church and assisted me from the car. Gale winds wrapped me like a cocoon in my gown and veil. George (usually a force to be reckoned with) was lifted, clinging to the church door while I practically hopped over the threshold to safety. So far, so good. A quick look around the rear of the church showed no sign of henchmen, and we went forward with renewed anticipation.

When we finally arranged ourselves for the procession, the organist had begun "Here Comes The Bride" for the third time. George, apparently no longer caring on which side he escorted me, took my left arm and away we went. I hardly felt a step as George guided me to the altar. The priest was a free spirit who flew small engine planes for a hobby, which convinced me I'd chosen the right man of the cloth. Peering at me he asked, "How'd ya come, by canoe?"

The ceremony began, and I, in a state of shock, tried zealously to place the ring on my groom's finger, without success. The priest stage-whispered to the groom: "Help her. Help her!" With a twist I was sure had dislocated a knuckle, the ring finally went on. He said he did, I said I did, and there was nothing left, save the priest asking, "If anyone knows why this man and woman should not be joined in marriage, let them speak now or forever hold their peace". No sooner had he spoken than a clap of thunder sounded above, equal to a sonic boom. It was loud enough to rock the pews and titter the stained glass. There was a noticeable gasp from the guests, as the priest raised his eyes upwards, then slowly gripped me in a long, hard, stare. He sighed once more and said, "I now pronounce you man and wife," but I thought I saw him shake his head, ever so slightly.

It was done. I was alive, as well as married, and there was nothing left to do but celebrate. The rain had stopped, the sun shone again on Carrol Street and all was right with the world. Back at the limestone, Connie waited on the stoop, Virginia Slim dancing languidly on her lower lip. She puffed a cloud through a big grin when she saw me and said, "Hey Babe. Ya made it. Looks like da grease-ball chickened out!"

I had the best reception, ever. It's been thirty-eight years and people are still talking about it. George still says it was the best one he ever attended. It began at one o'clock in the afternoon and lasted 'til six am the next morning. Naturally, there weren't enough seats so people had to use each other's laps, and that made for more familiarity than most receptions get with table arrangements. Somebody managed to sit in the bottom tier of wedding cake, and served butter cream from her derriere, to anyone who wanted a lick. My landlady, not to be outdone, managed to polish off a bottle of rye by herself. The last I saw of her, she was weaving out the door with one of the ushers, singing "He's my man, and I love him." I never had one complaint about the noise.

By six am the next morning, as I closed the door and surveyed the debris, George asked me, "Was that the last of them?" I nodded and sighed.

"Good. Then I can take this off." It was then that his insistence on knowing which side of the aisle to escort me became clear. He undid his tuxedo jacket and removed a shoulder holster. My mouth dropped.

"Hell," said George (sounding very much like John Wayne), "I wasn't going to let my kid sister get blown away on her wedding day!"

Well, that's it; the story of my very Brooklyn wedding. There is one small footnote. Several days later, an article appeared in The Park Slope Tribune:

"Brooklyn, NY. Park Slope – Five men were arrested at 'Lutheran Lamb of God' Church, last Saturday. The men were discovered lying beneath the rear pews of the church by a cleaning lady, early Saturday morning. Juana Chavez, of 259 Prospect Place, notified the 63rd Precinct. The men were arrested on illegal substance and weapons charges. They have been identified as members of a Serbian drug cartel, operating out of the Bronx. Bail was set at $100,000 dollars. They are being held in Brooklyn House of Detention, pending trial."

So it seems the Serbian Mafia went to the wrong church. My "ex" never was very good with directions.

My marriage didn't last by the way, but as experiences go it was worth the lesson learned. I think 1 know more about love now than when I lived in Brooklyn. There's an old joke about a man who's drowning at sea, and refuses the help of a boat and plane because he says that God will rescue him. When he drowns and goes to heaven, he asks God why he let him drown, and God says, "You Fool. I sent you a boat and a plane." Next time I ask for a sign, I intend to pay attention.

At any rate, it was a swell reception; the best Brooklyn reception in memory. Terrible marriage, wrong partner and rite of passage aside, it was a slice of life; the stuff memoirs are made of. If nothing else, it's a hell of a tale to tell the grandchildren, on a rainy day.

The Last Haircut
by Marlon S. Hayes

He didn't like to drive to the barber shop he'd owned for the last forty-six years, but Charlie Morris had decided to drive the six blocks today. Any other day, he'd have preferred walking, letting his mind and memories flow as he strolled in a relaxed manner through the neighborhood he'd loved and known all the years of his life. Today would be Charlie's last day of being a professional barber, and he had two matching suitcases in his trunk, suitcases his wife had insisted on only a year before.

"The old ones are used up and raggedy," Shirley had declared. "We ain't used up and raggedy, Charlie, and I don't like arriving at hotels or the airport with hobo luggage."

Of course he'd done his usual, and agreed to whatever she wanted. Charlie had only put his foot down about going to do the actual shopping with her. He had known only too well that Shirley would insist on going to at least three or four stores in search of whatever luggage she'd envisioned in her mind, and he knew his frustration would have turned him into a cranky old man. She'd have laughed at his consternation, and out of spite, she'd have had him drive back to the first store they'd visited to buy the luggage. He'd have been grinding his teeth by that time, so he'd flat out told her to go alone. She'd laughed at his response, knowing all of his reasons for not going. She'd bought a beautiful, burgundy set of luggage, which included two large suitcases, a smaller one, and a carry-on bag. They'd only gotten to use it once, and she'd been on his mind as he packed his most valuable things into the suitcases.

The neighborhood had changed so much in the years since he'd started working at the barber shop. He'd been twenty-one when the previous owner, Mr. Arnold, had given the young man fresh out of the Army a permanent job and a chair of his own, but that was because Mr. Arnold had been the one to push him into becoming a barber. Charlie had gone into the shop when he was fourteen and asked for a job. Mr. Arnold had sized him up, a teenaged boy with clean clothes, even if they were somewhat shabby. Charlie's mannerisms were polite and respectful, which impressed the older man, and he'd started sweeping up hair and polishing the chairs the very next day.

When he was twenty-five, Mr. Arnold had sold the shop to him. After the paperwork had been signed, Mr. Arnold gave him the keys to the shop, and put his hand on Charlie's shoulder. There were tears in the old man's eyes.

"I'd seen you around the neighborhood before you ever even came in the shop asking for a job," Mr. Arnold said. "I didn't know your name or anything about you, but from the raggedy haircut you had, I thought to myself that you must not have no daddy, because no man woulda let they son walk around looking like that. When you came and asked for a job, you were polite, and your clothes were clean. It made me think that someone must love you and that times was rough. I took a chance on you, and you turned out to be a good boy. You'll do fine."

Mr. Arnold had patted his shoulder, and left out of the shop. Charlie had never seen the old man again, but he knew he'd returned to Alabama, which he had left as a young man. Forty-six years later, the name painted on the front of Charlie's barbershop still read 'Arnold's,' in homage to the man who'd been a mentor and friend to a fatherless boy. Charlie grinned as he made a left turn onto the street where the shop was located. Part of the deal he'd agreed to with the new owners was a stipulation that the barbershop still be named 'Arnold's.' It hadn't been a problem at all.

It was only eight in the morning, but the parking spaces on the street in front of the shop were already filled. The three other barbers who worked in the shop worked by appointment only, and their days started at six in the morning. They were enterprising young people, all of them in their mid-twenties. As much as Charlie had taught them, they'd probably be surprised at how much he had learned from them.

He parked the late-model Lincoln at the end of the block. He stepped out of the car and just stood there, looking around. When he'd been a boy, there had been plenty of businesses lining the wide boulevard. There'd been a shoe shine and repair shop, a mom and pop grocery store, two soul food restaurants that had held lively competitive promotions, a tailor, a boutique, a pawn shop, two beauty salons, and of course, Arnold's. Now, the street had a few vacant lots, a payday loan store, a fried chicken joint, and the barbershop. There was talk of revitalization and gentrification, but Charlie wouldn't be there to see whatever it was that might happen. His plan was to hit the highway in the early evening, and drive for an hour or two before stopping at a roadside motel to spend the night. He had a long drive waiting for him, and he planned on relaxing and doing his best to enjoy the journey as much as he could.

The last time he'd undertaken this road trip, it had just been him and Shirley, the one-time they'd gotten to use the luggage. He'd left the shop in the hands of the three young barbers for two weeks, from before Christmas until after New Year's Day. They'd meandered down to Charleston, South Carolina, where their oldest boy Chuck lived with his wife and three of his four kids. They'd had an absolute blast, relaxing in the mild weather, and for Christmas, their other two children, Tracy and Adam, had arrived with their families. It had felt good to be fussed over, and his kids had asked him how much longer he would work. They all lived in, or near Charleston, and at the time, he'd had no immediate plans to retire, so he couldn't give them any type of answer. Sometimes life takes a left turn when it's least expected.

They'd been back from Charleston for a month, and he'd been wondering how much longer he'd be able to deal with the harsh, brutal cold of Chicago. He and Shirley had been discussing making the move, and even though they hadn't made a firm decision, he knew it would probably be their last winter in the only city they'd ever lived in. The house they lived in had been paid off for twenty years, and they had money in the bank. They talked of buying a condo, or maybe a small house in Charleston, where they could take walks along the ocean, or visit some of the restaurants where the kids had taken them to eat.

It had come out of nowhere; he told the doctors later. Shirley had woken up with a headache, which was odd, because she rarely had any kind of illness. She'd shooed him on his way, telling him she'd take an aspirin and maybe put a cold rag on her forehead. He'd went to the shop, and immersed himself in the talk of women, politics, the crap music the kids listened to, and the familiar rhythm of cutting hair. He called home around noon, and Shirley hadn't answered. He'd had an uneasy feeling all of a sudden, and he left the shop, walking home as brisk as his old legs would carry him.

He'd found his sweetheart lying on the kitchen floor. He dialed 9-1-1 immediately, and sat down on the floor, trying to revive her. Her hands had been cold to his touch, and he knew the light in his life had been extinguished. He bent over her, kissing her forehead, as his tears poured out of him. The paramedics had arrived within five minutes, but there hadn't been anything they could do. They'd enjoyed forty-eight years of marriage, and in a flash, it was over.

After the funeral and burial, he'd had a talk with his children about his plans. It wasn't so much a discussion as it was a statement. He would sell the shop and buy a small house near Charleston, where he could be close to them without living with anyone. He put his plans into motion immediately, and by the time he signed the paperwork to sell the shop, he'd already purchased a small townhouse in Charleston.

The shop was full when he entered, and they greeted him with almost a chorus of "Hey, Pops." One of his oldest customers, Quick Eddie, was sitting in his chair awaiting his arrival. He'd been cutting Eddie's hair for at least forty years, and the man had never changed his hairstyle, regardless of whatever new trend was happening in the world. The only difference in his hairstyle now was that it had gotten mighty thin at the top. Charlie put on his smock, and all thoughts of what lay ahead for him went out of his head, as the professionalism of his craft took over.

It was almost a routine day at the shop, as the hustlers came in, paying their respects to Charlie, while selling everything from phone chargers, Mexican corn, cigars, t-shirts, real cologne, and tamales. Charlie only had a few rules when it came to the peddlers, and they were strictly adhered to. Fake jewelry, knock-off products, and drugs weren't allowed to be sold in his shop. He also had a rule that any hustler who made sales in his shop had to deposit ten percent of whatever they'd made into his bucket before they left. No one complained, because on any given day, they could make a killing selling their wares at the barbershop.

Charlie took his time cutting Eddie's hair, and when he was finished, he brushed the hair off of him, and they hugged after Charlie had been paid. Eddie left, and Charlie's chair remained vacant for almost an hour. These days, he only cut the hair of his regular clients, and the heads of small children. On the average, he might give five or six haircuts in a ten-hour day, whereas the three young barbers who worked in his shop averaged three clients an hour. Each of them was skilled and talented, and Charlie marveled at how they did the crazy new styles with elan and efficiency.

He watched with a smile of appreciation, as one of them, a young woman named Cheryl, created designs on a young man's head, while at the same time keeping up a ceaseless flow of witty and engaging conversation. He beamed with pride and admiration as she cut the hair of young men and women (which he'd never thought he'd see!), getting them in and out of the shop like a well-oiled machine. He was positive that the young woman, the first to ever work in his shop, might be the best barber he'd ever seen.

Over the course of the rest of the day, he cut a couple of heads, gave a couple of shaves, exchanged handshakes and hugs, all while the conversation one could only find at a barbershop flowed without ceasing. Nostalgia threatened to make him cry because the conversations would be what he missed the most. The barbershop had always been a special place in the neighborhood, and he was positive that it held that same reverence in every Black community in America.

At a quarter to six, Charlie finished cutting the head of a local pastor, Reverend Smith. When they hugged, the reverend whispered a prayer in his ear for safe travels, and Charlie appreciated the gesture. The reverend had presided over Shirley's home going ceremony, and even though Charlie didn't attend the church on a regular basis, the man had come to his house to sit with him in the aftermath of Shirley's passing. Such things were not forgotten.

He cleaned his area with the same care and detail as he had for five decades. He packed up his equipment, and sat down in his chair, watching as the three young barbers finished their last customers. When the last person had exited the shop, Cheryl locked the door, and flipped the sign over from 'Open' to 'Closed.' She grinned at him, and he smiled at her in return.

The other two barbers cleaned their stations, gathered their things, then shook his hand and gave him heartfelt hugs before departing the shop, leaving him alone with the young woman. Their eyes met, and as she walked towards him, he dug in his pocket. When she was two feet from him, he held out the keys to the shop, the shop which she now owned. She blinked back tears as she accepted the keys. She put them in the front pocket of her jeans, and looked at him with her head tilted to the side.

"Can I give you a haircut?" she asked in a soft voice.

Without saying anything, he walked over to her chair and sat down. He'd been cutting his own hair since he was sixteen, and the only haircut he'd received from someone else had been when he'd arrived for Army Basic Training back in the late sixties. She covered him with a protective cloth, tying it securely, but not too tightly around his neck. Their eyes met in the mirror, and he closed his eyes when she turned on the clippers.

Her soft hand was gentle on his head, as she turned his head slightly. The soothing buzz of the clippers were almost hypnotic, and Cheryl began to softly sing an old, familiar song. The song was 'My Girl,' by the Temptations, and he immediately thought of his beloved Shirley. His mind flipped through the years, remembering their passionate courtship, their wedding, the births of their children, and later, their grandchildren. He felt the tears began to leak from his closed eyes, as his heart sang along to the soft words being spoken from the young woman's soul.

Cheryl stopped singing, and a few heartbeats later, she turned the clippers off. She turned the chair towards the mirror, and he opened his eyes. Their gazes met in the mirror, and he could see the tears leaking from her soulful, brown eyes, eyes that mirrored those of her grandmother's, his only sweetheart.

"Is it okay, Grandad?" she asked, her soft voice tremulous.

Charlie's smile went from ear-to-ear. He knew that she was his favorite grandchild, but he would never say that out loud. She'd been coming in the shop since she was a toddler, and he knew that he was her hero. He'd told her what the red and white striped barber pole stood for, and he'd showed and taught her everything he knew about his craft. When her father Chuck had moved to Charleston, she was adamant about staying in Chicago and working with her grandfather in his shop, which now belonged to her.

"You know what, Cheryl Lee?" Charlie asked. "I think this is the best haircut I've ever received. You'll do fine."

The young woman who'd been named after her grandmother, beamed at him, and he could see his Shirley in her smile. Life goes on, he thought, but 'Arnold's' barbershop was in good hands…

There He Is
by Michael Tuffin

There he is.

Not a surprise, not really. He was always there at that time. Gradually, I had grown to enjoy spotting him. Trying to be in the right place at the right time; making it a game. Although his presence could not have been described as "clockwork", exactly, there was always a comforting regularity to his travels. Come rain or shine.

And did observing that repetition, having fun trying to imagine the background behind the routine, give me a distraction to my own life? Possibly.

Even though I could not empathise with the man, was it wrong to take comfort, even feel some kind of superiority, whilst looking down on him? Absolutely.

To set the scene: I'd be washing dishes in the sink in the upstairs flat I shared with my girlfriend, Lauren. Whilst drying dishes over the draining board, I would glance at the digital clock on the microwave. I had a routine of my own back then; setting that clock to tick over the minutes exactly in time with my phone. And when the red digital numbers read anything past 11:00 I'd be keen to glance out the window in front of me.

And there he'd be, walking past on the other side of the quiet tree-lined street. I am no good at guessing ages, but I'd say late-50s. Uncaring in his gait, maybe even slightly determined. But oblivious to me watching, of course.

I'd point him out to Lauren, who usually took a passing interest in his routine, but not enough to wait around for the return trip.

I knew it would only be a matter of a few minutes until he was walking back. The amount of time differed slightly, depending, I assumed, on how busy the shop was.

There was only one in the direction he walked, and it was opposite a train station. At 11am, close to peak lunchtime hours, it would be busy with workers and commuters wanting sandwiches and pastries.

His walk back was always the same, too. No bag of groceries, oversized chocolate bars, frozen meat, wrapping paper, or novelty plush toys. Just a bottle of wine – always red – in his left hand, swinging slightly. Always just that one bottle of wine; until it became something else – a clear bottle and a clear liquid. Walking slightly more slowly, less steadily, with a head more bowed than on previous return journeys. Personally, I always wondered if he would have acted differently had he known he was being watched.

Probably not, I know now.

For some reason, I never mentioned seeing his return journey, or his single piece of shopping, to Lauren. Maybe there was some empathy, after all. Can a feeling of superiority birth a feeling of embarrassment for someone?

During that time back then I often wondered about following him. I'm not sure what that would have achieved, though. Just to see where he went, and what that place looked like? Would it add anything to my story of him? Maybe it would make him more "human", and not just some kind of organic metronome.

I bet his routine continues to live on as we speak, so I could easily go back to that street, at around the right time, and pick up where we left off. Maybe see what it is that he carries now.

To go back to that street.

Because as happens in life, Lauren and I eventually moved to a new home together. So for a while I forgot all about him, and the small details of the street I used to look out on slowly faded away. I became immersed in my new life, and new shift working patterns.

Once, after a particularly rough late-into-morning shift – maybe testing the waters of other's normality – I asked a co-worker (a non-shift working co-worker, I hasten to add) if buying beer at 7am was "wrong". She replied no, but drinking it at that time would be.

Ha. She didn't know the life of the shift worker. Spending your weekend evenings working, and coming home to the start of your own weekend at 7am on a Monday morning, just as your partner is getting ready to start her work week.

It's an odd concept, when considered against other people's weekends; the Friday 5pm whistle blowing and everyone downing tools. For post-work drinks, it doesn't matter what time it is really, it's more about your circadian rhythm.

And that was how I justified it to myself.

Regardless of the actual time, I had worked my hours. It was just a post-work "evening" to me (I bet there are shift workers reading this right now who feel the same; 0700 is a number to us. It's agnostic of day, night, brightness, or darkness).

What started as a cool beer at the end of a shift, became a beer and a glass or two of wine at the end of a shift. Then what started as... well, you get the picture. Anything after a shift, just became my normality. And increased.

And then things changed. Again.

Not unlike the changes with a house move, there are also changes with a job move; be it up (yay!), across (ok), or down (oh). I moved off shifts back to your common-or-garden 9 - 5 work, making this actually a move down in pay once shift allowance was removed.

And this is where being a creature of habit – euphemism – can alter your normality. The end-of-shift-early-morning-but late-to-me drink had been set as a routine. It was normal. And even though I was no longer on shift work, so didn't have a totally legitimate reason for visiting my local corner shop in the morning, I still did.

I'm right-handed. But on the way home, for some reason, it felt more comfortable to carry my bottle – back then what started as red wine is no longer adequate, so currently it is a much more clear, stronger liquid – in my left hand. And I had to plan the places to hide it so Lauren wouldn't see it. She sometimes did.

Now I saunter back to that empty house, head bowed. On the way I have to pass the outside of a very run-down butcher shop. With it being so dark inside, the windows have a reflective quality. I avoid looking. My left hand swinging would be directly reflected in the window, and I don't want to see it, even though I'm painfully aware of it.

Unknown to me, just as it was to him then, there is someone watching. Looking down.

That someone isn't washing dishes, nor conjuring up elaborate back-stories for a protagonist in their personal story; she's just a child, scribbling in a colouring book next to her bedroom window. And of course, like some kind of vicious inevitability, that window is also on the second floor.

Over a period of time, this girl also picks up routines and patterns. A stranger who appears at roughly the same time daily, and carrying something. She's too young to know what. I don't hurry. There's no need to rush, I have all the time in the world now; no job and no person waiting.

"Look!! There he is" she enthusiastically shouts to her uninterested mum, who's away in a different room.

There I am.

Going Home
by Daniel Amoah

For many young and mostly male migrants from the poorer parts of the world, the grass is always greener in the "West". For some, life in the "West" has been an unimaginable improvement in their personal and material well-being, but for others it has been a journey fraught with crises of belonging, identity, assimilation and on occasion even a questioning of the "greener pastures" appeal of the host country.

Flight BA078, on which Joseph Asante was travelling, landed on time at 05:30 at *Kotoka International Airport* in Ghana's capital, Accra. British Airways is renowned for punctuality so that he had expected. However, what Joseph Asante had not expected was such warm and humid weather so early in the morning.

It had been ten years since Joseph had won a scholarship to study Theology in England, a matter which pleased his parents enormously, as they had always prayed that one of their three sons would became a "man of the cloth". Joseph, being the youngest child, reminded his devout Christian parents of the Biblical Joseph, and his eventful but triumphant career in Egypt, rising from prisoner to Prime Minister.

In his early years in London he had written regularly to Dora, his girlfriend in Ghana, but the frequency and intensity of their correspondence had reduced over the years and had almost stopped. He had hoped to finish his studies in three years and then return home to teach at the Catholic seminary school near his hometown, but alas, Joseph hadn't fully reckoned with how hard he would have to work to survive life in London and pay his board and lodgings and his college fees. Three years had somehow expanded into ten. That was how long it was that he had consoled a tearful Dora at this same airport that three years wasn't a long time and he'd be back before she knew that he was gone.

Joseph had been lost in his own thoughts since the plane landed and hardly said a word to the taxi driver, beyond giving him his destination and throwing his coat on the back seat.

"I left Ghana in the prime of my youth for England to study Theology," he told the grey-haired smartly dressed taxi driver by way on introducing himself. "I was barely twenty when I left these shores, and now at thirty years old I have returned to my roots to settle down, if I can cope with this heat."

"Oh I see, you were young and adventurous then, but now you are a returnee man of God," the taxi driver replied, more out of courtesy than in agreement with Joseph that the weather was hot. "This is the harmattan season sir", he teased, "the winds blow south from wintry Europe, so this time of the year it is much cooler for us." He said "it is much cooler for us" with a Ghanaian nuanced expression that politely suggested a dismissal of his passenger's discomfort with the heat. The freezing winter temperatures in Europe are beyond most people's imagination in tropical Ghana.

Joseph loosened his tie and undid his collar button. The taxi driver offered to turn on the air conditioning in the car, for which Joseph was thankful, but it didn't seem to make much difference to him, while probably freezing his taxi driver.

Joseph was quietly optimistic about his future, and looked forward to seeing Dora whom he hadn't heard from for about four years.

They had written lovingly and regularly to each other in the first five or so years, long and tender letters about what was going on in their lives in their respective countries.

"Joe, you have been gone five years and your absence leaves me yearning and broken hearted, yet I have no idea when or if I will ever see you again. I can't stop loving you and I hope you are not taking me for granted."

Joseph's taxi finally reached his parents' house at Aburi, north of the city, to a tumultuous welcome. There was a lot of catching up to do, parents and siblings to explain to why it had taken him so long to return, new nieces and nephews to get to know, and of course reunions with old friends – especially Dora.

He had brought her some presents and planned to see her soon, perhaps on Saturday, which gave him a few days to acclimatise.

The night was mercifully cool and long entering that Saturday, but Joseph felt jittery and hadn't slept well all night. He had also been woken up early by the dawn chorus of cocks crowing throughout the entire neighbourhood, and the sound of a woman sweeping the compound whilst humming a popular church hymn. Joseph smiled and stretched himself in bed. This was home, as he had always known it.

Suddenly, he recalled a chat with his mum just days before he left for London, as she had sat at the foot of the same bed he was lying in.

She rarely came to his room except when his father, who never said much, was displeased with something or other the children had done and complained to her. She would then go and talk to the children to smooth ruffled feathers, so Joseph was a bit apprehensive when his mum came in that evening to talk with him.

"Joe, you know how I love to be a mother and grandma to all my children… If you brought me a half-coffee half-milk grandchild, I might not be able to be the best grandma I would like to be. I heard that those mixed blood children are delicate, they bruise easily, and they can't cope with our humid and warm weather. I overheard sister Mary say that…"

"Mum!" Joseph protested sharply, "I have not given a thought to marrying any European woman. You know I'll be back in three years to marry Dora."

Joseph's retort had surprised his mum. They both sat in silence for a while, and then she left.

He knew that his mum meant well, and wasn't speaking out of prejudice. She genuinely worried about the physical strength of mixed parentage babies. She simply wasn't that sort of person. As a devout Christian she kept an open house where complete strangers came to seek sanctuary and solace.

He couldn't believe that the conversation was ten years ago.

Joseph leapt out of bed as a fluttering flock of migratory birds landed on the mango tree behind his window and the birdsong and chirping rose to a deafening crescendo. He opened his window and it was a sight to behold, different species of birds all jostling for a place to perch. "Paradise," he muttered.

He stood outside Dora's house. It had been repainted and a metal gate installed. He wondered if the family had moved.

Nobody knows I am here and I would not be missed if I turned round and walked away, he thought, as he stood a few feet back. I am really an unexpected, maybe unwelcome visitor.

A blue crested bird with a bright yellow peak came to perch on the metal gates and started hopping and chirping noisily. Soon another similar one arrived and joined it with an excited and noisy display of their singing skills. Joseph took a few more steps back from the metal gate to enjoy the spectacle of what he assumed was a pair of courting birds flirtingly doing a love dance.

He stiffened his resolve, reminding himself that he hadn't come this far to give up outside Dora's house. He walked towards the gate, raised his hand to knock, but ended up only scratching his head instead.

With his thinning hair and a sprinkle of grey at his temples, Dora might not even recognise him. The thought filled him with dread and tilted the balance decidedly towards turning back and walking away.

The two lovebirds had quietened down a bit and Joseph could hear his heart pounding in his chest. The mid-day heat was getting to him and he perspired profusely and uncomfortably, a rarity if he imagined himself in London's December.

He walked back to the metal gate once more and took a deep breath while wondering if he had been arrogant, too self-assured in turning up unannounced. He flatly dismissed the notion. How could I have been, when I have brought a huge cargo of material comforts for both of them?

He banged on the gate with his clenched fist in a fit of impatience. The clanging noise reverberated through the metal and frightened the two lovebirds away. Joseph's heart was now pounding faster and louder as he waited. He worried he might have banged too hard but assured himself that it was a loud enough bang not to need a second one. He settled to wait for a while, then it suddenly hit him that Dora could be a happily married woman – after all it had been ten long years. What if her husband came to the gate? What if Dora herself came to the gate holding a baby in her arms? Too late to turn back, the die was cast. He was preparing himself to say "I am sorry but I knocked on the wrong door," if he was not welcomed by whoever came to the gate.

A passage from Dora's last letter flashed through his mind: "Joe, your absence leaves me heart-broken, yet I have no idea when or if I will ever see you again. I hope you haven't taken me for granted."

He pulled a handkerchief from his breast pocket and wiped his sweaty forehead and temples.

Just then, a pretty and smartly dressed young girl opened the gate. "Akwaaba" she said with a shy demeanour and a display of reverence that took Joseph by surprise, because he had prepared himself to expect the exact opposite.

He cleared his throat and swallowed hard. "I have come to see Dora," he said gently, hoping he managed not to sound stressed.

"Wait here please, I am going to get aunty."

Joseph mused at the "Akwaaba," (welcome) greeting from the young girl. Don't I look local enough? Good afternoon would have been just fine, but *welcome*? That is for complete strangers.

He caressed the gift parcel he had brought and imagined sitting next to Dora happily opening it.

It felt like eternity before a woman in her mid-thirties appeared at the gate. Joseph had sufficiently calmed himself down now and felt surprisingly confident and fluent.

"I am an old friend of Dora," he introduced himself. "We both attended the Catholic school up the hill, but I have been living abroad for..."

Just then a little boy of mixed race appearance came calling "Mummy! Mummy!" and wrapped his arms around the woman. His complexion was what his mum had referred to as "half coffee, half milk".

Joseph paused to let the woman give the child some attention. He was going to continue introducing himself, when the woman leaned forward and said softly, "Dora has gone home."

"Gone home," Joseph repeated absent-mindedly, "you mean, the family moved?"

The woman patted the little boy on the shoulder and steered him behind her.

"Dora died in childbirth three years ago," she continued, gently mothering the little boy behind her. "He calls me mummy because he doesn't know. His European father went back to his country soon after the baby was born."

Joseph gasped. He took a deep breath and was completely lost for words. With remorse and a sinking heart he realised he had indeed taken Dora for granted.

His distress must have been obvious to the woman, and as if to bring closure to the conversation, she whispered, "You must be Joseph."

Joseph's eyes filled with tears and his voice quivered as he bent down to take the little boy's hand and gently coax him forward. "What's your name?" he asked.

He replied shyly, "Joseph."

The Girl I Nearly Knew
by Lynn Braybrooke

I didn't give her a second thought until after I'd developed the film. She sort of sprang to life and demanded my attention like a spoiled brat, so that I couldn't rest until I'd remembered where I'd taken the shot. Every time I walked into my flat that picture tried to fall into my lap, or be the one thing I would see among the mountains of paperwork on my desk. I suppose she must have intruded on my thoughts for nearly a week, until I decided to enlarge the print.

I'd named her Sunny because I didn't know what her real name was. She was blond and tanned with freckles and seemed the kind of girl who smiled easily. Her face was somehow open and candid, and the more I looked at her photograph the more certain I became that she was the sort of person who fed stray dogs, liked absolutely everybody and probably talked to her plants. I wouldn't have minded a daughter like Sunny. All this I surmised from a postcard sized print that seemed to have a life of its own.

I'm not sure if I'm a journalist who likes photography or a photographer who likes to write. Either way I'm useful to the local rag on which I labour, in my capacity as both. My editor and I have long meaningful discussions about this that end abruptly the moment I mention money. We understand each other perfectly. He knows I love the job and so pays me as little as possible. Because I don't have a family to support I let him get away with it. He thinks he's cheating me, and I pick his brains all the time because there's not much to running a provincial newspaper that he doesn't know.

I suppose he had become a bit like a surrogate parent to me as my own parents were still living in the East End of London. They refused to be parted from Bethnal Green for more than two weeks of any year and thought me quite mad to want to live in the country. I couldn't share their devotion to the city, but I did miss them at times.

If I hadn't enlarged the photo of Sunny, I wouldn't have seen the man. I certainly hadn't noticed him at the time. I had been strolling around

Brighton in the sunshine, camera at the ready. It was Monday, my day off, and I was in no hurry nor in search of anything special for the paper, I was enjoying myself. I'd used a lot of film by the time I'd spotted Sunny. She was sitting astride a low brick wall eating fish and chips out of a cardboard tray. The wall was a circular affair, with heaps of shrubs within its perimeter, the kind of thing local councils feel enhance the landscape. She was so engrossed in eating that she hadn't noticed me until I was very close and had her in focus. She'd looked up then and laughed, holding out one single chip in offering, and I had taken the shot just like that. So here she is upon my wall, laughing at me and goading me into regret.

The man was on the far side of the circular wall and was in profile only. I thought uncharitably how much better my shot would have been if his profile had been on the other side of the channel. But for him, I might have been able to sell that photo. As it was, his gloom was such a contrast to her obvious love of life, that it just wouldn't do. I don't have any equipment to airbrush and as I quietly cursed him, my editor rang and I was dispatched to the police station A.S.A.P.

"Get down there Adam my boy!" He'd bellowed. "Find out what's going on, something's a-foot. Looks like another missing holiday maker, might be a drowning."

And I'd skipped breakfast and gone.

I already knew most of the local police officers and was pretty sure of getting a cup of coffee from one of them, but not so. When I arrived, there was only the duty officer at the counter and he looked as though he'd been there all night.

"Where is everybody?" I said.

"Bit of a panic on." He replied, throwing a look of despair in the direction of the DI's office.

"So," I said, "another holiday maker bites the dust?"

He was not in the mood for flippancy, he looked weary. I thought, I'd better get on with it.

"What have you got then?"

"Landlady reported one of her tenants has not returned since Monday last."

"Male or female tenant Bill? Part of a couple? People rarely go on holiday alone do they? How come it was the land lady who reported it?"

"She's not been seen since Monday," he said patiently ignoring my string of questions.

"Spoken to her parents, Bill? She might just have gone back home early. She could have gone off with some holiday Lothario."

Bill scowled at me as if I should know better than to ask such obvious questions. He was right but I had to ask.

"Is that it then?" I ventured.

"Yes, until the parents arrive we can't even circulate a picture."

"OK." I said, "Where was she staying?"

He gave me the address and I got as far as the door before I thought to ask what time the parents were due to arrive. Bill shrugged as if it was anybody's guess but there was a look on his face that I couldn't quite fathom. A kind of dread, maybe or fear – something I couldn't put a finger on, but I felt it.

Bill was not a complicated man. He was one of the very few policemen whose wife did not feel neglected and his pride in his daughters was almost a bore. Bill was a first class community copper, not MI5 material at all. His face told the story of his life. As policemen go, Bill was an open book. But there was something I'd never glimpsed before. I let it go and went to the address where the missing girl was staying.

The landlady turned out to be an enigma too. I judged her to be about fifty and she wore way too much makeup. She had a habit of smoothing her clothes all the time as if she were very particular about her appearance. The house was almost Spartan in its orderliness. "No children or pets," said the notice, and I believed it. She wore a blouse that was a flashy pink colour and had too many frills, the skirt looked like she'd been poured into it. But it was her face that startled, it was so cold. She wasn't going to let me into the building until I offered her a twenty pound note, then she hesitated just long enough for me to push the point.

"I only want to have a look in the girl's room," I said. "And the police have been and gone, it's not as if I'm going to touch anything." She stood aside, took the money then followed me into the room. Even though it was an intrusion into the girl's privacy, I wanted to look around by myself and anyway I didn't like that landlady. It wasn't just her cheapness, I'd known all my life that it usually masked characters with good hearts, but there was something soulless about her.

"You can't stay long," she said, pocketing my money. "The police might come back."

"The girl might come back," I reminded her. "What does she look like?"

"Well she's young," she replied with a bitterness I could almost taste.

"Is she on holiday alone?"

"She's not on holiday, she's a student. Been here two and a half months," she said. then added, "Art." There was so much contempt in that word, it made me shiver. I glanced around the room. There were some very good sketches of the local area, but apart from that the room was tidy without being quite like the rest of the house. It looked as if the girl had just gone out for a few hours. There was nothing to suggest she wasn't coming back, even the plants on the windowsill looked cared for.

I stopped dead, and somehow knew that this was Sunny's room.

"What's her name?" I asked, my mouth suddenly dry.

"Susan Gaskell." She almost spat the words.

I hesitated, then said, "Do you like her?" I was looking right into her face but my question didn't throw her at all.

"Oh, everyone likes her," she replied, smiling. It was the worst excuse for a smile I have ever seen. " Well she's blonde and beautiful and young, why wouldn't everyone like her? Just ask my husband," she added, as a man's footsteps sounded in the hall. So that's it, I thought.

The man who stood in the doorway was big with a surly expression that was tinged with something else I couldn't quite fathom. But I knew he was the man in my photograph and my heart sank. This was Sunny's room all right. He was carrying some old magazines, Playboy I noticed, and so did his wife.

"Been studying?" she drawled in a voice loaded with irony, "expanding your intellect? Must be all this intellectual influence here." She went on opening her arms to include the whole room. "I suppose a bloke as smart as you must long for a classical education eh?"

For a moment I thought he was going to hit her, but she was too strong for him. Not physically perhaps, but she had so much resentment festering away inside her that he would always shrink from her waspish tongue. There's a war going on here, I thought, with nothing as clean as armed combat. Theirs was a terrible battlefield, insidious, an undiluted poison. Whatever drew them together I couldn't begin to grasp and I wasn't sure I wanted to know.

"When was the last time you saw her?" I asked them both in an attempt to break through the tension.

"Last Monday morning," The woman replied, but her husband walked away giving no answer.

I wondered about that for a long time afterwards, and concluded that he didn't want to answer the question in front of his wife because unlike me she would know if he was lying. The painted face ushered me out. I didn't get much for my twenty quid, I thought. I decided to go to the college to see if I could find out more about the girl called Susan Gaskell. I desperately wanted to be wrong about this.

I passed the police station on the way there and decided to drop in. Bill was just going off duty as I arrived, and he didn't look any happier.

"Hi Bill," I called. "I've just met that couple the girl lodges with, what a win double they are." I shook my head. "You met them Bill? What a pair." He still had that vacant look on his face, but he turned then and looked at me.

"What do you mean?"

"Well I'm not sure." I said. "But I get the feeling that the husband knows more than he's letting on. God knows Bill, I didn't like the look of either of them. They're both a bit weird, sort of nasty. Hark at me I've no evidence just a gut feeling, what does the DI say?"

"Why don't you go and have a word with him Ads?" He said and went out the door. Clearly Bill had heard enough, I'd never seen him like this.

The station had become a hive of activity since my earlier visit, I just managed to grab the sleeve of a passing officer I knew by sight.

"Hey! Any news on the missing girl?" I said rushing to keep up with him.

"She's not missing, she's dead." He said matter-of-factly.

"But where? How?" He must have sensed the urgency in my voice, because he stopped then and looked at me.

"You don't want to know... really." He shook his head and moved away.

"For crying out loud!" I yelled. "How?"

"With a bloody crow bar by the look of her – well what's left of her." I could tell that he was as devastated as me. I felt sick, my head was swimming. I could have wept at the waste. What had I said? I wouldn't have minded a daughter like Sunny. I could see two shattered people as a door opened to my left and knew they were Sunny's parents. I wouldn't change places with them now. I sat down, I suppose in shock,

I didn't know what to do. Some reporter, I thought bitterly. I caught bits and pieces of conversation from time to time, they seemed to float in and out of my head along with Sunny's laughing face.

She had been found lying face down in a ditch, by an elderly man walking his dog. She had lost most of her blood through her injuries: She had been dead since Monday night: She hadn't been easy to identify: Her clothes were still missing: And I sat quietly and listened becoming more and more angry. How had she ever come to matter so much to me? I couldn't tell, I only knew I wanted someone to blame, someone to punish.

Eventually, I knew I'd have to go to work, a story is a story, however harrowing. But I didn't want to write this one in newspaper type copy. How could I express all this in jargon? An inner voice told me my feelings had nothing to do with it. Write the story; Go to work.

In my heart I knew the man in my photograph had killed her, the Playboy carrying landlord with the ghastly wife. The police would know this soon, they had ways of finding out, making the connections, collecting evidence. Yes they'd get to it, but I just knew. She would have been so easy to hurt, not like his hateful wife. Sunny would have been helpless, devoid of spite, vulnerable, easy to kill. In that moment I do believe I could have killed him myself. But what about the painted face? What about her part in this? Just who was responsible for the twisted mentality of that terrible excuse for a man.

I went home eventually and agonized all night between emotions of rage and despair. I know I didn't sleep. I got up about three-thirty and went for a walk. I don't remember how far I went or where. I saw the sun rise and thought, they'll arrest him today, but what of her? I found myself outside their house and fought the urge to go inside and murder them both. Instead I turned away, and as I moved, I saw movement behind the window. I walked on and waited out of sight of the house and watched.

The man who killed Sunny came out of the front door and got in his car. Where were the police I wondered, they must have this man under surveillance surely? The car pulled away, then speeded up and suddenly went out of control. I watched in disbelief as the thing careered off the road and hit the sea wall. It toppled over onto it's side and burst into flames immediately. No-one got out, it happened so quickly, I couldn't understand how, there was no other traffic at all. And like an idiot I just looked and did nothing.

Then I became aware of a car coming towards me. It passed the wreckage in slow deliberation, the driver looking intently at the blaze. It did not stop but slowly cruised away from the flames. As it passed me, I saw Bill smile quietly to himself.

The Case of the Worn Out Soap
by Slavko Mali

I've never been to a psychiatrist. And why should I? Like they know something? That drug addict Freud convinced the world that all mental problems are related to sex. And what am I missing?

I have never had sex, I am completely normal, I live nicely and stably. Mom and I drink tea with tea rings in the afternoon and watch series on TV. Then in the evening I put on my pajamas, and she puts on her nightgown, and we go to bed. We have the big double one, where Dad used to sleep with Mom, until he fell down the stairs and broke his neck. Since then, I have taken his place under the warm quilt.

Mom and I get along nicely. She strokes my hair like when I was little. Sometimes she lets me touch her naked warm breast. It reminds me of childhood and I fall asleep nicely.

The hardest thing for me is when I have to get up for work in the morning. My mother kisses me on the forehead at the door and says: "Be a good son today. Don't be afraid of them. They are just unfortunates."

He got up from the table and went to the sink, swallowed a couple of antidepressants and then started washing his hands. He rubbed the soap between his palms for a long time, until he created a huge mass of foam. Then he began to rinse them under a thin stream of warm water, slowly and thoroughly. He sat down at the table again.

And these psychotherapists are common tricksters. They put you on the couch, adopt a professional demeanor, take their notepads in their hands, and then they dig for your childhood ...

Did you hate your father? Did you love your mother more ...?

Well, it's perfectly normal to love your mother more. She gave birth to you. From that embarrassing thing between her legs. And she breast-fed you from her warm breast, which I can only touch in the dark when my mom and I go to bed ...

Yes, I hated my father. He dishonored and desecrated my mother, took away her innocence, that disgusting bully under whom the poor woman gasped and moaned, just for me to be born.

And why did I have to be born at all... like my existence helped someone? Like I fixed the world?

He opened the desk drawer and took out a small box of tranquilizers. He had already started to shake slightly. He went to the sink again and began to wash his hands. The soap thinned more and more each time, and kept slipping out of his hands, falling into the sink, which irritated him more and more.

"My mother is good," *he said, returning to the table.*

When I was little I had nightmares, and I would often get wet in bed. Then my mother would change my clothes and put me in her big double bed. I felt the warmth of her body calming me. Dad, who was sleeping next to her on the other side, was snoring like a pig, smelling of brandy and cigarettes.

And my mother smelled so nice, of lilac soap. That's why I only planted lilacs in the whole yard. As an eternal monument to my mother.

"Doctor, the patients are waiting for you," The nurse poked her head through the door. "They're already getting upset!"

"Let them wait, I can't help them anyway!"

He got up and nervously began to soap his hands. At one point the soap slipped from his fists and fell down on the white tiles. He moved backwards, stepped on it, and fell his entire length, hitting his head on the floor.

His consciousness blurred, and in his mind he saw the small worn-out soap on the floor in front of the wooden staircase in his house, on which his father had slipped. As he lost consciousness, he tried to remember how that soap bar was right there when his father died.

He heard relentless cries from the hallway: "Doctor, help me, you are a psychiatrist, no one believes me that I am not crazy ... it's not my fault, I'm not ... responsible ..."

Buddy Nickel and The Mistletoe Men
by Gareth Hywel Phillips

Part 1: Canteen

Buddy Nickel is an absurd name. When Buddy tells people, they say, "Buddy? Nickel?"

And he says, "Mm hmm". And they humph incredulously as if to say, *well, okay but I don't think that's your real name.* And he smiles, thinking (as the person who named him must have), *it is.*

"Come on, you must hear how it sounds! Like the frontman of a 50s doowop group or something," said his old boss when they first met, a great number of years ago. Buddy feigned ignorance and shrugged, the way he always responds to evaluations of his name. But he knows how his name sounds, and has always found it amusing that his name suggests he might be the frontman of anything.

Buddy believes that autobiographies should begin with a humorous reflection on one's name. He remembers hearing that your name is the oldest part of you – that is, the *you* that is rendered in the imagination of someone who hears your name. He believes that the other part of *you*, which is not named, is much older.

"The quiche," says Buddy, holding the exact change in his hand. The hot-food counter spread is pitiful: a tray of mucilaginous *brown*, seven straggles of dry oven chips, and a pale quiche. His right hand tingles from the emanating warmth of the hot-food counter, and his face seems to glow with seraphic light.

This is the present. He thinks and repeats. *This is the present. If I were to inexplicably finish my autobiography now, I could write no further than this present moment: feeling hungry, my hand tingling, and the sense that everyone in this canteen, to whom my back is turned, is looking at me. This is the present. I hand the cashier the money. The end.*

The cutlery rattles precariously on his plate as he finds a table. There are a number of available tables; the canteen is surprisingly quiet for lunching rush hour, but it would still be the busiest time of the day. Behind him, the soft clatter of cutlery and the sibilance of table talk encroach on his headspace, pleasantly dulling his thoughts. But this pleasing sound is broken sporadically with what Buddy has come to call *the sounds that don't belong*: fingers clicking impatiently, tongues licking violently, lips smacking and kissing – taunting him. On hearing these sounds, it takes a great deal of self-discipline not to turn his head to see what he hears. But he believes it is good practice not to look at things that aren't there. In the same respect, all the empty seats near to him are pushed tight to the table's rim, as they should be, so as to not imply that invisible people are sitting with him.

This is the present. He thinks and repeats, dissatisfied. *And now this is the present.* He realises that his autobiography would chase the present like some insatiable time-fondling *thing*; and the dust of seconds slipping through its fingers would make for an interminable ending. He believes that autobiographies should end with a coda, in which trivial details introduced at the beginning (such as an absurd name) are satisfyingly reprised with special significance. He does not yet know what significance is held by his name and, therefore, does not yet know when his autobiography should end.

He is thinking this way because nobody is sitting with him. Nobody is sitting with him because nobody knows him. He started working at The Warehouse two days ago and has made no active effort to make friends; he feels a little abashed about the reasons for his being dismissed from his previous job.

The supervisor of the Faircliff Nautical Museum informed Buddy that only his new employer would need to be notified. "Beyond that, it's out of my control", he said. Buddy hopes that his colleagues don't know and don't find out and don't sense his capacity for it; and most of all, he hopes he doesn't do it again.

Now that his autobiography is 'in the works', he wonders if he will include the reason for his dismissal. *It happened and however humiliating it is part of me now.* But if it had not been the structural marker for a new chapter in his life, bringing so much change and reassessment, he might choose to omit it. He won't, he knows. It deserves to have centrality within this new chapter, which began when he started work at The Warehouse two days ago. This chapter will be titled, 'Onset Days', referring to what he suspects are symptoms of a psychological malady, which he believes will blossom in the coming weeks and months.

A single act of exposure is what led to Buddy's dismissal, and the strange experiences that have followed. He knows that he (a responsible man, accelerating toward middle-age) has a duty to probe his mind and surmise a motive, and so he returns to the fateful moment via interview questions (designed to reduce culpability in the form of detached self-examination): *Why did you follow the cleaner into the underground-floor male toilets when you did not need to relieve yourself? Why did you stand at the neighbouring urinal to the cleaner and study her eyes for a loss of composure? Why did you think that she would not immediately report you to her supervisor, as she should, and did?* Why does the memory excite him? He experiences frisson at this moment and clumsily places his knife and fork at 2:20 on the plate. The phantom clicks and kisses emerge slowly from the sibilant background noise, as if they are always there and an unseen tormenter needs only to twist the volume dial for them to be heard again.

 Buddy catches the eye of a short, fat man sitting opposite him, whom he did not notice sitting down.

 "Alright mate?" says the fat man, to which Buddy nods, smiling. "My name's Trev."

"I'm Buddy."

"Buddy?"

"Mm hmm."

"You're new, are you?"

"Yeah, backdoor. You?"

"Deliveries, so you'll see me around" says Trev, dipping a chip in the *brown*. "Don't usually have my lunch here though. The food's shit, innit?" he adds.

"Yeah" says Buddy, catching the eye of the canteen cook.

"It's okay, I know it's shit," laughs the cook.

"I- I actually really liked your quiche."

"We get them frozen."

Part 2: Faircliff Nautical Museum

He remembers the precise moment the *sounds that don't belong* popped up in his awareness. It was the end of a long day, nearing the end of his shift and moments before staff started asking people to leave the museum. He was standing in the marine-life room looking at the *shark hole* from a distance.

 From the time Buddy visited the museum as a child, the marine-life room had boasted a 5 by 5 metre hologram screen on the floor by the furthest wall, called the *shark hole*. From the perspective of someone standing on the dark screen's glass, the screen reveals a 3D image of a life-sized basking shark – a shark breed primarily identifiable by its disconcertingly large mouth. The gaping mouth faces upward to the observer like a recreation of the famous Jaws poster composition. Children and parents alike would nervously laugh, and cling tightly to their composure as their eyes met the obscured outline of that enormous, gaping, toothless void beneath them. Buddy was often impressed by their cool act, but knew that an unheard part of them screamed.

 That's why he always looked at the shark hole from a distance. He has only ever seen the shark from the intended perspective once, and his old boss laughed heartily at his reaction. However, that particular evening, as he found himself alone, aimlessly looking for tasks, cleaning the clean cabinet glass, altering the fake scenery of the taxidermy cabinet, and replenishing the hilly piles of the leaflet table, he started daringly reducing his distance. When he reached the Devil's Toenail fossil cabinet, eight feet from the shark hole, he suddenly froze and listened. *Yes, there it is again,* he thought. He looked behind and all around and then to empty space, allowing his ears to see. *Is this a joke?* Was he being teased? He wondered. His eyes were foolishly drawn to the shark hole, as if the sounds originated there. *That is unmistakably the squeaking sound lips make when they kiss the air.* Were some teenagers making fun of him in that sexually aggressive way they tend to make fun of prudish, meek adults? He thought. *Are people clicking their fingers at me trying to discreetly get my attention?*

It was difficult to give much more thought than that to the sounds. He eventually assumed, as anyone would, that it was caused by some air-vent mechanism, or a draft disturbing some loose *thing* in some unseen crevice, or any number of other reasonable explanations. So after listening for a few more minutes, he hesitantly left and clocked out (a number of vital minutes later than usual).

As he approached the large, brass entrance doors of the museum, he saw the cleaner, on the far side of the foyer hall, descending the basement steps. There was a very brief moment of mindless hesitation, when he reached out and held the cold, metal door handle – not long enough to allow his better nature to push him through the doors and begin the walk home.

His heart was beating very fast. His footsteps echoed softly as he traversed the main hall floor. He descended the marble basement stairs and when he saw the door to the men's toilet was swinging shut, his face flushed. He waited a little while outside the men's toilets, looking at the deep-diving suit display and mentally buffering. The choice to keep the antique diving suit in the basement level of the museum could be interpreted as something close to a joke – but Buddy hadn't considered it before that moment, as his mind raced while he loitered outside the men's toilets. Before long, a single image pushed itself to the forefront of his mind, and monopolised his thought; he was imagining that when he opened the toilet door the cleaner might be kneeling at one of the urinals.

And she was, indeed, precisely where he had hoped. The door closed behind him and he wasted no time in unzipping his trousers and standing beside her and waiting only until then, as he held his penis, to turn his eyes down to meet hers.

Her name was Marion. She was a middle-aged single-mother of three whom he had seen floating in and out of cleaning closets and toilets, and occasionally observed on her hands and knees polishing cabinet glass at the end of the day. He is ashamed to admit that, before then, she had never once entered his thoughts after leaving the museum to go home. His actions were in no way premeditated, or the result of long-denied, repressed sexual feelings he harboured for her. But now he thinks of her daily. He had not apologised to her, but hoped that she was satisfied with the punitive action taken by her supervisor.

Buddy didn't put up any kind of defence when his old boss outlined the charges. He could not think coherently, and there were strange sounds coming from the peripheries of the office. After that final meeting, as Buddy exited the museum, he did not hesitate when he passed through the heavy, brass entrance doors. He left as quickly as he could, and didn't look back.

For the rest of that day, having no job to wake up to the following morning, Buddy wandered home from the marina to the bay and to the pier and the market and then through the town centre. He didn't stop. He kept walking this meandering route home thinking of what he had done and what he might do.

And so, for the past three days, Buddy has not spoken to anyone about the incident. He knows only one other person outside of his circle of colleagues at the museum. Her name is Peggy, and he would rather die than for her to know what he did.

Part 3: Lock-ins at Shore Side Coffee

He met Peggy as she waitressed in a café called Shore Side Coffee, a short walk from The Warehouse (three years before he would start working there). The first time he visited he heard her colleagues and some regulars call her Peggy Sue – a nickname referencing the famous song. After Googling the lyrics once (in order to someday make a shrewd reference to the song as he thanked her for coffee), he only ever seemed to remember the words, *pretty, pretty, pretty, pretty Peggy Sue*. He shoehorned these lyrics into one exchange, around their third or fourth encounter – he suspected she wasn't keeping count.

"Hello Peggy Sue, you're looking pretty, pretty, pretty," he said, writhing internally.

He didn't do that again but Peggy always smiled and twinkled her eyes at him anyway, until one evening she said, "I finish at 7."

They ambled about Faircliff harbour for a while, trying to find the right place, but finally decided to have a coffee where they started, at Shore Side Coffee. Peggy made coffee for both of them and served it with the same focus she would have if she were working a shift. When they left it was approaching 10pm and they both suggested that the Café lock-in should become a regular arrangement.

"Goodbye, Peggy Sue," he said.

"Goodbye, Buddy Nickel," she said.

He didn't walk directly home that night but wandered the cobbled streets, grinning uncontrollably. The night was grimly cold and the dotted Christmas lights sang bright and dreamy in the sea-misted air.

They had one more lock-in a week later. They were both tired from the Christmas rush for seaside coffee and the museum's inundation with holidaying families. Buddy had spent the day answering children's questions about prehistoric molluscs and maritime fishing practices, and the shark hole. Peggy spent the day washing cups and saucers and then pouring coffee and then retrieving the cups and saucers, and repeating – for 10 hours.

They had been talking for a while, freely and easily, as they had the first time. Then, as if bored by the agreeability of the interaction and the vagueness of their relationship, Peggy's eyes started to quizzically caress his.

"I can't work you out. I think of myself as a people person, able to get a read on people, but I can't with you," said Peggy.

Buddy was reminded of the countless other women in his life that had said the same or very similar things as their eyes caressed his, quizzically. He tried to stifle an implacable sense of pride that overcame him, but failed. His eyes involuntarily smiled and he stared off to a corner of the room trying to work out why her question made him feel so ridiculous. He seldom felt such a mixture of pride and humiliation, and didn't know what to do with it. He had no answer for her intrigue but supposed that he liked a woman looking at him so intently, searching for something.

Knowing she wouldn't find what she was searching for, he looked down at his hands and said, "I am a strange old man."

"Okay," she sighed.

"I don't know," he added.

"Okay."

"Someone says that in the book I'm reading."

"*I am a strange old man?*"

"Yes. It was a joke. I didn't know what to say so I said that."

"You don't know what to say?"

"No, I *didn't* know what to say."

Then they were quiet.

When Buddy remembers this conversation, he hears the sounds that don't belong and his heart starts beating very fast. He knows she was not attracted to him because she didn't ask what book he was reading. He has to be careful, he thinks, as he knows he cannot keep a woman's interest anymore merely by relying on his natural looks to sweeten his natural evasiveness. His natural looks have diminished, naturally; he has become slightly strange in appearance, as if the repressed inner world of his adolescence and early manhood has slowly risen to the surface.

He is passing Shore Side Coffee now, feeling very tired, and wishing he could feel that *wanting* he felt years ago when he memorised lyrics, and watched Peggy serving coffee, and talked with her for hours. *Wanting* might make him go in and see her again. He could recover from that one bad conversation they had when they were both tired three Christmases ago. He is sure that she feels the same way he does about it: vaguely sad – a missed opportunity. But the glow of the entrance passes him, as it had for the past two days walking home from The Warehouse – as it had for the past three years.

Ahead, he sees the tangent-lane he had taken the night of the first lock-in. He walks by trying to figure out what precisely is different about his conscious experience now compared to then. The idea of wandering through the side streets at night seems repellent now. Looking at the hazy lights and the lonely darkness behind the shop windows, he remembers grinning uncontrollably. What did he know then that he's forgotten now? What did the three-hour conversation with Peggy remind him of? *It is a lovely feeling to figure out what you want,* he thinks. He wants to want another lock-in with Peggy. He wants to want to go for a night-wander. He wants to want her. But he's too tired.

Part 4: The Mistletoe Boys

Buddy drifts into sleep the same way he has the past two nights, listening to the lazy syncopations of the sounds that don't belong. After lying under the cold sheets for about two hours, thinking of Marion The Cleaner and Peggy and other regrets, his body would start to tingle with the texture of sand sprinkled onto rolling sea waves, and then TV static would fade in from the sides of his eyelids. Soon the sounds would align to form crisp, resonant clicks at about 60bpm. This pulse would pave a pathway into his dreams.

He would see by a peripheral light that went dark if he tried to look with his eyes. Colours would soak up the light, and then objects would come into focus.

He is standing at a bar with circular windows. Waiting for someone, he orders a drink. Holding the drink, he watches the band. Everyone is dressed like they're wearing a costume of a suit or a dress instead of just wearing a suit or a dress. Later, there might be an anachronistic doowop group set. *Uncle Wynn's Christmas party*, he thinks.

A group of boys of around 8 years of age are waiting behind the bend of the bar, giggling – distant relatives or friends of his cousins. Buddy always met family he didn't know at his uncle's Christmas parties. The only people he remembers from these parties now are Uncle Wynn himself, and the group of boys hiding behind the bend of the bar.

Plastic mistletoe decorations are coiled around a brass pole that rims the bar's edge. Another boy is leading a girl of about the same age to the bar. This all occurs beneath the visual plane of the adult world, where the children weave and run and laugh through the forest of adult legs and bar stools, unconcerned with the higher plains of experience. Buddy takes a languid swig of his tasteless drink and watches.

When the girl is led to the rounded corner of the bar, beneath the plastic mistletoe, the boys each jump out and steal a kiss. The first is swift, perhaps a little forceful, and surprises the girl; the second comes almost immediately, followed by a third, more forceful than the first. Then she becomes very still, and red in the face, and she looks down and starts quietly crying. A tentative fourth kiss comes, and the fifth and final boy stops, looking around for witnesses or an imminent reprimand. He looks at Buddy with fearful eyes, and his bottom lip starts to wobble. The other boys whom had been laughing initially now wear rapidly dying smiles. Buddy takes another drink of tasteless liquid as the fifth boy starts sobbing and the girl dries her tears.

This dream is true to Buddy's early memories of The Mistletoe Boys. They would play this game every year, at every single one of Uncle Wynn's Christmas parties that Buddy attended. And every winter since, from adolescence to adulthood, he has wondered what became of The Mistletoe Boys.

In the later years of attending Uncle Wynn's parties, Buddy had noticed a change in the game's spirit; where once it had merely been a crass joke at someone's expense, it transformed into a game of etiquette and pantomime. The girls would be chosen based on attractiveness and popularity and would regard the invitation to play as an unambiguous compliment. Then, having accepted the veiled invitation, they would be led to the bend of the bar, keeping up a consistent act of innocence and ignorance. Before the kisses came, the girls would often blush and close their eyes expectantly, as if waiting for a crown to be lowered onto their heads.

Buddy watched like the adults sometimes watched: curiously, and slightly disconcerted. The Mistletoe Boys never asked him to join, and Buddy was never sure if he needed to be invited to play. *If I had waited behind the bend of the bar with them, would I have joined the kiss queue?* He wondered, decades after. He came to dislike the obliqueness of the game's rules. In the last few years he attended the parties, he missed the days when the game would make the girls cry – at least then he could be glad that he had no part in it. He had stopped going after the age of thirteen, when he had a little more say in his festive engagements. He was flirting with *wanting* then, specifically wanting for parts of another's body – and he believed that watching and not participating in the aforementioned game might heighten his *wanting-and-not-having* to uncomfortable levels.

The year he became a teenager, when his grandmother once again asked him if he wanted to go to Uncle Wynn's party, he said what he said every subsequent time he was asked: *not really*. And the two of them stayed in the house and drank Bucksfizz and watched television and played battleships and went to bed around 11pm; and he stared up at the ceiling in his dark room and imagined The Mistletoe Boys and the crying girls until he fell asleep.

Part 5: Pot-wash

Buddy is about to walk through warehouse B toward the backdoor to unload the morning deliveries, but is stopped by Mr Jenkins, his new boss.

"Hello Buddy, it's going to be a little different today. They need someone in pot-wash – in the café. So don't worry about the deliveries, we have plenty of staff – go to the café today and help them best you can."

"Okay."

When Buddy hears the word café, he thinks of Peggy. He thinks of something he could say to her about working in a café and feels the *wanting* stirring in him – impotent sparks, which ignite no flame. But there are sparks nonetheless.

When he enters the café he smells coffee and stale baked-beans, and feels the closest he has felt to Peggy since their last meeting, three years ago.

A juvenile looking man, who looks 19 but is surely older, approaches him and leads him through mock-saloon doors to a backroom of the kitchen where a large, deep sink occupies a poorly lit corner. A pair of yellow gloves is draped over the curve of the tap.

"Cheers for helping today. It's going to be busy and fast but I think you should get into the flow of it easily enough. Do you want a coffee?" says the young man.

"Yes, please." Says Buddy, oddly comforted by the offer of free barista-style coffee. "An Americano." He picks the easiest to make.

"No problem. So, rinse there and dishwasher there and stack there." says the young man, pointing imprecisely with his middle finger. "If it's slow, come out and smash the floor – bring anything dirty back here. What's your name again? Eddie?"

"Buddy Nickel," he says, unsure of why he chose to give his full name.

"Buddy Nickel?"

"Mm hmm."

"Okay, ha ha. I'm Dan."

Dan pulls out a piece of card from his pocket and writes *Buddy* on it; he then places it in a small plastic sleeve and hands it to Buddy. Buddy notices a pixelated image of an anchor on the nametag, beside his name.

"We all wear nametags here if we're around customers – the kitchen staff don't but you do."

"Okay," replies Buddy, noting that Dan's picture is a sand castle.

The busy routine of café work is enormously satisfying to Buddy. His mood has taken a palpable upward turn. He is occupied, indefinitely, with the task of washing every single item of cutlery and porcelain touched by customer hands. He cannot dwell on certain thoughts, or listen for the sounds that don't belong. The environment is too fast and too loud. The repetition of movement and the numbing wash of sound facilitate only the most dream-like tangents of free flowing thought.

As Buddy works, he is entertained by the baristas, cooks and waiting staff, who burst unpredictably through the saloon doors, expelling unprompted, and strangely heartening, complaints regarding the faults of humankind: *Why bring your entire fucking family and then complain that you don't have enough room! Of course I don't mind wiping down your table for three crumbs, it's not like I have anything else going on! Oh, I can't fucking stand people!* And Buddy is not obligated to pull-together engaging or humorous responses; they assume he is too busy. Sometimes he says *I feel the same way*, or nods to convey the same general agreement. And to this, his new colleagues usually laugh or flash him a look that suggests, to him, that he is one of them.

All of a sudden, as he wipes and scrubs and splashes and stacks and bends down to load the washer, he feels his mouth grinning uncontrollably. He thinks of how much he enjoyed working at the museum, and how there are other museums waiting for his employment in the future; then he thinks about Peggy, and he wants to tell her about this shift and that he (to his surprise) actually enjoys café work. He wants to meet more people like the charismatic, ironically name-tagged post-students bursting in and out through the saloon doors. He thinks about his home, the seaside town of Faircliff, and the places nearby that he is yet to visit. And he plans on going to see Peggy as soon as he finishes work, and wonders why he hadn't sooner.

Buddy understands that his current sense of wellness is finite. Soon the coffee will wear off, he thinks, and he will feel inexplicably afraid of things again. It seems cruel to him that he can be so agonisingly aware of this fact.

He is able to think this way due to a lull in the supply of dirty crockery. No one has burst through the saloon doors for about 20 minutes. The dirty stacks at his side are rapidly depleting. From what he can hear of the floor, things are significantly less bustling, and now there is time and sufficient stillness for him to listen to his thoughts. Of course, the sounds that don't belong begin their beckoning from the corners of the room. And as he looks into the murky water, into which his hands are completely submerged, he goadingly thinks about the shark hole; and if he were to extend his hand deep enough into the large basin, he flirts with the notion that he might be able to lay the tips of his fingers on the gums of a basking shark.

The saloon doors slam open. Buddy jolts and turns, and Dan is stopped in his approach.

"You okay, Eddie? Didn't mean to startle you," says Dan.

"Yeah, all good."

"Everyone gets a bit bugged-out in here! You're doing well though. Not long now."

"Will you need me here often?"

"No, I shouldn't think so, don't worry. We're getting some new staff next week – interviews this week. But now we know who to call if we need an emergency pot-wash."

"I quite like it."

"Yeah?"

"Yeah."

Part 6: The Sea

Buddy's fingers are wrinkled and sore. Under some of his fingernails the skin is very tender and aches when he relaxes his arms at his side, letting them fill with blood. His skin feels unusually loose and crisp around the creases of his hands, as if he is about to shed his skin, and he delicately dabs and stretches his fingers as he walks. This tender sensation, paired with his exhaustion, is quite pleasing to Buddy, and he hasn't felt it for a long time.

As he walks, he looks out to the sea and is able, for game's sake, to pretend that he is seeing it for the first time: *a big sink*, he says, *full of dirty water*. This is the prototype that the youngest children must reference in interpreting the sea, he posits. *You might think a big bath – children play with toy boats and fish and ducks in the bath, after all. But the bath, too, is just a big sink: the first body of water in which most children will bathe*. Buddy remembers, very distantly, this function of the kitchen sink; and it accounts for unusual impulses he has had in later life, to plunge his hands deep into the water when he washes dishes, and hold them there with bourgeoning hopes to, at any moment, dive in.

As he looks out, walking on the side of the road closest to the bay, he makes declarations with his eyes. *I've always loved water. I've always loved the sea. It's true because I've always felt it. This must be what it means to have an affinity with one of the archaic elements*. Although, he isn't sure if he had once heard that his own astrological sign was connected more with fire than water; and he usually stops listening when people try to tell him this or that about astrology. He believes that some wisdom is best kept mysterious, and necessarily looks a little silly when expressed in the cold-light-of-day's terms: codifications, aphorisms and charts. To him, something like an astrological chart brings to mind a certain kind of fish with billowing fins that looks angelic in the flowing suspension of water, but looks like a flaccid, slimy blob when pulled out of it. Leave it in the dense flow of mystery, he thinks.

He is distracting himself from the approach of Shore Side Coffee by looking out at the sea. He is looking very deliberately. Maybe he is trying to channel the eternal cool of the ocean, which moves always and for no one. Like Old Man River, he thinks; *he must know somethin' but don't say nothin', he just keeps rollin', he keeps on rollin' along.* The slave in 'Showboat' channels the eternal cool and steadfastness of the Mississippi, and feels empowered and even inspired to sing as he looks out on that particular body of water. But Buddy believes that the *big sink* is different from any river or waterway; the ocean has nowhere to *go* from or to, and nothing to *do* for or at. In the ocean, all flows and yet is somehow unmoving, emanating an impenetrable truth as effortlessly as it reflects the stars and might also bring to mind the bathing of a baby. *That's another sort of cool*, he thinks. *The sea wouldn't correct you if you called it the cosmos, or a big sink.*

Ordinarily, he would cross the road and pass the amber glow of the entrance to Shore Side Coffee, and allow for some moments of tempted impetuousness where he might turn abruptly and walk in – but, of course, for the last three years, he hasn't. Today, however, he has already declared that he will walk in and speak to Peggy. *It will happen*, he says.

The friendly sign beckons from the distance. On the right side of the sign, following on from the stylistic leg of the final 'e', there's an image of a man in a boat upon some wavy lines that represent ocean waves. It reminds Buddy of the pixelated nametag pictures. He tried to retain as many names and corresponding icons as he could, but forgot to remember. Now he can only recall Dan and his sandcastle, Penelope and her boat, and his own anchor. Maybe he will tell Peggy about the nametag art, and spur a game of *what picture are you?* In Buddy's imagination, he and Peggy are speaking in an empty café, but he knows that another lock-in is highly unlikely. What is more likely is that he will simply order a coffee and drink it very quietly in a corner as he plays through scenarios in his own mind (as he his doing now) of what he might say.

He turns and places his hand on the door and hesitates. An image of Marion The Cleaner comes to mind – her eyes looking up at him, embarrassed and a little afraid. As he pushes the door he imagines Peggy at the urinal, in place of Marion, and a knot tightens in his gut. He steps inside, feeling the warm glow of the orange lights, and hears the sounds that don't belong clicking at his heels and kissing just behind his ears. The ocean disappears into the dark backdrop seen vaguely through the windows, and people from the past wander into the foreground of his mind.

Part 7: Christmas Party

"Go on then, he's showed his. You've got to show yours now."

Buddy never liked Uncle Wynn, but until that moment he never had good reason. From the moment this sentence was uttered, as Buddy stood there next to one of the Mistletoe Boys, he felt a deep repulsion swell within. He was close to seven years of age, as was the distant cousin or son of family friends that accompanied him. They both stood in the doorway to the strange bedroom, looking up at the drunk, fat man they called Wynn. Though Buddy was young, he remembers quite vividly thinking: *Fuck you. Fuck you, Uncle Wynn.* And then Wynn spoke again:

"Go on. I've seen his. He's got a big one. What about yours?"

Buddy was surprisingly sensitive to the emotional artefacts of Wynn's face; he could see the pretence of cheeky humour, and the sly calculations of someone doing what they know to be wrong. But beyond that, what really discouraged Buddy or the Mistletoe Boy from leaving to go back to the party was the dark desperation in Wynn's large pupils. Buddy just looked up at him without moving, trying to be amiable without betraying his deep embarrassment, and wishing death upon the drunk, fat man with the saddest, oldest part of his soul.

Unsure of the forfeit of this game they found themselves playing, the Mistletoe Boy eventually turned to Buddy and said:

"Go on, just do it quick."

Wynn smiled innocently and took a sip from his wine glass. The air was very still, and the dying party seemed miles away. Echoes of dusty Christmas songs crept down the dark hallway, toward Wynn's bedroom.

Buddy needed to go to the toilet, Uncle Wynn's en suite bathroom, but he was caught in their gaze; both Wynn's and the Mistletoe Boy's staring seemed to be weighing down on his bladder, weakening him. *Why can't I not show?* He wondered.

"Go on, it's okay", said the Mistletoe Boy, once again. And Buddy pulled down his trousers and pulled them back up very quickly, and Wynn saw and smiled.

Later that night, when Buddy saw another girl being led to the bar's hanging mistletoe, he looked for his acquaintance in the group of Mistletoe Boys hiding behind the bend of the bar. Buddy found him waiting with the others, third in line. *In* the group but not *of* the group, thought Buddy. His acquaintance's eyes wandered to empty spaces and patches on the art deco carpet design. He didn't seem upset, and when the others looked at him he laughed giddily with them, but his eyes continued to drift vaguely about him until the girl was led under the mistletoe. When his turn came – third in line – and he kissed her on the cheek, he suddenly started to blush as much, if not more, as she did. It was a rare sight to see intimations of sexual bashfulness on the face of one of the Mistletoe Boys, and Buddy thought that it complimented the handsome complexion of his acquaintance. His blushing made her blush more and a beautifully nervous laughter curtailed the game, arresting all the children involved. Seeing his acquaintance this way made Buddy hate Wynn all the more, and he hoped that nothing else would happen in the doorway of Uncle Wynn's bedroom.

The next time Buddy and his acquaintance met was two Christmases after. And they didn't speak to each other again. They merely nodded at each other as Buddy watched the mistletoe game from afar. His acquaintance's eyes still drifted to empty spaces as he waited in line.

Part 8: Return to Shore Side Coffee

"Hello, Peggy."

"Hi, Buddy."

Buddy returns a clinical smile and orders a flat white and hands her the exact change. His responses are short and staccato, as his mind focuses not on the inflection or spirit of his voice but on what he should be saying, and isn't. As she operates the till, dropping the coins into their trays, he finds the words:

"How are you?"

"I'm very good, you? It took me a moment to recognise you. It's been a long time," says Peggy, flashing a look at the door as another patron enters.

"I'm good too. Yeah – It feels like a very long time since I saw you last."

"Does it feel like two or three years?" she says, flashing him an ironic look.

"Longer."

"I looked for you on Facebook, but couldn't find you. I thought maybe Buddy Nickel wasn't your real name."

"It is. I don't have anything like that. I'm-"

"-*a strange old man*?" says Peggy.

Buddy laughs and takes the cup and saucer in his hands, which have started shaking a little. He must be careful not to spill the drink, so that he doesn't look foolish, he thinks. He looks up and smiles at her once more, as a sign off, but she has already turned her attention to the next customer, patiently waiting.

The teaspoon rattles precariously on the saucer as he finds a table in the corner, as he had implicitly planned. As he sits down, he feels a sort of warmth emanating within him and welling up to meet the sleepy, comforting haze of the room. He is glad he has come. *It is important to visit the places that glow for you,* he thinks. It is fear that keeps him from visiting the places and people that make him happy, he thinks. *Why?* He asks the echoing hallways of his mind. *What am I afraid of?* One mildly strained conversation was enough to repel him from Shore Side Coffee for three years. He sups his coffee and thinks about that. He wonders if his theoretical autobiography would include an analysis of this implacable sense of fear.

This is the present, he thinks. *This is the present. If I finished my autobiography now, it might end with this visit to Shore Side Coffee, and my personal reflections, and the vague promise of change: the moment things started to get better.* A hopeful ending.

Peggy continues to talk with the customer who had waited behind Buddy in line. They talk as if he were, at the very least, a regular. He is quite tall – taller than Buddy – and sinewy, and his cheekbones are notably quite high and pronounced, and he smiles often, but calmly; and Peggy smiles and twinkles for him, and her gestures are endearingly less controlled than Buddy remembers, and she sends her gaze up to the top corners of the room, wondering something or saying *maaaybe,* hiding a coy smile with a pout.

Buddy wonders if she is saying, or has said, "I finish at 7". He sups his coffee and thinks about what he had wanted from her three years ago, and he imagines her on her knees while he pulls down his trousers. And when she looks up at him with her eyes twinkling he imagines slapping his penis on her face, her blushing and her loss of composure. And he imagines looking out to sea with her. Then, he imagines the man to whom she is talking towering over her or holding her small wrists with his large hands. Buddy imagines talking to her at another lock-in and saying, *let's go for a walk by the bay,* or, *would you like to go for dinner sometime,* or, *there's a secret place I can show you by the rocks in Faircliff Bay.*

Without his full consent, Buddy's consciousness has started trying to glean what Peggy and the tall man are talking about. And like little gremlins waving at him from the shadows, he hears the sounds that don't belong once again. They're almost too quiet to hear, but he knows they're there clicking at him and sending their squeaky kisses carelessly into the air. His heart starts accelerating its rhythm and he feels his eyes checking empty spaces. He wonders how he looks to the small number of customers sharing the café with him. Does he look like a man who is listening to sounds that can't be heard? Peggy glances at him and his eyes return to his hands clutching the coffee cup. *Don't look at me for the moment, Peggy,* he thinks.

When he becomes alone with the coffee cup, losing sense of the table and the floor and the café and the ocean, silently churning in the distance, his thoughts start to whisper. And they whisper strange things, and make suggestions, and ask him unusual questions. He wonders if there is a basking shark in the window directly behind him. He wonders if Peggy has heard about his dismissal from the museum, and if she asked why it happened; and the orange lights start to burn, and he wants nothing more than to be outside in the fresh sea-air, channelling the eternal cool of the ocean.

He finishes the coffee grain froth at the bottom of his cup and stands up, and the teaspoon falls to the floor. He leaves without picking it up or saying goodbye to Peggy.

"Goodbye, Buddy," she calls after him, peaking over the shoulder of the tall man.

Part 9: The Mistletoe Men

It is 10pm, and the sounds that don't belong have followed Buddy all the way home without relenting. He brings his laptop onto the bed and types into a search-engine: *hearig sdounds that arent there*; and, shortly after exhausting a few pages, he types: *cant sleep becausde of audtiory hallcinations*. Buddy reads about various conditions and tentative referrals to see a doctor, but his heart beats faster as he reads and after a few minutes of reading he turns from the bright screen and looks down at his sheets and his shaking hands, and then checks his pulse and listens to his breathing. He knows he mustn't think of Marion The Cleaner or Peggy or the basking shark or Uncle Wynn or the fallen teaspoon, and so he inevitably thinks of nothing else. He lies back, ever listening to the sounds that never fully disappear. Lying back helps, and he takes long breaths that tremble on their release. Then he taps his leg in time with the clicks and very slowly feels his heartbeat subsiding.

He turns once more to his laptop, exits the previous websites and types in: *sleep sounds for loud thoughts and unhappiness*. Sometimes he likes to make very specific requests of the search-engine in the hope that he finds exactly what he is looking for. And he does. He finds a video entitled, "Guided meditation for sadness and spiralling thoughts". He clicks on the video, sets his alarm clock, switches off the bedroom light and lies back with the glow of the laptop screen dimly limning the back of his left eyelid.

A soft male voice has been speaking for just under a minute and when he attunes to the voice, and focuses on nothing else, he hears the words:

"...Your time to relax, and put the pressures of daily existence to one side. Find a still, quiet place to sit or lie down and if you like, close your eyes. Listen to the sounds around you. Allow the sounds to flow through your consciousness. Listen to your body, and feel the floor or the seat or the bed beneath you. Hear how it interacts with your body."

Buddy very much likes the priority the voice gives to listening.

"If your mind wanders. Let it wander. Watch it wander, and then gently guide it back to the present: where you are now and when you are now and what you hear now, and what it may make you feel. If your thoughts wander to a place they don't usually like to go, let them be. Listen to your body and how those mental spaces might make you feel. Are those places dark or light? It doesn't matter. Nothing needs to be hidden or silenced and pushed away. Wander to the dark places, if you like, and switch on the light."

With that, Buddy starts smiling. Not because of any perceived beauty in the phrasing or depth to the words' meaning. It is a sudden feeling washing over him, triggered by the simple words coming from his laptop. He feels momentarily unshackled, like a filter has lifted from his ears letting every sound sing for him. Now he is laughing, in the darkness of his room, with his eyes closed, stifling tears welling in the creases. *I should have listened to this earlier,* he thinks.

He doesn't remember drifting into sleep. For the first time in three days, the sounds that don't belong did not dictate the rhythm of his dreams. But at this moment, nearing the end of his cerebral travels, he becomes aware of where he is.

He drinks his tasteless drink and watches the band. The band is a doowop group of five singers dressed in very attractive sea-green suits. A dim light shines on them from below, highlighting the contours of their expressive faces. Plastic mistletoe decorations hang from the stage lights.

They've grown up, he thinks. They're handsome, talented – they radiate poise. *The Mistletoe Men*, he says, laughing. *Mistletoe Men.* He enjoys saying the words. There is something humorous about the epithet; he hears a sort of ineffable punchline in it. *Mistletoe Men.*

He is alone with them. There are no partygoers or children, and Uncle Wynn is nowhere to be seen. The Mistletoe Men gaze at him, smiling and rocking gracefully and clicking their fingers at about 60bpm. When they eventually finish their set, Buddy plans to go and congratulate them, and say how good it is to see them. But until then, he will watch and listen, and bask in the glow of their arresting performance, which exists just for him. The wordless music flows like syrup from their lips; beautiful harmonies, suspensions and melodic decorations delivered in velvet tones.

To the right of the stage, Buddy sees a glass cabinet containing an antique deep-diving suit. The same cabinet display acts as the centrepiece of the museum basement – outside of the male toilets. Sure enough, Buddy sees the familiar man-icon for the male toilets behind it. The door is swinging shut. The music has drifted into memory, and the stage is suddenly empty.

With the half awareness that he is dreaming, Buddy is careful not to encourage the dream to be unnecessarily unkind – he does not look out of the dark circular windows and does not will the wrong people to wander in. He tries to will his grandmother to enter his dream. He has not spoken to her in years and wants to see her and tell her how much he misses her.

An old woman drinks beside him, but it isn't quite his grandmother. She is surly and shifty and Buddy tries to wake up before she can turn to look at him. He knows the dream has turned. She presses herself against him and he becomes unsure if this old woman is merely a haggard figment from the recesses of his mind, or – somehow, simultaneously – Uncle Wynn. The dreamscape loses its clarity and when he starts looking with his real eyes (and not his mind's eye) the visual field dissolves into the darkness of his eyelids. He is left with an afterimage of her gawking eyes and mouth lurching into his face. He can still hear the old woman (or Uncle Wynn); she tongues at his left ear and whispers angrily into it as the sound of a buzz saw rapidly crescendos on the surface of his ear drum. This, he hears with perfect clarity. She says:

"Did you see? Did you see it?"

And then she screams over the sound of a wailing buzz saw:

"Did you see it you saw it you see it you see it you see it did you see it you saw it you see it you saw it you saw it you saw it!"

Part 10: The Backdoor

Buddy unloads the delivery crates from the truck and tries to stack them by type. This will help with his next task, which is to sort the crates' contents into cages ready to be taken and unloaded on the shop floor of The Warehouse.

At no point has he stopped thinking about his dream, and the moments of tentative release he glimpsed while listening to the voice from his laptop and the Mistletoe Men's performance.

It was unusually pleasing to see the adult figments of those characters of his childhood. While knowing it to be absurd, he sourced a deep well of pride as he watched them sing. It was a sincere affection that he had forgotten his facility for, but it flowed from him in abundance. He wonders what other kind of pride might be hiding within him ready to leap forth at the call of beautiful music or old acquaintances.

His efforts to lift and carry feel lighter and easier than they had previously, and he breathes in the cold, musty air of warehouse B, sourcing the dregs of that well of pride and positivity. The hall is still and quiet, save for his echoed shuffles, which ring out peacefully over the sea of crates and cages.

He knows he must make plans fast, as he is sure his pride will wane rapidly. Like he had the day before, he will make a declaration of action while in the thralls of wellness. When fear and the sounds that don't belong creep on him in the coming minutes or hours, he will cling to his declaration – like he had concerning the visit to Shore Side Coffee.

When considering this new personal assignment (the declaration of action), he finds his memory keeps returning to the old woman's screaming. He mutters the words under his breath: *did you see it?* And in the very same moment, an image of Marion flashes over the projector in his mind, as if he is asking her.

Something hits the side of his head very lightly. He looks down and sees a rolled up chewing gum wrapper. He looks up and around and behind him, and hears movement behind the large stack of plastic-wrapped crates.

A chubby face peaks over the top and smiles – a bright, smug smile that, in the same instant, loses all confidence.

"Hi! Buddy?"

"Trev," says Buddy, attempting to look less irritated.

"Can I tell you what happened there?"

"You thought I was someone else."

"I did."

Buddy smiles as Trev jumps down and comes around the crates to greet him.

"Sorry about that – they said the backdoor guy was late, so I thought you were Pete. Pete's always late."

"No harm done. Distractions are always welcome."

"Ha ha, good good. How're you finding it?"

"It's fine. They had me in pot-wash in the café yesterday – I think I prefer it there."

"Aye, it's pretty lonely at the backdoor. You're lookin' more settled than last time I saw you anyway," says Trev, sheepishly.

Trev is quite a short man but his bodily weight gives him presence, and his discerning eyes keep Buddy on his guard. Buddy has tentatively started peeling off the plastic on one of the crates, revealing a jenga-stack of boxed desk lights in varying designs.

"So, Saturday night – any plans?" says Trev, unwrapping another piece of chewing gum.

Buddy pulls up an empty cage and lets the loose metal cage-door swing open. He doesn't know what he will do tonight; he hasn't yet made his *declaration of action*. And though he is fond of Trev, Buddy's feeling of wellness has waned considerably since his arrival, and he senses the pressure of an undefined time-constraint. *Did you see it?* He thinks, as if he is contriving a vaguely symbolic connection between Trev's question and the old woman's question. *Did you see it?* He repeats into the echoing hallways of his mind. An image of the men's toilet door swinging shut repeats like the singularly remembered refrain of a song. The deep-diving suit cabinet waits, in the song-less silence, beside it.

When he looks up, Trev is looking back at him, amused but with a slightly impatient furrow in his brow.

"*I'm goin' out a'paddlin'*," says Buddy, as a smile glows on his face.

"I didn't peg you for a drinker! Where are you thinking of going?"

"Wherever the current takes me," says Buddy, laughing like a schoolboy.

"Ha ha, well me and a bunch of the boys are going out to watch the match. We'll be in The Lonely Anchor for most of the night. You're welcome to join us."

Buddy looks at Trev, and nods earnestly. Trev nods back and starts rolling the stacked empty crates into his truck.

Part 11: Bayside Walk

In this last hour of his shift, the sounds that don't belong have emerged very softly, like a simmering pan of oil in another room, starting to spit. As he walks to the clock-out machine, he tries not to synchronise his steps with the accelerating clacks, ticks and squeaks, but fails.

Wellness feels now like an abstracted memory, and he wants nothing more than to let the sounds push him home, to bed and into another dream, which would end, no doubt, at Uncle Wynn's party. His declaration of action seems to him to be one of the most absurd ideas he has ever conceived. *It is utterly strange,* he thinks. Could he pretend to himself that the verbal declaration made and sealed with Trev merely concerned going out for a drink? He wonders. The idea present in his mind then, and now, has not yet been expressed linguistically – not even in thought. But Buddy would be lying if he claimed ignorance of the meaning of his strange phrase, *goin' out a'paddlin'*. He remembers the expression from the book, Moby Dick. And given the thoughts and symbolic *mood* that led to the use of this phrase, the meaning was unambiguous.

Buddy has always been ensnared by an unfaltering awareness of his own absurdity; and, to a degree, it has recalibrated his gauge of what should actually be regarded as absurd. He is aware that the current mental space he finds himself – a dark room leading from the echoing corridors of his mind – is a disconcerting place, with paranoid scribbles on the walls and rumblings under the floorboards, but he is sure that he still doesn't fully appreciate how absurd he is being. *It will happen,* he says, *however absurd.*

Night has fallen and the air is bitterly cold – colder and darker still, having just exited the bright hallways of The Warehouse. Buddy waves goodbye to Trev's stocky figure waddling off in the distance, toward The Lonely Anchor. At this moment, the sounds that don't belong align and pulse at around 60bpm, like they do when he is in bed, or like a band might before they begin a song.

It is grimly cold, he thinks; and it might have taken all the fight out of Buddy had he not already made his declaration of action. The thought of going for a drink with Trev is actually very attractive to him. He enjoys the way certain pubs glow in winter, and believes that alcohol can sometimes make him shine in ways that coffee does not. But a trip to the pub isn't what he said, or meant. His deeply rooted intuitions of what the words *goin' out a'paddlin'* meant even specify a certain location: the small, sand-capped inlet by the lighthouse. It is the act of burglary preceding the *paddle* that will require the majority of his focussed planning, he thinks.

He follows his legs now as they stride, in time with the spectral clicking, from The Warehouse toward the direction of the museum. He walks on the side of the road closest to the sea and looks out, making declarations with his eyes. He speaks, quietly so that no one walking near him might hear: *I'll try not to do anything stupid tonight. But, obviously, I'm in no position to guarantee it. I suppose it's up to you and where you want to take me.*

He considers the point of entry. All of his keys had been returned following his dismissal. However, having worked there for close to five years, he is aware of a back-entrance door that has a faulty alarm. That is, the alarm was faulty during the time Buddy worked there, and he is assuming that his old boss has, of yet, gone no further than giving the same empty assurance that it *will* be fixed. This is his point of entry. Beyond that, luck will determine whether or not the security guard or a cleaner spots him, or hears him when he uses brute force to breach the cabinet glass.

There would be no other way to access the suit; finding the correct key in the security office would take too much time. He needs to take a blunt object to force his will on the display cabinet. He will look for something around Faircliff Bay: a rusty chunk of metal or an optimally shaped rock that tapers to a point and provides some protection to his hand. Had he given any prior thought to this plan, he would've brought a tool from home – but that isn't the way he's doing things.

On the other side of the road he can see the glow of Shore Side Coffee, and a long queue leading from the counter to the front door. *Peggy's busy*, he thinks. *Next time*. The Mistletoe Men's clicking has set a steady pace for his strides, and the stiff sea breeze pushes him on.

Part 12: Break-in at Faircliff Nautical Museum

He stayed out on the bay for longer than intended, and didn't keep to the rocks as he planned. Seeing only by moonlight, the search for an appropriate blunt object was very time consuming. He wandered around the rocky cliff-base beneath the lighthouse and eventually found a rusted pipe trapped in the intersection of some large boulders, sticking out like a small flagpole. Then he walked the length of the next bay and washed the pipe in the frothing tide. When he reached another rocky escarpment nearing Faircliff Harbour, he listened to the violent waves crashing and growling in the echoing cave passages beneath him. And in that darkness, he imagined large eyes and mouths waiting calmly behind the fierce waters, and so he kept his back close to the rock-face and wouldn't venture too near the edge, where the water spat at him. There were times when the sea seemed like a *big sink*, but it was not one of those times, he thought.

This is the present, he thinks and repeats. *This is the present.* He kneels in front of the open door assessing the damage he has inflicted on the locking mechanism, hoping that it would not be too costly. A draught blows through the doorway into the basement corridors of the museum creating a ghostly howling. A thin coating of wet sand softens his footsteps as he starts walking through the narrow hallway.

He feels tired from the exertion of strength required to climb the coastal rocks and dislodge the rusty pipe from the clamped stone and break the back entrance door – in addition to his nine-hour shift. He redirects the focus of his thought to the declaration of action, and how, in the following minutes and hours, it would be realised.

A security guard is likely stalking a route on the ground and second-floor levels of the museum, where valuable and historically significant items are displayed. Two thick doors separate the basement toilets from the ground floor, in addition to a lengthy stairwell. So Buddy is hopeful that in the basement, he will be safe to break the unalarmed cabinet glass without alerting the guard.

Buddy comes to the place he has visited in memory every day since he was fired. The men's toilet door looks strikingly innocuous in contrast to the ominous weight it holds in memory. *It's just a door,* he thinks. On the furthest wall of this restroom foyer section, the deep-diving suit strikes a curious underwater pose. The suit is much larger and more intricate than in Buddy's imagination. Buddy visualises lugging it down to the bay, and sees the jagged rocks and the darkness and hears the growling waves. He decides in this moment that he will instead go to one of the harbour slipways, about a 10-minute walk from the museum. He takes note of how quickly his plans can change.

He opens the door at the foot of the stairwell and turns his ear to the echoing darkness leading to the ground floor. *Nothing.* Then he secures the door shut and turns to the diving suit cabinet. It doesn't matter how or where he strikes the glass, it would need to have tremendous force and would inevitably be very loud.

His right hand, clutching the rusted pipe, comes down in a swift arching motion as his left arm shields his face. The breach in the shattered glass is surprisingly localised to the point of impact, and he is just able to fit his arm through to unbolt the lock from the other side. Straggling loose shards rattle and fall as he opens the cabinet door.

Before undressing the mannequin, Buddy opens the stairwell door once again, and turns his ear to the echoing darkness leading to the ground floor. At first, he hears nothing, as before. Then faint footsteps approach and make his heart flutter and the sounds that don't belong start beckoning from above and behind and all around, and he can no longer separate these sounds from the approaching footsteps.

With little thought, Buddy slots the pipe through the brass handles of the stairwell door, creating a makeshift blockade. He then topples the mannequin, quickly unbuckles the helmet, and uses its weight to bash the ends of the jammed pipe so that they bend around the handle, locking it in place.

An overweight man dressed in a white shirt and black tie emerges from the dark stairwell and looks at Buddy through the door's glass, and then looks at the bent pipe, and then tests the blockade with a tentative nudge, and then looks at Buddy once more.

"Buddy. What on earth are you doing?"

"I'm taking the suit, Phil."

"Why?"

"Because I'm going diving."

"Why didn't you just ask to use it?"

Buddy has turned toward the mannequin and begins delicately disassembling the deep-diving suit. To his surprise, he notices that the mannequin is female, indicated by the prominent plastic breasts and feminine contours of the featureless face. He doesn't hear any further questions from Phil; the sounds that don't belong are snapping and screaming in his ears.

There is a lot to carry. He finally secures the helmet under his right arm and pinches the boot cuffs in his left, and then looks at the stairwell door for the first time in about two minutes. Phil still watches him, full of contempt for the person who complicated his Saturday night, and resentment of the notion that he should (but isn't going to) run round to the back-entrance of the museum to face-off with Buddy.

Buddy stands there with the cumbersome folded fabric, boots and helmet, studying the emotional artefacts in Phil's face.

"What happened?" says Phil. His eyes cease their darting back and forth from Buddy to the mannequin, and they rest on Buddy's white knuckles.

"Don't follow me, Phil. Call the police and all that, but don't follow me. I won't give up," says Buddy, making additional declarations and threats with his eyes.

When Buddy looks back at the filleted cabinet and the naked mannequin and the broken glass on the floor, he thinks: *this image might be the front cover of my autobiography.* And then he leaves, feeling excited, like a child who's collected his favourite toys before bathing.

Part 13: Slipway No. 4

Now this is the present, he thinks and repeats. *This is the present.* His love of *the big sink* diminishes with every movement of his body, lifting and pulling and clasping the suit upon himself, as the icy air assaults his skin. Lights from distant shores dance on the water, roiling and churning, the colour of black coffee. He stands at the top of the slipway watching the dark water lapping slowly against the stone as if that particular entryway to the ocean is licking its lips. He remembers his grandmother saying that the sea scared her because it always seems hungry. As he hesitates, full of vague fear, he remembers hesitating at the brass doors of the museum entrance. In the nebulous dark before him, he finds her form, Marion, descending into the basement of the sea. He secures the helmet, finding her once more through the tarnished circular visor, and follows. His heart pounds in his chest. His throat tightens and breathing becomes a laborious task.

Then, he hears it (he thinks): voices singing in harmony, as one. The Mistletoe Men are very quietly serenading him in maudlin, crooning tones – the same song they sang last night at Uncle Wynn's Christmas party. Buddy couldn't help but grin, sensing, once again, that ineffable punchline and sourcing the deep well of pride. He descends the slipway, stepping in time like a musical promenade, and then starts singing with them, but a little louder maybe, sometimes breaking into laughter. *Ahh doowop doowahh ha ha!*

Water is at his waist when the music stops, and the deathly cold creeps on him, seeping softly through the aged linen. All he can hear now is the black water's heavy breathing; he tries to calm the water and himself by placing his gloved hand flat on the water's skin and breathing with it. As he continues the descent, he finds himself hoping that Phil called the police or might have followed, or that a stranger spots him and becomes concerned and might ask him what he's up to and might ask him if he's all right and then ask him to get out of the water. Soon his head and that heavy helmet will be completely submerged. He isn't looking forward to that.

Slipway no. 4 is always empty, save for the rotting skiff that has bobbed by the decayed docking post since he was a boy, and even an unknown number of eons before, when men fished and ate the fish they fished and slept in shacks and then did it all again. Buddy has chosen this particular slipway because it is old, unused and forgotten; the symbolic imagery of his being there would be unclouded by slipway obstacles, like *no swimming* signs, buoys and ropes. It is just he, the old skiff, and a clear, slow slope to the sea. The image of his descent might be on the front cover of his autobiography: the moment he turned it all around. Like the laptop voice said: *go to your dark place, and turn on the light.*

He can't see a thing. His thoughts race in blindness, and he is struck by an unhelpful notion: his *dark place* is the museum basement, or Shore Side Coffee – or maybe even Marion herself – not the ocean. A simple apology would be far more meaningful than this confused and tenuous gesture, he thinks; and as he descends deeper into the coffee-coloured murk, he starts to feel very silly. "There's clearly something wrong with me", he sighs into his cold helmet, which is rapidly, and quite dramatically, filling with salty water. Why doesn't he go on a scuba diving course – see the ocean with the lights on? He thinks. Why is he trying to terrify himself like a child that won't stop wandering, alone, to the shark hole and then running away to find his parents? *If I saw the basking shark with the lights on, would I be afraid?* Almost certainly.

His foot reaches out and suddenly finds no ground beneath. He stops and places it back beside the other. He feels as if he is standing at the precipice of an underwater cliff, looking out at a vast, theoretical abyss. He soberly replays scenes from his dream of The Mistletoe Men, and wills their figures to manifest dimly in the water before him and their music to fill the song-less darkness.

He has stared into the black for so long that, now, wandering phosphene ghosts inhabit the imagined space. His eyes sting. He hasn't taken a breath for a number of seconds and finds that when he purses his lips, his mouth slowly fills with sharp liquid salt. His thoughts slow. Dimly illuminated pink and orange phosphene clouds swoop and swoon above and below. Their outlines gradually sharpen, miraculously; like giant, iridescent stingrays, they fill the vast underwater expanse with effortless and impossibly beautiful gliding motions, and they flock like sparrows and plunge downward, lighting a path to the yawning mouth at the bottom of the ocean – or the plughole of the big sink. His eyes follow them down. Soon he will need to breathe. *Do you see it?* He asks the echoing corridors of his mind. He understands the cryptic language of his thoughts. *Yes, I see it. It's big.* His foot lifts from the ground it can no longer feel. *I should go back,* he thinks, *to breathe.*

He feels weightless.

Part 14: Last Lock-in

The entire evening felt, to Buddy, like a long, slow descent. As Peggy spoke, she blinked languidly and smiled clinically, and Buddy's words could do little to brighten her eyes.

Peggy switched off the lights. And when they approached the door to leave, she stood in front of him for a moment, facing the frosted glass, and then looked back over her shoulder and said:

"Is Buddy Nickel your real name?"

"It's what my grandmother called me," he said.

Peggy's eyes softened, and the playful suspicion in them faded. But she had no intention of speaking, and waited for Buddy to continue.

"We weren't related by blood; her maiden name was Moss and after that, Lightfoot, and from what I could gather, she never had children. As I grew up, her mind got more and more unwell – she couldn't give me any information about my parents; she didn't have any of my documentation or anything. The details about how I came to her got very hazy, and in conversation she would usually just say, *the time I found you...*"

Peggy's gaze was so unwavering that it made Buddy self-conscious. She encouraged him, again with her silence, to continue.

"To start work at the museum, I needed to apply for a late registration of birth. Knowing my grandmother's mind, it always seemed unlikely to me that *Nickel* was my family name, but I went with it. I went through the first half of my life without any record that I exist – it's crazy really."

"Why did she call you Buddy Nickel then?" said Peggy, patently unsatisfied.

"I have no idea," he said, chuckling.

Then they were quiet. Their thoughts were muted as a voice might be in water, and neither could kick their way to the surface to think or speak for a number of drawn-out seconds. And then Peggy gave-in and said, smiling: "It sounds like the name of a singer or something."

"Does it?"

"Mm hmm."

Without the orange lamplight, their faces were illuminated only by the moon's reflected, second-hand luminescence. Peggy eventually turned to the door, hesitating when she touched the handle, and said: "Sorry I've been a bit off tonight – I'm tired. I've been so tired recently."

She unlocked the door and let in the cold night-air as she opened it.

"I like you, Buddy – so let me know if you want to see me again."

"I do."

About the Authors

Omma Velada
author of *Lillya*

Omma Velada read languages at London University, followed by a masters in technical translation at Westminster University. Her short stories and poems have been published in numerous magazines and anthologies. She founded Gold Dust magazine, a literary journal that ran from 2004-2020 and has published three novels, *The Mackerby Scandal* (UKA Press, 2004), *Sun, Sea & Pilots* (Lulu Press, 2006) and *How to Steal a Goat (from a witch)* (Lulu Press, 2006). She now works full-time as an Editor.

About the Authors

James Bates
author of *The Jump*

James lives in a small town twenty miles west of Minneapolis, Minnesota. His stories and poems have appeared online in *CafeLit, The Writers' Cafe Magazine, Cabinet of Heed, Paragraph Planet, Nailpolish Stories, Ariel Chart, Potato Soup Journal, Literary Yard, Spillwords (Dec, 2019, Author of the Month), The Drabble, The Academy of the Heart and Mind, World of Myth Magazine, The Horror Tree, The Terror House, Fox Hollow Stories* and *Bindweed Press*. In print publications: *A Million Ways, Mused Literary Journal, Gleam Flash Fiction Anthology #2*, the *Portal Anthology* and the *Glamour Anthology* by Clarendon House Publishing, *The Best of CafeLit 8* by Chapeltown Publishing, the *Nativity Anthology* by Bridge House Publishing, *Forgotten One's Drabble Anthology* by Eerie River Publishing, *Gold Dust Magazine, Down In the Dirt Magazine and* the *Oceans Anthology and the 20/20 Anthology* by Black Hare Press. His collection of short stories, *Resilience*, with be published in the fall of 2020 by Bridge House Publishing. You can also check out his blog to see more:

www.theviewfromlonglake.wordpress.com

Geoff Nelder
Perplexed Eye of a Sufi Pirate

Geoff Nelder lives in Chester with his physicist wife, within easy cycle rides of the Welsh mountains.

Geoff is a former teacher, now an editor, writer and fiction competition judge.

His novels include Scifi: *Exit, Pursued by Bee*; *The ARIA trilogy*; *The Chaos of Mokii*; The *Flying Crooked* series with book one, *Suppose We* released 2019, followed by *Falling Up*.

Thrillers: *Escaping Reality*, and *Hot Air*.

Historical fantasy inspired by the mass abduction by pirates of the population of Malta's Gozo in 1551. Those 5,000 spirits need justice: *Xaghra's Revenge* (July 2017).

Collections: *Incremental–* 25 surreal tales more mental than incremental.

Geoff's website is at: **http://geoffnelder.com**

David Gardiner
Author of *The Summer of Dust*

David is a former science teacher and electronic technician (plus many other things), now retired and living in east London with his partner Jean.

For 16 years he helped to run the literary magazine *Gold Dust*, and has published two novels and two short story collections, as well a large number of shorter works in magazines and newspapers. Having been a student in Belfast during the rise of the IRA and the descent of Northern Ireland into civil war (although it was never called that) a lot of his fiction uses that era as background and draws on actual events, highly fictionalised.

His most recent novel, *Engineering Paradise*, charts what would now be called the "radicalisation" of a Belfast schoolboy who is seduced into a Faustian bargain with the IRA from which there can be no escape. David has turned this into an as yet unproduced (very dark) stage musical with a great deal of help from other people.

All of David's full length books are available from Amazon in both printed and Kindle editions. Search: "David Gardiner author Amazon" or buy from his website at **davidgardiner.net**, where you can also read a lot of his stories for free.

Introduction to *The Summer of Dust*

Like a lot of my stories, based on real events. This one deals with the collision of two cultures and the hurt it can cause. It is probably the saddest story I have written and I think my absolute best.

Kevan Youde
Author of *A Cautious Man*

Kevan Youde (pen name) was born in Derbyshire and has spent most of his professional career in Europe, working as a marine scientist and writing fiction in his spare time. He has had his fiction published in books, literary annuals and magazines.

Priti Mehta
Mrs Joshi Doesn't Cry Any More

Priti Mehta has lived a life across cultures. She is an outspoken representative of her gender; still unsure whether she represents liberation, or equity. She writes short fiction, satirical pieces, and poetry. Armed with majors in finance and economics, Priti finds inspiration for her stories and poetry in odd places. Priti currently lives in Mumbai, India.

Introduction to *Mrs Joshi Doesn't Cry Any More*

Set in Mumbai, India, in the year 2006, the story narrates the events of the fateful day that changed the course of life for Mrs. Joshi - July 26 - seven bomb blasts in eleven minutes in running trains, which ripped apart the lives of hundreds of families in an instant.

Jane Seaford
author of *Dead is Dead*

Jane Seaford is the Competition Secretary at Takahē Magazine in New Zealand. (**www.takahe.org.nz**)

Her novels *The Insides of Banana Skins* and *Archie's Daughter* and her short story collection *Dead is Dead and Other Stories* have received excellent reviews. Several of Jane's stories have been placed, highly commended or short-listed in international competitions. Many have appeared in anthologies or magazines. Others have been broadcast. As a freelance journalist, she had a column in *Bonjour* magazine and sold pieces to the *Guardian*, the *Independent* and other British publications. Her website is: **janeseaford.com**

Introduction to *Dead is Dead*

Dead is Dead stems from a real incident. It was the first story that I submitted to New Zealand's National Radio (I live in New Zealand) and to my delight it was quickly accepted.

The character of Tim is based on my brother. He is a fan of my writing but *Dead is Dead* is his favourite piece. "I don't know if it's because it's good, or because I'm in it," he says.

Not many of my stories have their origin in real life. This one has: the events it portrays were dramatic and deeply disturbing, and for me stem from racism and colonialism.

Shawn Klimek
author of *Pregenisis*

Shawn M. Klimek is the internationally published author of more than 170 poems and stories. His first book is *Hungry Thing*, an illustrated dark fantasy tale told in five melodic poems. He lives in Illinois with his wife and their Maltese.

Website: **http://blog.jotinthedark.com/**
Facebook: **@shawnmklimekauthor**
Twitter: **@shawnmklimek**

Introduction to *Pregenisis*

Originally published in *Carrier Wave: The Inner Circle Writers' Group Comedy Anthology 2018,* it was voted by readers as the best in the anthology. Reactions seemed to vary by geography, from North American readers, who found it humorous, to English and Australian readers, who found it humourous.

The original publisher, Clarendon House Publications (CHP), featured it a second time in *Gold: The Best from Clarendon House Anthologies Volume One: 2017/2018.* Despite being available only on Kindle (or POD via Lulu.com), all of the CHP anthologies sort as the priciest in my Amazon catalog, and therefore remain the least exposed.

G. Allen Wilbanks
author of *Teach a Man to Fish*

G. Allen Wilbanks is a member of the HWA and has published over 100 short stories in *Daily Science Fiction*, *Deep Magic*, *Mythic*, *The Colored Lens*, and other places. His writing has also been featured in several internationally best-selling anthologies. He is the author of two short story collections, and the novel *When Darkness Comes*. For more information, please visit the author's website at:

www.gallenwilbanks.com

Introduction to *Teach a Man to Fish*

The story is the tale of a grandfather passing on a somewhat unique tradition to his grandson while fishing in the middle of a remote lake.

Mark Kodama
author of *Land of the Pharaohs*

Mark Kodama is a trial attorney and former newspaper reporter who lives in Washington, D.C. with his wife and two sons. He is currently working on *Las Vegas Tales*, a work of philosophy, sugar-coated with meter and rhyme and told through stories.

More than 150 of his short stories, poems and essays have been published in anthologies, including those published by Black Hare Press, Clarendon Publishing House, Eerie River Publishing, Escaped Ink Press and Devil's Party Press.

His stories and poems have appeared in *Writers and Readers Magazine*, the *Academy of Hearts and Mind Magazine*, *Café Lit*, *Commuter Lit*, *Dastaan World Magazine*, *Dissident Voice*, *Jakob's Horror Box*, *Indie's Nest*, *Inner Circle Writers' Group Magazine*, *Literary Yard*, *Magazine of History and Fiction*, *Mercurial Stories*, *Portland Metrozine*, *Potato Soup Journal*, *PPP Ezine*, *Spillwords*, *Tuck Magazine* and *World of Myths Magazine*.

His stories and poems appear in *Ancients, Apocalypse, Blaze, Cadence, Unravel, Dragon Bone Soup, Enigma, Fox Hollow Stories, Glamour, Hate, Tall Tales and Short Stories, Gleam, Fireburst, Latin Anthology, Maelstrom, Pride, Tempest* and *What Sort of Fuckery Is This?*

Land of the Pharaohs won Story of the Month at *World of Myths* and *The Summer Camp* appears in *Potato Soup Journal*, Volume 1, Issue 1 (Best of).

https://www.facebook.com/xkodama
http://www.amazon.com/-/e/B07Z2HHKR6

Glenn Bresciani
author of *Medicated Success*

Glenn Brisciani works as a support worker in community aged care. Fantasy and Sci-Fi are his favourite genres that he enjoys reading and in which he wants to write . His wish is that the process of writing a short story should be the same as eating a bowl of ice cream– every spoonful a pleasant experience, and it's all done in five minutes.

Jean Duggleby
author of *Land of Elephants*

Jean Duggleby, a retired primary school teacher who eventually specialised in teaching hearing-impaired children, discovered her talent for writing at the mature age of 73. It came about as a result of attending a writing course run by her partner, ostensibly to make the tea at break time (!). Intrigued by the notion of subtext, she tried her hand at writing herself and produced a story that was immediately accepted for magazine publication. Before this she claims that she struggled composing a postcard and at school the only good mark she received for a story was for one that she had copied.

She has now completed around 100 stories, several of which have been published in *Gold Dust* and elsewhere, and has self-published 25 of them in a collection entitled *It's Never Too late*. Copies can be bough for £5 plus postage by emailing her at: **jean.duggleby@talktalk.net**.

Introduction to *Land of Elephants*

The story was inspired by a holiday in Kerala, southern India, where she saw the man who inspired the story in a bus station. The story teaches the lesson that we should never make assumptions about people based on appearances.

Andrew Parker
author of *Shadow Angel*

Andrew Parker has been writing fiction for four years, nonfiction for decades. His writings are comprised of an eclectic mix of novels, short stories, poetry, commentaries, and narratives. A discovery writer, he often finds himself surprised as the first reader of his works, as plot twists and character development unfold. A love of words and a desire to bring positive to readers motivates him to continually pound on the keyboard.

Andrew's 'day job' for the past 28 years has been as a mental health and substance use treatment therapist. While he won't ever completely give that up, he hopes to shift more of his time and energy into writing.

Introduction to *Shadow Angel*

Shadow Angel is a story inspired by an internet image of the shadow of a girl on the shadow of an empty swing. A girl who died in her youth, but who remains stuck between this life and the hereafter. It is the story of a loving friendship between her and the boy who comes into her existence, to be both saved by her and to save her. A tale of fear and loneliness, hope and love, service and selflessness, and sharing and letting go.

Paul B. Cohen
author of *The Projectionist*

Paul B. Cohen read English at the University of Leeds, took a Master of Arts in English at Vanderbilt University, and gained a Master of Professional Writing from the University of Southern California in Los Angeles. Recent short stories have appeared in *Prole, Here Comes Everyone* and for Fairlight Books. His tale 'Lecha Dodi' was a first-place winner in the Moment-Karma Foundation Short Story Contest, judged by novelist Alice Hoffman. 'Tea and Biscuits' took third place in the Ryedale Book Festival Short Story Competition and he was the joint first-place winner in Writer's Atelier 2019 Short Story Contest for 'Interruption' which was published as an eBook on Amazon. His novel *Tales of Freedom* was released in February 2019 and is also available on Amazon.

Introduction to *The Projectionist*

Originally published in *Prole* (2015) I've always felt it was one of my best and would love to see it again in print and, more importantly, feel that it'll reach new readers. The story was loosely inspired by *Cinema Paradiso*. I was teaching A-Level Film Studies and had chosen the film for the course.

Ann Christine Tabaka
author of *The Fire Eater*

Ann Christine Tabaka was nominated for the 2017 Pushcart Prize in Poetry. Winner of Spillwords Press 2020 Publication of the Year (Poetic), has been internationally published, and won poetry awards from numerous publications. She is the author of 10 poetry books. She has micro-fiction in several anthologies. Christine lives in Delaware, USA. She loves gardening and cooking. Chris lives with her husband and three cats. Her most recent credits are: The Black Hair Press (*Unravel Anthology*, *Apocalypse Anthology*, *Hate Anthology*); Fantasia Divinity Publishing (*Winds of Despair Anthology*, W*aters of Destruction Anthology*, *Earth of Oblivion Anthology*); *The Siren's Call* (drabbles); *Potato Soup Journa*l: 10-word stories.

Website: **annchristinetabaka.com**

Introduction to *The Fire Eater*

The Fire Eater is a fiction and love story written to encompass the Native American culture, and to bring attention to the fragility of the Earth and all her creatures.

David Bowmore
author of *Sins of the Father*

David Bowmore has worn many hats in his time: chef, teacher and landscape gardener.

Now, he is an award winning author, living in Yorkshire with his wonderful wife and a small white poodle.

David is included in the *Who's Who of Emerging Writers 2020*.

His collection of connected short stories *The Magic of Deben Market* published by Clarendon House is available in paperback and Kindle through Amazon. His website is at: **www.davidbowmore.co.uk**

Introduction to *Sins of the Father*

(More of a back story really.)

Sins is the first story I had published back in 2018. It surprised me that it won best in book, thereby granting me the opportunity to have a collection of my stories published by Clarendon House.

Despite a successful couple of years, in which the previously mentioned collection was released, people still take time to remind me how much they like "Sins of The Father".

On the 25th June 2020, it was given a virtual theatre enactment starring Garry Cooper, Leslie Ash and David Sterne. The recording can be viewed at **https://vimeo.com/432756822**.

It's a story I am very proud of.

DC Diamondopolous
author of *Billy Luck*

DC Diamondopolous is an award-winning novelette, short story, and flash fiction writer with over 200 stories published internationally in print and online magazines, literary journals, and anthologies. DC's stories have appeared in: *34th Parallel, So It Goes: The Literary Journal of the Kurt Vonnegut Museum and Library, Lunch Ticket, Raven Chronicles, Silver Pen, Blue Lake Review,* and many others. Among DC's many awards and honorary mentions are: two time finalist for ScreenCraft's Cinematic Short Story Contest and nomination for *Best of the Net Anthology*. She lives on the California central coast with her wife and animals. Her website is at: **dcdiamondopolous.com**

Lesley Price
author of *Family Business*

Born on the outskirts of London, Lesley Price is Scottish by blood and tradition. She moved abroad at an early age and has spent most of her life in Belgium where she still lives with her three children, French partner, his son and two demanding cats. Lesley enjoyed a long and successful career within IT before founding her own coaching, training and consulting company in Luxembourg. Although writing is not her day job, it was Lesley's childhood dream and occupies much of her spare time. She regularly writes short stories, often exploring the darker side of humankind, and occasionally tries her hand at flash fiction. In 2017, Lesley self-published her first full-length novel, book one in the Glasgow-based *Cathy Stewart* crime series, with significant contributions from her father who sadly passed away since. Book two is currently a work in progress, squeezed between Lesley's day job, family commitments and other interests.

Lesley's website is at: **www.lesleyprice.lu**

Patric Mauzy
author of *The Night Life*

Patric Mauzy is a writer from Fort Wayne, Indiana. His stories have been published in the *Dark Solstice* anthology, and also local journal *Indiana Voice*.

About the Authors

R.L.M. Cooper
author of *The Vanishing of M. Renoir*

RLM Cooper is a *summa cum laude* graduate of the University of Alabama in Huntsville. A former computer scientist, she now spends her time writing poetry and fiction. Her work as been published in online magazines, literary reviews, and print anthologies both in the United States and abroad. She lives in the Pacific Northwest with her husband and a well-loved Tonkinese cat. Her first novel is due to be published in the latter part of 2020. For links to her other work, please visit her website at: **rlmcooper.com**

P.C. Darkcliff
author of *The Wandering Corpse*

P.C. Darkcliff has been writing fiction ever since he learned his letters, and his first attempt was a tale about a talking dog. Then he discovered the world of fantasy and paranormal fiction – and he never looked back.

P.C. has released two novels, *Deception of the Damned* and *The Priest of Orpagus*, and co-edited a fantasy anthology called *Dragon Bone Soup*. His short stories have appeared in various publications.

In September of 2020, he's going to launch *Celts* and the *Mad Goddess*, the first installment of *The Deathless Chronicle*.

P.C. has lived in six countries and on three continents, and many of his adventures have spilled into his stories. He has settled with his wife in southwestern Spain where he goes swimming and cycling whenever he isn't too busy writing.

Join his VIP reader list to get his novels for free:
https://mailchi.mp/c5550d315607/pcdarkcliff

Find him anywhere on social media in one click:
https://plu.us/p.c.darkcliff

Belinda Brady
author of *Howl*

A bookworm since childhood, Belinda is passionate about stories and after years of procrastinating, has finally turned her hand to writing them, with a preference for supernatural/thriller themes; both often competing for her attention. She has had several stories published in a variety of publications, both online and in anthologies. Belinda lives in Australia with her family and has been known to enjoy the company of cats over people.

Peggy Gerber
author of *Saving Aaron*

Peggy Gerber began her writing career in order to fill the void created when she became an empty nester. Along with several friends, she co-founded the group Champagne Writers, a group specifically created for writers of a certain age. Peggy has been published in *Daily Science Fiction*, *Spillwords*, *Potato Soup Journal*, *81words.net* and the anthology *Poetry in the Time of Coronavirus*.

Introduction to *Saving Aaron*

What lengths would you go to, to save the life of your beloved child? Well, if you were Maggie, you would do just about anything.

Kristy Kerruish
author of *Ghost-maker*

Kristy Kerruish (pen name) was born in Edinburgh and currently lives in Europe where she combines her work as a historical researcher with her creative writing. She has had her fiction and poetry published in books, literary annuals and magazines.

Introduction to *Ghost-maker*

Ghost-maker was originally published in Gold Dust. The story is inspired by a small, unobtrusive portrait hanging in Mauritshuis, The Hague.

Adele C. Geraghty
author of *A Very Brooklyn Wedding*

Adele C Geraghty is a citizen of both the US and the UK. She is the recipient of the US National Women's History Award for Poetry and Essay and author of *Skywriting in the Minor Key*, a poetry collection. Adele is also an illustrator and graphic designer and member of both the New York ensemble "The Arts Soire" and the writing site UKAuthors.com. Adele is Publisher of BTS Books and Founder & Publishing Editor of *Between These Shores Literary & Arts Annual*. Adele's work has been published in numerous anthologies, magazines and journals, and performed on radio in both her countries.

Marlon S. Hayes
author of *The Last Haircut*

Marlon S. Hayes is a writer, poet, and author from Chicago, Illinois, USA. He likes traveling, cooking, and lazy, rainy days. He's the author of six books, and has had his work featured in multiple magazines and anthologies. His upcoming novel *Eleven Fifty-Nine* will be published by Oghma Creative Media in autumn, 2020. He can be followed on Amazon, and on Facebook at "Marlon's Writings and Voices from the Bleachers".

Introduction to *The Last Haircut*

An elderly Black man named Charlie reflects on his life as he embarks on his last day as a professional barber. He's watched as the world has changed from when he was a teenager in the 1960's, to the fast-paced urban setting that is no longer where he wants to be. His wife, Shirley has been his life partner for the majority of his adult life, and their shared daydream of a simpler life down South is the dangling carrot he needs to enter into his retirement. His barbershop represents his life's work, and he worries that his legacy will not be understood or carried on by the shop's new owner.

Michael Tuffin
author of *There He Is*

A former Royal Navy officer, Michael now lives in Gloucestershire. He has not had any work published and was not under the illusion that he would. This story was a test to see what the response – if any – to his writing would be.

I think I have made the appropriate response.

Introduction to *There He Is*

The story is a look at how easy the slide into addiction can be, and a look at the effect it has on you and others.

Daniel Amoah
author of *Going Home*

Daniel Amoah volunteers on Saturdays at the Harrow Green Community Library in Leytonstone, east London, partly to serve his local community and also to meet some of the many different people within the community, an opportunity which his day job doesn't offer.

His background is in accountancy but during the course of his career he has re-invented himself and qualified as a Microsoft Certified Professional and now IT and photography, which he finds quite symbiotic, are two of his other passions after reading.

Daniel likes reading and has always wanted to write his own story, but just didn't know how or indeed when. So when the community library started a Writers' Group he thought he'd give it a go. The many people he has talked to during his volunteering sessions at the community library leave him in no doubt that every person has a story to tell, but few manage to do so. He hopes that his short stories will be the first step on a journey that will lead to fulfilling his wish to write his own story.

Lynn Braybrooke
author of *The Girl I Nearly Knew*

Lynn Braybrooke ~ born and educated in Leyton, east London, has loved stories as far back as she can remember. She has found the Harrow Green Community Library Creative Writing group a great stimulus for writing stories instead of just reading them. All the jobs she has done. from machining garments to shipping cargo, have been a way of earning money while the children grew up and the mortgage got paid. Along the way she went back to school for "O" and "A" level English because what she really wanted to do was write. She loves to cook and swim and believes that she has a strong creative streak that propels her to make things. But the story is the thing. One way or another, she must be in a story.

Earlier this year she published her first novel "After the Loving" through Amazon. It concerns a particularly ugly and unfair divorce looked at from the point of view of the man. The stuff of nightmares.

> Google "After the Loving - Lynn Braybrook - Amazon"
> Paperback: £7.99, Kindle: £2.99

Slavko Mali
The Case of the Worn Out Soap

Slavko Mali creates illustrations, graphic stories, written stories and poems which are frequently published in domestic and foreign electronic and printed magazines and journals. Until it ceased publication this year he was an illustrator and editorial board member of *Gold Dust Magazine* (London) which also published many of his illustrations, short stories and a guest editorial.

He was one of the two founders of the BTS publishing house in Sheffield where he held the post of Editor-in-Chief of illustrations on their magazine/yearbook *Between These Shores Annual*. His artwork appeared on most pages, and the magazine ran a major article about his work with an interview and a large number of illustrations and photographs, as well as one of his stories and a poem.

He has received several awards as an artist, cartoonist and writer. His work has been included in more than a dozen anthologies of various types of art, as well as placed in many poetry and short story competitions.

He won first prize for poetry in the international competition run by the magazine *Ulaznica* ("Ticket") in Zrenjanin, Serbia.

Among the places where his illustrations, short stories, graphic stories, mail art and poems have been published are: *U - Direct* (Chicago, USA), *Farrago* (Australia), *Kairan* (Osaka, Japan), *Obsolete* (New York), *Homeless Diamonds* (London), *Gold Dust* (London), *BTSA* (Sheffield, UK), *Dream Magazine* (Nevada City, USA), *Andromeda Quarterly* (Pittsburgh), *Pouët Café* (Montreal, Canada), *Komikaze* (Croatia), *West Herzegovina* (Bosnia and Herzegovina) and *Urban Comics* (Macedonia). His fanzines published by "Sticky" were successfully sold in a store of alternative publications in the subway in Melbourne, Australia.

He is currently involved in journalism and writing short stories and poems. His collection of short stories *Nije Čovjek* (He is Not a Man) is published by AUC Zeleni konj (Green Horse) in Belgrade.

Gareth Hywel Phillips
Buddy Nickel and The Mistletoe Men

Gareth Hywel Phillips was born and raised in Carlisle, North England, though his family is proudly Welsh (hence the name). He studied English and Music at the University of Birmingham, taught English and tutored guitar in China, and is currently based in Cardiff studying an MA in Forensic Linguistics with the hope of eventually completing a PhD in Forensic Speech Science. He is an avid musician who daydreamed many stories from a very young age, and has recently decided to start publishing them.

Introduction to *Buddy Nickel and The Mistletoe Men*

This piece explores the roles of dreams and nightmares in personal-development, the effect of time on relationships, my honest reflections on what could be termed 'toxic masculinity', and the significance of one man's audio-hallucinations in understanding his darker impulses. In writing this short story, I have drawn from personal experience of sleep disorders and mental illness. I should also note that the piece contains mature/explicit themes that I believe were essential in telling the story right.